HER PERFECT

DEDICATION

For M. Our imperfections are what make us beautiful. You're perfect exactly as you are.

CONTENTS

PROLOGUE

COLBIE

"You're making something out of nothing. I promise."

"You need help, Colbie."

I grabbed Jess's wrist when she tried to leave. "I'm fine." I enunciated those two words certain she'd understand how seriously I meant them.

Jess was going to make herself sick if she didn't stop twisting her neck. And the tears. "It's all there. The pieces fit together. I can't believe I've been so stupid that I didn't notice."

"Jess, I'm not kidding. Lower your voice." I'd clamp her mouth shut or shove a wash cloth into it if I had to. I was not above gagging my best friend.

The door to the hall stood open from where she'd entered, and her tone rose with each word. She had me trapped, unable to bypass her much less keep everyone else from listening.

"No. If you didn't have anything to hide, you wouldn't be worried about anyone hearing me." Snot ran from her nose, and she hiccupped when she talked. "How long have you been doing," she waved her hands in circles, "this?"

I took a deep breath, unable to come up with a response to settle her. The truth would only make matters worse.

"Is this what happened that night Eli came to get you at my house?"

I shook my head and stared at her shoes.

Still I didn't respond.

Jess stomped her foot on the ceramic tiles, but her shoe didn't make nearly the noise her voice did when she shouted, "Answer me, dammit. Tell me why you're killing yourself." Her fists shook at her sides, but I couldn't determine if it was anger or disappointment that made her tremble.

The stampede had begun at the bottom of the stairs, closing in rapidly.

I tried to push her out of the way, but she latched onto the doorframe and held on for dear life. "You're being ridiculous."

"This is why you've lost so much weight, isn't it? And why your parents are freaked out. They just don't know it's the catalyst for all the other stuff." As if she needed each person in the house to hear every word she said, her clarity didn't come quietly.

My defensive walls went up thick and strong. If she wouldn't shut up then I'd shut down. Which was precisely what happened when Caden stumbled through the door, followed by my brothers and parents.

Caden spun Jess toward him. The change in his expression gave way the second he had realized she was crying. Chasity appeared confused. And none of my brothers said a word. My parents brought up the tail end, but before either could express concern or question, Jess sobbed into my little brother's chest.

"She's going to die, Caden. I've told you a hundred times there was something wrong, and you wouldn't listen." Jess's fist beat on Caden's shoulder as her knees decided to quit holding her weight.

It was a melodramatic performance to say the least. I rolled my eyes as Caden caught his girlfriend's weight and scooped her up. He sat on the bed with her in his arms, and all I could think of was the way I felt when Eli cradled me.

God, I missed him.

"Colbie, what's going on?" My mother's prim yet surprised voice barely made it through the commotion of the multitude of people now hovering in the entrance to my bedroom. She glanced at Jess and Caden and back to me for an explanation.

I crossed my arms. "Nothing."

"It's not true." Jess was a blubbering mess, and Caden needed to get his girlfriend under control. "Look at her face."

I swiped painful strokes under my lashes to remove mascara residue, knowing it was futile. I hadn't gotten to wash my face before Jess went into hysterics. The water still ran next to me. In fact, she'd thrown my entire sequence out of order.

"Look at her eye, Dr. Chapman." She sniveled, and I wanted to wring her damn neck. "Just look."

My father pushed through the group, but before I could slam the door—that Caden had removed Jess from—and hide behind it, he slapped his palm against the wood and forced it open. I couldn't remember the last time Daddy had put his hands on me, but he grabbed my chin so he could see my face.

Jess continued to wallow from the bed. Meanwhile, my family waited with baited breath to see what Jess referred to. My dad was a doctor. If Jess had seen it, he would instantly. He tilted my chin to the side and used two fingers to pry my lids apart.

He went from looking *at* my eyes to looking *in* them. "Colbie, what's going on?" The gruff tumble of my father's gravelly voice had taken on a softer, concerned tone. It was the voice of my childhood, the one that had tucked me into bed at night. I hadn't heard that man in years, and I realized I missed him as much as I did Eli.

I shrugged him off, but trying to get by him was pointless. And even if I had, there was layer after layer of people between me and freedom. "Nothing, I'm fine." If I'd taken a gentler approach than snarling, I might have convinced my father that was true.

"It's not true, Dr. Chapman. Ask her what she was doing. Ask her what she does every time she leaves the table."

My brother tried to calm his girlfriend. "Jess—"

"Ask her!" Jess was on the verge of hyperventilating, and my dad's medical expertise would be better suited toward getting her under control before she passed out.

"Shut up, Jess. Nobody cares." The walls breathed in, stealing my air. "Shut up." The room rotated, side swiping my equilibrium. "Shut up." Gravity squeezed every inch of my body, ripping apart my flesh. "Shut up." I no longer knew if I'd continued yelling the same words on repeat or if that was an echo smothering the bathroom. I didn't care.

Pandemonium had ensued, and I lost my grip on reality. Brother after brother leaned into my face and disappeared to allow the next to demonstrate their disapproval in my mind's funhouse mirror.

None of it was real, or maybe all of it was.

1

COLBIE

FOUR MONTHS EARLIER

"Colbie," my mother called from the bottom of the stairs. "Sweetheart, it's the first day of your senior year; you don't want to be late."

"Coming, Mama." Pacifying her was easy.

Of the seven kids, I was by far the one she worried about least. Smack dab in the middle at birth number four, I was the only girl in a vast sea of boys. I never gave her or my dad any trouble. My brothers would never have allowed it, anyhow. We were raised in the deep south by God-fearing Christians. Our family ate dinner together, we said grace before meals, attended church on Wednesday nights and Sunday mornings, said "sir" and "ma'am" as much as "please" and "thank you," and as a whole, lived a life most envied. My daddy was a doctor, and my mama a homemaker, both of which had come from generations of old money. We wanted for nothing and had everything. But somewhere in the midst of that perfection, I'd gotten lost in the shuffle of my siblings' sports careers. In the heart of Dixie, football was king, and my brothers were heirs to that throne.

When I reached the bottom of the steps, I kissed her on the cheek. "Bye, Mama."

"Don't forget your brothers have practice after school today. I told them you might be a little late if your piano lesson ran over."

I wasn't normally charged with the responsibility of my younger brothers, Caden, Clayton, and Collin, but my oldest brother, Caleb—who also happened to be our high school's football coach after a stellar college career at the University of Georgia—had to go to the courthouse after school today and wouldn't be there to bring the three stooges home. He was finally tying the knot with his childhood sweetheart in the wedding of the century before the season really started, and they were picking up the marriage license today. Nothing ever interfered with football in this town—lives were planned around home games for tailgating, away games for parties around a huge television, and the possibility of attending a bowl at the end of the season. Add spring and summer training to that schedule and there was virtually no window of opportunity where football wasn't front and center.

Luckily, Chasity, my brother's fiancée, had been a cheerleader and lived the life of football right alongside her soon-to-be spouse. She was the monogram-wearing, pom-pom waving, sorority type who ate that stuff up. The amount of pep that girl had made me wonder if she ever shut down. But she made Caleb happy, and that was all that mattered. Although I prayed like hell they chose a new letter besides C for their kids' names. Caleb and Chasity Chapman were enough. I would never know what possessed my parents to make such a choice, but I swore the curse would end with me.

"I know, Mama. I won't forget to pick them up."

Caden was a month shy of turning sixteen and getting his license. This responsibility would fall to him at that point, but in the meantime, I was expected to fill in. My mother had community obligations that kept her busy now that we all had our own social lives. She was the epitome of a Southern belle and had an image to uphold. Our family ran like a well-oiled machine, and no one ever saw any chinks in the Chapman armor, not that there were any...besides me.

The drive to the school was short, and while I attempted to listen to the radio, my brothers bickered about things that didn't interest me. Once in the parking lot, we all exited and went our separate ways.

I just had to make it through one final year before escaping this town, and I started counting the days today. Two hundred and eighty to go before graduation, including holidays and breaks. I'd gotten early acceptance to Vanderbilt and planned to follow in my father's footsteps—I just wouldn't be returning here after med school.

"Colbie, wait up."

I turned at the sound of my name to see my best friend rounding the back of her SUV. Our parents had been friends since Lucifer fell from grace, and I'd known her since birth. Six days older than me, we'd both turned eighteen just before school started and had been friends since we first saw the light of day. She was the closest thing I had to a sister and the only person in the world who adored me in spite of my sports ineptitude and the fact that I had a vagina. Don't get me wrong, my parents loved me, but when I showed no interest in cheering like Chasity and therefore wasn't on the football field at every game, I slid down the totem pole until they forgot I was actually on it.

"Hey, Jess. I thought we were meeting in homeroom."

"I had to come back out to get my phone. I left it in the car."

Jessica McLean and I had been cut from the same cloth. Both honors students, vying for the valedictorian title, and incredibly smart. We were blessed with beauty and brains, although she didn't have to work nearly as hard at maintaining the beauty part as I did. People said the two of us could pass for twins, but I never saw it. Her raven-colored hair was much more striking than my mahogany brown, her porcelain skin didn't have the small splattering of freckles mine did, and where my eyes were a pale blue, hers were as rich as sapphires. While we wore the same size four, I was just a hair taller. And though both of us were popular with the opposite sex, neither of us bothered with dating them.

"Have you seen the new AP English teacher?" Her ruby-red lips parted into an award-winning smile.

"No, what happened to Mr. Talley?"

"I can't confirm the rumors, but the word in the hallway is that he had a heart attack over the summer and retired early."

"That's awful."

"You won't think so when you walk into third period." She veered off to her locker, sporting a mischievous grin, and I went in the opposite direction to my own. My friend waved over her shoulder as I shook my head. Clearly, Jess had a new zest for life and our senior year, although I had no idea what had brought it on.

My class schedule was grueling. I wanted to get in as many advanced placement courses as I could to gain as many college credits as possible, but I also wanted the boost in my GPA. Salutatorian wasn't good enough. Jess could have that honor; I had to be number one. AP Calculus, followed by AP Physics, and two hours into the day my head was already swimming. I stopped by my locker to drop off the textbooks I had acquired during the first two periods of school before racing off to AP English on the other side of the campus.

English was by far my favorite subject. If I could make a living doing something with a degree in that field, I'd go after it—but I didn't aspire to teach...I just loved to read. I arrived just after the bell rang and tried to sneak in the door unnoticed. I had no sooner taken a seat in the front row and leaned over to get a notebook and pen from my book bag than the man who'd been standing with his back to the class, writing on the board, turned.

"You're expected to be in your seat and ready to learn when the bell sounds. That doesn't mean sliding in under the radar, thinking you're any different than the rest of the students. Your tardiness prevents their learning."

When I sat up with my pen in hand, I realized his warning was issued directly to me. My eyes went wide, mortified that he would call me out on the first day in front of my peers. My stare met his, and the chocolate-brown irises did their best to instill fear. I saw red and wondered who the hell he thought he was.

"I'm Dr. Paxton." He spoke directly to me as though he'd read my thoughts. "I'm filling in for Mr. Talley until the district finds a permanent replacement, but make no mistake, I am not a substitute...." His gaze roamed the room momentarily before landing back on me. "And I will not go lightly on you." The fact that he felt the need to enunciate that point in my direction only further served to escalate my agitation, and my classmates snickered at his insinuation. "My job is to prepare you to *pass* the AP exam at the end of the year, not just take it." He turned away from the class and uttered his final words before starting the lecture. "Think seriously about whether you can maintain the workload outlined in the syllabus. If you can't, excuse yourself now, find the nearest guidance counselor, and cry to them before you request a drop."

My jaw hung loosely in dismay, but I kept my lips closed to prevent anyone else from seeing just how far off my straight line Dr. Paxton had managed to knock me. Within seconds, I realized I had to forego my disdain for the man at the front of the room and focus on the words coming from his mouth. I'd taken pages of notes by the end of the fifty-minute period when the bell rang, interrupting his sentence. He reminded us to check the syllabus for homework assignments due tomorrow and dismissed the class.

I quickly gathered my things and zipped my backpack as Jess stepped up to my desk. But before she got a word out, Drill Sargent Paxton interrupted.

"Ms. Chapman, can I see you for a minute, please?"

The glance I gave Jess indicated my confusion, which mirrored her own.

"How does he know your name?" she whispered.

I shrugged, wondering the same thing.

"I'll see you at lunch, Colbie." The look of pity she threw my way didn't ease my apprehension.

My feet carried me to the dictator's desk where he now sat casually on the corner with his ankles crossed and his hands firmly planted at his sides on the edge of the old wood. And I waited.

"I expect you to be on time in the future." He'd made his point at the start of class; reiterating it was unnecessary.

"Yes, sir." I held my head high and waited.

"You don't know who I am, do you?" The rigid tension washed away as though relief flooded him.

Other than the pompous ass who'd embarrassed me in front of my classmates, I didn't care who the hell he was. "No, sir. I do not."

"Eli Paxton." He said his name as though he were some pop icon I should instantly recognize, but it was still just as foreign as before. "You *are* Caleb Chapman's little sister, right?"

I ground my teeth together, biting back the comparison I often received. "Yes, sir." Years of etiquette training and classes in poise had me at my Southern best. Even though I raged inside, I wouldn't give him the pleasure of knowing he'd garnered a rise from me.

"I played ball with Caleb at UGA. We roomed together for four years before I went to grad school."

My eyebrows rose in question, encouraging him to get to

whatever point he tried to make before he caused me to be late to my next class.

"I'm sorry. You must think I'm a total ass. I thought Caleb told you I'd be teaching the class. I talked to him about it last week when I saw your name on my roster. And I'm embarrassed to admit, I assumed you'd know who I was since your brother and I are pretty tight."

I continued to stare at him—the way his brown eyes softened like melted chocolate almost had me mesmerized—but when he continued to talk, notably flustered by my indifference, I stayed focused on his words.

"I didn't want you to have the impression I'd let you slide just because of my relationship with your brother."

"With all due respect, sir, your relationship with Caleb isn't my concern and holds little interest in my life. I don't make a habit of arriving late, but even more so, I don't *slide* in anything academic. Where my brothers want to be star quarterbacks, I'm aiming for valedictorian, and I didn't get there by resting on my laurels or my brother's friendships. Vanderbilt doesn't give a shit who Caleb Chapman is."

He gave me a curt nod of understanding and tilted his head toward the door to excuse me. Two hundred and seventy-nine more days before I could wave goodbye to that cocky bastard...and counting.

Jess scared the hell out of me when I rounded the corner, exiting Dr. Douche's classroom.

"Holy crap, Colbie. What was that about?"

She kept up with me as we traversed at break-neck speed across the school to AP Chemistry. As hard as it would be to make these trips in the few minutes we were allotted between classes, I was grateful for the bit of cardio thrown into my day. "He's friends with Caleb. They played ball together at UGA." I had a bad habit of rolling my eyes. It wasn't lady-like, and my mother hated it, but that one action said so much that words couldn't.

"Jesus. He's so intense. I can't imagine Caleb being friends with someone like that. But you have to admit, his broody personality is sexy in a dark way. Did you see his eyes? And if he's friends with your brother and he's into football, that means there's a badass body beneath that Polo shirt and khaki pants."

"Yeah, but let's focus on the only part of that sentence that matters...he's into football." I let that statement hang in the air for a minute. She knew what it meant. Guys like that weren't into girls like us, and girls like us quickly grew bored with guys like that. "And don't forget, that would make him at least twenty-four."

"Age is just a number." She shrugged with indifference, but I knew her well enough to know she was anything but flippant.

"So are the years handed down in a prison sentence. Don't be stupid, Jess."

Just before we crossed the threshold to our next class, my best friend turned her head toward me with a dopey grin and a glazed look in her eyes. "Can't we fantasize about his being an intellectual?"

"Daydream all you want. I'm not interested. I don't appreciate being called out in front of the entire class or told he wasn't going to let me 'slide' because of Caleb."

As we took our seats and waited for the bell to ring, Jess kept talking. "He said that to you?"

"Yep. And seemed a little put off that I wasn't aware of who he was."

Men always thought everything was about them. I wondered if the guy had bothered to think of how little I had in common with a brother that was six years my senior, a college football star, and every girl's wet dream. Although, he clearly knew who I was, which made me pause. I couldn't imagine Caleb had ever mentioned me to his friends at school. Those I knew back home were by default because I'd grown up around them. I could only recall a handful of times I had talked to Caleb when he was at UGA, and I'd only seen him when he'd come home for holidays. The notion that my brother's friend even knew my name shocked me almost as much as the warning he'd issued in his class. The few times Caleb, Carson, or Casey had brought anyone home from school—which hadn't been often—they were always surprised to learn there was a sister they'd never met.

My parents and my brothers traveled in packs to UGA games. They were all die-hard Bulldog fans. But even as a child, I'd begged to stay with a friend or relative while they were gone. Nothing about football interested me. I hated the noise of the crowd, thought the game was insipid, and couldn't fathom why anyone would want to watch guys run around on a field and slap each others' asses. If I didn't look exactly like the female version of my six siblings, I'd question my heritage. But as it stood, my lineage couldn't be denied.

"Earth to Colbie." She waved her hand in my face to get my attention. "Where'd you go?"

"Are you surprised he knows who I am?"

Before she could answer my question, the bell sounded, and the class started.

After school, I gathered my books for hours of homework and made my way out the front of the building to the parking lot. Before I reached the doors, my name being called grabbed my attention. When I saw Dr. Paxton, I waved and kept walking as though I hadn't fully understood he'd wanted me to stop. I knew from traveling these halls for the last three years, he'd get bogged down in the crowd and not be able to reach me before I was long gone, and I took full advantage. The final bell had rung—

he couldn't keep me here. And I hadn't done anything wrong... other than cuss in front of him. But it was warranted, and my record didn't have a blemish on it. If he had an issue, it wasn't like he couldn't reach out to his good-buddy Caleb to pass along a message.

My early acceptance to Vandy was based on academics, but I'd decided to minor in music, and my piano lessons were just as important as any AP class I was enrolled in. With my fall recital only a few weeks away, I was working on some of the most difficult pieces I'd ever played, much less performed. Perfection wasn't an option; it was a must. I worked with Dr. Chalmers, my music teacher, tirelessly and spent a minimum of an hour a day with him five days a week.

He was well compensated for his time, but I was also his star pupil. I'd been under his wing since I was seven, and there were occasions I had spent more time with him than I did anyone else in my life. Dr. Chalmers knew if I got into a difficult passage and struggled with it, I wouldn't leave the practice room until I'd conquered the notes. My parents had waited hours in the parking lot of the university where he taught for me to emerge on more than one occasion. At some point, he had started taking me home until I was old enough to drive myself.

Today was one of those days where I needed to stay and work. My entire recital would be comprised of Chopin pieces I'd slaved over, and "Étude in A Minor" was causing problems it shouldn't. I had known the étude was difficult when I'd chosen "Winter Wind," but there was no point in playing if I didn't push my limits and test my skills. The notes raced on the page, and my fingers strained to keep up. I needed to spend hours here but had to leave to pick up my brothers from football.

"Colbie, it will come. Stop putting so much pressure on yourself. And if it doesn't work, then we'll pull it before the recital."

Dr. Chalmers's words were meant to soothe, yet they only served to send my nerves into overdrive.

I'd never pulled a piece, and I wasn't about to start now. I tucked my dark hair behind my ear and then gathered the sheet music to slide it into my bag. "I'll get it."

His frail fingers met my forearm, and I turned my eyes to his grandfatherly gaze. "Even the greatest concert pianists make mistakes. Perfection is an illusion; don't try to achieve something that's unobtainable."

My head bobbed in agreement, but nothing could be further from the truth. He worried about me and the pressure I heaped on my own shoulders. When I was younger, he'd listened not only to my fingers on the keys, but hours of my confused chatter as I'd tried to navigate my way in a family that didn't know what to do with me. Dr. Chalmers was acutely aware that I believed the only way I could prove to my family that something existed outside of football was to be better than great—I had to be flawless.

My stomach growled on my way to pick up Caden, Clayton, and Collin. The downside to my grueling class schedule and piano afterward was hunger. Couple that with a stressful day, and it was a recipe for an incident or hours on the treadmill. I stared at the clock on the dashboard and mentally calculated whether or not I had time to grab a snack before dinner, and with each passing moment I waited on the Chapman clan, that notion became a fantasy. I couldn't snack on the way home and then eat dinner thirty minutes after I arrived. Instead, I pulled a room-temperature bottle of water from my backpack and chugged it in the parking lot next to the stadium. It would have to tide me over.

My agitation grew, and my leg started to bounce. My fingers ran the imaginary keys on my steering wheel as I mentally worked through the étude. The stress of the first day, as well as the encounter with Dr. Paxton, acted as mental blocks on my ability to allow the music to flow. The sooner I eliminated that obstacle and regained control, the faster I'd work through the piece.

Caden joined me first. He startled me by throwing his backpack onto the floorboard before climbing into the front seat. "Hey, Maestro." Of all my siblings, Caden and I were the closest, and he was the only person I'd ever let tease me about music or anything else he deemed comical.

"Hi. Where are the Bobbsey Twins?" The three of them traveled in a pack, and it was rare to see them apart.

"They had laps after practice for smarting off to the coach. I wouldn't want to be either one of them when Caleb finds out."

Blatant disrespect was something not tolerated in our family—by anyone. My parents didn't allow it to them or between any of us, and my brothers enforced it down the line. Caleb sure as hell wouldn't permit it happening on his field to one of his colleagues.

Before I could ask any questions, my youngest brothers joined us. The chatter amongst the three started almost instantly, so I just put the car in gear and drove home. Clayton and Collin raced from the backseat before I came to a complete stop, but Caden only moved to face me.

"You okay, Cole?"

His intuition at fifteen was astounding—not that he couldn't see the visible distress on my face at the moment, but it wasn't just when we were together. Caden and I were connected almost like the twins. We didn't even have to be in the same state, and he'd sense something was wrong and call. That was great when I wanted or needed someone to talk to. It had become a liability in the last six months. And every time I lied to him, I lost a piece of me I would never get back. Part of secrecy was deception, and I'd become a veritable Pinocchio.

"I'm good. Just got a lot on my plate."

His jaw clenched, and his head bobbed slowly in acceptance, but he was leery. Caden knew something was off, yet for the first time in his life, I wasn't able to confide in him what it was. Our father was a doctor. I was intelligent. I knew the consequences of my choices if I took it too far, but once I'd started, I hadn't wanted to stop.

"I'm here when you want to talk." *When*, not *if*. My little brother wouldn't out me, but if I weren't more careful, he'd certainly become a hurdle.

Caden grabbed his bag, and I followed behind him. I hadn't seen my brother's truck outside, but there stood Caleb and Chasity in our dining room just the same. They were the picture of perfection. Both gorgeous in their own right, they were as American as apple pie. I'd be lying if I said it didn't sting to watch my mother and father embrace Chasity in a way they never had me, even though the two of us were different. And regardless of how much I envied the attention she received in my home, I wouldn't want to be her for all the money in the world. She wasn't shallow per se; she just lacked depth.

As the family gathered around the dinner table, yammering on about how the Bulldogs were shaping up for the season, I excused myself without notice to do homework until I was called for dinner.

"Colbie, where are you running off to?"

I didn't have any desire to be bosom buddies with Caleb's fiancée. We had nothing in common, no shared interests, and talking to her bored me. She taught kindergarten, an admirable profession, and coached the local middle school cheering squad. I didn't like kids or football, and I doubted she could recall the last bit of literature she'd read that wasn't written by Dr. Seuss or found at the cash register of the nearest grocery store.

"I have homework to do and need to practice for my recital." My tone didn't reflect my feelings. I kept up the manners instilled in me since birth.

"You've already gotten into college. Stop being so stiff and come hang out." She meant well.

"Yeah, Critter. I haven't seen you in ages. Don't leave. The books will be there tomorrow."

I detested the nickname. One of Caleb's moronic friends had given it to me when I was a toddler because I scurried away from the people that were always in our home. Neither he nor anyone else in my family understood being an introvert or an outcast. And I was both.

I snickered. "Yeah? You might want to let your buddy, Dr. Paxton, know you told me to leave the books for another day...you know, since he's not going to let me 'slide' just because I'm your sister." Mentally, I counted backward...three, two, one—

"Colbie Chapman, you apologize to your brother this instant. What's gotten into you? That tone is unbecoming of a lady."

Insert internal eye roll. "Sorry, Caleb."

He knew I wasn't, but it pacified my mother and allowed for my escape. I found solace in the retreat of my bedroom. The noise that floated through the house having seven people downstairs made me feel like part of the whole without actually being in it. For so long, I'd wanted to be involved, to fit in, just like the rest of them, but I gave up years ago.

There was a light tap on my door just before it opened. "Dinner's ready, Fido. You coming down?" Caden acted as though not attending was an option.

I closed the textbook after marking my place with my pen. "Yeah."

"What's going on with you, Colbie? You never lose your cool like that, especially not with Caleb."

"Nothing. I'm fine." And I was. I knew what I wanted and how to get it. I just refused to let anyone stand in my way. I wasn't a child anymore.

"You're a liar, but I'm not going to press. For now."

Mama had obviously known Caleb would be around for dinner tonight. We were having chicken and dumplings, which was his favorite. The wedding was only a few days away, and then she'd be saying goodbye to her oldest boy and handing him over to another woman. And while she made the best dumplings in the world, I'd grown to hate anytime they showed up on the table.

There was no color variance. The chicken, the dumplings, the thick liquid they swam in...it was all beige...off-white. They appeared as bland as the life around me did, and I couldn't stand it. I'd have to find a way to add carrots or a salad to my plate. When I swung open the refrigerator door, the beets immediately caught my attention. I grabbed them along with another bottle of water, sat them on my placemat, and took a seat. Meals in the Chapman house were served family style. Bowls were passed around the table, and each person took what they wanted before handing it off.

While the color wasn't appealing, the taste was that of pure comfort. Each bite made my brain hum with pleasure. I tuned out the conversations around me and focused on the way I felt and the joy that settled inside me. There was little these days that brought me serenity, but every now and then, dinner did. Until someone stole the emotion I coveted.

"Where do you put all that food, Colbie? I wish I could eat like that and stay as tiny as you are." I stopped chewing and met my sister-in-law-to-be's grin across the table. "Be careful developing eating habits like that. Your metabolism tanks in your twenties. You'll have to exercise twice as often to eat half as much."

I angled my head to the side just slightly, my brow furrowed a bit.

"What am I talking about? You're the only Chapman who doesn't do anything sports related. You really are blessed." She winked at me to indicate her teasing was just that, but my chest heaved with restrained anger.

I didn't bother pointing out the hour I spent running every morning before I even started my day. Chasity saw what she wanted to.

"Oh yeah, Mama said you have one of your little recitals or something coming up." And as quickly as Chasity had ruffled my feathers, Caleb deflated my balloon.

My shoulders dropped, although I doubted it was visible to anyone other than Caden, whose jaw ticced in agitation.

"It's the weekend of the UGA-Auburn game," Daddy piped in.

I anticipated that comment. There was always a game. I just quit planning around them.

"So we don't have to go to her piano thing?" Collin looked to our father, hopeful for confirmation.

He ignored the twins, and instead, addressed his answer to me. "Sorry, buttercup. I wish you had picked another weekend."

Clayton and Collin met between their chairs with a loud high-five that clapped and echoed around the table. Caleb and Chasity had already lost interest, and Mama rattled off her tailgating plans for that weekend. But Caden's stare held mine down the long table. And it was the first time since he was a child that I witnessed his eyes brim with tears. He would be expected to attend the game with everyone else, and even if that's where he'd have more fun, he knew my heart broke with their dismissal. I refused to force him to face my disappointment, and instead, asked to be excused.

"Of course, sugar, but don't you want dessert? Your mama baked a peach cobbler."

"No thanks, Daddy." I loved him. I would always love him. And one day, I hoped he'd brag about me the way he did his sons.

"Cole?" My little brother's plea rattled me, but I didn't stay.

I knew what Caden was capable of, how quickly he could

blow his top, and it just wasn't worth it. I gave him a feeble smile as I fought the emotion burning my eyes.

When I reached the top of the stairs, I went straight to my room and locked the door behind me. They'd stolen the happiness the dumplings should have brought. I lingered in discomfort and willed myself to maintain control. When my emotions were finally in check, then, and only then, would I allow myself to relax.

And purge.

2

ELI

It took Caleb longer to reach out than I'd anticipated. After the blunder with his sister, I had dreaded that call all afternoon. I'd half expected him to find me before the day ended, but when I went by his office in the gym after the final bell, his light was out and the door locked. Then I'd seen Colbie in the halls and tried to stop her, but even when she had looked right at me, she had waved me off as quickly as she had after she put me in my place.

The last thing I wanted to do was piss off my best friend or his family. The Chapmans had been good to me while I was at UGA and treated me like one of their own anytime they were in town. My parents hadn't been able to make it to many games during my career. Not because they hadn't wanted to, but circumstances had prevented it. They watched every televised broadcast and bragged to all their friends. I knew they were proud even if they couldn't be there. But the Chapmans welcomed me as though Caleb and I had known each other all our lives.

With Caleb's wedding this weekend and the rehearsal dinner on Friday, I didn't want to have tension between any of us, including Colbie. I couldn't pull my thoughts away from how I'd completely screwed up that introduction. Never in my wildest dreams had I figured she hadn't ever heard my name. Not because I had been one of the fastest running backs in UGA's history, rather because I was tight with her family. And they were tight. Foolishly, I'd assumed when I told Caleb she would be in my class that he would have given her a heads-up, but that hadn't happened. And as a result, I stuck my foot in my mouth and now had to do damage control.

When my phone finally rang, I sat on my back porch with a beer in hand and a citronella candle burning on the table next to me in hopes the mosquitos didn't eat me alive.

"Hey, man. I hear you met Critter today."

"Critter?" I chuckled at the reference and thought of a woodland creature, which Colbie was anything but.

"Yeah, it's my sister's nickname. Guess it doesn't really suit her anymore."

He was correct in that assumption, but I didn't voice my opinion.

"So, how'd you manage to ruffle her feathers? She's a good student...I know she didn't do anything to get in trouble."

I groaned, knowing how stupid this would sound. "She came in late."

"And?"

"And, nothing. She was late to class, and I made sure they all knew it wasn't acceptable."

"How'd you go from her coming in after the bell to insinuating she expected an easy *A*?" Caleb was humored by the situation. I, however, was not.

"I never said she expected an easy *A*." My fingers tangled in my hair, and I pulled at the roots instead of expressing my frustration. "I kept her after class to apologize to her. At that point, I might have mentioned our friendship and that having no bearing on my expectations of her."

The sound of his laughter had never grated on my nerves in the past, not even on drunken nights at frat parties. "Did you not listen to a word I said about her when we were in school, man?"

That right there was the problem. Caleb's description of his sibling had been far from accurate. And the last picture I'd seen of her, she couldn't have been more than twelve or thirteen. "You almost never talked about her, but what little information you offered about her said she was a music nerd. I could give you the stats of all five of your brothers from the time they started playing ball, but dude, you didn't talk about Colbie."

"Huh." He paused, seemingly to contemplate the notion. "I guess not. We aren't close. She's tight with Caden, but I didn't see her much after I left home. And when I came back, Chasity came with me. My time is still spent on the field, and hers is still spent at a piano or with her nose in a book."

"That would've been good information to have had...*yesterday*. Shit, Chapman. You're killing me."

"You don't have to worry about Colbie expecting any kind of special treatment. And you won't have to worry about her putting in the work in your class. She's a brainiac, and the only girl I've ever known who was more interested in education than socializing."

"Seriously?"

"Yeah, she and her best friend, Jess, swore off guys right before their freshman year. I thought it was the dumbest thing I'd ever heard and laughed when she announced it at the dinner table one night when I was home from school."

"Was there a reason?"

"She wants to be a doctor like my dad. And the two of them, Jess and her, are neck and neck for the valedictorian title at graduation. Personally, I don't get it, but she wants it, and knowing Critter, she'll do whatever it takes to make sure she gets top billing."

Jesus, I wondered if I could have insulted her any more than I had. Telling an honor student you weren't going to let them slide was like the coach threatening to bench a star player during their rival game.

"Is she pissed?" I had to know how much I needed to do between now and Friday night to smooth things over.

"Dude, who cares? She's a kid. You're her teacher. Don't sweat it."

But I *did* care. Colbie Chapman wasn't the Critter that Caleb portrayed. Somewhere along the way, her big brother had missed her growing up. And she might be a bookworm, but I admired anyone who set a goal and went after it. And for a thirteen- or fourteen-year-old kid to set their sights on being the number one student in their class, and then achieving it…that blew my mind.

I hung up a few minutes later but remained on my porch, listening to the crickets chirp as the sky went dark. Colbie Chapman plagued my mind. There'd been fear in her eyes when she looked up from her backpack, then embarrassment flushed her pale complexion when the other kids in the class snickered. At the time, I'd had no idea what I'd done. She was the girl the nerds chased. There is a hierarchy in every sect of the high school population from the band to the jocks, and she was it for the intellectuals. Couple her brain with her insanely good looks, and you had perfection.

I could only imagine she'd never been chastised in class, and I'd done that to her for no other reason than to prove a point that hadn't needed to be made. Kids like her thrived on perfection, and I'd pointed out a flaw—publicly. Although, I had to give her credit. She had brass kahunas. The same demure smile I'd seen on her mother's face a thousand times and the polite way she'd said "sir" had thrown me. She'd been raised with Southern grace, but there was a streak of piss and vinegar in there, too. And when the time came, she had put me in my place…right before she walked out my door.

I STRUGGLED THE NEXT COUPLE OF DAYS NOT TO FOCUS ON her in third period. Part of me wanted to give her the opportunity to shine, but the other thought it might be better to ignore our first encounter and treat it as though it had never happened. Yet I knew the night I graded their first assignment, this girl was in a league all her own. Even her friend Jess was no competition academically. As much as I wanted to believe the quality of work she had turned in was an effort to prove a point, I quickly learned through teacher-breakroom gossip that wasn't the case. Colbie Chapman was every faculty members' best student. Analytically, she was years ahead of her classmates. Her writing was beyond a college level. And she could critique literary works well beyond her years. This girl wasn't just after valedictorian; she wanted to conquer the world.

Even though she engaged in class, she refused to engage with me. Colbie had no problem debating theory with other students, yet when I challenged her, she shut down. It had only been a few days, but I'd never had a problem warming the hearts of my students. Quite the opposite—I'd struggled, and still did, with the females. Only being a handful of years older than most who sat in the chairs in my classroom, coupled with being male, always led to at least one or two trying to get closer than they should. The workload usually squashed any notions of romance they might have, and if that didn't, their grades on the first test did.

Third period was my only AP English class, and it should have been the most enjoyable. These were all bright kids, and I wanted to push their boundaries and encourage them to think beyond a textbook. We'd covered a lot of material in the first week of school, and romantic poetry wasn't a topic that excited very many high school seniors, at least not when they thought in the context of Wadsworth, Byron, or Shelley.

"Assignment for the weekend." Unlike my other classes throughout the day, I didn't get a lot of grumbling from the AP students. "Find a song released in the last twenty years and outline the romantic elements. It should provoke emotion, celebrate nature and beauty, and hone in on the critical fundamental elements of the period."

Kids like these needed more structure, more direction in the assignment. Before the questions started, I answered what few I would in order to guide them, but a large part of the task was figuring out how romanticism still existed in modern-day...even if it wasn't written in iambic pentameter.

"There's no set page requirement. I don't care what type of music you pick. You will read the song to the class on Wednesday, and fifty percent of your grade on this assignment will be determined by your ability to convince me of the romantic-era roots in the lyrics."

Mouths dropped while I spoke. It was unconventional, and it would give me a glimpse into who they were as individuals. The song they chose would be largely defined by the music they listened to, yet what they idealized in the words would open them up to more than just singing a popular song.

Hands went up all around the room. One by one they asked questions I refused to answer. There was no right or wrong choice in what they picked or how they interpreted it. Music, like poetry, is all subjective. With a minute before the bell, the class chattered about the assignment, some with excitement and others, nervous hesitation.

Colbie stared straight ahead.

"Ms. Chapman, is everything all right?" I straightened papers on my desk as I spoke, but when I hadn't received an immediate response, I glanced up to meet her gaze. There was something in her eyes I couldn't place—haunting almost.

"Yes, sir." And there was the canned response I anticipated.

She raced out with Jess at her side as quickly as the bell allowed. My gaze followed her and her friend out the door. I'd spent a good deal of time with every other member of the Chapman family, and Colbie was nothing like any of them. If she weren't the spitting image of her siblings, I'd swear she'd been adopted or even switched at birth. But Colbie looked just like her brothers, only in a much more attractive, female version. As far as I could tell, that was where the similarities stopped. It would be interesting to see if she were really that vastly different when they were all in the same room tonight.

I'd been to enough weddings since I graduated from college to know they were a big deal in the South. Caleb came from a large family, and they came from money, as did Chasity. I was *one* of eleven groomsmen. Their wedding party was enormous and the guest list even more extensive. Although, the number of people standing at the altar with Caleb and his fiancée wasn't what surprised me. It was the fact that his sister wasn't one of them.

With twenty-two bridesmaids and groomsmen, two flower girls, and a ring bearer, the sanctuary of the church was a madhouse. As I stood in my assigned spot waiting for instructions —because walking down an aisle and then back up with a woman on my arm was difficult to do without coaching—my attention waned from the wedding organizer calling out demands. I scanned the room, taking in the effects—the pews, the stained-glass windows, the crowd. My eyes drifted from one person to the next—noting those I hadn't seen since graduation—when they landed firmly on the dark-haired woman in the middle of an empty pew.

She was hard not to notice and not just because of the isolation. Colbie didn't dress to stand out at school and wore very little—if any—makeup, but tonight, she might as well have been a beacon. Even as far off as she sat, it was easy to see Caleb's sister wasn't a child, she was a stunning woman. Albeit, she appeared sad and terribly lonely, but maybe that was because she was the only member of the Chapman family who wasn't in the wedding party. Or possibly because her parents sat on the front row, beaming with pride at Caleb and Chasity, while their only daughter waited silently. It was possible she hadn't wanted to be in the wedding, although something told me she hadn't been asked, not that she'd refused.

I lost track of her momentarily as the people in the processional moved outside the sanctuary to run through the motions again, but when we came back in and I resumed my spot, she still sat stoically on the wooden bench. Not on a cell phone, no book in hand, not engaging with any of the one hundred people here. And I couldn't help but wonder why. The wedding planner finally seemed satisfied after our fifth run-through, and the group moved to the country club where the Chapmans were members for the rehearsal dinner.

Colbie spoke with her parents briefly and left with the rest of us. While everyone else rode with several others, she'd gone by herself. I hung back with the rest of the guys I knew and had gone to school with, waiting on Caleb. He kissed his bride, promising he'd meet her there, and she left with her friends. His brothers made their exit soon after.

As Caleb and I walked to my truck, I asked the question that was none of my business. "Hey, man. Why isn't your sister in the wedding?"

"She and Chas just don't click."

"And your parents were okay with that?"

"What were they going to say, Eli? It's not like they're paying for the ceremony. Plus, it's not Colbie's cup of tea. Trust me, she doesn't care."

The conversation ended there. It wasn't my place to pry, and I didn't need to create undue stress. If I could have gotten out of wearing a penguin suit for this event, I would have, so maybe he was right.

The club was reserved for the Chapman party, and they offered the largest buffet of food I'd ever seen. I kept spotting my student through the crowd, always alone. None of her family members, immediate or extended, appeared to do more than briefly interact with her before moving on, and even that was in passing. I shouldn't be concerned about it, yet somehow, I was dumbfounded by how the rest of the family was this tightly woven cloth while she hung on like a tattered thread.

I'd envied the Chapmans since I'd met them my freshman year. They did everything together, supported each other, hung out together. From the oldest to the youngest, when I saw one, they were all there. It never dawned on me how odd it was that the only female in a menagerie of males was never present. Since I hadn't met her, I hadn't had any reason to give it any thought, yet now that I had, it baffled me.

Caleb had never given any indication that she was a troubled teen, but when I looked back at the conversations with or about his family, her name almost never came up.

With a plate of food in hand, I searched the room for an empty seat and found my mind's subject sitting at a table with a smattering of vacant chairs. No one occupied the space to her left or right. I shouldn't do it, but something about her called to me, drew me in. Not surprisingly, Colbie didn't even give me a sideways glance when I joined her.

"Hey. Mind if I sit here?" I tried to keep my tone light. For all I knew, she'd had a fight with someone and didn't want to be here.

My heart nearly stopped when her head turned in my direction. Her eyes were the palest blue I'd ever seen, and I silently questioned if they'd be sensitive to light without more pigment to protect them against the harmful rays of the sun. The smoky makeup accentuated the shade of her irises and made her creamy complexion appear flawless.

"No, sir." A flicker of something passed over her expression, but she had an incredible poker face.

I knew nothing about her other than a few useless facts and couldn't think of anything to say. My silence resulted in her focus returning to the massive plate of food in front of her.

"Please, call me Eli." The words came out before I realized what I said.

"That's probably not appropriate."

It wasn't; nonetheless, I desperately wanted to draw her out of her shell. And maybe if she didn't see me as her teacher, at least not tonight, she might let me in just a little.

"Dr. Paxton is pretty formal when we're not at school, but I can't think of anything you might be comfortable with."

Without missing a beat, she shot back, "Oh, I can think of a laundry list of things I'd be comfortable with, but Emily Post might roll over in her grave if I used them."

Her bite was entertaining. There weren't many people who attempted to put me in my place, certainly never students, and rarely a woman. "Do tell."

"Hitler, Douche, Dr. Dictator, Castro, Stalin...the list is endless." The side of her lip quivered as she fought a smile.

I set down my fork and wiped my mouth with a napkin. "I'm sorry, Colbie. My behavior the first day of school was over the top. It's tough being a new teacher. Add relocating at the last minute to work at your best friend's alma mater, and it becomes a bit intimidating. I was worried the faculty would question why I'd been given the job, and with four Chapman kids in the school, I didn't want favoritism to be thrown around. It wasn't fair to you, nor was it your fault."

Dark waves fell as she took a bite, but she quickly swiped it back behind her ear. "Thank you." It was always the right side of her hair that bothered her, yet she always moved it with her left hand, crossing her body.

The awkward silence fell between the two of us again. I should have gotten up and moved to a more appropriate seat, but I couldn't bring myself to leave her secluded. "Have you thought any about the assignment?" It was lame, but I was desperate to open up the dialogue.

"No, sir. I have piano every day after school. And from there, I was wrangled into a dress and makeup and then herded to the church."

"Not big on weddings?"

She just shrugged.

"How long have you been playing the piano?"

"Since I was little. I don't know. Ten years or so."

I'd stumbled on the topic Colbie was willing to discuss. "Is that what you want to go to Vanderbilt for?" I already knew she wanted to go pre-med, but I'd ask the same questions a hundred different ways to hear her excited.

"No, though I am going to minor in music."

"That's a pretty big time commitment, isn't it?"

"No more than football." And I'd struck a chord.

"Do most people take lessons every day? I thought it was a once-a-week kind of thing."

She shrugged again. "I guess for the majority that's true. But I wouldn't say they're lessons so much as intense practice sessions that go on for hours with a classically-trained concert pianist at my side."

"That's impressive."

And just as quickly as she'd gotten enthusiastic, her flame

extinguished. "You don't have to pretend to be interested."

I touched her forearm with my hand, and my fingers ignited before I jerked them away. She giggled when she realized what I'd done and seemed to think my paranoia was humorous.

"I'm not pretending. I love music. I wish I played an instrument, but football was always the priority in my house."

"Mine too. But I'm sure you already know that."

Before I could respond, an older woman stopped next to Colbie and pretended to fawn over her in the way fake women did. "Colbie, dear, you're stunning this evening. Turning into quite the beauty. Is this your boyfriend?" The lady glanced at me while waiting for Colbie's response.

"No, Aunt Nancy. I don't have a boyfriend. This is Eli. He's one of Caleb's groomsmen." The sickeningly sweet, prim girl returned to address her family member.

"You know, honey, you're never going to get a man with your nose in those books. And your mother tells me you're missing the Auburn game for a recital." She tsked and clicked her tongue. "Boys aren't hanging around in music rooms."

"I suppose you're right."

Her aunt lost interest quickly and hugged her awkwardly before racing off to bother someone else.

"Your parents are going to miss a game?" My shock rang through my voice.

"Are you kidding? That would be sacrilegious." The way she tried to play it off told me just how much she was hurt by it, though not surprised.

"Where do you do your recitals?" I wasn't sure why I'd felt the need to continue the line of questioning, other than something told me this girl needed someone in her corner.

She placated me throughout the meal, answering my questions with as little information as she could offer without being rude, but her distance was forced. Colbie would catch herself opening up, and I could visibly see her shut back down. Her refusal to allow me to get too close waved all sorts of red flags, but she didn't give me enough to pinpoint the reason.

When she finished eating, she drank a glass of water, dabbed her mouth, and folded the napkin neatly on the table. "Excuse me. I need to use the restroom. I'm sure I'll see you at the wedding tomorrow."

3

COLBIE

The next morning, I got up early to work on homework before the wedding instead of my morning run. I'd played the piano when I came home from the rehearsal dinner until my parents forced me to stop because of "the noise." I'd read for a while after, still nothing held my attention. Somewhere around one in the morning, I finally gave in to sleep.

At five, I got up and made sure all my assignments had been completed with the exception of the poetry dissection for Dr. Paxton's class. It would take longer than I had to find a song, and while I was sure my classmates would go for things like Bob Dylan or The Doors, I wasn't interested in something so trite. My choice would be a careful selection that I didn't make lightly. I really wanted to push the boundaries of the lyrics. And since I had a day full of sitting in silence, feigning interest in my brother's nuptials, I figured I'd have time to scour the internet in a corner unnoticed.

With the size of our family coupled with the breadth of the wedding party, multiple limos were picking people up. I assumed I would drive myself since I wasn't actually participating in the event, but at the last minute, Mama told me to ride with the boys. I considered arguing so I'd be able to leave at the earliest possible point, but just as I opened my mouth to protest, the stern look I received kept me silent. I had my iPad in my purse, so even when the morning turned into an unbearable night, I could work on my English assignment.

We all clamored into the black limo—me the only female in the gang of boys. My brothers were worse about talking than any woman I'd ever known. They gossiped liked old women in the beauty parlor, and it started the moment they opened their eyes in the morning. I had no idea how long it continued, but it hadn't stopped when we arrived at the church.

Caden had been unusually quiet, and I expected him to say something about last night, but he never did. We hadn't talked about it, but he'd had a rather heated discussion with Caleb, and then my parents, about excluding me from the wedding party. And I'd seen him watch me all evening at the rehearsal dinner from his seat with the other groomsmen. Instead of bringing attention to my isolation, he kissed my cheek just before we went our separate ways.

My brother's friends hollered our last name when they saw him, and a hint of a smile crept across my lips. He was a good guy, and everybody loved him. But truth be told, there hadn't been a single Chapman male to grace this town that *hadn't* been adored by everyone they met.

Somehow, that grace hadn't extended to me. People were nice enough because they were Southern and it was expected; nevertheless, I didn't miss the little jabs. They didn't happen in front of my parents, and people like Chasity were confident I'd never repeat them. It was far easier to keep the peace than create a greater divide.

"Colbie, honey, I know you're bored in here." Chasity's tone was condescending, and the way she fluttered her eyes made me want to slap the fake eyelashes off her face. "Why don't you go see if the staff needs any help?" The smile dripped from her mouth—it was as plastic as her nose.

The way she excused me from participating might have seemed like a favor to an outsider, but in my family's circle, and Chasity's too, the family and the help didn't co-mingle.

"Sure." There was no reason to point out just how tacky it was. Everyone within earshot heard it, and their eyes had gone wide at the suggestion.

But relief washed over me the moment the door closed at my back. I wasn't interested in playing the role of little sister to Caleb Chapman any more than Chasity wanted to pretend she cared for me. I didn't know what I'd done to her, or why a grown woman had such disdain for someone so much younger than herself, but it had started their freshman year of college and had gotten progressively worse.

When they were still in high school, she would never have gotten away with treating me the way she did now because my parents would have seen it. While they tended to overlook me, they would have discouraged Caleb from dating a girl who didn't love his little sister. But that was before Caleb hit celebrity status at UGA. And Chasity was openly a fan and supporter of all my brothers, so the entire family, minus Caden, assumed the tension was my fault. I didn't bother to acknowledge it, much less correct it.

Walking toward the sanctuary—hoping to hide in peace for as long as possible—I lifted my gaze just in time to see Dr. Paxton and several of the other groomsmen coming my way. Before I could avert my attention, he caught my eyes and held my stare. I didn't intend to stop to talk but politely said hello to the group.

"You guys go ahead. I'll catch up in a minute." He waved off his friends, who seemed confused by his desire to talk to me. "Hey, Colbie. Where are you heading?"

"To the sanctuary to find a seat." I chewed on my bottom lip just slightly, waiting to be excused.

He chuckled. "The ceremony doesn't start for almost three hours."

I lifted my gaze from his knees to his eyes. "Yes, I know."

His brow furrowed at the lack of humor in my response. "You're going alone?"

"It's not a big deal, Dr. Paxton—"

"Eli."

"Eli," I corrected myself. "It really isn't a big deal."

"What are you going to do for three hours?"

I smoothed the skirt of the soft-yellow silk dress, uncomfortable with the attention he showed me. And when my hair swept across my face, I tucked it behind my ear. "I have an assignment to work on for my English teacher that's due this week. I'll be fine."

A tender smile tugged on the corners of his lips, and the light caught his eyes, making them dance with animation. "Must be a real slave driver."

"He can be a bit of a tyrant."

"You sure you don't want to hang out with us?" He threw up his hand, motioning in the direction of the guys who'd left him standing with me.

"No. Thank you, though." I didn't give him time to protest before adding, "It was good to see you. I'm sure Caleb is grateful you're here."

His forehead crinkled, indicating his desire to say something else, but whatever it was that lingered on his tongue never came out of his mouth. "Good to see you, too. I'm sure I'll see you at the reception."

With a slight nod, I left him standing where he'd stopped. I could sense his eyes boring into my back, but I refused to turn around to see why he hadn't moved. When I finally reached the double doors to the sanctuary, I was able to glance in his direction without being obvious—he stood stock-still with his hands in his pockets, watching my every move until I disappeared from view.

I really wasn't bothered by the time alone to work on my English project. It proved to be far more difficult than I had anticipated. Coming up with song choices wasn't hard, but picking one that said nothing about me yet conveyed romanticism was. I considered myself an upper-level Googler. I didn't just use a word or two typed in; I'd perfected Boolean searches. Identifying one to use that met the criteria for the assignment should have been an easy task, yet every song I started to pick ended up giving away a secret I hid. Secrets I couldn't share with anyone, much less Eli. Or maybe that was the perfect thing to do—give him lyrics that told him everything about me so he'd assume they were meaningless.

His name tumbled around my thoughts. He was like two different people—Eli and Dr. Paxton. While I knew the latter would turn out to be an incredible teacher, the idea of Eli being an equally valuable friend threw me for a loop. I couldn't separate the two, and it seemed vastly inappropriate and strangely alluring. The practical side of me won out in the war inside my mind. I had to please the teacher, not the man, and to do so, I had to choose a song.

I don't know how long I'd been sitting there or how many songs I'd pored through, but Caden sliding into the pew at the back of the church scared the crap out of me. I jerked the headphones from my ears and met my little brother's stare.

"What are you doing in here, Cole?"

"Homework. Why?"

"Do you ever stop?"

"I have an assignment due this week, and it's not like my assistance or attendance is needed anywhere else. Why not kill two birds with one stone?" I shrugged as though the explanation was obvious and everyone did schoolwork while waiting for their brother to tie the knot.

"I just wanted to check on you. Chasity said you bailed shortly after we got here—which I'm sure is a variation of the truth."

"I'm fine, Caden. Promise." My little brother wouldn't buy the lie I was selling. I could only hope he chose to ignore it.

Being squished between two people I didn't know and hoped never to have the pleasure of smelling again, for what I believed was only a twenty-minute ceremony, seemed more like an hour. I stood and sat with the rest of the congregation at appropriate moments, and I tried to focus on the words our minister spoke. My attention repeatedly drifted from the older man with gray hair I'd known my entire life to the one I'd just met who appeared to be having the same issue I was. His gaze lingered with mine for just a fraction of a second too long before returning to the man in front of him. He no more paid attention to Caleb and Chasity than I did, although he was far better at concealing it. I wasn't close enough to see the intricate details of his eyes; still, I caught myself fantasizing about the depths of brown with streaks of black and gold that I'd tried so hard not to notice during our interactions.

As the processional filed out of the sanctuary at the end of the service, my brother and his wife radiated happiness. I watched as my parents followed behind the line and a slew of other people in the parade. Pew by pew the guests retreated behind them, and I finally caught sight of Jess with her parents. They kept her on a short leash, even though there was no reason to. She'd vowed the same life of celibacy in high school I had, and being at the top of the class was just as great a goal. Her parents didn't seem to get it any more than mine did if they thought she'd jeopardize that for idiotic, teenage drama. She offered me a meek wave at her side as she passed, and her father tipped his head in my direction.

I joined the herd and followed the leader to the entrance of the church. The reception wasn't far from here, and I hoped to get away with walking the few measly blocks. It hadn't taken much to get left behind with the masses. My parents were concerned with their guests, my brothers with their friends, and the wedding party with each other, which all suited me just fine. I made a stop in the restroom to freshen up in anticipation of being the last to leave. Yet when I stepped through the ladies' room door, I ran into a wall of muscle covered in black rayon and white cotton. My gaze traveled the pearl buttons, one by one, to the bow neatly tied at a thick, corded neck, over a chiseled chin and perfect nose, to warm chocolate-brown eyes staring back at me. It took me a second to realize Dr. Paxton's hands rested on my biceps, and I was lost in him. Instinctively, my palms hit his chest to brace myself against falling, but the heat radiating through the fabric beneath my fingers quickly scorched me, causing me to peel back.

"I'm sorry, Dr. Paxton. I didn't think anyone was still here."

"Is it coincidence or intentional?"

"Excuse me?"

"Your isolation."

My brow hitched a fraction of an inch before I steadied my expression. "Both, I suppose." I managed to keep my voice from shaking and giving away the anxiety his presence brought.

He stepped back, realizing I wasn't going to fall. "Any particular reason?"

The corners of my mouth pulled down as my shoulders went up. "It's easier for everyone this way."

"How so?"

I cocked my head, taking in his features—most importantly, his eyes. There didn't appear to be any ulterior motive for his questions other than curiosity, and for the first time, I noticed a hint of tenderness I hadn't seen before. It might have been the golden hue that mingled with the chocolate or the crow's feet that etched his skin when he grinned, but something in the way he regarded me warmed my insides.

"I don't know. My parents are good people. So are my brothers. I just ended up with the wrong family. Like there was a boy being born at the same time I arrived, and God got us mixed up." I shrugged for the second time in a matter of seconds. "Clearly, I don't fit in."

"I think you do."

"Then you're blind. I bet you money not one person in my family knows I'm still at the church. Except for Caden; he might have picked up on it."

"Maybe you just haven't found your niche yet."

I shook my head. "I've found my groove; it just doesn't have anything to do with cheerleading or football. You'd think since my dad's a doctor that my education would be equally as important as the boys playing a sport, but in some weird twist of fate, it's not."

"Your parents are proud of you, Colbie. So are your brothers."

"Yeah? How many times did you see me at UGA?" I held up my hand when he started to answer. "Better yet, how many years did you know Caleb before you realized he had a sister you'd never met?" I cocked my eyebrow, waiting for his answer.

He pursed his lips the way boys do without really committing to it, and the truth was written all over his face.

"It's okay, Dr. Paxton. It's not a surprise." Rather than face any more of this titillating conversation about my inability to mesh with my family, I turned toward the doors to exit the church. I left with the grace and dignity my mother raised me to have—with my head held high and my shoulders back.

"Cole."

My head whipped around to stare over my shoulder, stunned by his brazen use of my nickname.

"Wait. You don't have to do everything by yourself. Let me walk with you."

My scowl softened as he trotted down the church stairs to take a place at my side. He extended his elbow as though he were escorting me. I almost warned him about the gossips in this town but decided it was the one day I could safely get away with being on a man's arm and not arouse suspicion.

"You don't like anyone calling you Cole, do you?"

"Caden is pretty much the only one who does. It just caught me off guard." I was oddly confident strolling down the sidewalk at Eli Paxton's side. Boys normally made me uneasy. I wasn't sure what to do around them other than debate. Yet somehow, he set me at ease while ratcheting my anxiety in an entirely different way.

His free hand rested on top of mine holding his arm. Something akin to a static shock ran up my arm, but he didn't seem fazed by it. "The two of you are close?"

"Very." I didn't know how to elaborate on that. I couldn't explain my connection to my little brother—it just existed, and it was my most prized possession outside of my brain. Neither would impress a guy, so I kept my mouth shut.

"I think it's cool. I don't have any siblings. I've always admired how close your family is."

I pinched my lips with my teeth, biting back the words I wanted to say. He didn't have any idea how left out I felt, how isolated, how lonely. Just like everyone else, he saw the big picture —the portrait the Chapmans painted. It was a beautiful, Southern family. It was also very one dimensional.

"Do you wish your parents lived closer?" I didn't know where he was from, but his attachment to my family indicated either he wasn't close to his own—which I doubted—or that they weren't close enough to see often. I'd hedge my bets on the latter based on what remained of his northern accent.

"At times. I've been gone for several years now. I left right after high school, went to UGA for undergrad, and then I fast-tracked my masters and doctorate program. My family didn't have the money for me to fly back and forth to Michigan, so I got used to not seeing them much. They sacrificed to help me pay for grad school so I wouldn't be saddled with student loan debt."

"How on earth did you finish your doctorate in six years?"

"I went to school year-round and took more credit hours each semester than the average student." His blasé attitude about his accomplishment was either arrogant or humble, I wasn't able to discern which. Regardless, it was impressive.

"And still managed to be hailed as one of the University of Georgia's fastest running backs in the school's history? Wow. I thought I was an overachiever." Mumbling didn't prevent him from hearing my thoughts.

"Is that what you are? An overachiever?" He'd stopped walking to look me in the eyes as I answered. "Or are you a perfectionist?"

I chewed on my lip and gave him a slight shrug. "Neither. Both."

Dr. Paxton lifted his free hand to tuck a stray piece of hair behind my ear. "There's something that drives you." His pupils surged, distracting me from the topic, although not far enough that I didn't know where this would lead.

"You say that as though being driven is a bad quality for a girl to possess."

"On the contrary, it's just unusual at your age."

"It's who I am, Dr. Paxton. I don't know what else to tell you. There's no big secret I'm hiding or shortfall I'm trying to mask." Unless my lack of a penis or my disinterest in football counted.

He regarded me with care, searching my features as though he were memorizing them before he blinked several times, and the corners of his mouth alluded to a smile. "Fair enough." Dr. Paxton didn't believe a word I'd said, but hell, neither did I.

The two of us fell into a quiet stroll the remainder of the walk. When we reached the country club, there were still a large number of people congregated outside.

"Pax, man, over here," Caleb called over the crowd to his friend, waving him in his direction.

Dr. Paxton acknowledged my brother before turning his attention to me. "Would you like to join me?" The apprehension in his voice indicated his question was a polite gesture, not a real request. And it shouldn't be.

"No. Thank you for walking with me."

He held my eyes but said nothing before gently squeezing my hand in his and then releasing it. It was brief, not more than a second or two, but the moments his fingers had adorned my skin filled my soul. The only other person in my life who ever managed to release the gag that strangled my heart's ability to beat naturally was Caden. I trusted my little brother implicitly, and for some reason, Dr. Paxton garnered that same internal response. My breath hitched with the realization. Not even Jess had that knack.

I refused to consider the why behind the emotion. It wasn't rational or appropriate. That man could no more be my friend than I could play football. My face flushed with heat, and I pressed my palms to my cheeks, hoping no one bore witness to my frustration. The racing beat of my heart threatened to bring my confusion out in tears. This was not the time nor the place for me to lose my composure or control. I closed my eyes and took several deep breaths to clear my mind. The sting of my nails piercing my skin under the force of a closed fist kept the anxiety at bay. I didn't know how long I'd stood there trying to find my center before I rejoined the world around me, but when I did, I was alone.

The crowd had gone inside, leaving me to find myself deserted on the sidewalk of our small, Southern town. I chose to take solace in knowing no one had seen me. Until I made eye contact with Dr. Paxton through the window in the club.

There he stood with a drink in his hand amongst a group of his friends, but his gaze was cast on me, concern marring his brow. I released my clenched fingers and stretched them out while attempting to appease him with a forced smile. I wouldn't swear to having seen him shake his head, and even if he had, it had been just slightly. He lifted his drink and tipped his chin in acknowledgment but made no move to come in my direction. I couldn't release his gaze. It should have been awkward; instead, I found it more captivating than unnerving.

"Colbie?" The sound of my mother's voice knocked me out of my daze.

"Yes, ma'am?" I didn't have to wait for her to answer. I knew what she wanted. I was expected for pictures, although I wasn't sure why since I wasn't in the wedding party. My feet carried me as if they had a mind of their own. Obeying my mother's silent commands was second nature.

Thankfully, the photographer was adept at dealing with large groups and cantankerous brides. The shuffle in and out of shots should have been like herding cats, but somehow, it worked more like a choreographed dance executed to perfection. The men, then the women, the wedding party, then the family. While my presence was required, I was in very few shots and spent most of the time off to the side. Dr. Paxton ended up on the outskirts next to me; how, I was unsure, though his presence calmed the anxiety these types of situations brought me—even without words.

With him at my side, the photographer motioned for the group to squeeze in together. I slid uncomfortably toward the perimeter. Everything else blurred the second his arm went causally around my back, and his hand landed on my waist. The heat of his touch singed my skin through the silk of my dress. The instant I glanced up at him with uncertainty, he stared down at me with a tender smile, and the flash of the camera caught that moment for eternity. Even knowing how inappropriate it was, I couldn't turn away from his gaze. The warmth of his kind eyes, the way his nostrils flared just slightly, and the hint of a squeeze from his fingers captivated me.

Suddenly, the photographer clapped loudly, thanked us, and people started to move...and so did Dr. Paxton. I instantly regretted his absence, but I couldn't think of a logical reason to call him back to stay by his side. Reminding myself he wasn't here for me did nothing other than cause a longing in my chest—one I'd never experienced or cared to repeat. When Chasity's glare caught my attention, I quickly excused myself, hoping she hadn't witnessed the emotion that crossed my features in Dr. Paxton's presence. He was dangerous and completely off limits.

"Hey, Colbie." My best friend was a welcome distraction.

"Jess."

"Why are your cheeks so flush? Do you feel bad?" She put her hand on my forehead, and I backed away.

"I'm fine. Next thing I know, you're going to lick your thumb and wipe something off my face."

"You're ridiculous. Come dance with me."

"Seriously?"

Jess handed me one of the two glasses in her hand and then leaned in close to my ear. "Drink that, and then we'll dance."

Pulling back, I stared at her, wondering what she had up her sleeve...until I went to sip what I assumed to be Diet Coke. The stench of liquor nearly knocked me off my feet. "Jess," I hissed, but she just raised her eyebrows and then cocked her head toward Chasity.

She knew how tedious the act of perfection could be where my family was concerned. "Just loosen up a little. Have fun for once. We never do anything reckless."

"Somehow, I don't think getting drunk is the answer." Yet, I still put the glass to my lips and sipped at the concoction.

No one paid the two of us a bit of attention. My parents were busy playing host and hostess while my brothers talked football with Caleb and his friends. It seemed as though everyone here was involved in some secret club Jess and I weren't members of.

"No one said anything about getting drunk. One drink won't send you over the edge, but I bet you won't mind hitting the dance floor, either."

I considered her offer for a fraction of a second. She was right. There wasn't a soul here that cared what the two of us did. Her parents had even let her off the leash in favor of working the roomful of social connections. Throwing caution to the wind, I took another sip before I drank the strong mixture in a couple of large gulps.

When I wiped my mouth with the back of my hand, I looked up to see Dr. Paxton watching me from across the room. As though I'd been caught with my hand in the cookie jar, my cheeks warmed, and I averted my gaze.

"Dr. Paxton is staring at you, Colbie."

He was. And I liked it far more than I should. It should have creeped me out. Instead, it seemed to awaken a piece of me that had been dormant, one I'd chosen to allow to hibernate through high school. I didn't need distractions—that's precisely what boys were. But Dr. Paxton wasn't just a boy—he was all man.

"Come on." I grabbed her hand, ignoring her comment, fearful of what she might have seen in him and terrified of what she might see in me.

Jess and I shared a bond, not like the one I had with Caden, but we were close. I wouldn't be able to conceal whatever it was I currently felt, and I wasn't prepared to dissect it.

Just before we reached the dance floor, I set the empty glass on a table. "What was that?"

"Rum and Diet Coke." She set hers down next to mine.

In less than five minutes, the alcohol had warmed my insides and relaxed my mind. The two of us danced to songs I couldn't identify and those I didn't care for. Nevertheless, I was having the time of my life, laughing with my best friend as the two of us danced without a care in the world. When I got hot, I tried my luck with the bartender, not thinking he'd serve me, but wondering how Jess had secured drinks. To my surprise, not only did he not question me, he dropped a cherry in each glass with a wink.

I'd downed mine before I made it back to the dance floor. If I were legally able to consume alcohol, I would complain to my parents about how cheap they were being with those tiny glasses. As it stood, that probably wasn't the best idea. It didn't take Jess long to drink hers, either. She left my side to get rid of the cup just as the song started to change, and the first ballad of the night played through the speakers.

"May I?" Dr. Paxton stood next to me with his hand out ready to take mine.

Jess had returned and waited a step behind him with wide eyes. When she eagerly nodded to accept his invitation, I did.

"Of course." I placed my hand in his, and he wrapped an arm around my lower back, pulling me in. Dr. Paxton didn't press me to his chest or squeeze my hand. He held me as though my father would if he were to dance with me. It was the way his pupils grew before quickly shrinking and the slight sweat of his palm that told me something no one else could see.

"You seem to be having a good time."

"I am." It was true. I had dreaded this event for months, but Jess made it fun. The liquor helped.

"Have you been drinking?" The accusation came in the form of hushed words. Concerned.

There was no point in lying, and I didn't care to justify myself to my teacher or my brother's best friend. "Yes." Short and sweet.

"Colbie, you're underage."

I couldn't stop the grin that tugged on the corners of my lips when his brows dipped and creased a line between them. It was cute...endearing.

"I am."

"You need to be careful." His whispered warning heated my ear before he pulled back to meet my eyes.

"I'm always careful, Dr. Paxton." I talked to his shoulder and then took in the other people in the room before directing my attention back to the man who held me in his embrace. "Just once, I'm letting go." I wasn't sure if I was still talking about drinking or the thoughts running through my mind about all the things I wanted this man to do to me.

He didn't say anything else as he expertly moved me around the dance floor. Then, just before the song ended, he leaned down and pressed his cheek to mine. His thick fingers curled more firmly around my own, and my heart swelled with his proximity. "Please be careful, Colbie." No one would have heard what he said regardless, but there was something in the way he issued his plea that tugged at my heart. As though it were a secret we shared.

My naiveté and the two mixed drinks I'd had were the only things that could possibly lead me to believe there was anything more between us, but I'd managed to blur the lines...even if it were only in my mind. Jess seemed unaffected by his presence or his desire to dance with me. She resumed her spot on the dance floor as quickly as he exited.

Two drinks turned into four, and when dinner was served, Jess sat with her parents while I took my fifth adult beverage to the patio of the country club. Alone with my thoughts and the lake surrounded by endless stretches of golf greens. The ice clinked as I dangled the glass between my fingers and stared at the waning sun. It was surprisingly quiet for the mass of people just beyond the doors behind me, but not even the wind seemed to stir. It was as if Mother Nature herself was paying her respects to Caleb Chapman, recognizing his greatness. I rolled my eyes at the thought of the world conspiring to offer a Chapman praise.

In the silence, I suddenly became hyper-aware of my own actions. I wondered if the universe considered my intoxication an abomination or if it overlooked my indiscretion the way my family did me. The final sip of rum left my lips wet and my throat warm. As though I were seducing myself, my tongue snaked out to grab every last drop that might have lingered, and then my teeth caught my bottom lip, tugging briefly before releasing it.

With nothing left to drink, I turned to go back inside. Caden stared at me with an edge to his expression I hadn't seen directed at me before. "Cole?"

"What are you doing out here, Caden?" I proceeded toward him, knowing my isolation issued the invitation, and the only way to get him to relax was to return to the reception. Two steps forward and I stumbled on my heel and landed in his arms.

"Are you drunk?"

"No. My heel twisted. I'm fine." I made certain not to meet his eyes and directed my mouth away from him. My only hope was that he didn't smell the alcohol. If he told my parents, I couldn't imagine what they'd do.

"I'm not stupid. Can you even stand up straight?"

"Of course, I can. Don't be a brat." The instant the word came out of my mouth, I regretted it. He was the only member of my family who'd tried to pay any attention to me tonight. He didn't deserve my sassy disposition. "I'm sorry. I didn't mean that."

"Why don't you go in and get something to eat?" His suggestion was meant to sober me, not because he worried about my being hungry.

Only, I wasn't hungry, and I didn't want to sober up. I wanted this night to end. Jess had abandoned me and would be stuck with her parents for the rest of the evening. The moment we stepped inside, Caden would get sucked into the gang of men surrounding Caleb and my brothers, and I'd be alone. There wasn't a soul here I didn't know. There was no possibility of meeting new people. I'd grown up with or was related to everyone beyond those doors. And the only person who didn't fall into either of those qualifiers was also the one person I needed to stay far away from.

Instead of arguing with my little brother, I nodded and let him help me over the threshold and back into the party. After kissing his cheek, I assured him I would be fine on my own and that I would get a bite to eat. He knew I wasn't driving, so it wasn't like I was a physical danger to anyone. If my parents caught wind, it might get ugly, but that certainly wouldn't take place here.

Most of the guests had danced along with the bride and groom and the wedding party. The music was upbeat and lively. Only a wedding in the South would lend itself to people clogging at a reception, yet sure enough, there were several people on the floor putting on quite the show. Caden watched me, making sure I went toward food. He even made eye contact with me as I picked up a plate. Satisfied, he turned away and joined his friends. I promptly set down the plate and went back to the bar.

I had alternated between the bars around the room, so no one got suspicious. The bartenders didn't care. I guess they all assumed if I were asking for alcohol, I was old enough to drink. With my rum and Diet Coke in hand, I stepped into a shadow the dimmed lights left against a wall where I continued to sip the night away. It was probably a good thing I didn't have easy access to liquor. Even I recognized how much easier things were with a little liquid courage. My troubles faded into the distance, the stress eased from my shoulders, the isolation seemed unimportant, and I was just Colbie.

Lost in peaceful serenity, I missed the person standing next to me—until he took my glass. "I'm not sure what number you're on, but it's safe to say, you've had too many, Colbie."

My eyes fluttered in annoyed frustration. Trying to roll them drunk and irritated was far more difficult than it was sober, and I couldn't imagine how mortified my mother would have been to see that sight. "Dr. Douche returns."

"Are you *trying* to get in trouble?" Dr. Paxton's concern was misplaced.

"In order to get in trouble, someone would have to be aware of what I was doing. Hell, they'd have to know where I was. And other than Caden, there's not a solitary person here that remembers I even attended the festivities." My words slurred just enough to give away my level of intoxication, although I believed I did a pretty good job of concealing it.

He set the glass on the empty table in front of us and stepped back into my hideout with me. "Clearly that's not true since I'm here."

"Did Caleb send you to warn me of my unladylike behavior? Or maybe the disrespect I was showing him and his bride on their wedding day?" My voice carried farther than I'd expected, and a couple glanced over their shoulders to see what was going on.

Suddenly, Eli's fingers wrapped around my bicep, and he hauled me away from the group and toward the back door I'd just come in. I struggled to keep up with him without falling on my face. His grip was tighter than I cared for, and I wasn't interested in whatever lecture he'd been sent to impart. Dr. Paxton didn't stop once the door closed behind us, although he did look around to see who might bear witness to our exchange and kept moving —dragging me—until there was no chance we'd have an audience.

"What are you doing, Colbie? This isn't like you."

I scoffed at his assumption and huffed as though he were clueless. "You don't *know* me. Don't pretend you do just because you and Caleb are attached at the hip." My lip curled into a sneer at the same time I jerked my arm from his grasp.

His fingers no longer made my heart soar or warmed my insides; they now felt as condemning as everyone else who had ever dared to touch me.

"That's not fair." If he were hurt by my words, he didn't allude to it. "I don't want you to do something you'll regret. I'm sure Chasity would have a field day finding you like this, and I wouldn't wish that on anyone, much less you."

I sat in a sanctimonious show of disrespect. "Like you're any better than they are." My defenses reared their ugly heads—the wall went up to keep him out.

Dr. Paxton sighed and ran his fingers through his hair before taking a seat next to me. With our backs to the patio, we were cloaked in shadows. He leaned up against the building and angled his legs toward me. I crossed my arms over my chest and pressed my knees together. While he appeared to be relaxed for a conversation between friends, I was defensive and ready for battle.

"You're different than the rest of your family."

Thank you, Captain Obvious. "A bit."

"Want to talk about it?" He reached out and touched my forearm with the back of his pointer finger.

My traitorous body responded like it had on the dance floor. I didn't pull back, and neither did he. His nail trailed slowly down to my wrist, and I watched with rapt attention, unable to focus on the question at bay. When he pulled back his hand, my gaze followed as though the world were proceeding in slow motion.

"You know they love you, right?"

I realized I'd never answered his last question. When I met his eyes again, the prickly agitation I'd held onto as he pulled me out the door vanished. And the rambling began. "They don't know what to do with me. Ignoring me is the easiest way to address it."

"I'm sure it's hard being the only girl."

I shrugged. "I guess."

The silence lingered for what seemed an eternity while he waited for me to continue; although, in reality, it wasn't more than a minute or so while I attempted to collect my thoughts. I wanted to believe I wasn't interested in sharing with him, that no part of me desired to connect with him on a different level—the only problem was, *every* part of me wanted to connect with him on a level I'd never connected to anyone. Emotionally, physically, spiritually, and any other way I could.

"I used to think I'd been adopted or switched at birth."

He snickered. "Had you never looked in a mirror?"

"Sadly, that is the only irrefutable evidence I have. As far back as I remember—four maybe five years old—I didn't fit in with them. It was more than just being the only girl, though." My thoughts swam as I tried to organize them through the fog and my thick tongue. It took effort to speak when all I cared to do was memorize the way his mouth moved and how he moistened his lips.

Dr. Paxton's attention didn't waver. His eyes studied mine, waiting for more—as though he needed my past like he needed water or air.

"The years and additional brothers only compounded the already cataclysmic differences. By the time I was seven, I had given up trying to fit in. I remember sitting on a piano bench with my teacher, crying."

"About what?"

"Even then, I believed the only way I'd ever get any of their attention was to be perfect."

"At the piano?"

My eyes drifted from his mouth to his gaze in silence. And for a beat, I considered what he had asked and wondered if he'd get the significance of my answer. "Everything." The pain I'd shared with Dr. Chalmers that day rushed back as though it took place in the present. "Being the best wasn't enough. Great wouldn't crack the surface. Exceptional was the only option."

The expression on his face shook me as profoundly as the fact that I'd willingly shared my most intimate secret with a man who had no business having this discussion. He didn't interrupt or try to dissuade my perception. The only move he made was to loop his pointer finger with mine, as though he thought I might float away if he didn't ground me. The intimate gesture spurred my confession.

"Now perfection is expected, and it never got me anything more than what they were willing to give.... Funny how that happens." I shrugged one shoulder, careful not to move the hand he held for fear he'd drop it.

"Colbie..." Reverence clung to each syllable of my name as they moved past his lips. Or possibly pity.

"Don't."

The one finger he held wrangled the others into a full embrace. "Don't what?"

"Feel sorry for me." I straightened my spine and pushed back my shoulders with more confidence than I actually had.

"I don't feel sorry for you. I'm in awe of your strength."

I couldn't stifle the chuckle that escaped until I met his stare. A pensive glare softened into something unrecognizable. Even in the darkness, I could see his pupils shrink and his nostrils flare. I didn't have any experience with men, but I'd watched enough romance movies and read enough smut to know he fought what I felt with an equal amount of vigor.

Leaning closer to him, I pulled the hand he held onto my lap, and my other went to his cheek. I closed my eyes and touched my mouth to his. The electricity was cosmic. I'd never kissed a boy or a man, but when his lips parted and his tongue slipped next to mine, the way they tangled together in an erotic dance had me flying. Or I was more inebriated than I thought.

He pushed back, and my eyes flew open just in time to catch the drunken look lingering in his flushed features. "We can't do this." Then he wiped his mouth with the back of his hand in disgust, and I realized I'd misread every signal I believed I'd seen. Dr. Paxton appeared mortified by my actions.

Without thinking any further, I stood and raced down the stairs hoping to stave off the tears until I was safely away.

"Colbie," he shouted, but I didn't chance looking back to see his rejection. "Colbie. Stop."

Running in heels was far different than Hollywood made it appear—even if they didn't do it intoxicated. Tears stung my eyes and burned my cheeks as they trickled down my face. Embarrassment was not an emotion I cared to experience—ever. And losing control of myself was a close second in comparison.

4

ELI

I COULDN'T RISK COLBIE NOT MAKING IT HOME SAFELY. Caleb would kill me for following her, but if something happened, I wouldn't be able to live with myself. They didn't live far from here, ten or twelve blocks, but it was far enough that something could happen and Colbie not be found. It wasn't a chance I was willing to take.

She'd crossed the line tonight, and that was something I'd have to deal with when she was sober. Unfortunately, it wasn't something I could address with her brother or any other member of her family. As I ran back into the country club to grab my keys, I noticed how right she'd been. No one seemed the wiser as to her whereabouts. It hadn't been any different at the rehearsal, either. It was the first flaw I'd ever seen in the Chapman clan, and it was one that shook me to the core. Not because of how it affected my friend or his brothers, but because of how it affected Colbie. The passion I'd felt flow from her skin to mine with just the brush of a finger was nothing compared to the pull of her lips, the way her tongue ignited something inside me when we kissed. And as my student, every bit of it was wrong, even thinking it—acting on it could not only cost me my job but my relationship with Caleb.

Standing there, staring at her family, the guests, my friends, I realized I was wasting time. Colbie's safety was far more important than anything going on here. Once I shoved my keys into my pocket, I took off out the front door. My car wasn't here, and I wasn't sure how long this would take. Coming back to find everyone had left and I didn't have access to my vehicle wouldn't bode well.

There was no point in running. I doubted that she'd continued jogging once she believed I hadn't followed. A formal dress and shoes wouldn't have made it easy—add in the alcohol and she was on an obstacle course of her own making. I expected to find her fairly quickly. To my surprise, we didn't meet on the street. When I caught up to her, she had made it home.

The place was lit up like a Christmas tree. Every light on the first floor of their plantation-style house was illuminated. It was a sight to behold itself, yet the image that caught my attention was the woman at the piano in the window. The sidewalk ran parallel to their front porch, and I followed it until I was directly in front of her. There I stood with my hands in my pockets and listened to the most beautiful music I'd ever heard played. It was as if she were putting on a concert for one—me.

The glass of the windows muted the notes, although not enough to prevent the melody from reaching me—just from disturbing anyone else. She sat perched on the bench in front of an instrument as gorgeous as the beauty playing it, and in that moment, she transformed into something resembling an angel. Instead of white wings extended to soar, hers appeared broken. Colbie's long hair hung below her shoulders, and her delicate fingers danced on the keys. I was mesmerized by the way she made love to the ivory while exuding pain.

I wanted nothing more than to knock on the door, to hug her, reassure her, tell her how special I believed her to be—how exquisite she really was. Unfortunately, doing so would only serve to encourage the behavior she'd exhibited tonight—the kiss, not the drinking—and regardless of how it felt, it couldn't happen. I didn't even want to think of what Caleb would do if he found out I'd ever touched his little sister. My job was another story. I'd never work in a high school again if I were caught with a student.

At some point, I'd have to explain that to her, share with her. Tonight wasn't the time. My heart ached at the notion of being another person to push her away, let her go, make her believe she wasn't worth my time. In truth, I didn't know much about her—just enough to know I wanted more. With every note that flowed through to the street, my will waned. Everything about her was stunning, and witnessing Colbie uninhibited in her environment, doing what she loved brought a smile to my face.

I didn't know how long I watched her performance. I lost count of the number of songs she played. It wasn't until she stood and seemed to meet me eye for eye through the distance that I realized I needed to leave. Colbie paused, staring at me on her sidewalk. The light behind her erased her features, leaving nothing other than a silhouette that lingered briefly, then the room went dark as did each of the others downstairs. I followed her through the house from the sidewalk until the last bit of illumination disappeared, and so did Colbie.

She'd made it home safely and in one piece. I wasn't so sure I'd be able to say the same for myself. I'd crossed a line I wasn't positive I could come back from or even wanted to. I had approximately thirty-six hours to figure it out before she walked into my classroom on Monday morning.

Colbie ignored me, refused to make eye contact, for days. I didn't have a clue how to break through or fix things when she wouldn't acknowledge me. She had quit participating in class discussions, didn't answer questions, and I hadn't been willing to call on her to force it. There hadn't been a single time she'd made eye contact with me since the exchange through the window on Saturday night. She'd have to engage tomorrow when the class presented their songs or take a zero. And while she hadn't joined in the literary debates, Colbie hadn't missed an assignment. I couldn't imagine her taking a zero. It would eliminate her run for valedictorian completely—she wouldn't give me that. I wouldn't let her.

Thankfully, I hadn't had to deal with Caleb. He and Chasity were on their honeymoon and wouldn't be back until next week. I had a handful of days to get shit straight with his sister. At some point, I'd have to come clean with her brother, it just didn't have to be today. I didn't know anyone else here, so my evenings had been quiet and filled with reflection. What I should have done with a student. How I needed to fix things with my student. And each solution brought more frustration. Although I wasn't sure if it was because I couldn't try any of them with her ignoring me or that I didn't want to. She was an eighteen-year-old kid. There was no way in hell I could risk throwing my career away. Nonetheless, she plagued my thoughts and had started haunting my dreams.

Every way I imagined trying to resolve our current predicament or my inappropriate behavior came to fruition when I closed my eyes—only in my sleep, her pain racked my own body. I'd wake in a cold sweat, chest heaving, heart throbbing, and it took several minutes for me to recognize it wasn't reality. This girl had me in unreasonable knots I couldn't unravel.

As much as I looked forward to today—hearing her voice—I dreaded it just the same. I worried about what song she'd chosen, thinking it might be a message for me, a safe way for her to deliver it. Then on the flip side, I worried it would tell me nothing. Without being obvious, I watched her in class. I listened when she talked to other people. If I saw her in the hall, I observed her body language and how she interacted. I craved something personal from her, and it pained me that she'd given me nothing other than indifference.

When second period ended, my stomach turned itself in knots in anticipation of her arrival. Colbie was here; I'd seen her in the hall this morning from the safety of my classroom. She came strolling into class with Jess at her side. The two laughed and the radiance of Colbie's smile ruined me. And for the first time since her brother's wedding, when she took her seat, she looked up. As she pulled her notebook and a pen from her backpack, her gaze met mine. The sadness that lingered in her pale-blue eyes was there like always, but when the smile fell from her lips, my heart plummeted. It was dangerous to risk staring at her as other kids entered, yet I refused to steal my attention from her as long as she willingly received it. And I didn't—not until she looked away.

My line of sight shifted to the other kids in the room, and I found Jess's hard stare honed in on me—unforgiving. I couldn't dwell on what she might know. I had to assume Colbie hadn't shared with anyone else that she'd kissed me or that I'd held her hand. Hell, everyone at the wedding had seen me dance with her. I raked my hand through my already disheveled hair, and Jess just shook her head with a snide look on her face. Colbie might not have told her anything, but she definitely knew more than was safe for me.

I didn't waste any time when the bell rang. "All right." I clapped my hands together. Normally, this was one of the most fun days of the year. It gave me a chance to learn a little about my students, and they typically enjoyed it. Today, I was nervous. "Who's first?" I scanned the room waiting for an eager student to raise their hand. I pointed to the first volunteer. "Jeremy, you're up."

Jeremy was a good student and seemed to be a good kid. He'd equate to middle management where he was a yes man. He aimed to please and didn't have the gumption to lead. The world needed people like Jeremy. He'd done exactly what was asked of him with little imagination. I'd bet money he'd Googled song and romantic poetry instead of listening to his iPod to find something that represented him.

The same was true of the next four students. Perfectly executed. Exactly what they thought I wanted; except, I wanted them to give me what *they* wanted. Each had expertly outlined the romantic elements in the lyrics and argued what made the song fit into the period we studied. They just did it without any heart—there was nothing in their presentation that was part of who they were. The truly analytical minds, the creative ones, would make me feel their approach, understand the music—I'd hear the song in my mind being played by their emotions. Thus far, I hadn't gotten that.

"Colbie, you're next." I didn't look in her direction when I called her name. I made my way to the back of the class to watch her without hesitation or distraction. When I reached the last row, I took one final step to turn and lean against the wall. "What song did you choose?" With my ankles crossed and my hands behind my back, I appeared casual and unaffected—I was anything but.

"'Invisible'"—her eyes bored holes through me—"by Hunter Hayes."

Interesting. I wouldn't have dubbed her a fan of country music. I hadn't heard the song and made a mental note to look it up the moment the bell rang.

Colbie held my attention from the moment she started speaking and never looked away. Not once did she roam the room or act as though there was anyone else in her audience. She directed every word at me, to me, *for me*. The pain in my chest grew as she spoke of the rejection of social convention and the force of emotion on the inner world—the ache of a lonely teenager.

A lump formed in my throat, knowing she'd picked this song as a representation of who she believed herself to be. Yet her determination to move past the labels she'd been dubbed with, daring to be something different—this song was Colbie's autobiography. I just hadn't heard it sung. Somehow, she'd found inspiration in the loss, the hurt—her melancholy. Every word she spoke as she made her way through each stanza and then the chorus was perfectly executed and poignantly placed.

Colbie knew what she was doing.

There wasn't a doubt in my mind that she wanted me to hear her.

She'd done precisely what I'd hoped for. Colbie dug deep and made herself vulnerable to those around her. Twenty other kids had just witnessed her expose her torment—the pain she carried down the halls daily. She was idolized by her peers, the intellectuals. There were other students with tears in their eyes, likely because they related. Once again, I stood in awe of this girl. She was lightyears ahead of those around her. All I wanted to do was grab her and scream how vibrant she truly was. Make her see herself the way those around her did. I wanted to make her pain invisible by erasing it.

When she was done, the class clapped as they had for everyone who'd gone before her. I couldn't move or speak. And when she turned to retake her seat, I wiped the emotion from my features. Before I could call on anyone else, Jess jumped up.

"Me next!"

I hadn't heard a word she said. Thankfully, each presentation was accompanied by a paper outlining the same thing. I hadn't been able to engage in anything else after Colbie took her seat. Never had a student affected me the way Colbie Chapman had. *Did.*

And if I didn't get my shit together, she might destroy me before it was over.

When the bell rang, I gathered the papers as the seniors left the classroom and shut the door behind the last one. Fourth period was my planning period, and the first thing I did was get out my phone to look up the song that shattered Colbie, and then me.

If I were a man prone to tears, that song would have brought them to my eyes—or at least how it related to Colbie. Her perception of herself hit me so profoundly a lump formed in my throat that I had a hard time swallowing around. High school was a cruel place, and Colbie was strangled here. She knew who she was—it just wasn't someone appreciated in this tiny Georgia town. She was destined for greatness. And when she found it, those who had underestimated her would regret not being a part of the blinding light she'd shine.

Another day had passed without my addressing the situation with Colbie. I started to wonder if maybe that was best for us both. Although, I wasn't so convinced that I hadn't gone looking for her during her lunch period. I'd tried to keep her after class. When she asked if she could meet me at lunch, I'd almost said no, knowing it would put the two of us alone. Then she indicated she had a test in AP Calculus, and I was afraid if she were late to class it would affect her grade, so I let her leave.

Now, here I was searching the halls when I didn't find her in the lunchroom with Jess. I checked the library next. The last place I'd gone had been a total crapshoot. I'd gotten her schedule from the office and knew she took music, and the closer I got to the band room, the more confident I became that I'd found her.

Her back was to me when I reached the open door. I leaned against the frame and listened—without her knowledge—to what sounded like an incredibly difficult song. She flowed through it without a hitch, and I got lost in the notes just like I had on her sidewalk after her brother's wedding. Colbie hypnotized me with each key she touched. I wondered how she didn't recognize she'd reached the perfection she strived for.

Her hands beat on the keys, suddenly frustrated. Then her fingers flew to her hair, clutched at the strands, and pulled.

"Damn, damn, damn."

"Colbie?" It probably wasn't the best time to interrupt. I'd just admitted—without saying anything—I'd witnessed whatever mistake she'd made in her performance.

She spun around on the seat, clearly shocked anyone had been watching. "Dr. Paxton." The irritation quickly changed to something akin to surprise. "I'm sorry. I forgot about our meeting." It took her less than five seconds to turn back to the piano, close the keyboard, and then stand. She pointed with her thumb over her shoulder toward the instrument. "I was trying to work through the étude." Colbie fumbled with an explanation I hadn't asked for. She finally dropped her hands to her sides and exhaled, slumping her shoulders in defeat. "Did you still want to talk to me?"

"Please."

She grabbed her backpack from the floor next to the piano and slid it onto her shoulder. Following closely behind me, Colbie didn't utter a word on the way back to my class. I wanted to leave the door open to prevent gossip, but she closed it after walking through.

Hovering mere inches from the door, she'd struck a defensive posture with her feet shoulder-width apart and her arms crossed.

"You want to have a seat?"

Her tongue snuck out from between her lips just before she chewed on the bottom one. Then she proceeded to the desk she sat in during third period, the Chapman poise firmly in place. I could see her mom all over her. They didn't look alike; it was in her expressions, the way she held her hands and bit her tongue—she'd been schooled in the art of diplomacy. Only Colbie did it with a grace her mother would never have—because Colbie was pure class. She just didn't know it, and her humility only made her light more radiant.

"You know we have to talk about Saturday night, right?"

Her eyes tilted up to acknowledge me, and her brow lifted slightly. Still, she said nothing. The innocence on her face nearly drove me to the brink of insanity.

"Colbie..." Her name came off as a plea.

"I understand, Dr. Paxton. Is there anything else?" The innocence left her eyes and was replaced by harsh indifference. The girl I'd met the first day of school had resumed occupancy in front of me.

"I'm sorry." I wanted to tell her if she weren't my student, if she were out of school, if she could wait a year—if, if, if. There were too many stipulations, and none of them were safe for either of us. I didn't have any options regardless of what I wanted. Playing with Colbie was playing with fire, and it was one I wouldn't be able to extinguish once it was lit.

"Don't be. I'm the one who should apologize. I hope you'll forgive me." Her canned response was cold and stole my breath as intended. She was embarrassed, and in her mind, I'd turned her down.

Without admitting everything I couldn't say, I wouldn't be able to change her perception. All I could do was tell her that I hoped there were no hard feelings and that we could keep it between the two of us. She nodded her agreement. There was no discussion, no real dialogue. That was it.

I had just shamed her to save my own ass. The way she felt everyone did. Colbie believed she was invisible, that she hadn't affected me or left a lasting impression. She was so far from the truth, and yet, there was nothing I could do to assuage her guilt or hurt.

She stood and walked to the door. With her hand on the knob, she didn't turn to face me while she looked at the floor. "I won't tell Caleb, Dr. Paxton. I hope you don't, either."

I didn't respond. And with my silence, she opened the door and left.

It was Saturday night all over again. My desire to run after her, tell her she was mistaken, show her just how wrong she was nearly overtook my common sense. Instead, I dropped to my chair and banged my head on the desk several times. I'd managed to take a flower that just needed a little water and light and drown it to the point that it wilted under the heat of the sun.

5

COLBIE

"What were you doing in Dr. Paxton's room during lunch?" Jess asked as she caught up with me in the hall.

"He just wanted to talk to me about my essay." I hated lying to her, but I hadn't told her about kissing him at the reception and didn't plan to.

It wasn't that I thought she'd overreact. I didn't know what she'd do. My greatest fear was that Jess would think *he'd* done something wrong. I couldn't let Dr. Paxton get in trouble for my drinking, much less taking it upon myself to plant one on him. I was doing my best to pretend it hadn't happened. The only time that became difficult was during third period...and now.

"I think he likes you."

"What? He does not." I realized how loudly I'd responded to her, and the look of shock must have been humorous because she died laughing.

"Oh my God. You have a crush on our teacher, don't you?"

I hit her in the arm playfully, hoping she'd drop it. "Hardly. Now keep it down." And then I rolled my eyes to punctuate my disinterest.

"You totally do. It's so cute. You better be careful going to see him outside of class. You don't want to get him in trouble."

"Jess, seriously. He's just a good-looking guy. He's also my brother's best friend and...*old*." He was anything but old. Gorgeous, intelligent, built, sweet—*old* never entered the equation. Older, yes. Off limits, absolutely.

She held her hands up in surrender. "If you say so." Then she winked, keeping it playful. "What are you doing after school? Hot date?" Jess broke out in giggles again, and I stopped to stare at her, showing her just how little humor I found in her jokes. "Okay, I promise, I'm done."

"I have piano. The same thing I do every day. Why?"

"After that?"

"Homework, I guess. Is there something you're getting at?"

"Just wondering what my best friend was doing. Why do I have to have motivation to be curious about your plans?"

"I don't have any. Do you want to come over?"

Before Jess could answer, Caleb stopped us. "Hey, Jess. Sorry to interrupt you guys. Colbie, is there any way you can pick up your brothers after practice this afternoon? I want to take Caden out for a while."

"Sorry, I can't. I have practice with Dr. Chalmers. Why don't you ask Mama?"

He waved me off. "No big deal. I'll drop the twins off first. Or get Chasity to." My brother punched me lightly in the arm with a smile I'm sure won ladies over but only served to make me roll my eyes. "Better not let Mama see you do that." He laughed as he backed down the hall. When I stuck out my tongue, he replied, "Critter, have you learned nothing about etiquette in the South? You're never going to land a husband doing that kind of thing." His teasing wasn't appreciated. Before I could respond, he turned and walked away.

"Remind me how he ended up with a hag like Chasity." Jess

had never hidden her infatuation with Caleb. And Caleb had never hidden his irritation with her interest.

"She's not so bad."

"Are you kidding me? She treats you like a dog."

"Okay, she's not so bad to everyone other than me." I snickered. Jess was right. Chasity had two very different personalities—one of which seemed to be reserved for me. "So do you want to come over when I get home?"

We started moving toward my locker when she blew me off. "Nah, I guess not. Maybe another time." She raised her eyebrows suggestively, yet somehow, I'd managed to miss her innuendo. "I'm sure I'll talk to you later."

After two hours with Dr. Chalmers, I drove home and spent another hour practicing the étude before Caleb dropped off Caden, Collin, and Clayton. Whatever plans he'd had with Caden hadn't happened, although I didn't bother asking why. The boys all appeared to be in good moods, so it must not have been important. When Daddy came in the door, Mama called us all to dinner, and I finally rose from the piano bench.

"Cole, that sounded wicked. What are you working on?" Caden no more cared about classical music than I did football; he just loved me enough to pretend.

As we neared the dining room, the smell of fried chicken overwhelmed my empty stomach. I had skipped breakfast to catch up on the homework I hadn't done last night, and skipped lunch to work on the étude so I could focus on my time with Dr. Chalmers this afternoon.

"Chopin."

"Will you play it for me sometime?"

I stopped dead in my tracks. My little brother had never, in all the years I'd played, asked to hear anything. He might not know the details, but that request proved he knew how much I hurt inside. When he realized I wasn't still on his heels, he turned back.

"You coming?" he asked.

I just smiled and caught up to him. He slung his arm over my shoulder and rolled me into his chest to wrap me in a bear hug. I wasn't an overly affectionate person and couldn't remember the last time anyone other than my dad had hugged me. But being tucked into the security Caden offered not only reminded me that I had a safety net, but he was getting big. My little brother was now several inches taller than me and had a solid hundred extra pounds of lean muscle. He even smelled like he'd grown up, but I couldn't identify which scent of Axe it was on his shirt.

He assumed his spot at the table, and I took mine. For the first time in ages, I missed Carson and Casey. The rest of the family saw them at UGA games. Carson was in his first year of grad school, and Casey had just started his junior year. True to the Chapman legacy, they, too, bled for the Bulldogs, and there was no way my parents would ever miss a game Casey played. Just like they hadn't missed any of Caleb's or Carson's. And they'd never miss Caden's, Clayton's, or Collin's...as long as they played for Georgia.

There were now three empty seats at our table, and their absence suddenly stung for some reason. I'd be the next to leave, and as much as I wanted to pretend like I wouldn't miss my family, the truth was I would. I hadn't ever wanted to be away from them; I'd wanted to be a part of them. If that couldn't happen, then I wanted to make a life for myself, one where I felt loved, cherished.

As the food was passed around the table, Collin shoved a chunk of chicken into his mouth and then tried to talk through it. "What was Jess doing at practice today, Critter?"

I took a deep breath to keep from responding to the nickname.

"I didn't know she was there. What was she doing?" For all I knew, she had some project due that she was using football statistics for.

"Watching." Food fell out of his mouth and onto his plate.

I glanced to my mother, hoping she'd address his foul table manners, but she was wrapped up in a conversation with my dad. "She had to be doing more than watching. Did she have a notebook or anything with her?"

Jess detested football with as much vigor as I did, and she wasn't one of those girls who ogled the players.

"Nope." He continued to shove food into his mouth while trying to carry on a conversation.

"Collin, please. Don't talk until you've finished chewing." The grimace I made in disgust only fueled his fire as he hung his tongue out with mush clinging to it.

My mom finally decided to interject. "Collin, stop. That's so unbecoming." And she went right back to addressing my father.

He snapped his trap shut and then grinned at me.

"How long was she there?"

He shrugged. "I dunno. I saw her after warm up, and she was still there when we left. She talked to Caden."

Caden's head popped up at the mention of his name, obviously uninterested in the conversation at hand. "Huh?"

"Did Jess say why she was at practice?" It shouldn't bother me. I had my own things going on. It was just odd.

"Not really, but I wasn't paying much attention to her. I think she just wanted to stop by and watch. Lots of girls do it."

"Not girls like Jess." My sentiment was true.

Something about her attendance at the football field unnerved me, especially since she'd asked about coming over and then bailed after Caleb interrupted us. I wasn't going to press my brothers for information, and cell phones weren't allowed at our dinner table, so contacting Jess would have to wait.

"Maybe the vow of celibacy has been lifted." The smartass look on Clayton's face made me want to reach across the table and smack him.

"You should certainly know what celibacy looks like." Caden didn't often get shots in on the twins, but I couldn't stop my smile.

"All of you better be intimately acquainted with celibacy until you're married." My mother could be cute. She believed we were all the pictures of virtue because that was what she needed her friends to think. The Chapman kids were the standard all others held their children to—even if it was an illusion.

I didn't have the heart to tell her Caden had lost his virginity in ninth grade, and based on the rumor mills in the high school halls, the twins weren't far behind. I prayed to God none of them got some girl pregnant—my mother might have a stroke just before she was committed.

"You can't be serious, Ma." Clayton must have a death wish.

"I most certainly am. Forget diseases, do you realize what a teenage pregnancy would do to your future? You could kiss UGA goodbye!" She huffed as if his comment were preposterous and the threat of not attending the family alma mater would keep him from getting his dick wet. Silly woman.

My giggle brought her attention to me. "That goes for you, too, missy. You may not have dreams of football, but no man wants a woman who isn't pure."

"Guess it's a good thing I'm not after a man," I mumbled.

"Are you after a chick?" Clayton cocked his head in question, waiting for my response.

I threw a roll at him, which only served to further ignite my mother's spirit.

"Stop it. Both of you. What's gotten into you guys tonight? This is not appropriate dinner-table discussion."

"So you think Jess is trying to get lucky with one of the guys on the team?" Collin looked right at my mother with a grin the size of Texas on his face. He loved to goad her and was the only one of us who successfully got away it.

The rest of us settled down when she gave him a disapproving glance.

After dinner, I made sure to find out what my best friend was up to. She finally answered on the third ring when I'd almost given up.

"Hey. What are you up to?" I didn't want to come right out and grill her.

"Just doing homework. You?" I could hear the television in the background and wondered how she ever got anything done with that racket.

"I'm about to start mine." There was a moment of silence. I doubted she recognized it between books and sitcoms. "So Caden said you hung out at the football field after school today."

"Oh yeah?" If I didn't know her better, I'd say her tone was overly optimistic.

"Were you working on a project?"

"You could say that."

"...Are you going to tell me what?" The fact that I had to pry information out of her and she wasn't forthcoming told me more than I wanted to admit.

"I don't know. Not really a project for school."

"Then what kind could it be?"

She let out a sigh. I'd heard it before. It was the one that said I wasn't going to like whatever came next. "Aren't you tired of doing nothing but studying and playing the piano?"

I didn't respond because she wasn't really asking me a question. This was her lead into a confession.

"We're seniors, Colbie. We have nothing to show for it. The two of us really have no other friends, just study buddies who want to use us to make better grades. Neither of us has ever dated or even gone to a dance, much less prom. And at the end of the year, we're both going to separate colleges where we will be little fish in an enormous pond with zero experience."

Please God, no. She can't like a football player. Anyone else. "I'm okay with that."

"No you aren't or you wouldn't have been hugged up on Dr. Paxton at Caleb's wedding. You're just as curious as I am. You're just unwilling to admit it."

She was right about that. There was no way in hell I'd admit to having interest in my teacher who was six years older than me... and *my teacher*. Even before uttering it out loud, I was sure I would regret asking this question. "Who is it?"

"Don't get mad."

I was already mad.

"Promise?"

I refused to make a commitment I couldn't keep. It was ludicrous to ask someone not to be upset about something when they didn't know what it was they were agreeing to. "Sure." *Lie.*

I heard her intake of air and then the release. "Caden."

"As in my fifteen-year-old brother?"

"Almost sixteen." She took a deep breath. "He's really sweet, Colbie."

"I know. He's my brother. He's also off limits. What are you thinking?" I didn't have a clue when this had developed. First Caleb, and now that he was truly off the market—not that he was ever a viable candidate—Caden. Nope. "Wait. Was that why you wanted to come over after school?"

"Not the only reason. Don't be upset. Please."

"He's my little brother, Jess. This violates every girl code on the books."

"I can't help that your parents populated more than their fair share of the student body. Plus, it's just a crush. Caden doesn't see me as anything other than your best friend."

"Thank God for someone's loyalty."

"You said you wouldn't be mad!"

"I lied."

Jess wouldn't understand. She was an only child who didn't have to compete with six other boys for attention. Sharing her with one of them was more than I could deal with.

"That's not fair."

"Neither is you scoping out my little brother. Damn, there's no one else in the school you can follow around?" The sneer in my tone crossed a line I shouldn't have crossed. I justified my anger and outburst even though it wasn't warranted...not to this extreme.

"Wow. Nice to know how you really feel."

"Ugh. Jess. It's not that—"

"Then what is it? Afraid he'll like me better than you?" That hit landed below the belt.

"Gross. No. I hope my brother never looks at me as a piece of ass. Thank you."

I waited for her comeback; however, after a couple ragged breaths, I realized the line was dead. Jess had hung up. Over my little brother. No, that wasn't true. She'd hung up over my reaction to her lusting after my little brother. Of all people, she picked the only member of my family who knew I existed beyond the dinner table and taxi service I provided. It hurt, and I was pissed.

I had homework to do, but there was no way I could focus with the pent-up energy surging through my veins. Instead, I quickly changed clothes, laced up my tennis shoes, and went to find solace on the pavement.

THE SKY HAD LONG SINCE LOST ITS COLOR BY THE TIME I stepped foot outside. One of the benefits of living in a small town, jogging after dark or in the early morning before light was just as safe as mid-day. I knew the owner of every single house I'd pass, and if I ever had a problem, one of them could hear me yell from the sidewalk. I had no doubt there were an equal number casting judgment along with their gazes onto me from inside, but I didn't worry about it. I found comfort in the pain of pushing my body beyond the point it wanted to go. I controlled how far, how fast, and how long, and every jog I took, I stretched for more. If nothing else, by the time I reached my doorstep, I'd be so exhausted that the argument with Jess would be a distant memory.

But sleep evaded me that night, and fatigue clung to my soul like a monkey to a tree the next morning as I struggled through the homework I hadn't done. When I laced up my sneakers for my morning run, my mind was foggy, and it didn't clear by the time I got back. A shower did nothing, and the clock on the wall taunted me when my stomach growled. I hated to rush eating, and being late to school wasn't an option, but with the weight of failure on my shoulders, I felt a binge coming on that I wasn't certain I could stop. With a binge came a purge. Time wasn't on my side.

Mama had a spread on the table like she did every morning. With six growing boys, she always prepared for an army to eat. Even with three gone, she hasn't cut back much. Eggs, bacon, biscuits, sausages, fruit...it was all there, and it ran the length of the dining room table. I hated how much I craved the fat-laden options before me. And even more that I knew how happy they'd make me, until the consequences came crashing down. I longed for that pleasure, and then I'd seek the pain.

It was a vicious cycle, but I loved to love food and then push it away. I relished having a secret no one could take from me. Every mouthful should have been a deterrent; instead, each calorie brought me satisfaction. A smile lingered as I wrapped my lips around a forkful of eggs, and I couldn't stop the grin when I chewed. As my stomach expanded to accommodate my happiness, peace settled my chaotic mind. I swirled the last bite of my biscuit around in the bits of food left on my plate, plopped the buttery goodness into my mouth, and then leaned back in my chair to swallow. My hands rested on my bloated belly, and I rubbed over the smooth surface of my shirt.

But I didn't have time to enjoy the current utopia. I hated to rush the process. As soon as the notion hit, I glanced at the clock and dread settled in with my biscuits and sausage and eggs until it gurgled and the guilt became too much to bear.

"May I be excused? I need to go wash up before school." I slid my chair back, not waiting for Mama's reply.

She blotted her mouth with a napkin—not that she had anything on it—and glanced at my brothers. None of them stopped talking or shoveling food into their mouths, so she nodded. "Of course, dear. But don't dawdle."

Dawdle. I wasn't five. I didn't dawdle. "Yes, ma'am."

As much as I wanted to race up the stairs, taking them two at a time, my mother would have a heart attack. For the boys, that was perfectly acceptable behavior—not so for a lady. I held the stair rail as I took each step with a straight spine, and the moment I passed the wall so she couldn't see me, I raced as quietly as possible to my room. I softly closed my bedroom door, snuck into my bathroom, and then locked the door behind me.

My ritual was as effortless as it always was and just as fruitful. Sparks of light drifted across my line of sight with each heave, my eyes watered as I released my pain, and my heart pounded with joy when I flushed the toilet. The next fifteen to twenty minutes were the moments I craved. My brain still believed I was full, I knew my stomach was empty, and the endorphins that bombarded my body had me on top of the world. I craved the pain, I loved the secret, and the control sealed my ability to make it through another day in Tiny Town.

Whether the crash came when Jess snubbed me in the parking lot, or the snub caused the crash, I couldn't tell. But the high I'd left the house with sent me tumbling down an emotional mountain when my best friend not only didn't say hello in the school parking lot, but she glared at me. Worst of all, she smiled at Caden, who was oblivious to it all. He clearly didn't have a clue that Jess and I were on the outs, nor did he appear to know the reason why. At least she'd done one thing in my favor, she hadn't alerted my little brother to her affinity. I didn't want to consider the possibility of his returning her ardor.

"Hey, Cole," Caden called after me as I raced toward the front steps of the school. "Wait up." He grabbed my elbow when my foot landed on the stair.

Reluctantly, I stopped and donned my best poker face. "What's up?" I tucked my hair behind my ear and raised my brows in question.

He jerked his head toward the direction I'd seen Jess disappear. "What's up with you and your shadow?" Maybe he was a little more astute than I cared to give him credit for.

With a casual shrug and a nonchalant shake of my head, I blew him off. "Nothing. Why?"

Caden's forehead wrinkled as he searched my face. I gave him nothing but a blank stare. Thankfully, the first bell sounded, alerting us that we had five minutes to get to our first class. I kissed my brother's cheek and squeezed his arm. It took seconds for the crowd to sweep me away, and I didn't look back. The less Caden knew, the better. Jess was a gorgeous girl. My brother was a good-looking guy. The age difference shouldn't bother me, and the truth was, it didn't. What ate at my soul and devoured my spirit was the idea of losing him to her.

Envy.

Greed.

Gluttony.

I had three of the seven deadly sins in spades, nearly halfway to hell. Envy was semantics—I was jealous. I wanted Caden to myself, and a girlfriend coupled with football would take what little time we had. The third—gluttony—didn't need to even be addressed. My internal eye roll was strong today and even resulted in an external groan.

I should encourage my best friend to spend time with my little brother. She was just as fabulous as he was, but I feared losing them both to each other. It didn't matter that fear was irrational. Caden would always be my brother, and Jess should always be my best friend. If only I could force myself to dream of her being a sister by marriage, yet I couldn't. That thought nearly had me in the bathroom, gagging. It was selfish as hell. He was mine. She was mine. Both were all I had.

"Good morning, Colbie."

I nearly knocked Dr. Paxton over when I barreled into him, my eyes trained on the ground. A gasp escaped my lips when his fingers wrapped around my biceps to steady me, and when I accidentally peered into his soft brown eyes, a sigh followed. His touch shocked me, sending electric currents down my arms and straight between my legs. The path didn't even follow logical biological direction, but it was there nonetheless. With people swimming around us like a school of fish, I had faltered far too long. His tongue snaked out, discreetly moistening his full lips, and I realized I bit my own to stifle what would have been an embarrassing groan.

I blinked. Twice.

And then, I regained my composure. Casually, I shrugged him off—or as casually as I could with heated cheeks and wet panties—and cleared my throat. I forced myself to straighten my spine before I spoke. "Good morning, Dr. Paxton."

A gentle smile crept up the corners of his mouth.

"I'm sorry. I should've been watching where I was going." I didn't give him time to respond, because there was no response he could give that would change the way I felt about him. And it was wrong. My body should not react to a teacher—no, a *man*—the way it did to Eli Paxton. I'd made a fool of myself days earlier. I didn't need to do it again. If I stood here any longer, not only would I not be able to conceal it from him, the entire student body would witness my lust. "I'll see you in class." I tucked my hair behind my ear and stepped around the man in my path.

Thus far, I was less than ten minutes into my morning, and I'd already dodged two bullets. Or maybe I hadn't missed either. I'd run into both Jess and Dr. Paxton. One wasn't eager to see me, and I wasn't eager to see the other. There were way too many days left in the school year to be dealing with this kind of drama. Somehow, I had to smooth things over with my best friend and squash my embarrassment over my teacher. Unfortunately, that didn't happen during first or second period, and Jess created a divide that everyone saw in third period.

She sat on the other side of the room. And never glanced my way.

When Dr. Paxton opened up the discussion to the class about Stephen King's *Christine* and the romantic elements of the book, what started out as a healthy banter amongst several of my classmates turned into an all-out verbal brawl between Jess and me. Somehow, she used the car in the novel as a metaphor for our relationship. Before I knew it, she was standing and yelling at me about how I'd become the possessed car in the book.

"Whoa, ladies. Not sure what's going on here, but let's dial it back several notches." Dr. Paxton stood in front of Jess, blocking my view of her.

She was the only one shouting, yet he addressed his comment to me. His eyes pleaded with me to let it go, while his mouth blamed me. And then it clicked. Dr. Paxton believed her comments were about him, not the blowup she and I'd had about Caden. Figured, men always thought everything was about them.

I rolled my eyes, crossed my arms, and turned toward the front with a huff.

I managed to keep my mouth shut the rest of third period, and I had planned to leave without any further fanfare. I just wanted the day to end, and thus far, it wasn't off to a great start.

"Ms. Chapman. Ms. McLean. Can I see you both, please?" Dr. Paxton requested our presence as the rest of the class filed out after the bell. With his back to us, his voice remained stern—that no-nonsense man who'd barked at me on day one. Yet when he turned to face us, he caught Jess's stare first and then mine. His pupils surged and the brown softened. And then it was gone. "I don't care what cat fight the two of you had before class, you will not use third period as a verbal sparring ring. Understood?"

Jess didn't respond.

I knew better. The last thing I needed was Caleb on my ass about being disrespectful, a lecture I'd probably already get based on the outburst. "Yes, sir." I ground my teeth together as I allowed the two words to slip out, the fake smile I'd mastered years ago firmly set in place.

Jess nodded and turned toward the door. We'd both taken a couple steps when Dr. Paxton spoke again.

"Colbie, do you have a moment?"

I stopped in my tracks, wondering how brazen he'd be at school. My heart raced when Jess cast an accusing glance over her shoulder. She glared at me and then at Dr. Paxton. *If she only knew.* Thankfully, none of her speculations had been confirmed, and she left.

Students for his fourth period would be here soon. I checked the clock, knowing he'd make me late for my next class and that he'd seen me do it.

"You want to tell me what that was about?" He had to be joking.

We weren't friends. He wasn't my buddy or my boyfriend. I

wasn't about to divulge the inner workings of the teenage drama to anyone, much less him.

"I'm not sure what you're referring to, Dr. Paxton." I didn't fidget or shuffle my feet.

His lips parted as if he were about to say something and changed his mind. Instead, he nodded toward the door, dismissing me. I didn't dare look back, but I could feel his stare when I exited the room. I was so focused on leaving without giving anything away, that I didn't see the train barreling toward me.

Jess McLean was on a war path, and I stood directly in her crosshairs. If I'd ever doubted Jesus or his redemption, in that moment, He renewed my faith. Caleb Chapman stepped in front of Jess, diverting her path...for now.

I didn't hear a word my brother said through the ringing in my ears, and I gladly accepted his accompaniment to fourth period to vouch for my inevitable tardy. I could only hope the day got better.

It didn't, and neither had the rest of the week. I wasn't sleeping, homework was increasingly more difficult with each day that I didn't get a decent night's rest, my legs ached from pushing them on my morning runs, and Jess still hadn't talked to me. She'd done a lot of glaring and even more avoiding, but after the incident in Dr. Paxton's class, she'd kept clear.

Walking to my car, thankful for the weekend, I caught a glimpse of her. Her long hair blew behind her as she strolled to the bleachers in front of the football field. My stomach churned, and then it nearly came out of my mouth when Caden stopped to talk to her. It was the first time I'd ever seen Jess so...vapid. My jaw dropped as she flipped her hair over her shoulder, and I saw red the moment she laid her hand on my little brother's arm. It was classic flirting, and she was stunning. My shoulders slumped as Caden's face lit up. When she laughed, he followed. Even from here, I witnessed the pink tinge of his cheeks and knew he was flush with excitement. I wanted to be happy. The possibility of the two people I loved most in the world coming together should excite me, but instead, it crushed what was left of a dismal week.

I climbed into my car, unable to delay leaving any longer. My brother and Jess would have to wait. Dr. Chalmers and the étude were up next. I tried to relax as I drove across town, but it was pointless. I was strung tighter than a harp, and if I wasn't careful, one of my strings would break.

"Colbie, stop." Dr. Chalmers ran his hands through his silvery hair and closed his eyes. His nostrils flared as he took a deep breath, yet when he looked at me again, there was nothing but calm staring back. "Slow the tempo of the entire piece until you master the notes. You're racing the runs."

My right hand needed to move as effortlessly as the wind while my left struck like thunder. It was an intricate balance, and the more frustrated I became, the choppier my wind blew and more brazen my thunder became. My hands weren't working in harmony. It was a mess. Instead of getting better, something as simple as a scale within a handful of measures was throwing me completely off balance. I should be able to run the keys blindfolded at breakneck speed, but today, nothing worked.

I tried again, and again. And after two hours, my fists hit the ivory keys. Dr. Chalmers called it a day.

"Colbie." He sat on the bench next to me and encouraged me to face him. "You've been off all week. I don't know what's going on, but if you want to talk about it..."

I shook my head. I didn't want to talk about it. I refused to admit how ugly I'd been to Jess and how selfish I was not wanting to give up my little brother.

"All right, then. If you want to master this piece before the recital, you need to take a couple of days and get your head in the game." He took a deep breath, and I knew whatever came next would be his version of fatherly advice. "You've been on edge all week. You have dark circles and bags under your eyes, both of which tell me you're not sleeping. Your mind can't be sharp without proper rest. Plain and simple. So you either get it together, or we pull the piece. I'd start with some sleep." He patted my leg and stood.

Dr. Chalmers gathered his things, turned off the metronome, and offered me a weak smile just before he walked through the door. Even if he hadn't said anything, his thoughts were written all over his face. He wanted me to succeed as badly as I needed it, but he wouldn't stand by while I withered away doing it. I knew him well enough to know, he would shut me down completely, recital and all...if he had to.

That I couldn't let happen. I shuffled the pages of my music together into an unorganized stack and stuffed them into my notebook. I didn't bother putting them in properly. Dr. Chalmers was right, I needed a reset. And that would have to start with Jess. My week had spiraled out of control since she'd hung up on me. The two of us had always been like peanut butter and jelly. I refused to let a little bread come between us.

I rehearsed what I'd say in the car on my way home, thinking I'd call her after dinner. But as luck would have it, at least the way my luck ran these days, I wouldn't have to call her. She sat at the dining room table with Caden and Mama when I walked in.

"Hey, Cole." My brother's voice wavered when he greeted me. "I invited Jess for dinner." His expression was a plea for acceptance and understanding.

I glanced to Jess whose brow was furrowed and then my mother who clapped and held her hands together.

My mother spoke before I could. "I'm making chicken and rice."

And in that moment, I conceded the best I could. My lips rose in a smile no one would realize was forced. "That's great. I'm glad you're here, Jess. I wanted to talk to you."

She shifted nervously in her seat. Caden glanced at her and then back to me. I couldn't tell if he was aware of our phone call last week or if he was confused by my lack of extra enthusiasm.

"Cole?"

My heart melted at the sound of my little brother's nickname for me, and a piece of my resistance softened. "Let me go put my stuff in my room. I'll be right back."

Relief shown in his eyes and Jess's. My mother still didn't have a clue anything was unusual about my brother inviting my best friend to dinner on a Friday night. Bless her heart. She probably still thought Carson and Casey were virgins. Her naivete was endearing.

The footsteps I heard behind me didn't belong to my heavy-footed brother, nor did they click like the heels of my mother, which meant Jess had followed me. I set my backpack on my desk and began to dig through my drawers for a tank top and a pair of running shorts. After I apologized, I would need a few miles of concrete to clear my mind and accept whatever lay in my future.

I heard her come in and close the door. I knew without looking that she'd taken a seat on my bed and put a pillow in her lap the way she always did. So after I changed and found her exactly where I expected to, I wasn't surprised, even though she hadn't said a word.

I climbed onto my bed with socks in one hand and my tennis shoes in the other. I needed something to fiddle with while I talked to keep my hands and arms from speaking for me.

"I'm sorry, Jess. I should have been supportive." I intended to say more. I'd rehearsed more. But nothing came. That was the sum total of what I had to offer. It was sincere. And it was honest. It just wasn't much of an apology.

She twisted a lock of her hair between her fingers, and her eyes glistened with unshed tears. "I should have been more sensitive to your feelings about it. I kind of sprung it on you without any preparation."

"So what do we do from here? Are you dating my brother?" I kept my tone soft and unassuming. I couldn't live without Jess or Caden, and if they'd already decided to date, then I didn't have a choice but to go along with it or lose them.

Jess didn't answer right away, which told me more than I wanted to know. "He kissed me, Colbie." Her entire face erupted in unbridled happiness. It was an expression I'd never seen on her before, and while I wanted to cringe and tell her to shut up, I had to listen. "I felt it in my toes." Her eyes had gone to a far-off place where unicorns crapped glitter and rainbows colored the world. "Caden was my first kiss, but I can't imagine anything ever comparing." She leaned back and sighed.

"I'm happy for you, Jess. I really am. I can't say that it won't take some getting used to, but I promise to try to be a better friend about it."

She sat back up and threw her arms around me. "Thank you, Colbie." She squeezed me like she needed the air in my lungs to breathe.

"Just promise me that we'll make time for us...without Caden. Please."

Jess nodded vigorously when she pulled away. "Of course. Of course. Nothing between us changes."

But everything had changed. She just didn't realize it. I, however, did. I'd prepared myself for changes after high school. I hadn't thought it would happen before.

With nothing left to say, and a hole the size of Georgia in my heart, I finished tying my shoes and then stood. "I'll be back."

"You're going running before dinner?" Her look of giddy glee melted into confused sadness. "You only run at night when you're upset." We'd been friends for far too long, clearly.

"I had a really rough piano lesson. Dr. Chalmers wants me to get my crap together or he's going to pull the étude." I shrugged, but Jess knew what that meant in my world. Devastation.

She hopped off the bed and raced around the edge. For the second time in less than five minutes, she threw her arms around my neck and clung to me like a sloth to a tree. "Oh, Colbie. I'm sorry." She stepped back but kept her hands on my biceps. "Go. Run your little heart out. Then we'll eat, and maybe the three of us can hang out and watch a movie. Get your mind off it. I bet by Monday, you'll be good as new. You've never pulled a piece, and this won't be the first one."

The words were right. Everything she said was what I needed to hear. Unfortunately, none of them fixed anything. She and Caden were going to do whatever it was they were doing. And the étude still taunted me like a bully in the schoolyard. I didn't even want to think about the mounds of homework I had waiting for me.

So I didn't.

I put in my headphones, turned on my favorite running playlist—which happened to include "Winterwind"—and then I stepped out onto the sidewalk. Twenty minutes and two miles later, my afternoon went from dismal to unfortunate. Without crossing the street, which would be an obvious avoidance, I couldn't keep from running into Dr. Paxton. Even from a block away, when he turned the corner toward me, I could see every vivid detail.

Sweat glistened on his bare chest, which was even more sculpted than I'd imagined. His hair was damp from exercise, and holy hell, the man had the sexiest legs I'd ever seen. Just the right smattering of hair trailed from his navel to beneath his shorts, and he'd obviously caught me ogling him. When my eyes met his, there was a roguishly delicious smirk tilting one side of perfectly pouty lips. I didn't know if men were supposed to have full lips, but Eli Paxton did, and I'd never wanted to suck on one as bad as I did in that moment.

He came to a stop in front of me and leaned over with his hands on his knees. I'd venture to guess he'd been pushing himself harder than I had. I needed monotony; he apparently needed a workout. When he stood, he pulled the buds from his ears, and I mirrored him, assuming it would be rude to sidestep his glorious body to keep jogging.

Dr. Paxton had a difficult time speaking through his ragged breathing, which just made him more appealing. "You run, too? I shouldn't be surprised."

"Nerds can't run?" Unlikely what he meant, but I wasn't in a great mood.

He cocked his head to the side. "Not at all what I said. It makes sense. You're tall and lean." His gaze grazed me from shoulder to toe and back up, and I'd hasten to say, it wasn't in an appraisal a teacher should make of his student.

"I don't think running has anything to do with my height, Dr. Paxton."

"You know what I mean." Now he was flustered and winded. "And call me Eli. Please."

I propped my hands on my hips, trying to conceal just how awkward all of this felt. "Okay, *Eli*."

His Adam's apple bobbed in his throat when he swallowed. He wasn't trying to be seductive, but damn, every move he made sparked a synapse in my brain that hadn't fired before. If this was what Jess felt like around Caden, it was no wonder she hadn't been able to stop herself. Too bad Eli was off limits.

"Do you run every night?" Dr. Paxton now refused to look me in the eye, or maybe he was keeping watch for witnesses to our interaction.

I should be more concerned, but if word got out, it could easily be explained by his friendship and ties to Caleb and my family, or the simple fact that I ran into my teacher. Walking off would be rude. "No. I run every morning. I only run at night when I've got things on my mind." I'd shared far more information than I should with a man I barely knew. "Sorry, TMI." I rolled my eyes at my own stupidity. By continuing to speak, I only made things worse.

"So you run every day, you take piano lessons every day, and you maintain the highest GPA of any student in the school?" He'd been taking notes. "When do you do anything fun?" He chuckled, but I didn't find any humor in his question.

I'd listened to those kinds of "jokes" for years, and I didn't find them any funnier then than I did now. "Being driven is its own reward."

"Is everything you do a job?" He'd sobered, and the conversation had changed tones quickly.

I wasn't sure how to respond, so I didn't. I pulled my ponytail tighter, grabbed my earbuds, and got ready to put them in. I donned the same smile my mother was famous for. "It was nice to see you, Dr. Paxton. I really should be going."

The music drowned out whatever he said after. I just waved.

6

ELI

I CONVINCED MYSELF I HADN'T GOTTEN UP EARLY ON A Saturday to try to catch Colbie on her morning run. I didn't know her route, nor what time she would be out on a weekend, so it was easy to lie to my guilty conscience about my motivation for setting an alarm and walking out my door at seven. It did occur to me to wear a shirt this go around, though. As much as I loved witnessing Colbie go weak in the knees, it was a dangerous thing to let myself dwell in, much less encourage.

I knew better than to pursue her, yet for whatever reason, my mind wouldn't let her go. I wanted to blame the connection via Caleb, but that didn't exist—there was no connection other than they shared a last name. They certainly weren't close. I hadn't been privy to personal information about her from my best friend over the years. It was her snark, her wit, her intelligence. She was a model student by any standards, and as a teacher, those things appealed to me. What shouldn't cross my mind were her long legs or her dark hair, and I definitely shouldn't have the color of her eyes memorized. But I did.

The school year lasted roughly nine months. We were a

couple weeks into it. After that, my interaction with her wouldn't matter, but then, she would move to Tennessee. The only future I might have with Colbie Chapman was in the principal's office as he handed me my pink slip, or worse, in a courtroom where I stood trial. Nevertheless, I jogged down the sidewalks of Brogdon, Georgia, attempting to appear normal while scoping every cross street and intersection for any sign of Colbie.

I'd traversed miles and every street in her neighborhood. There weren't a lot of positives about small, country towns, but this was one. Neighborhoods blended with each other, and a brisk walk would take me from one city limit to the other. I peered down at the GPS on my watch and sighed. Five miles was far beyond my normal jog, and I was out of places to try. Either she wasn't out, or I didn't have a clue how to find her. I dipped past her house—on the opposite side of the street—and rounded the curve toward the park. Having given up, my pace slowed. My feet hit the pavement harder, jarring my knees, and my arms jerked at my sides. Exhausted was an understatement. Add disappointed and fruitless to the list of adjectives, and I was a veritable ball of sweat and anger.

Then, the clouds parted and the sun shined like a beacon on the inky-haired beauty dancing toward me. The light reflected off her silky hair creating a halo around her, but unlike Pamela Anderson, nothing bounced on Colbie. Every carefully sculpted muscle tensed with each stride, the definition like art. I stood in the middle of the sidewalk, unmoving as she approached. And even under her already crimson cheeks, I witnessed the blush that crossed her face when she recognized me. In a word, she was radiant. And when I allowed my eyes to drift, I realized she was wearing the tiniest running shorts coupled with a sports bra...and that was all that covered her, or rather, left her exposed.

Her skin was shiny with perspiration, and her ponytail swung behind her. I watched as her tiny fists pumped in front of her with each step she took. It wasn't until she stopped, inches in front of me, that I realized I blocked her path.

She pulled down her earphones. "Hey."

It wasn't much of a greeting, but she had stopped instead of going around me, and she had spoken first. Jesus, it was like high school all over again. I didn't miss analyzing every action a girl made to determine her interest. I already knew Colbie was interested. I also knew I couldn't have her. This should have been cut and dry. Case closed.

"Hey!"

She giggled and reached out to remove the buds from my ears. "You don't have to yell."

I felt like a moron, but if my stupidity garnered that smile from those lips, I'd play the clown anytime I could. "Sorry."

"What are you doing out here?" Her fingers touched her neck beneath her jaw. She had on a watch that tracked her pulse, so the gesture was odd. "I thought you jogged at night?"

This was brilliant. Not a terribly well-thought-out plan. "I have a thing tonight." *A thing.* Not only did I not have plans, but that was as nondescript as one could get, and she clearly caught my lie.

"Oh yeah? Do you do a lot of those?" Humor danced in her blue eyes like glitter.

"Things?" I couldn't stop the smirk that tugged on my lips when her brow lifted in question. "Yeah, pretty much. What about you?" This was worse than high school. I had game in high school. Now, I was a loser trying to pick up a girl who was so out of my league and shouldn't be on my radar...and failing.

She shook her head. "Nah, I'm not big on *things*."

"No plans with Jess?"

And just like that, her face crumpled, and the sparkle turned to murk. Without thought, my hand lifted her downturned chin. Electricity flew from her through me, and I snatched my hand away like I'd been burned. "Something happen?"

Her lips pursed, and then she chewed on the bottom one. "Not really." Colbie's shrug said differently.

I shouldn't pry. And I damn sure shouldn't take her hand. I did both. "So, the incident in my class on Monday isn't related?"

The two had gone at each other. Colbie had managed to do a much better job of remaining calm than Jess had, but regardless, claws came out. Two bright young ladies attacking each other with metaphors and book references was a new one. I had picked up on it immediately. Oddly, most of the other students seemed to believe the two were just that passionate about Stephen King and the Romantic period.

Colbie fidgeted under my stare. From the moment I'd first laid eyes on her, she'd had brass balls and nerves of steel. There wasn't a bit of uncertainty in her, yet insecurity and hesitation now held her expression captive.

I glanced around to find that we were alone in the park. There wasn't a car or person in sight. I let out a sigh and pulled her toward the nearest bench. She didn't hesitate to follow, although she still hadn't spoken. The metal was cool on my leg when I turned to face her. We sat there in silence for a moment, her staring at my shoe and me staring at her. Her long lashes mesmerized me, and when she finally peered up through them, my heart nearly pounded out of my chest. The innocence stole my breath. Eighteen-year-old girls didn't possess that these days.

"I'm not going to tell anyone what you say, Colbie." I brushed a piece of fallen hair away from her face and behind her ear.

Her lips parted, but words didn't come. I waited. If she were formulating a thought, interrupting her or leading her down the path I believed she wanted to go wouldn't get her the relief she appeared to need. And I wouldn't be any closer to knowing a damn thing about her than I currently was.

She licked her lips, moistening them with an appealing shine, and I had to will my dick to stand down. I closed my eyes in the effort.

Colbie stood, having misread the action as frustration or maybe disinterest. I grabbed her by the wrist and pleaded with her not to leave, without saying a word. She hesitated, and then resumed her spot next to me.

"My guess is that Jess has a date with Caden."

If I'd had anything in my mouth, I would have spit it all over her. "Your little brother?" That was not at all what I expected to hear.

"Yes."

Come on, Colbie...offer me more.

Nada.

Damn, this girl was nothing like any other member of her family. Any one of the Chapmans would have launched into a diatribe about how it had come about, how it would come across to their friends, whether their parents would condone it, or just their overall approval or disapproval. Not Colbie.

I didn't have a clue which angle to go at this. From what Caleb had said, Colbie and Caden were really tight. In fact, he was the *only* member of the family she connected with. And from what I'd seen, Jess was her only friend, best friend. I couldn't verify that because I didn't follow her around, but I'd never so much as seen her eat lunch with anyone else.

"Ouch." It wasn't profound, but it verbalized what I imagined she felt without picking a side.

"I have homework to do. It's not a big deal." There was the indifference she typically carried. "I'm cool with it."

She lied through her teeth. I didn't doubt the homework, but there was no way in hell she was "fine" with her best friend dating her fifteen-year-old brother.

"He's sixteen. Just turned."

Shit. I hadn't meant to say that out loud. I also didn't know how I'd missed a Chapman birthday. "Still. Why Caden? And I thought you two had a pact of sorts?"

If looks could kill, the one she'd just given me would be lethal. "Caleb needs to learn to keep his mouth shut."

"For what it's worth, I think it's admirable." I had no idea why she'd be embarrassed.

"Yeah, nothing like the dork swearing off boys who never would've been interested in her to begin with." Sarcasm dripped from her words, and I wanted to shake her. She had to see what everyone else did—they were intimidated by her, not disgusted. Beauty, brains, body...Colbie Chapman was a wet dream walking the halls of Brogdon High.

"That's a conversation for another day." I couldn't begin to tell her just what she did to the male species. I'd pitch a tent in my running shorts, and all hope would be lost. "Are they dating?"

"They've kissed. And he had her over for dinner last night."

In my book that was dating, but I didn't know what it meant for kids these days. "Hard to deal with?"

She fiddled with an imaginary something in her hands to keep from looking at me. "I didn't handle it all that well when she told me. I should have been more supportive..." But she wasn't. It didn't take a rocket scientist to figure out that, in Colbie's mind, she'd just lost them both. And for a perfectionist, failure was crippling.

"Knee-jerk reactions happen sometimes."

Her head bobbed in agreement, but I could see that her thoughts were miles away from this bench. And when she met my stare, her delicate fingers tucked the same stray strand of hair behind her ear, crossing her face with her left hand the way she always did. If I could have given her my heart sitting on that bench, I would have handed it over. No questions asked.

"Pax!"

I jerked away from the trance Colbie had me in to find Caleb Chapman standing with a group of guys in the park's football field. Colbie tensed next to me as Caleb took a couple steps in our direction.

"Critter? Is that you?"

"Hey, Caleb." She sounded as uninterested in his presence as I was.

Thankfully, Caleb didn't seem to notice—or care—that I sat alone with his sister on a park bench at nine in the morning. "Pax, you wanna play?"

I didn't, but turning him down in favor of playing footsie with his sister might raise a few red flags I didn't care to see fly. "Yeah, man. Gimme a minute."

Satisfied with my response, Caleb rejoined the group with his back facing us. He'd never been one for gossip, much less spreading it.

"Give me your phone."

Colbie stared at me through wide eyes, and I stuck out my hand. She looked to Caleb—who still wasn't paying attention to us—and then pressed it into my palm. She allowed her fingertips to linger a moment too long, and I relished it as much as I wanted to believe she did. Her touch. *Fuck*. Her touch.

I quickly added my name and number into her contacts and sent myself a text. "In case you need to talk." I handed the device back and stood. "Have a good day, Colbie."

I walked away without glancing back. If she still sat on that bench, I'd have to tell her brother to kiss my ass. There was no way in hell I could stand to see hurt in her eyes. And since I couldn't make that choice, I didn't allow myself the opportunity.

By the time we'd divided into sides and I'd huddled up with my team, she was gone.

The bench was empty.

And so was my heart.

I'd only thought I'd escaped any questioning from Caleb about being with Colbie on Saturday. Thankfully, he hadn't done it when anyone else was around or even that day. No, he waited until he caught me alone before school.

The instant I saw him materialize in my classroom door, the expression on his face told me he wasn't here to socialize.

"What's up, man?" I closed my grade book and leaned back in my chair.

Caleb closed the door behind him, and suddenly, my room felt like a vacuum, not only devoid of sound but oxygen. My heart hammered in my chest, waiting for him to speak. I had spent days thinking about how I would handle this and still hadn't come up with a viable option.

"I didn't want to say anything, but I talked to Chas and feel obligated to."

Pretending I didn't know what was coming was pointless, but I tried anyhow. I sat up straight and contorted my face into one of concern. It felt ridiculous, but I either acted like I didn't have a clue what was going on or admitted that I'd crossed a line with a student. I opted for the first since the last could get me fired and beaten up. "What's on your mind?"

He sat on the desk directly in front of my own with his arms locked at his sides and his fingers curled tightly around the edge. His knuckles turned white, and I wondered if he was trying to keep from hitting me. "What were you doing in the park with Critter?"

I waved him off and let out a huff. "We ran into each other jogging. Why? Is everything okay?" If he bought this shit, I should consider an alternate career in acting.

His head moved side to side as he considered what to say. It was painful to watch my best friend struggle to approach the topic. "I just think maybe you're getting a little too close to your students."

My brain quickly picked apart his word choice. He hadn't specifically stated his sister, just students in general. "Finding that balance is tough. There are so many bright kids here. It's hard not to get caught up in discussions with them."

His jaw ticced ever so slightly. "I'd hate for anyone to get the wrong idea. This is a small town, Eli. People talk. I know your intentions are professional, but you probably should keep the conversing to classrooms and high school hallways. Anything else these kids want to talk about, they should ask their friends or parents." Caleb was so cavalier about the whole thing, as if none of these kids might need more than what they at home.

"And if they don't have either of those available?"

I wondered if he'd get the insinuation. Caleb was far from dumb. Actually, he was quite intelligent, yet when it came to the inner workings of his family, he seemed to be oblivious. I didn't live with them, and even I could see Colbie screaming for attention.

He chuckled and stood. "They all have someone. It just shouldn't be you."

I should have kept my mouth shut. I should have allowed him to walk out the door without further fanfare. I should have put my head down, taken the warning, and moved on. "Is that what you do with your players? Tell them to ask a friend or find someone else to talk to?" I knew it wasn't, because he'd told me about kids he'd helped out of school and off the field.

"That's different."

"Because it's football? Or because they're boys?" I was treading on thin ice. I didn't have a leg to stand on here. If he prodded into who all I had conversations with outside the school walls, the answer would be one, and only one. Colbie.

Caleb turned back to face me and crossed his arms over his chest. "You know as well as I do—whether it's right or wrong—it's different. That line isn't worth blurring. If you have female students who need extra help, send them to Chasity or one of the other female teachers. Keep your hands and your reputation clean, Eli." Caleb's eyes darkened, and I didn't miss the flare of his nostrils. "High school drama hasn't changed since we were there. They all get over it. It's called graduation."

Chasity. That was laughable. She was a cheerleading coach and a kindergarten teacher. And she didn't like Colbie. A fact that Caleb had himself admitted.

He stepped closer and hit me on the bicep with a smile. It was a punch intended to lighten the mood and cut through the tension. It fell short. "If you're in need of people to talk to, why don't you come over and spend time with Chasity and me? We can grill out. Have a couple beers. I forget that you're new here." He started back toward the door. "I'll talk to Chas, and we'll figure out a day to have you and some of our friends over so you can meet people our age."

"Sounds good, Caleb. Just let me know. My calendar is pretty empty."

Anger boiled in my chest, and I could feel the heat rising in my cheeks as I worked to keep myself under control. A student shouldn't cause this sort of visceral reaction. Caleb was right, about all of it, which only pissed me off more. Add to it that it was his sister who needed the attention, and I was ready to blow my top when a student walked into first period.

"Whoa, Dr. Paxton. You look like you're about to stroke out."

Jonathan Powers craned his neck back and stared at me. "You need me to get the nurse?"

I shook my head and took a deep breath. "I'm fine, Jonathan. Have a seat."

He held up his hands in surrender and lingered with his buddies until the bell rang. I was only minutes into my first class, and I was already prepared to call it a day.

7

COLBIE

All week I'd wished—and even prayed—I'd meet up with Dr. Paxton again on my daily runs. Yet every morning passed the way it had for years—alone. I'd wanted to believe that last Saturday had been intentional, but maybe he really did have a *thing* that night. I ran harder when I realized his "thing" might quite possibly have been a date.

Oh Lord, he hadn't wanted to tell me. My mind went wild, thinking my teacher would worry that I'd become a crazy stalker, or maybe cry, or worse, talk about me in the teacher's lounge to other faculty members. My breath was jagged from sprinting as I warred with worry, and my lungs burned for more oxygen when I questioned why he'd given me his phone number. None of it made sense, and for once, I regretted not listening more when my brothers talked. They could have provided valuable insight into the male mind.

The truth was, Eli Paxton occupied far too many moments in my thoughts. I had enough on my plate with school and piano. I didn't need distractions, and that was exactly what this had become. My pace slowed as I forced myself to accept that I needed to refocus. The man who visited in my dreams couldn't take up residence in my days.

The familiar white house I'd grown up in came into view, and I debated on whether to turn right to add another mile to my Saturday jog or go home. More distance wouldn't get my homework done, nor would it help with the étude. It had helped clear my head and put me back into the headspace I needed. Discipline always proved fruitful...and one step closer to perfection.

The front door was locked, and the garage was closed. I went around to the back and retrieved the key. The house was empty. I didn't know where UGA played this weekend, but Mama and Daddy had loaded up Caden and the twins to go to the game while I was gone. I assumed it was a home game since they hadn't left last night. I would love to see Carson and Casey, but sacrificing an entire day of studying and piano wasn't worth competing with UGA football to do it. Instead, I fired off the same text message to both brothers that I did for every game I missed. I told Carson that I was sorry I didn't get to see him and to come home soon. And I wished Casey luck in the game and that I missed him.

Neither responded. They never did.

I tried to imagine what college life was like so I didn't take it personally. They were both wildly popular and involved in all kinds of clubs and activities. Carson not only had grad school, but he was a teacher's assistant and had a steady girlfriend that my parents swore he'd marry. I got it. They were busy.

A chill rose on my damp skin when I opened the fridge to grab a bottle of water. And when I lifted my arm to drink it, my stench reminded me I needed to shower. I tossed the now empty bottle into the trash compactor and jogged upstairs to my bathroom. There the inspection began after I toed off my shoes. Facing the mirror, I crossed my arms and tugged the wet sports bra from my chest and over my head. My shorts and panties joined it on the floor seconds later.

My fingers pinched at the skin on my stomach and then my sides. I angled my body in every direction to chronicle every imperfection, every extra inch and bulge. Then I turned and lifted onto my toes and stared over my shoulder at my butt and thighs. No matter how many miles I'd ran, there was a dimple on my right cheek that simply wouldn't budge. The sight of it left my heart heavy, and despite the fact that food put that cellulite there, all I wanted to do was comfort myself with a donut. My gaze traveled up the knots of my spine along with the guilt I felt for wanting to eat my way into happiness. The bones of my hips protruded but still had a round edge to them that wasn't quite lean enough, and I could only count four ribs on either side. I closed my eyes and sank back down onto flat feet, chastising myself for not pushing through another mile or two before I came home.

Disappointment was like a noose, but every day was another opportunity to get it right. I forced myself to face my reflection with open eyes and pick something I liked. It was a battle. I could find flaw in every aspect, but my teeth were straight, and people always told me what a beautiful smile I had. My lips tilted upward, even though I wouldn't agree with them, and when the happiness didn't reach my eyes, I couldn't pick that feature. I unwound the tie from my hair and let my locks cascade past my shoulders. It was a bit duller than normal, but that was just because I needed to wash it. Overall, there wasn't anything I would change about it. I fluffed it up in the mirror a bit, giving it a little attention, and decided I liked my hair...for the sixth time this week.

With that settled, I reached into the shower and turned the knob. It didn't take long for the water to run hot, and when I stepped in, the heat soothed away the aches of my morning run and cleared my head of the fog. By the time I got out, dried my hair, and got dressed, homework was no longer a dreaded task. It was just next on my to-do list.

Several hours later, my stomach growled, and I smiled at my ability to keep myself from gorging on donuts this morning. I hadn't eaten all day, and I had a renewed sense of clarity that always came from denial. Light on my feet, I raced downstairs to the piano and pulled out the sheet music to "Winterwind."

As the sun began to fade and the streetlights came on, I played through Chopin's étude without mistake. Albeit, not at the pace I needed, but it was the first time I'd made it through the entire piece without a blunder. I glanced around, hoping someone had witnessed my accomplishment, but the house was as empty as it had been all day. My parents and my brothers were nowhere to be found, just like they wouldn't be the day of the recital. And what felt like a win faded into a loss.

But my drive wasn't dependent upon them. And I had to increase the tempo to be ready to perform. Just because I'd hit every note once didn't mean I was in the clear. I took a deep breath and shifted on the bench. Then from the window, I noticed Dr. Paxton standing on the sidewalk with his earphones in his hand, watching me.

I wondered how long he'd been standing there. He didn't appear winded, and based on his attire, he had been running. When he smiled and nodded, I knew.

Eli had heard.

I couldn't avert my gaze. I didn't care to. Every fiber of my being wanted to get up and run to the door and beg him to tell me, to confirm I hadn't missed a single key. I would throw myself into his arms, and he'd hug me tightly and tell me how proud he was just before he took my mouth with his. Before the fantasy could become reality, he waved, and then he was gone.

The silence hung in the air and in my chest. I'd never realized the weight of such emptiness. It was vast and painful. It stung. My phone vibrated on the piano, interrupting the quiet. Expecting a text from Jess, I was surprised at what I found.

Eli: Beautiful.

One word. It could mean so many things. Although, I was certain he referred to the music. I debated responding, but in the end, my need for acknowledgment beat out my need for self-preservation.

Me: How much did you hear?

Minutes went by, and I wondered if he'd text back. Staring at the screen was like watching water boil.

Eli: Would you be mad if I said all of it?

My heart jumped into my throat and tears filled my eyes. This wasn't something to be so emotional over, yet I couldn't stop the light-headed feeling that took over or the warmth that spread through me.

Me: Depends.

I had no idea where I was going with this. I didn't have the first clue how to flirt, but I knew I didn't want him to stop talking, either.

Again, the long moments between texts exacerbated my anxiety. I'd never been good at this kind of thing. The only people I ever texted were Jess and my family. Jess sent instant responses, and my family never needed a reply.

Eli: On what?

Okay, this definitely wasn't a very good plan.

Me: Whether or not you're going to tell anyone.

Eli: Haha. It's safe to say I'm not going to tell a soul that I stood outside your house and peeped through the window for an absurd amount of time.

My cheeks hurt from the size of my grin.

Me: An "absurd" amount?

Giddy. That was the only word to describe what I felt.

Eli: Sounded like you nailed it. Is that the piece you said you were having a hard time with?

He ignored my request for verification of just how much time he'd actually spent on the sidewalk.

Me: It is. It still needs work. The tempo should be considerably faster, but I've definitely made progress.

Eli: I'm confident you'll get it perfected.

Perfect. That word stuck in my brain and lingered on my tongue as I said it out loud. And the ache in my face subsided as my lips fell.

Me: Is that what you expect? Perfection?

Eli: Not at all. I know it's what YOU expect.

Before I could respond, the front door swung open. Collin and Clayton came bounding in the door followed by my parents. Their excitement filled the foyer, and I turned on the bench. It was easy to see that Georgia had won. Each of them talked about plays they'd found particularly spectacular, none of which I understood. Football had its own language, and I'd never learned to speak the vernacular.

Just as I was about to resume practice, the door opened again. This time, Caden came through...holding Jess's hand. My jaw went slack, but I managed to keep my mouth closed even if my eyes were wide. I hadn't heard from her all day, but I just assumed her parents had her on lockdown. Never in my wildest dreams did I imagine she was with my family at a football game.

"Hey, Cole." Caden closed the door behind his girlfriend.

I didn't trust my voice, so I donned the Chapman smile of familiarity and waved in silence. Jess avoided my stare, and I let her. Caden's greeting caused my father's recognition. Still talking to the twins about the "big game," he strolled into the living room and closed the lid on the piano.

"That's enough for tonight." His authority left no room for negotiation. "Your mama's gonna warm up leftovers for dinner."

I wasn't sure if that was an invitation or just a reason for me not to bother them by "banging on the keys." They'd told me countless times that it was difficult to carry on a conversation over the instrument. I'd never bothered to point out that the piano was across the house from the dining room and couldn't possibly be anything more than background noise.

The others had wandered off, and Jess let go of my brother's hand when Mama asked her if she wanted to help in the kitchen. I still sat motionless on the bench.

"You coming?" Caden waited expectantly.

I shook my head. "You guys go ahead. I didn't know when you'd be home, so I ate earlier." *Lie.* "I need to start working on my homework." At this rate, my growing nose would knock him over.

His brow dipped, but he didn't call me out. Instead, he bit his lip and nodded. Caden glanced over his shoulder. When he didn't see anything, or maybe he saw exactly what he wanted—no one—his long legs carried him to where I sat. He joined me and wrapped his arm around my shoulders.

"You okay with all this?" Caden didn't have to tell me what "all this" was.

Jess appeared before I could respond. Her hands were loaded down with silverware and napkins. "Caden, your mom asked us to set the table." And just like that, she had a seat next to my brother at the table and a place in my mom's heart. Not that she hadn't always been welcome in my home; it was just different now. She was part of Caden, which elevated her to a noticeable status. As *my* friend, she'd been as invisible as I was.

Caden's face lit up when she had entered the room. "Okay. I'll be there in a second." He waited for her to disappear before speaking to me again. "You know you're still my favorite, right?" His hand dropped from my shoulder to my side, and he dug his finger into my ribs to get me to laugh.

I gave him what he wanted, even though I didn't believe it. "I know."

He kissed my temple and popped up off the bench like a jack-in-the-box to join the rest of the family. The conversation and laughter flowed from the kitchen. I sat in silence and listened to the sounds of happiness and togetherness, and then I walked up the stairs to my room.

The light knock on my door didn't surprise me. The person on the other side did.

Caden peeked his head through the crack. "Can we talk?"

I set my novel down and sat up, crossing my legs on my bed. "Sure. What's on your mind?"

He could no longer sneak through a tiny crack. He had to open the door full swing. Caden's shoulders had broadened in the last few months, and he'd put on a solid bit of muscle. He was already tall, but now, he was filling out. I'd caught glimpses of the man he was turning into, but where they had been few and far between, there was less of the boy I loved than the man he was destined to be.

He launched himself through the air and landed on the mattress next to me in a pike position. I rolled my eyes and giggled. I hoped some things never changed. This had always been our thing, although it had matured a bit over time. He no longer tried to bounce me off the bed by repeatedly jumping on it or tickle me until I peed; however, the amused look faded when he rolled onto his side to face me.

"Ugh. You're going to force this, aren't you?" I had no desire to talk about Jess with Caden. I didn't care to talk to Jess about him, either.

He hit me with a stray pillow. "Yup. She told me what happened."

I closed my eyes and took a deep breath before opening them again. "Of course she did." I meant to mutter to myself, but with Caden jammed up next to me, it hadn't come out all that quietly.

"We tell each other everything, Colbie."

He was right. It was what separated my relationship with him from everyone else in our family. We'd always talked, shared secrets. "It wasn't my place to tell you."

He snickered. "No, silly. I mean Jess and me. We tell each other everything."

Well, that wasn't what I thought he'd meant. "Oh." They'd been dating for like two minutes, and suddenly, they're BFFs. I hadn't gotten the memo, clearly.

Caden sat up. His face was pale, and all humor had disappeared from his eyes. "I need to tell you something." This was serious.

"Okay...." I hated the nervous anticipation I got when I was filled with dread.

He cracked his knuckles and bent one knee, both signs of his apprehension. My heart raced, wishing he'd just spit it out.

"If you're going to be mad, I need you to direct that at me and not Jess. Promise?"

Jesus. "No. I don't promise. How can you even ask me that?" I couldn't assure him of anything when I didn't have a clue what he might divulge.

Caden's Adam's apple slid down his throat and back up when he swallowed. I'd seen this before when he'd fessed up to something we'd done as kids. It was never good. "Jess and I had sex last night."

I pulled back like I'd been slapped. "What?"

He had to be lying. Jess would have told me. She never would have left that to Caden, not to mention, they'd been dating for all of, like, a day.

I unfolded my legs and got off the bed. Standing next to it, I crossed my arms, ready to tear my little brother apart. He knew better than to lie about girls that way. Caden would destroy Jess's reputation if that kind of gossip got out. "Caden Chapman! I don't know what game you're playing, but you better not tell anyone else that lie. I can't believe such filth just came out of your mouth." I hissed the words through my teeth, trying to keep my voice down so my parents wouldn't hear the conversation.

His face turned the color of a red Skittle when he got to his feet and stood so close I could smell his breath. "What the hell, Cole? Why would you think I'm lying?"

I blinked. Once. Twice. Three times. He had to be joking.

"Well?" Caden threw his arms in the air.

"She's a virgin, Caden. She's not just going to have sex with the first guy who pays her a little attention a week after they start dating." It got increasingly more difficult not to yell, although I wasn't certain why I vehemently refused to believe what he said.

"It's been four months."

There was no way. I quickly did the mental math. Jess had only mentioned it a couple weeks ago. I laughed and tossed my head back to emphasize just how funny that was. "You're so full of it. Two weeks ago was the first time she mentioned you."

He stuffed his hands into his pockets, and a smug grin lined his lips. "Where was Jess all summer, Colbie?"

I gave him a half shrug. "Her parents wouldn't let her do anything."

"Or maybe that was just what she told you so she could do something else."

I hadn't given it a second thought. Her parents had always been strict, so when she told me she couldn't do anything, it wasn't unusual. I still saw her, just not as much as I had in previous summers. "What are you saying, Caden?"

"That I've been seeing Jess since the end of last year."

It all fell into place. This was why she'd been so forward about giving up the pact the first day of school. She'd already quit; she'd just been lying to me about it.

"Say something."

I straightened my spine and dropped my defensive posture. "What would you like me to say?"

He pulled on the roots of his hair and turned in a circle. "I want you to tell me you're okay with it. That nothing has to change. I want you to call your best friend and tell her you're happy for her and mean it." Caden stared at me and waited. "Colbie?"

But I couldn't give them a free pass. "You want me to lie the way the two of you have?"

"That's not fair, Cole." He must live in an alternate universe.

I huffed out a sarcastic laugh. "What about that isn't fair?" I walked toward my door and then wrapped my fingers around the knob. "The two people I'm closest to in life have kept secrets from me and lied to me, not once, but repeatedly...for *months*. I'm not okay with that, and four months ago, you wouldn't have been, either. But I guess getting your dick wet was more important than honesty and loyalty. Congrats, Caden, you're officially another member of the male species and an asshole to boot." I opened the door and jerked my eyes toward the opening, inviting him to leave.

It took him three steps to reach me, and one more to push the door closed. "Maybe if you weren't so damn hard to get through to, then people wouldn't feel like they had to lie to you in order to protect you." He waved a hand in front of my face. "Earth to Colbie, the world doesn't care about your overly sensitive heart."

"No, but my brother should." I couldn't do this, and I wouldn't.

If he refused to leave, then I would. I locked myself in the bathroom and waited. It didn't take long for Caden to stop cussing and slam my bedroom door.

By the time I emerged, my hands shook, and I fought every urge to cry. I glanced at the clock, and I knew it was too late to eat my feelings or go running. Stuck, I did the only thing I could think of.

Me: You busy?

8

ELI

I WAS HALF ASLEEP ON THE COUCH WHEN MY PHONE DINGED on the coffee table. Even groggy, seeing a text from her put a smile on my face. It was nearly eleven, but I refused to admit I was an old man who couldn't stay awake long enough to get through the news...or that I even watched the news.

Me: Just lying on the couch, watching TV. You?

It wasn't an outright lie, just a tiny stretch of the truth.

The bubbles appeared and stopped. Then appeared again and stopped. But no text came through. The longer it went on the more worried I became that she wasn't just wanting to chitchat, and there was indeed something wrong.

Me: Talk to me. Is everything okay?

Job and I would not be competing for any patience awards. If Colbie needed something, I had no idea how I'd provide her with it, which only made me anxious.

Beautiful: I had a bad night.

It hadn't been that long since I'd seen her. Granted, through the window didn't really count, but she had seemed okay when I texted her.

Me: What happened?

At this rate, I'd have another birthday by the time I knew what was going on. My heart was in my throat, and this girl had me tied in unreasonable knots.

Me: Colbie, I need to know you're okay.

Beautiful: I guess that's relative.

This is where age became an issue. Problems to an eighteen-year-old weren't the same as those to a twenty-four-year-old. Not that they were any less significant in our respective worlds, but a bad hair day in high school was detrimental. It was expected as an adult.

Me: You've got to give me more to go on.

Preferably before I went bald and got a senior citizen discount. No teenager texted this slowly, which meant she was considering every word before she typed it and then reconsidering it before she hit send.

Me: Stop overthinking this, and tell me what happened.

Maybe taking off the gloves was the best approached. She fought hard when anyone bucked up to her. Treating her like a delicate flower probably wouldn't get me anywhere.

Beautiful: Caden and Jess had sex.

Beautiful: And they've lied about how long they've been dating.

Beautiful: Clearly, I'm naïve.

Beautiful: And the only virgin left at Brogdon High.

I snickered at the last text, but at least she was talking, even if I still didn't know what actually happened.

Me: First of all, being a virgin is not like having the plague. It's a gift. Keep that shit as long as you want to, and don't give it to a man who's not deserving.

Please don't give it to anyone. Not yet.

Me: Second, how did you find all this out about Caden and Jess? Did they tell you?

Beautiful: You have to say that. You're a teacher.

That was a reminder I didn't need right now.

Beautiful: Caden wanted to "talk" to me tonight. He wanted me to call Jess and tell her I was fine with all of it and be happy for them.

Beautiful: You really should encourage Caleb to drug test the football players. Caden has to be smoking something.

There were so many sides to this girl. I was quite fond of the snarky one and definitely enjoyed the intelligent one, but the vulnerable, innocent one was by far my favorite because no one else ever got to see it.

Me: How long have they been dating?

Beautiful: Since the end of last school year.

I didn't know the details of how they'd pulled that off without Colbie finding out, but I could imagine how badly it would hurt to learn the truth. And with what little I knew about Colbie, I'd bet my savings account that she felt deserted.

Texting wasn't my favorite way to communicate, although I recognized the limitations I had to deal with. I'd told her if she ever needed to talk, I'd be there. Colbie had reached out, and I wasn't going back on that. I also couldn't risk getting caught with her on the phone, so calling was out of the question. Never in my life had I felt so helpless. It wasn't the end of the world, but it was the end of Colbie's world. And *that* gutted me. Almost as much as the realization that I wouldn't see her until Monday.

And when she finally succumbed to exhaustion, or maybe just got tired of texting, she said goodnight. But I couldn't leave it at that.

Me: I have a thing tomorrow night, so I'm going running in the morning. Maybe I'll see you.

I prayed she got the reference.

Beautiful: Oh.

Oh? That wasn't the response I'd expected or wanted.

Me: Oh?

Beautiful: You have a date.

I was lost. I scrolled up and read through the text messages—there were hundreds after two hours of talking. Nothing indicated anything of the sort.

Me: A date? No. A "thing."

Me: Why would you think I have a date?

Again with the damn bubbles.

Me: Spit it out, Cole.

It was a risk, both the command and the nickname.

Beautiful: I just assumed that's what you meant and didn't want to discuss your dating life with a kid in your class.

She was jealous. I shouldn't relish it, but every bit of me did. I also wouldn't play on her vulnerability. She'd laid herself out there, trusting I wouldn't crush her with my response. And as long as she gave me that kind of honesty, I'd guard it with my life.

Me: I'm not dating anyone. I haven't since grad school.

Beautiful: I leave my house at six on Sundays because church starts at ten. I go through the park.

Me: Sleep tight.

Beautiful: Goodnight, Eli.

My chest swelled, and in my head, I could hear her say my name. I wished she were lying next to me and had whispered into my ear just before I turned out the lights, but since that couldn't happen, my imagination was the next best thing.

I watched the clock all night. Six couldn't come fast enough. At five, I gave up and got dressed. Thirty minutes later, I walked to the park and sat on the same bench Colbie had shared with me a week ago. I swear, I didn't have to see her come around the corner. My body sensed hers, and every hair on my neck stood at attention when she came near.

Colbie stopped long enough to pull one bud from her ear. "You coming?"

This was probably the closest I'd ever get to seeing her in the dark, and she didn't disappoint. Her shorts barely covered her butt, and her sports bra was minimal. She wasn't indecent; I was just a pervert. I had no idea how she kept her milky complexion when she ran every day in the sun, but it was alluring. She wouldn't have looked right with a tan, and somehow, it made her more appealing.

I stood and joined her. Colbie put her earbud back in and started down the path. If I'd had my choice, we would have sat on the bench and skipped the whole exercise bit, but that would've led to things she wasn't ready for and I couldn't do. So I kept her pace, but when we started down the old gravel road that led out to the country, I reached over and pulled on the cord attached to her ear until the bud fell out.

"Where are we going?" According to my watch, we'd already logged three miles. There was nothing but desolation down this stretch of road.

She didn't slow down, not even when a car came up beside us. "Down one fifty-three. It's only a few miles."

I grabbed her wrist and pulled her to my side to keep her from being run over. "Jesus, Colbie. You almost got hit."

Her pale blue eyes searched mine in the early light of morning. I'd hurt her feelings, but she wouldn't tell me.

I resisted the urge to wrap my arm around her slender waist and show her why I didn't want her to get hurt. Instead, I tucked a stray hair behind her ear and softened my tone. "How far are we going?"

The birds chirped around us, but there wasn't another human in sight. The car that had sped past was long gone.

"Seven more."

"Miles?"

She must have found humor in whatever expression I made. Her giggle was like spring air, a rainbow after a storm, fire on a snowy night. "Yeah. I do ten on Sundays."

"Why?" Three I could do with ease. Five I could handle but didn't want to. Ten was just punishing my body.

Colbie tensed and panic laced her wide eyes.

I cupped her jaw and the back of her neck in my hand, stroking her cheek with my thumb. "Hey. You can talk to me. Nothing has to be a secret if you don't want it to be." That was dangerous, and I absolutely didn't care.

She stared over my shoulder at something in the distance. I didn't have to be a genius to know that she couldn't look me in the eye when she made whatever confession she held, and I didn't press. I also didn't let her go.

"To stay in shape."

There was more. I could sense the hitch in her breath, the hesitation in her voice. I just had to give her the time and patience to offer me the rest.

"It's not as easy for me as it is for the other girls at school. I have to work for it." A tear slipped past her cheek as my brain registered her whispered words. "I should do more, but my parents make me go to church, and it's not safe to go out any earlier than six."

Wow. She truly didn't see what anyone else saw in her. "Colbie?" I doubted nature had heard me speak, but Colbie did.

Her eyes flicked to mine. Pain was etched into her face and her gorgeous blue eyes. Whatever was going on was so much deeper than the argument she'd had with Caden. Running was a ritual, and there was no doubt she had more of them that she hid. It was easy for her to do when no one bothered to note where she was or what she did as long as she showed up for dinner and church.

"I wish you could see yourself through the lenses of your classmates." *And mine.*

She shook her head and dropped her gaze to our feet. Her shoulders trembled, and I lost the fight. Pulling her to me, she came willingly. When I wrapped my arms around her back, she tucked her arms against my chest, but she didn't use them to put distance between us. Colbie coiled into my embrace like she needed protection. I rested my chin on top of her head and inhaled the scent of her shampoo. I didn't know shit about flowers, but it was definitely floral and altogether the essence of Colbie.

I'd never desired to fill a void of silence, yet with Colbie, I couldn't escape the sense of failing her. She needed more, but I didn't know how to give it to her. Not yet. Not for months. And even then, I was clueless if I could make it happen. I acted like I'd been in love with this girl for years when I'd known her for weeks. But I couldn't shake my feelings or where they were headed.

There, on the side of the road, we stood for an undetermined amount of time. I didn't check my watch because I didn't care. I just held her as tightly as I could and stroked her spine with my thumb. Eventually, her arms slipped around my waist, and all I could think about was having this perfect woman safe with me.

When she finally pulled back, she didn't let go. Her hands stayed on my hips, and I locked my fingers together behind her. Her tongue snuck out and moistened her lips, and I prayed like hell she didn't feel my dick twitch when she did it. I couldn't let her kiss me, but I wouldn't stop it, either. Instead of my mouth, her affection landed on my jaw. And I closed my eyes to enjoy the way she lingered there on her toes.

"Thank you, Eli," she whispered into my ear.

I had no idea what I'd done to deserve her praise, but hearing my name pass her lips was even better than I'd dreamed. Sultry, yet innocent. Warm and inviting. Soft and heartfelt. One syllable, three letters. No one had ever arranged them on their tongue the way Colbie Chapman just did, and I never wanted another woman to utter them with affection.

Standing on the side of the road last weekend, I'd known something shifted in Colbie. Everything in me had believed it was good. She'd trusted me, let me comfort her. Her tears had wet my shirt, and her fingers had clung to my sides. The desire in her voice when she thanked me wasn't something I'd fabricated. I'd seen how she looked at me before she went home. It was absolutely there.

Until Monday morning.

Colbie had given me a meek smile when she'd walked in, and then proceeded to sit in silence. Not once did she raise her hand, and when I called on her, she told me she didn't know the answer to my question. Seven—I counted—heads turned in disbelief to stare wide-eyed at the smartest girl at Brogdon High. But when she refused to maintain eye contact, I couldn't begin to guess what was going on. And when the bell rang, I was at the back of the class, and she rushed out the door.

But that night, once I got home and thought it was safe to message her, it seemed nothing bothered her.

Me: You were practically mute in class today. And you didn't know an answer. How can you tell me nothing's bothering you?

Beautiful: I just had an off day.

An off day. It was possible, but who was I to question her.

Beautiful: I had a headache.

She should have led with that. It would've been more believable, and now it just seemed like a lie.

Me: Are you feeling better?

Beautiful: I was sick after dinner, but I'm better now.

Beautiful: How was your night?

None of this even sounded like Colbie, although I couldn't imagine who it would have been. It was casual in a way that wasn't her.

Me: Okay. You running in the morning?

Beautiful: Every day.

I wouldn't just go find her, not again. She had to want to see me and tell me where she'd be. And if she didn't, I'd sleep an hour later and run tomorrow evening the same way I planned to do tonight. In this heat, I only worked out before dawn or after dusk; otherwise, I'd have a stroke and pass out. I might be in good physical shape, but Georgia was no joke when it came to humidity.

I tossed my phone aside and gave up on getting any more from her tonight. Not being able to call or just show up on her doorstep served as a reminder of why her brother had warned me away from my students. None of this was appropriate.

I laced my tennis shoes and continued to beat myself up for crossing countless moral boundaries. No matter how many points I made in favor of dropping whatever this was with Colbie, I came up with twice as many to argue against it. And as my feet hit the pavement, I understood how cathartic miles could be. Until every song that came on reminded me of her.

So much so that when I came down the hill in the park, I swore she sat on our bench like she waited for me. I wiped the sweat from my eyes, but it didn't remove her image. The closer I got, the more real she became. I slowed and pulled the buds from my ears.

"Cole?" I needed to slap myself and lay off the casual familiarity.

She lifted her hand and wiggled her fingers, but there was zero emotion in her expression or her eyes.

I squatted in front of her and tried to catch my breath. "You all right?"

Her head bobbed up and down. My chest heaved, but I was no longer certain if my heart raced from the exercise or her presence. I couldn't deny the effect she had on me. Everything about her was potent, or in my case, toxic.

She sat with her long legs crossed elegantly and her wrist propped on her knee. With my elbows on my knees, I took her hand in mine without bothering to check for onlookers. It was a dangerous game, yet when I was with her, I threw caution to the wind. Her pupils grew when I looked into her eyes, and her cheeks blushed a delicate pink. But she didn't look away.

"What are you doing out here? Do your parents know you're not home?" I sounded like an overprotective big brother. "Sorry. I didn't mean for that to come across that way."

Colbie blinked, and I fidgeted until I released her fingers. And when she giggled, I couldn't stop the tilt of my lips. "Are you always this awkward?"

I shook my head and sat next to her on the bench. "Only around enigmas." And she was every bit that.

She shifted to face me. "You think I'm mysterious?"

"Why does that surprise you? You don't think you're an anomaly?"

"You mean surreptitious?" Her brow quirked.

I raised my own at her acknowledgment of the nature of it all. "Touché, but no. And you still haven't answered my question."

"Which one? I've avoided answering them all."

In truth, she had. "Do you always sit on park benches alone at night?"

There was whimsy in her body language and amusement in her eyes. I loved seeing her this way, but for whatever reason, she never showed any of this if there was another soul around. Yet if it were just the two of us, her eyes glittered, her smile sparkled, and she beamed.

"Actually, no. This is a first."

I prayed she waited for me.

"You really should jog in the mornings. This heat is oppressive."

I chuckled. "Then why are you sitting in it?"

"Because I didn't know where you ran."

Colbie had zero game, and I loved that about her. There was no pretense, no hiding. She either didn't know she wasn't supposed to give herself away or she wasn't interested in playing the games most girls did. It was likely a bit of both.

I leaned against the bench and watched a lone car pass the park. "You could have sent me a text to ask."

Colbie burst out laughing. It was melodic and hypnotizing. "That probably would have been a lot easier." She wiped tears from her cheeks as she regained her composure. "See, I'm not as smart as you think." Her giggle settled into my chest and wrapped itself around my heart.

I didn't have a clue where to go with this. I wanted to ask her what had upset her this morning and made her sick this afternoon, but there was no sign of either. I feared bringing it up would tear her down, and I couldn't do that to her. "How's the étude going?"

A car slowed in the street and honked. It spooked Colbie, but I didn't recognize the vehicle. "Do you want to walk?"

Telling her I'd follow her anywhere probably wasn't the manliest of answers, so I didn't. "Sure."

We wandered the park, and she regaled me with details of her recital. Her hands danced in the air when she described the movements, and she spun in a circle when she admitted she'd continued to play the étude faster. "You have no idea what a relief it is to *get* it. I've worked for months on that one piece."

"How long do you have before the recital?" I already knew the time and place and date, but Colbie needed someone to show interest. It wasn't like I had to pretend. Anything that made her happy had me intrigued, and she could go on forever about music.

"A few weeks. But I'll make sure it's perfect."

That wasn't a surprise, either. Everything Colbie did redefined the word overachieving. Although, I hated to admit, I wondered at what price that perfection came. She'd had circles under her eyes the last couple of days, and while I hadn't seen her naked, I had seen her in some pretty skimpy running attire. She verged on being too thin. That in itself wouldn't be an issue. It was the miles she jogged seven days a week because she "had to work harder than the other girls" that scared me. It might just be stress. I wanted to believe it was stress, because stress would ease after the recital, and she would get breaks from schoolwork at holidays and vacation. But I couldn't deny that her home life definitely played a part.

I didn't know the extent, yet I was certain it did. This shit with Caden and Jess was tough for anyone, but to someone like Colbie who had a small circle of people close to her, it was devastating. Regardless of what she said or didn't say, I saw her in the halls. I'd witnessed her brother and best friend walk by without speaking to her. More often than not, she now skipped lunch and hid in the piano practice room because her best friend sat with the football players and their girlfriends. She and Jess had been cordial in class, but I'd have to be blind not to see the strain between them.

And there was nothing I could do.

The breakdown when we were jogging was a fluke. Colbie's armor didn't crack, and she kept that pain close to her vest. The best I could do was to seize moments like these and help keep her in them longer. My hope was to give her enough to carry her through the times I couldn't be a part of.

"Do you ever go to the games?" Colbie's question came out of nowhere, and then I realized, I'd drifted off into my own thoughts.

"UGA?" I didn't know any other games we could be talking about.

She swatted playfully at my arm. "Yes, silly. Remember my recital is the weekend of the Auburn game."

That cleared up how we got on the subject of UGA football, which I was well aware she hated. "I go to a fair number of them, but not all."

Colbie stared off into the darkness. "The rival's a big game."

"I haven't missed one since freshman year. Even away games. This year's is at home."

She had lost some of the pep in her step and the playfulness in her tone. "I'm sure you're excited about it." Colbie assumed things she shouldn't. "Do you ever miss being on the field?"

A laugh bubbled in my chest and erupted from my mouth. "No. I miss being part of a team, but I'm too old to be beaten up on a daily basis. Football is rough on the body."

"I doubt that." A jovial lilt returned to her tone as she denied me.

"Doubt what? Have you ever been tackled by a two-hundred-and-fifty-pound linebacker? That crap hurts." I chuckled, but it was the truth. I did not miss constant bruises and sore muscles. I missed the camaraderie that I hadn't had since I graduated and we all went separate ways.

In some ways, Colbie and I were in similar situations. Her family was absent, as was mine, although for different reasons. I had one friend in town, and he'd gotten married. She had Jess, who had coupled off with Caden. And both of us were counting down the days until she graduated.

"Obviously, I haven't had that experience, but I was referring to you being too old. You're only six years older than I am."

And when she put it that way, it didn't seem like a lifetime of experience that separated us, only a few days on a calendar. Every day I added another justification to my list of reasons why this wasn't wrong and crossed another one off.

Somehow, we'd wandered in a huge circle and had come close to her house, although I hadn't noticed until she stopped and stared across the street. There weren't any lights on, and when I glanced at Colbie, her eyes hinted at the sadness that we'd chased away while we'd been together.

Hidden in the shadow of a large hedge and the cover of night, I reached up and cupped her jaw. She shifted her gaze to me. The vulnerable innocence I only caught glimpses of stared up at me through her pale blue eyes, and I stroked her cheek with my thumb. "You okay?"

Colbie nodded, although she didn't speak or look away. I could drown in her beauty and not once bother to fight for air. I wanted to soak up her pain, pull her from the situation and take her home with me. The need to protect Colbie could suffocate me if I weren't careful.

She closed her eyes, and in a brazen move, slipped her arms around my waist. I didn't hesitate to use my hold on her to pull her cheek to my chest and wrap my other arm around her shoulders. There I basked in her scent. When she pulled away enough for me to look down, I fought the urge to capture her mouth. Instead, I pressed my lips to her forehead. In my opinion, it was more intimate than a chaste kiss, and there was no way in hell I could take what I wanted from her, standing on the sidewalk. Yet when I leaned back, her eyes were closed, and she wore a contented smile.

"I need to go." The strain in her voice told me she didn't want to.

I brushed her hair behind her ear. "If you need to talk, you know how to reach me."

Her nod was almost imperceptible. Something else lingered on her tongue, but I wasn't sure what. "I like having someone to run with...if you wanted to work out in the morning."

The shy side of Colbie was endearing.

"I could probably arrange that."

Colbie's grip on my hips tightened, and she lifted onto her toes. She could make a habit of kissing my jaw. "Thank you, Eli." And she could whisper into my ear anytime she wanted.

She held my hand as she walked away until the last finger dropped. Then she turned toward her house, looked both ways, and crossed the street. I didn't move until she waved from the front porch and I saw her safely inside.

Just as I got home and toed off my shoes, my phone dinged with a text.

Beautiful: Goodnight.

Me: Night.

I was in deep shit, and I didn't have a clue how to get out of it. Colbie was a siren, and I'd become a sailor. The lure irresistible, and the future inevitable, yet I was too drunk on the melody to assess the danger. But even if I had, there was no possibility that I could walk away.

Either I had to get myself in check, or Colbie and I needed to have a serious discussion about what we were doing.

9

COLBIE

SUNDAY DINNER USED TO BE SOMETHING I LOOKED FORWARD to. Years ago, it was always the time that everybody was home, and I felt like part of the group even if I just sat and listened to the others talk. Now, I dreaded it. If Caleb came, he brought Chasity with him, Carson and Casey never showed up, and Caden had attached himself to Jess like she was an arm he couldn't function without. After the last argument with my little brother, I couldn't hide the tension anymore, and I didn't try.

"Jess..." My dad had taken a sudden interest in my best friend. "Are you going to join us for the Auburn game?" He sliced his roast and then put a chunk into his mouth, waiting for her answer.

Jess glanced at Caden with a smile. "If you have an extra ticket, I'd love to."

Caden slid his arm around the back of Jess's seat. "Of course we do. Dad always buys a season ticket for Colbie, but since she never goes, that leaves an open seat. You should come."

Daddy didn't give her a chance to refuse. "It's settled then. The ticket is yours." And he turned the conversation to my mother, discussing a patient of his.

Across the table, I peered at Jess and Caden through my

lashes and tried to avoid eye contact. Jess had always come to my recitals, and either she'd forgotten it was the same day—which I doubted—or she'd chosen Caden over me.

"Can you pass the potatoes, please?" I asked Mama. "And the roast." If I couldn't address my feelings, then I'd consume them instead.

My mother smiled and sent them down the table through the twins. "I don't know where you put it all, Colbie. I guess it's all that running you do."

"Why don't you join the track team, Cole?" It was the first thing Caden had said to me since he'd stormed out of my room.

Jess interjected, "Or cross country. I hear Dr. Paxton is going to be the assistant coach." Her smug grin said she knew more than I cared for her to. Thankfully, no one else saw it.

"Oh, Colbie, sweetheart. That would be fantastic. He and Caleb are very close." My mother was so naïve. "It would be great to have that on your resume." She grinned and patted my dad on the arm. "Wouldn't that be wonderful, Phillip? Another athlete in the family."

"Certainly wouldn't hurt. You should give it some thought."

I slanted my head to the side, wondering what planet they all lived on, and why Jess had tried to inconspicuously throw me under the bus. But the only one who still took notice of me was my best friend. The rest of them had moved on to another topic. Her eyes narrowed, and I wondered about her end game.

My chest heaved with anxiety, and two helpings turned into three. When I reached the point that I thought I'd burst if I put one more bite into my mouth, I leaned back to enjoy the contentment. My stomach pressed against my ribs, and each breath I took was more labored than the last. There was no point in asking to be excused before the dishes were cleared, so I hopped up and grabbed everything I could without drawing anyone's attention.

With the dishwasher loaded, the rest of my family lingered over dessert.

"Mama, can I be excused?" I prayed she didn't insist I stay since we had "company."

She took my hand in hers and stared up at me from her chair at the table. "Don't you want any dessert?"

I puffed out my cheeks and put my hand on my stomach in an exaggerated display. "I can't eat anything else."

"But what about Jess?" My mom apparently hadn't caught the tension between us, nor had she realized Jess and I hadn't hung out in quite a while.

Jess saved me, although I had no idea why. "Go ahead. I'll come up after cake." She waved me off, but I didn't miss the squint of her eyes. Jess had never been a vindictive person, but she had something working in her brain.

Daddy finally gave me the green light. "Go ahead, sugar."

My mom dropped my hand, and I walked to the stairs. Once I was hidden behind the wall, I raced toward my room. The comfort of food had transformed into the pain of guilt. The rush of emotions came as fast as the need to purge. I pushed my bedroom door closed behind me and locked the bathroom once I was inside.

THE LID LIFTED EASILY ALONG WITH THE SEAT. I BENT AT THE waist, put one hand on the edge of the bowl, and started my ritual. The meal had been good, but this would be better. My eyes focused on the still water as I inhaled deeply, exhaled, and then swallowed the tips of my pointer and middle finger, inducing my gag reflex. My stomach jolted but didn't rebel, not yet. That first spasm, the clenching, was almost as satisfying as the first bite of food. My eyes watered before the tears fell, and they wouldn't fall until at least the third time I wretched. I hadn't drunk enough water during dinner, making everything more painful. If I wanted it badly enough, I'd suffer through it. It was my choice. I was the keeper of that destiny. And I coveted the emptiness that remained when I reached it. I jerked my hand from my mouth between each gag and relished in emptying my body, ridding myself of the calories that had tasted so good going down.

Saliva hung from my fingers and lips, yet I never made a sound. The taste of bile when there was no more food signaled another triumphant win.

After I peed and flushed, I washed my hands. My eyes were more bloodshot than usual, so I splashed a bit of cold water on my face to cool them. It hadn't really helped, but no one would see it regardless.

Or so I thought. I turned off the light and opened the door to find Jess facing the bathroom and staring at me. "Hey. I didn't know you were in here." I glanced around to see if she was alone—she was—and if she'd closed the door to the hall. She had.

For the first time in weeks, concern marred her expression instead of hostility. "What's going on, Colbie?"

I scrunched my face and pulled my head back as if I didn't know what she referred to. "With what?"

She raised her brows and tilted her head. "Do you do that a lot?"

"Do what?" I'd planned for this scenario in case it ever happened. I just hadn't planned on it being Jess I had to lie to.

Jess crossed her arms over her stomach and sat up straighter. "Did you just throw up?"

I did my best to appear mortified. "Oh gross. No. My stomach is pretty upset." I paused so she'd believe I had to think about how to put this. "I had diarrhea." My stomach gurgled to back up my lie. I pressed my palm to the site the noise had come from. "You probably don't want to go in there for a while." I used my other hand to point toward the bathroom.

But I'd prepared for that, too. If she chose to go in, she

wouldn't find anything in the toilet or trashcan. She would, however, be overwhelmed by the deodorizer I'd used to cover up the smell of bile. In fact, she might choke on it as she inhaled.

Her expression softened, and her mouth quirked to the side the way it did anytime she needed to say something she was uncomfortable with. "Can we talk? Or would you prefer to save it for another time?"

My head wanted to tell her to take a hike, but my heart missed her. I warred between the two, and in the end, I gave way to emotion rather than reason. "Sure. What's on your mind?" Maybe I could diffuse whatever came my way by acting nonchalant.

Jess took a deep breath. Her complexion had taken on a rather green hue, and I worried she might need the bathroom next. "I need to apologize to you." She held my stare and refused to look away.

"For what?"

She laughed, although not because she believed anything was funny. Jess was uncomfortable. "Everything I've done since the end of school last year."

I chewed on my lip and waited. No part of me had expected an apology. At best, I'd hoped we'd forget about it and find a way to move on that worked for all of us. "Okay..." I sat next to her.

Jess turned on the bed, drawing one leg into her, and took my hands. It was a bit odd. Nevertheless, sincerity danced in her eyes even though she hadn't said a word. "Will you hear me out without interrupting? Then you can ask whatever questions you need to or say whatever you have to. I'll listen if you'll give me a chance to explain."

I wasn't sure I wanted to hear any of it. Nothing justified all the lies she and my brother had told. I'd be happy if we pretended it had never happened. "You don't have to do this, Jess."

Her fingers squeezed mine, and she nodded almost imperceptibly. "I do." She took another deep breath and started. "Caden needed help to pass his math final last year. If he didn't pull a *C* or better, he wouldn't be able to play football. One day after school, a couple weeks before the semester ended, he asked me if I'd tutor him."

"Why didn't he say anything? I would have helped him." This probably wasn't the time or place to get my feelings hurt over my brother needing a tutor.

"You said you'd hear me out."

I held up my hands in apology. "Sorry. Go ahead." I laced my fingers together so I'd be able to fidget and keep my mouth shut.

"He thought your parents would pull him off the team over the summer and make him go to summer school if they found out." Jess's facial features went soft in sympathy for Caden. "He's not like us, Colbie. Caden has to work for every *A* or *B* he gets, and in math, he works his tail off for a *C*."

My heart sank. I should have known this, but Caden's grades had never come up, only his success on the football field. In all fairness, my grades only came up when one of my family members made fun of my drive for valedictorian.

"Don't do that. I see you mentally berating yourself. He didn't *want* you to know. You didn't just *miss* it."

Tears welled in my eyes, and I nodded so she'd keep going.

"Caden came by every night after football practice. I tutored him for an hour or so, and after a couple days, my mom started asking him to stay for dinner. I swear to you, Colbie, it all started out so innocently." Wrinkles formed on her forehead and between her eyes. She huffed, and I knew this was where she admitted how things changed. "My mom and dad were at some charity thing, but they agreed Caden could still come over. I got the lecture about no boys in my bedroom or behind a closed door, blah blah blah." She rolled her eyes, and I knew why. Jess had still been committed to our pact at that time—the warnings were pointless because she wouldn't have entertained an advance from a guy.

A tiny chuckle escaped my lips as I thought about how preposterous it would have been for my mom to say the same thing to me. At the sound of my laughter, the lines of worry eased on Jess's forehead.

"I'm not going to lie to you, Colbie. I was attracted to Caden and had been for two years. But girls like us don't date guys on the football team, much less ones as popular as the Chapman clan. And with only a year left, I didn't see risking class rank for any boy."

All of it made sense thus far. "What changed?"

"He kissed me. It was the night before his exam, and he thanked me and pecked me on the cheek. I stood there like a moron. My eyes had to have been the size of saucers. But Caden didn't pull away. It was like slow motion when he leaned in to kiss me on the lips."

I stuck my finger in my mouth, pretending to gag.

Jess pushed my shoulder playfully. "Stop it. You know I didn't have a clue what was going on. I'd never kissed a guy, and when he opened his mouth, I lost all coherent thought."

"Eww. That's still my brother you're talking about."

She stopped and raised her brow. "You can't tell me you don't know what I'm talking about."

I ignored that comment. "Go on."

Jess flopped onto her back on my bed. "We're coming back to that, so don't think you're getting out of it just because I'm currently the one in the hot seat."

I leaned on the pillows against my headboard. "Fine." The two of us had done this so many times that if the topic weren't Caden, this wouldn't be different than any other night.

"I thought the whole thing was a fluke, honestly. Caden Chapman could have any girl in school, and it made sense for it to be a cheerleader or someone in his class. Not me. I fought how the kiss made me feel and promised myself that I'd never breathe a word of it to you, since it would never happen again. The next day, Caden's math teacher graded his exam while he waited after school. And after practice, he stopped by to tell me he'd gotten a B." She lifted her head to see me. "If you could have seen how proud he was of himself.... Anyway"—Jess dropped her head—"he picked me up in a bear hug and swung me around, thanking me. Then when he finally set me down, the kiss was as natural as the hug had been."

She proceeded to tell me that she still didn't think it had meant anything, and while she had enjoyed it, she certainly didn't expect it to continue. Jess knew she had violated girl code. Nevertheless, Caden kept stopping by all summer, and before she realized it, they were dating exclusively. By then, Jess was in so deep that she didn't know how to get out. Her first attempt was in the parking lot on the way into school. And I knew the rest from there.

"There's nothing I can do to erase the deception, Colbie. I just hope you'll forgive me and we can move forward."

Trying to be a hard ass was pointless. I missed Jess and Caden. Somehow, I had to find a way to make things work so we all got what we wanted. I just didn't have a clue how. "I do. And as much as I don't like you dating Caden, at least I know he's not a jerk." I had so many questions I wanted to ask my friend about kissing and making out and sex, but when it was my brother on the other end, I couldn't bring myself to probe.

Jess sat up and scooted next to me against the headboard. She took a pillow and hugged it to her chest and drew her legs in with it. When she turned to me, she rested her cheek on her knees. "You ready to tell me what's going on with you and Dr. Paxton?"

My neck jerked faster than I could register shock. "Huh? What are you talking about?"

She hit me with the pillow she'd been cuddling. "Come on.

I'm not stupid.... And I may have seen the two of you jogging together last weekend."

"What were you doing out that early on a Saturday morning?" Deflecting was my best defense at this point.

"Driving to your house to go to the game with your family. So, stop avoiding the question. What gives?"

I shrugged. "There's nothing going on. Occasionally, he joins me on my morning jogs." This was not good.

"He joins you on your morning jogs?"

"Are you a parrot? Yes. Sometimes he does." There was no hope of getting out of an interrogation.

I needed to put some physical distance between the two of us. I got up and turned on some music. It wasn't loud, so we could keep talking. I just prayed she took the hint.

She did not. "Isn't that illegal or something?"

I plopped down on the corner of my mattress, and my shoulders slumped. "I don't know, Jess."

Jess scooted down the bed next and leaned on me the way she always did when I needed comfort. "Has anything else happened?"

Here I sat between a rock and a hard place. I was also in the same position Jess had been in with Caden this summer. The difference was, Eli could get in serious trouble if anyone found out, yet lying was still deception, regardless of who it was to protect.

"I've seen the way he looks at you, Colbie. It's not the way a teacher should view a student." If Jess saw it, I wondered who else had. "Don't worry, I noticed it on you long before I did him. I doubt anyone else has a clue."

I swallowed past the lump in my throat, and my palms got clammy with sweat. "We talk a lot through text messages, and we jog together most days."

"Is that it?" Her tone indicated disappointment, not condemnation.

I craned my neck to see her eyes. "He's hugged me a couple times." Regardless of how honest I wanted to be, I couldn't risk Eli taking the blame for me kissing him. I would take that secret to my grave. "Is he really going to coach track or cross country? He hasn't mentioned it."

She cackled and held her stomach when she couldn't catch her breath. "No. That was just me being a bitch. I didn't know how to bring it up since we've barely spoken."

"You realize my parents are going to think I'm joining one of the two teams now, right?"

Jess shooed me off and continued to chuckle as she talked. "Hardly. He won't be coaching either so they won't think anything of it." Clearly, she didn't know Phillip or Elise Chapman as well as I'd thought she did.

My phone dinged on the nightstand. I glanced at my watch and knew exactly who it was.

Jess nudged me again. "Is that Prince Charming?" She quit giggling when I pushed her and she lost her balance, falling onto the floor.

"I have no idea."

She scrambled on her hands and knees and grabbed my phone before I could stop her. "Eli? Do you call him that?" Jess said his name a couple more times, each one changing the inflection of her tone to make it more seductive. "Wow. I can definitely see how Dr. Paxton just doesn't hold the same appeal." Her eyes widened, and she held out my cell. "Umm, he wants to know if you're going to be in the park tonight."

Crap. Crap. Crap.

"You meet him in the park? Aren't you afraid of being seen together? Colbie, you guys aren't thinking straight. You might not believe this is a big deal, but he could get fired. If he does, he'll never get another job teaching. That's like the blacklist of all blacklists. Men don't recover from that."

I snatched the phone a little more aggressively than I should. "You act like I'm underage. I'm an adult."

Her face went blank followed by confusion. "And he's your teacher."

My jaw hurt I'd clenched my teeth so tightly, and my nails dug into the palms of my hands. I counted to ten in my head and blew out a breath. "He's also my brother's best friend and a friend of my family."

She stood and crossed her arms, coming face to face with me and calling my bluff. "Okay. Do your parents know the two of you run together?"

I cocked my head to the side and raised my eyebrows as high as I could. "Seriously, Jess. My parents don't know I'm even gone most of the time. As long as I show up for dinner each night and they get proof of life, they don't ask what happens in between."

She knew all of this. She'd known it for years. We had, in fact, joked about what all I could get away with if I were a different type of kid. Where her parents had always kept her on a tight leash, mine had let go of the reins the day I announced my pact with Jess. I'd never given them any reason not to trust me. And in my opinion, I still hadn't.

Jess sighed, knowing everything I said was accurate. "I'm just concerned...for *both* of you."

I covered my face with my hands, and the dam broke. "I don't know what to do, Jess."

"Hey. Shh." She wrapped me in a hug. "Why are you crying?"

I couldn't articulate my emotions or thoughts. My heart had tied itself around Eli Paxton, and I was fairly certain his had done the same. I knew the look Jess referred to and how my chest swelled each time I saw it. Eli and I talked more than Jess and I ever had. I'd confided things in him that no one else knew. He was more than just a companion, and I couldn't deny how unsafe that was for him. If we got caught, I wouldn't face repercussions; only he would. Yet there was no way on God's green earth that I'd let him go willingly.

"Colbie, talk to me."

Every part of me wanted to tell her that I'd fallen for him, to admit to someone what I'd denied to myself. In the split second I had to make the decision, my loyalty to Jess was outweighed by my love for Eli. I squashed my confession and bit my tongue. Instead, I gave her a different truth. "I don't want him to get in trouble for being my friend."

My phone dinged again, but this time, I didn't have to worry about anyone else seeing whatever Eli had sent in private. And when my tears finally stopped, Jess wiped my cheeks with the sleeve of her shirt. "You should talk to him, Colbie. The two of you need to get real about the liability of your relationship." She held my shoulders and stared me in the eyes.

I nodded.

Jess brought me in for one final hug. "I need to get going, but the two of us need to make plans. Just us. Okay?"

"Yeah." I needed her to go so I could respond to Eli. "Let me know what works for you."

"Text me if you want to talk." And with that, she closed the door behind her.

The moment I came into view, concern crossed Eli's face. His eyes hardened as did his lips. "Have you been crying?"

I couldn't get away with anything today. Any other time, I concealed my feelings like I'd locked them in a vault. Not tonight. "I'm fine."

"That didn't answer my question." Eli stood in front of me,

close enough for me to smell his woodsy scent. He used two fingers to tip my chin and force my eyes up. "Cole, talk to me."

All I wanted to do was melt into his arms and press my body to his chest. Nothing else in the world offered the same comfort, not even food. "Are we going to run?" After all, that was the ploy that brought me to our bench.

"Would that make you feel better?"

I didn't bother denying that I was upset. And he already knew that I took to the pavement the way most women ate ice cream when they had emotional breakdowns. They had Ben & Jerry's, and I had Adidas. Without glancing away, I nodded.

He swiped his thumb over my cheekbone and searched my face for a second. "Okay. No headphones."

I hadn't brought any. Eli liked to talk and jog, so I had quit carrying them. It was just something to get in the way, and I had nowhere to put them when I took them off. My phone was strapped to my bicep, but there was no room for them there.

He let me set the pace, which was a bit more vigorous than normal. "Wanna tell me what we're running from? You took off like the police were after you." The chuckle I'd hoped to hear didn't follow.

"I talked to Jess tonight, after she told my parents that you were going to be coaching track or maybe it was cross country. I don't remember which." The sounds of our sneakers on the sidewalk took on a cadence of their own. I could have easily gotten lost in the rhythmic beat had Eli not interrupted my count.

"Why would she tell them that? I'm not going to coach either team." Even his labored breathing was attractive, and I could only image how my name would sound passing his lips in a different kind of activity.

By telling Eli the truth, I risked losing him. Holding on to it, I risked his safety. And as much as I cared about him, I couldn't do the second and had to face the possibility of the first. "She saw us running together last weekend."

He stopped, and by the time I'd realized he wasn't next to me, I was several strides in front of him. When I turned back, Eli was hunched over with his hands on his knees, trying to catch his breath. I didn't catch sight of his brown eyes or supple lips because he stared at the ground. "Did she tell your parents?"

I approached him hesitantly. My fingers curled around his wrist, and I pulled him upright. Whatever crossed his eyes, I had to see it. I touched his jaw and let my hand slide down his sweaty throat and stop on his chest. His heart beat wildly beneath my palm, and my lips erupted into a smile. The situation was nothing to be happy about, although the way he looked at me, even under duress, filled me with hope and happiness.

"No. It was her way of telling me *she* knew."

His hand closed over mine on his pec. "Knew what?"

It seemed insignificant now that I tried to find words to express it. Maybe I'd misread everything between us. I didn't have any experience with boys, much less men. I stepped back, taking my hand with me, and my lips fell. My heart trembled inside my chest, and my worst fear stared me down—rejection. "That we run together."

"Jesus, Colbie. Why are you backing away from me like I might hurt you?" He closed the gap I'd created. "Hey." He tucked the hair that had fallen from my ponytail behind my ear and used that as his opportunity to let his hand grab hold of my nape. "I'd never lay a finger on you in anger."

"I'm not going to break, Eli. You don't have to talk to me like I'm made of glass." When all else failed, aggression was my default.

He snickered under his breath and shook his head. "You're one of the strongest people I've ever met. I promise, there's not a single part of me that believes you're going to break." He still hadn't let go of my neck, but he dropped his hold when another couple approached us.

We stepped aside to allow them to pass, and neither of them glanced our way, too caught up in their own conversation to pay any attention.

I took a deep breath. I wanted to hold on to as many moments with Eli as I could, but the longer I kept from telling him what happened, the harder it would be. "She said she's seen the way we look at each other. And she asked about our relationship."

Eli crossed his arms, and the sleeves stretched taut against his biceps. The definition in his forearms and the vein that ran across the top made me want to drool. I'd never heard of anyone being turned on by forearms, but Eli's did it for me—well, his arms in general. Although, now wasn't the time to analyze that. I couldn't read him, but his body language didn't appear happy.

And then the corner of his lip tilted up as did one eyebrow. "Oh yeah. How does she think we look at each other?"

My cheeks heated, and I had no doubt they were tinged red. I could only hope the physical exertion masked the embarrassment. "I don't know." I sucked at this. For someone with a vast vocabulary who was supposedly verbally gifted, I sounded like a moron.

His smirk eased into a full-blown grin, and he waited.

"Ugh. Fine. She thinks we look at each other like we're in love." I rolled my eyes and turned my head. I refused to see him laugh at me, or worse, think I was immature. There was a difference between maturity and experience. I had one and lacked the other.

Eli dropped his militant stance and grabbed my hips. I still refused to look anywhere other than the tree line on the far side of the road. Even when he rocked his hands and my lower half twisted with them, I still wouldn't make eye contact.

"What did you tell her?" His tone was playful, and if I chanced a glance, I imagined his irises glittered with amusement.

"This isn't funny, Eli." Pouting had never been my thing, but I was left with little choice when I insisted on avoiding him.

He leaned over, inserting his head between mine and the trees I was so fascinated with. "You're right. It's not. But before we address what Jess does or doesn't know, she's right—at least from my perspective." That got my attention. Eli couldn't possibly be saying what I thought that meant. "Why do you look so shocked, Cole? Surely you see it, too."

My lips parted. Words didn't come out. Like a fish gasping for air. Open. Close. Repeat.

"This probably isn't a conversation to have standing on the sidewalk, but since I can't take you home to have it privately, how about we sit on the curb?"

Eli took my hand, and I followed him around the corner and off the busier street. He chose a spot shrouded in shadows where we were less likely to be seen and took a seat. Thankfully, he took the lead, because I wouldn't have been able to speak. "I don't know how or why it happened, but my feelings for you have gotten out of hand. Knowing that doesn't change them though." The animation had left his tone, and things had taken a turn toward serious in the blink of an eye.

If emotional whiplash were a thing, I had just experienced it in a handful of sentences.

I pulled away, wrapped my arms around my waist, and leaned into my knees. I made myself as small as I could to keep as much of me protected as possible.

"I've told myself for weeks that I needed to pull back, and I've justified spending time with you because you're Caleb's sister. My career is on the line, and you're leaving at the end of the year." He ran his fingers through his dark hair. "But no matter what consequence I consider, my heart tells me you're worth the risk."

When I turned my head, Eli stared at me with truth written

all over his beautiful face and sadness haunting his warm brown eyes.

"I don't know how to get through this year, Colbie. It's almost the end of October, but that still leaves seven months of risk. And what does that look like after graduation?"

"What do you mean?" I could barely get the words out for fear of what his answer would mean for us.

He huffed out a laugh I wouldn't have heard had I not been sitting next to him. "I mean you're young and beautiful. The whole world awaits you in June."

"And you think that world doesn't include you?" If he couldn't hear the confusion in my tone, he should certainly be able to see it in my body language.

"Honestly, I'm not sure I want you to tell me. Because if the answer is no, I'm going to spend an awful lot of time licking my wounds."

"But what if it's yes?"

He took my hand and pressed a kiss to the top. "I think I need to let you figure that out, without me as a distraction."

I shook my head back and forth. "*What*? That's the *dumbest* thing I've ever heard. How am I supposed to figure that out without you?"

If he didn't want to risk his career, I understood that. If he was afraid of Caleb's response, I wouldn't like it, but I would understand. But to say that I needed to figure out his place in my life while he was absent was just ludicrous.

"I'm not going anywhere, Colbie. I'll wait seven months."

I snatched my hand away from him. "What does that mean?"

"It means that I care enough about you not to steal your senior year, and that I love you enough to wait on you so neither of us has to face our reputations being ruined." Eli delivered the words in a way that conveyed his heartache over having to say them, while leaving no real room for argument.

"That's it? I don't get a say?"

"Cole, don't be like that. You have no idea how hard this is. I hadn't planned to have this conversation. In fact, I have avoided it as long as possible. But if Jess is onto us, it's only a matter of time before another student is and the whispers begin in the halls. Then we're both called into the principal's office. Soon your parents join us, along with Caleb." He turned into me and tried to calm me with a touch on my arm. He relented when I jerked away. "Please don't shut me out."

I stood, barely able to contain my urge to cry. "The way I see it, you're the one who closed the door." And with that, I walked away.

"Colbie, wait."

But I didn't turn around. "Goodnight, Dr. Paxton."

10

ELI

Colbie walked away without so much as a glance over her shoulder. I hadn't intended for the conversation to turn that way, nor had I meant to alienate her. Somehow, I'd done both in the span of a few minutes, and Colbie wasn't the type of girl who'd let me take that shit back. I'd pushed her to open up, and then I used it against her. Whether it was intentional or not, Colbie was hurt, and I had no way to fix it.

I followed her home to make sure she got there safely, yet she never realized I was behind her. Or if she did, she never looked back. Her shoulders shook with sobs that gutted me. I fought my instinct to run to her, wrap her in my arms, pick her up, and carry her home with me. My throat clenched, and I struggled to swallow around the lump that formed there.

She stopped in front of a hedge on the side of her yard, and there I watched as she wiped at her cheeks, pulled her shoulders back, and straightened her spine. Colbie, undoubtedly, had just cleared all emotion from her face so no one would ask questions when she stepped inside. Her ribs expanded with the deep breaths she pulled in and constricted as she exhaled. Merely a few feet away, and I had to let her keep going...without me.

Once she was safely inside, I turned and ran in the opposite direction for as long as I could. There weren't enough roads in Georgia to alleviate the ache in my chest, and it wasn't from exercise. My calves and thighs burned with each step I took, but nothing overrode my loss. And when I'd gone so far I couldn't go another foot, I looked around and realized I was miles from home, and it was nearly midnight.

If choking myself would have put me out of my misery, I would have done it standing there in the road. Unfortunately, even if I managed to make myself pass out, I'd just end up getting hit by a car or waking up. Neither of which would eliminate my problem. There was no way I could walk back, which left me two options. Caleb or Uber.

When I opened the app, there wasn't a car anywhere near my location, and it estimated it would be over an hour to get one here. I'd be asleep in a ditch by that time. I wondered who I'd pissed off to be stuck in this position. Nothing like calling your best friend to come pick you up because you had to "break up" with his little sister who no one knows you're "seeing" anyhow. The entire situation was fucked up, and I had made it that way. I knew better than to get involved with any student, much less her. Even knowing that, I didn't regret a second other than telling her I'd wait for her, because I already missed her. I couldn't bear the idea of not getting texts from her, not meeting her to jog in the morning, not stealing glances when I could. Most of all, I hated to think I didn't get to hug her or hear her whisper my name after she'd kissed my jaw.

The phone rang three times before Caleb answered. "Everything okay?" No hello or what's up. Straight to the point.

I had to tap dance around this quietly. "Yeah, I'm good. But I could use a ride."

"Have you been drinking? Where are you?" The sleepiness in his tone had cleared, and now he sounded irritated.

A heavy sigh filled the line, and I realized it was my own. "No. I went for a jog and ended up a long way from my house. I tried Uber—"

"Where are you?" Frustration wasn't an easy emotion to hide, although Caleb didn't bother trying.

I told him roughly where I was and explained that without mile markers on county roads, I couldn't be certain. Assuring him that he wouldn't have a hard time finding me didn't win any points.

"That's got to be ten or twelve miles from your house. What the hell were you doing?"

Mentally, I didn't have the energy to have this conversation. Caleb could either come get me, or I'd start walking. "Are you coming or not? I could do without the lecture." I hadn't meant to snap, but Jesus Christ, if I had any other option, I wouldn't have called him.

Caleb was silent for a minute, and then his words were unsure. "Yeah.... I'll be there in a few."

I didn't say goodbye, I just started in the direction Caleb would come from. The lining of my socks had rubbed blisters on my heels, and the balls of my feet sent sharp pains up my legs each time they touched the pavement. It made for slow progress.

Headlights appeared in the distance, so I stopped to wait. A minute or so later, Caleb's truck turned on the road and pulled over. I climbed into the cab, wincing as I went, and closed the door.

Caleb took one look at me, shook his head, and whatever anger he'd been ready to unleash, he let go. "Wanna talk about it, Eli?"

I buckled the seatbelt and stared out the passenger window. "Nope."

We rode in silence—not even the radio played—to my house. He pulled up to the curb, and as I reached for the handle to get out, he said, "Whoever she is, she's not worth it."

I opened the door, hopped out, and turned to face him. "That's where you're wrong. Thanks for the ride. I owe you one."

He nodded. I closed the door and watched his taillights disappear down the street. Caleb didn't even know who he was talking about, and it still pissed me off. Colbie got dismissed by everyone in her life, and I couldn't be the one person who stood beside her. Her brothers—the ones that should protect her—were blind. And for the life of me, I didn't understand how her parents could see her daily and not recognize that she'd lost weight, had bags under her eyes, and overworked herself mentally and physically.

I slammed my front door behind me and went straight to the liquor cabinet. There was no point in using a glass; the bottle worked just fine. I kicked off my shoes as I uncapped the bottle, then pulled off my sweaty-ass socks, and hobbled over to the couch where I proceeded to drink until I passed out.

When my alarm went off to meet Colbie to run, I silenced it and promptly threw my phone across the room. The room spun when I sat up. Yet the headache was the least of my concerns. I didn't think a substitute could find a sub, so calling in wasn't an option. And the idea of seeing Colbie nearly tore me in half. Being an adult sucked ass.

A shower was my best bet toward a less painful day, until I tried to stand. It was like someone whacked the bottoms of my feet with a sledgehammer. I fell back on the couch and pulled my ankle toward me. There were no bruises to be seen, but the blisters had ripped open and the slightest touch to my heels was brutally painful.

Any movement I made today would be a reminder of last night. And an agonizing one at that. Crawling to my bathroom wasn't my finest moment, and it certainly wouldn't work at school. Nevertheless, I had to get to school to even worry about that issue. Right now, I needed to soak in a hot tub for as long as I could in hopes of it releasing some of the sore muscles and easing a bit of the hangover.

God answered that prayer, at least enough for me to bear walking. I had enough cotton balls taped to my heels that socks and shoes didn't touch the open sores. My head had settled into a dull throb. My heart...that was another situation entirely. It didn't beat right, like it skipped because it was no longer in sync with hers.

I'd become a fucking pansy who needed to have his ass kicked. I thought about taking up boxing just so someone could pound the shit out of me, hoping it would also knock sense into me. It hadn't even been twenty-four hours since I'd seen her. I had to shake this shit off. I had a job to do, which included Colbie. Unless I wanted to ruin my career, I had to get myself in check.

That would have been a hell of a lot easier to do if Caleb hadn't decided to insert himself into my morning before first period.

"You look like shit, Eli."

I gave him an apathetic glare. "You don't look so hot yourself."

Kids milled about in the hallways, and for the first time, the noise they made grated on every one of my nerves.

"Yeah, that tends to happen when you get woken up in the middle of the night to pick up a friend who doesn't want to talk."

I didn't respond. Nothing had changed; I still didn't want to talk. The next seven months would be pure hell without Caleb prying into it. He took a seat on the edge of my desk and proceeded to act like his nosey wife.

"Are you going to tell me what's going on?" He crossed his arms and shifted to get comfortable on the wood.

"There's nothing to tell."

He chuckled. "I didn't know you were seeing anyone? Is it that chick, Annabelle, you told me about from grad school?"

The warning bell sounded, meaning kids would start rolling

into my classroom in roughly five minutes. "Annabelle? No. God. We were in a study group together. I was never interested in her."

"You're not going to tell me anything, are you?"

I stood when the first student came in early and took a seat. "There's nothing to tell, Caleb. Thank you for helping me out last night. I'll make it up to you." And that was all the information my best friend would get.

Caleb clapped me on the shoulder with a smile. "Anytime. You know where to find me."

"Thanks."

Three girls from first period came racing through the door. "Hey, Dr. Paxton." The sound of the trio swooning caused me to roll my eyes at Caleb.

"Good morning, ladies."

Caleb shook his head with a laugh. "You've got your hands full. I don't envy you." And then he pushed through another group taking their seats.

Third period was worse than I had expected. Colbie not only didn't give me the cold shoulder, she didn't show up. Instead, Jess pranced in—like she knew everything that had happened—stared me in the eye, and handed me a note from the principal. As I read it, Jess pulled Colbie's essay from her backpack to turn in. I didn't have a clue what was going on other than Colbie was helping the administration this period, and I was to send any assignments or materials home with Jess.

Oddly, I didn't worry about Colbie exposing me. She wouldn't. The fact that she'd been so hurt by last night that she couldn't face me and risked missing a lecture that could affect her run for valedictorian was what sent up red flags. And those flags were so huge, they might as well have had flashing neon lights. She was spinning, and I prayed it wasn't out of control.

When I got home that night, unable to strip thoughts of her from my mind, I wondered if Colbie was trying to challenge me. I had a stack of essays to grade for AP and assignments for all of my other classes as well. I typically saved AP for last so I ended my day on a high. Not today. I went straight for third period. Colbie's essay was at the bottom of the stack since it was the first handed in. But the poetic words that typically filled her pages were rather bored and stagnant. She'd done the assignment, and even after reading all the other essays, including Jess's, it was heads above the rest. But for Colbie, it was C quality at best, and that was being lenient.

I held off on marking it with a grade. I didn't have to return the papers to the students the following day, although I typically tried to. This went beyond my expertise. I needed someone with tenure to give me advice on how to handle what I considered a delicate situation.

The next day, I went to the teachers' lounge during my planning period instead of staying in my classroom.

I hadn't considered how to inconspicuously approach the subject with another member of the staff. Initially, I'd thought one on one might be best, but when I had gotten to the lounge and five of the upper-class honors teachers sat at one table, I decided a general question to a group would be best.

"Hey, Eli. Have a seat." Kendra Cross welcomed me with a smile when she pulled out a chair next to her.

The conversation stopped when I joined the group, and the women all stared at me like I was prey. Maybe this wasn't such a great idea. "Ladies, it's nice to see you all." I opened my lunch and took out an orange. It gave me something to fidget with so no one realized how apprehensive I was.

A chorus of hellos flooded the table, followed by glassy-eyed looks of longing. *If only they knew just how unavailable I was.* It took effort not to grunt and laugh. Instead, I stuck my thumbnail into the rind and began to peel.

Susan Markey leaned forward with her elbows on the table, catching my eye. Of the five, she was by far the most attractive, not just physically. She was smart and quick witted. If she weren't ten years my senior and I'd met her before I met Colbie, things might have been different. As it stood, there was nothing between us. "What brings you in here? Don't you usually spend the period in your classroom or in Caleb's office?"

I didn't question why she'd kept tabs on me or knew how I spent my time. It didn't matter. The opening presented itself, and I needed to take it. "Actually, I was hoping I could ask you guys a question."

Eyebrows went up and expectant eyes grew wide. It wasn't like I planned to ask any of them out, especially not in a group, so I didn't have a clue what they were excited about. The room had gotten entirely too quiet, and with students in class, there was no noise coming from the halls, either. It was an illusion, but the absence of sound somehow made the walls seem like they were closing in.

"Have any of you had any experience with an exceptional student suddenly turning in mediocre work?" I scanned the faces around me, and each of them had fallen from hope to disappointment or possibly confusion.

Kendra sat back. "I have." She licked her lips, and her eyes filled with tears. "There was a boy about five years ago. Honors student. Well-liked by the student body. Popular. Athletic. Overall, great kid. It seemed like overnight he went from assertive and outgoing to introverted and shy. He went from *A*s to *C*s and *D*s in a couple weeks."

"Did you go easy on him?"

Kendra shook her head. "He was one of those kids whose *C*-

quality work was still *A*-quality for the rest of the class. But I never believed in grading kids based on the class as a whole. I graded subjective work by the student's capabilities and effort." Her voice broke, and she swallowed hard. When she swiped falling tears from her cheeks, I wondered if I wanted to know how this story ended.

Susan put her hand on Kendra's. "Are you talking about Michael Martin?"

That name didn't mean anything to me, yet it clearly did to everyone else. "What happened?" I asked, taking note of each woman's solemn expression.

Kendra had a hard time getting out words. "I gave him the grades he earned." She'd drifted off into a memory I knew nothing about. "I'd give anything to go back and talk to him. Ask him what was going on. Why things had changed." The tears flowed faster than she could catch them.

Like a CD stuck on repeat, I parroted my last question. "What happened?" Two words croaked into the mostly vacant room and echoed off the walls.

Susan answered when her friend couldn't. "He committed suicide."

"Jesus." I hadn't expected that. "Does anyone know why?"

Susan and Kendra exchanged glances while the other women at the table chewed on their lips or stared at their lunches. "He'd been sexually abused by a family member. Because he was a minor, most of the details were kept from the public. Kendra found out more than she should because her husband is an investigator who was assigned to the case."

Each breath I took burned the back of my raw throat, and my jaw hung open, not quite sure I understood how it all connected. "He didn't tell anyone? The kids I mean." It was a stupid question, but I couldn't wrap my mind around abuse of any type.

Kendra regained a bit of her composure, and after a few sniffles and a napkin blotted under her eyes, she gave me more of the story. "He told his best friend who happened to be the quarterback of the football team. It got out to other players on the team, and rumors started that called Michael's sexuality into question. It snowballed. Fast." Her head bobbed slowly, and she let the silence linger in the air for a moment. "Kids are cruel, Eli. Especially when one at the top of the pack falters. They see the weakness and pounce."

"Do you regret the bad grades? Or not asking him what caused them?"

Kendra took a drink of her water and contemplated my question. She adjusted her body in the hard, plastic chair, but I doubted it was the seat that had her fidgeting. "A bit of both. I contributed to his downhill slide. And I wonder if I could have helped him had I known what was going on."

The other ladies at the table disappeared from my focus, and it was as if Kendra and I were talking, just the two of us. "What if he had told you? What would you have done?"

"Legally, we're required to report abuse. But this is a small town, and the truth is, I probably would have tried to talk to his parents first. See if we could get him help. But I know for sure, if I ever come across it again, I'll turn the world upside down to save a student." Kendra stared me straight in the eyes with absolute resolution marring her stern expression.

And that was a sucker punch to the gut. I already knew the truth behind Colbie's pain, and I was quite certain about where the slope got so slippery that she could no longer manage the terrain. What I didn't know was how to go about addressing the situation without confessing the amount of time I'd spent with a student outside of school. The problem started in the Chapman house and trickled down a rocky path to me. But Colbie had been *okay* when I had met her. It wasn't until I cut her off that the status quo changed, even if what had been wasn't perfect.

The other teachers talked around me, remembering Michael in his prime. I zoned out, thinking about the girl in my present. The mere thought of something happening to her caused panic to settle into my chest and my head to throb.

By the time the bell sounded, ending my planning period, I'd convinced myself it was only one paper. I refused to tarnish her GPA over one missed mark. Instead, I tried to watch her like a hawk. To my dismay, she became a hawk who didn't want to be watched and flew the coop anytime I got near.

Within a matter of a few days, dark circles appeared under Colbie's eyes, and her clothes hung looser than they had a couple weeks ago. She would answer questions when called on, yet she never raised her hand anymore. Gone were the debates between her and her classmates. Colbie and Jess appeared to be okay, and even though they never ate lunch together, I'd catch Colbie smiling in the halls or huddled up with her best friend in the library after school.

No matter how hard I tried to stay away, during lunch I lingered near the practice rooms on the music hall, although not close enough that anyone would know I sat there to hear her play. And I managed to catch glimpses of her when she ran. I had hoped like hell she would text me or call, acknowledge my existence in one way or another. Throw me a bone to choke on. I would have taken a note from a carrier pigeon—anything to set my mind at ease. I got nothing other than deteriorating school work that, at some point, I'd have to address. I couldn't keep looking past it.

I'd just about reached the point that I refused to stay quiet any longer. Each assignment Colbie handed in was worse than the last. It shouldn't matter that it was still better than everyone else's, regardless of my justifying giving her *A*s because of it. I clenched my jaw when it occurred to me that she might be testing me. None of the other teachers had mentioned her work slipping, and they talked about students all the time. Or possibly, they were all like me—giving her the benefit of the doubt and not wanting to be the first one to raise their hand about the star student. The muscles in my face ached from grinding my teeth, and a headache had formed at the base of my neck that worked its way up the back of my skull and rooted itself in my temples...throbbing.

"Pax, what's got you pissed off?" Caleb hadn't bothered to knock since my door stood open.

I covered Colbie's paper with my grade book and set my red pen on top of the stack. I forced myself to relax and smile. "Just grading papers." I glanced down as if he didn't know what I meant. "Be glad you teach P.E. and don't have to deal with this." The chuckle at the end made it come across light-heartedly.

"I tried to tell you that in college."

Sadly, he had. He'd insisted being a physical education teacher would be so much easier—and more fun—than anything academic. And while I loved sports, and he might have been right, I loved English and literature more. It had a staying power that football didn't. My body was proof of that every day when I got out of bed and something hurt.

"You going to the game this weekend?" He sat on the top of the same desk he always did. "Most of the team is going to be tailgating. You can ride with me and Chas. Save on gas."

The UGA Auburn game was the day after tomorrow. I'd gone every year since I'd finished undergrad. This year, I'd made other plans—plans I hadn't shared with Caleb or anyone else. "I appreciate the offer, but I'm staying home." Jesus, I'd give anything for a student to storm through that door, needing assistance.

The bustle outside continued without interrupting us, and I wondered if I could get to the fire alarm and pull the handle without arousing suspicion. Since it wasn't in my room or under my desk, it was safe to say that couldn't happen. Nevertheless, I begged God for a distraction.

Caleb reared his head back and his brows knitted together. "What? You're kidding, right?"

The breath I drew in expanded my chest, and when I exhaled, tension went with it. "Nope. I don't even have a ticket."

He locked his elbows beside him. "Dude, if money's the issue, my dad will get you a ticket."

Money wasn't a factor. I hadn't even considered using it as an excuse because I'd hoped no one would ask where I was until *after* the game. "Caleb, I appreciate the offer. I just wouldn't feel right."

"You're like family, Eli. My parents wouldn't think twice about it."

I'd never taken handouts from them in all the years I'd known Caleb. It had been a bone of contention between us when he went skiing over winter break or to Jamaica in the spring. They weren't trips I could afford; therefore, I didn't go. Caleb had always offered, and I'd politely refused. "Not going to happen, Chapman. And you know it."

He huffed when he stood. "Pride cometh before the fall, man."

I didn't try to stifle the laugh as I walked to the hall behind Caleb. "Somehow, I don't think I'm going to fall if I don't take a free ticket to a football game." I clapped him on the shoulder. "I will, however, take you up on that free dinner you offered to cook at your house."

"Crap. I totally forgot to mention that to Chas." He pointed at me as he walked backward into the sea of students swimming down the hall. "It's a date. Promise."

One of the players on the team tackled Caleb, knocking him off balance. I'd gotten out of that too easily. My heart still raced after he'd left, and I worried I'd get caught.

But not so much that I changed my plans.

I'd changed clothes three times, and I still wasn't happy with what I had on. I didn't have a clue what to wear to this type of thing. It was in a church, so I assumed that meant dressier than casual, but that could be anything from slacks to a suit. If it were black tie then I was just screwed. This was what invitations were for. But I hadn't gotten one since I wasn't technically invited. And if they asked for one at the door—or my name—I'd get turned away. Nevertheless, I planned to attend.

With one final glimpse in the mirror, I settled on a white dress shirt with the top two buttons undone, grey slacks, a black belt, and dress shoes. The look was classic. I could roll up the sleeves if I were overdressed, and if I got into the parking lot and saw men in suits, I could add a jacket and tie with ease. I had to admit, I cleaned up well. The haircut I'd gotten last night helped, as did the hot shave.

Traffic had turned the twenty-minute drive to the church into thirty, and I'd stopped by a florist and picked up flowers. Yet standing in the parking lot, it seemed foolish and maybe even inappropriate. Although, there were others carrying arrangements, and my attire was spot on without the tie or jacket. It was the first time I'd ever thanked Chasity—albeit silently in my head—for the nagging she'd done with Caleb. Even if she had been a bit overbearing, she'd imparted—inadvertently—a great deal of social knowledge and class structure in small-town Georgia. Caleb had known the dos and don'ts of polite society. He'd just chosen to ignore them. I'd soaked it up like a sponge. Michigan was a very different place than the deep South.

I locked the truck and made my way to the steps of the unfamiliar church. I'd never know how small towns in the South could support churches on every corner. A woman in a long, black dress greeted each person at the sanctuary and handed out programs. The rows of pews appeared infinite and surprisingly full. I'd only arrived about ten minutes early, not realizing there'd be standing room only.

"Just one, sir?" A girl, about ten or eleven years old, stared up at me.

I'd missed the question through the muffled voices around me. "I'm sorry?"

"Do you need a seat for one?" She too wore a long, black dress and a gentle smile.

I nodded. "Yes, please."

"Follow me."

She moved down the center aisle, I assumed to show me to a seat; however, I stopped mid-way to stare at the lone grand piano that sat center stage. The pulpit had been transformed from a place to preach to a podium to perform. The sleek, black piano sat elevated, surrounded by carpeted steps on three sides.

"Sir?"

I blinked and looked around for the little voice. Even the balconies were full. "Sorry."

She sat me next to an older couple on the end of a pew. "There will be a reception in the auditorium following the performances. I hope you'll join us."

I didn't know what I'd expected, but this was far more grandiose than anything in my mind. I'd been to concerts that weren't this well attended.

"Good afternoon." An older man stood at a microphone to the side of the piano. "I'd like to thank you all for attending our fall recital." He had a warm smile that reminded me of my grandfather. "I have the pleasure of teaching an amazing group of students who are all gifted musicians. This year is no exception. But rather than me tell you about them, I'll let you listen for yourself. Please welcome Maggie Chan." He bowed off, clapping as an Asian girl took the stage.

She practically had to climb onto the bench, and her feet

didn't reach the peddles. I prepared myself for a fabulous rendition of "Mary Had a Little Lamb" or "Twinkle, Twinkle Little Star." Maggie situated herself and straightened her black dress. And thunder struck when her tiny hands hit the keys. I glanced around, expecting chatter about this tiny wonder who pounded out an intense, dark piece of classical music. Yet no one seemed the least bit surprised. Or the girl who followed her or the boy after that. Each one was better than the last, and their ages varied from five or six to seventeen or eighteen.

I glanced at the program. There were twelve students performing today, and Colbie was the finale. If I'd thought she were breathtaking at Caleb's wedding, it was nothing compared to today. Colbie appeared out of the same door at the side of the sanctuary that all the other performers had. Poised, elegant—everything her mother would be so proud of—she held her shoulders back and her head high. Colbie was in her element. She also believed she was alone.

When she faced the audience, her beauty rendered me speechless. The gown she wore accentuated her sleek shoulders and cinched waist while hiding her long, muscular legs. Her hair was pulled into some fancy hairdo that highlighted her neck, and all I could think about was kissing her from ear to nape.

She bowed and then quietly took the bench, spreading the skirt of her dress as she went. God, she was stunning. What I wouldn't give to see just how mesmerizing she was out of it. My mind began to disrobe her before I mentally slapped myself back in line. In all the times I'd heard Colbie play, there'd only been once that she'd played a song from start to finish. She'd work the same section of a piece for so long in the practice rooms that I'd almost convinced myself I could play them. Other than "Winterwind," none of the other titles listed under her name in the program were familiar to me.

Less than a minute after she began to play, the man beside me leaned over to whisper, "She's a prodigy. We come every year just to hear her play." He eased back against the pew and closed his eyes.

I glanced around to see more than one face covered in peace, eyes closed. People *felt* her. As much as I didn't want to take my eyes off her for a second, I allowed my lids to drift shut and my heart to accept the emotion she poured into the piano. A lump formed in my throat that made swallowing difficult, and my chest constricted. Her parents had missed this. They didn't get to see the way people viewed their daughter. They didn't get to hear the accolades sung in her name.

Her parents missed her perfection.

And when she played the first notes of the étude, I prayed they'd missed one more glimpse and she pulled this off without a hitch. Colbie desperately wanted this execution to be spot on. Her fingers raced the keys at a pace I couldn't keep up with. Her hands were a blur, and her shoulders and torso jerked in front of the instrument. She put her entire body into playing Chopin.

When she'd finished, her hands hovered just inches above the keys, and Colbie allowed the music to fade before she stood. Tears glistened just under her pale blue irises, and her chest heaved the way it did when we ran. At that precise moment, she noticed me in the audience.

Flawless.

Fucking flawless.

I was the first to rise, leaving the flowers on the pew. Her eyes never left mine—even as hair fell from her up-do into her face—from the first clap through the standing ovation. She closed her hands in front of her mouth, overwhelmed by the audience, and bowed again before she exited the stage.

The man beside me elbowed me. "Bloody brilliant, right?"

"She's amazing." But I wasn't just referring to her musical talent.

Colbie Chapman was the whole package. Beauty, brains, talent, gumption, drive, wit, and God, did she have the capacity to love.

"This is her last year. She's leaving for college this summer." A stranger appeared disappointed by the loss of a girl he didn't know, yet her family remained oblivious. "Maybe we'll see her on the stage with an orchestra one day." He and his wife scooted out of the pew and spilled into the aisle where everyone had started to exit.

I'd missed anything her teacher had said after Colbie had left the stage. The line to get out of the sanctuary was a mile long, so I sat in the pew to wait. And even after the audience had left, I remained there, unsure of what to do next. My heart longed to see her, hug her, be close to her, even if just briefly. My head told me it would set her back and to stay away.

I hadn't heard anyone else in the room until she stood next to me.

"May I?"

I couldn't discern her tone, but I slid over nonetheless.

"What are you doing here, Dr. Paxton?" Confusion mixed with innocence sprinkled with love.

Sitting sideways on a wooden pew, I faced her and tucked the stray lock of hair behind her ear out of habit. "Did you think I wouldn't come?"

She'd never asked me. In fact, other than her telling me about the work she put in, there'd been little mention of the recital since the weekend of her brother's wedding.

In a manner that would have her mother reeling, she snorted out a huff of a laugh. "I didn't think you'd even remember much less miss the game to be here." She glanced at her hands in her lap and started to pick at the skin around her nails.

"I'll never choose anything over you." Talking to her head wasn't ideal, but Colbie all but refused to look up.

"Except your career." It was nothing more than a hushed whisper.

I'd managed to keep from touching her—well, other than the hair thing—since she'd sat down. Until now. Instinctively, my fingers tilted her chin. "I didn't choose my career over you, Cole. I chose your security over my happiness. And there isn't a day that goes by that I don't wish I could do something different."

Desperation marred her brow and wrinkled her forehead. "But you can..." She had no idea how badly I wanted to give her everything she asked for.

The blue in her eyes swirled with feathers of gold and strings of intoxicating sapphire. And when she licked her lips, I wanted to seal my mouth to hers. I let go of her chin, hoping to break the spell that surrounded us. I was seconds away from throwing caution to the wind and Colbie over my shoulder. "It seems like graduation is a lifetime away. I get that. I really do—"

"Don't say anything else. I understand."

"Clearly, you don't." My voice had risen, and I had to pause to collect myself so we didn't end up with company. "You think I don't *want* to be with you. That this is easy for me."

The girl I'd met on the first day now sat before me. "Isn't it?" Her words were crisp, her expression staunch, and her wall was higher than it had ever been.

I dared to take her hand in mine, and she didn't resist, even if she didn't reciprocate. "No. No, it's not. In fact, it's by far the hardest thing I've ever had to do in my life." I searched the sanctuary for witnesses or anyone who might be within earshot. "Do you have any idea how much I agonize over not being able to touch you? Or see you?" I ran my free hand through my hair. "God, Colbie. I sit down the hall while you work in the practice rooms just to be close to you. I catch glimpses of you running but stay far enough behind that you don't see me." I shouldn't admit any of this. "I type out text messages and never hit send."

"Why?"

"Because I *miss you*. Every day." I couldn't hide my frustration any longer, and it came through in my desperate tone. "I miss talking to you, running with you, texting you. Jesus. I miss the way you whisper my name in my ear after you kiss my jaw. It's everything, Colbie. It's *you*. I don't feel like I can breathe right and like my heart beats just half a beat behind because yours isn't there to beat with it. But until you graduate, I can't erase any of that pain for me or you. And I *hate* it."

Either I'd stunned her into silence or she'd had a brain aneurysm. Since she was still upright, I guessed it was the first.

"Colbie, sweetheart. There you are." A voice boomed from behind us. "I've been looking all over for you. Come join us at the reception. Bring your friend." He continued toward us as he spoke.

Colbie stood and stepped into the aisle to greet him. All her practiced charm came front and center. "Dr. Chalmers, this is my friend, Eli Paxton." She turned to me with a demure grin, but the joy didn't reach her eyes. "Eli, this is my piano teacher, Dr. Chalmers."

I shook the man's hand. "I've heard a lot about you. Colbie speaks very highly."

He clapped me on the shoulder and slid his arm around me in a fatherly embrace. "Son, I wish I could say the same. This one"—he tilted his head toward Colbie affectionately—"hasn't ever mentioned a special someone."

Colbie tried to interject, "Oh, no—"

"I can't tell you how glad I am to meet you. Colbie is a fantastic girl." Nothing other than love showed in the lines of age that marked his skin. "I knew when that special someone came along, he would have to be perfect." Dr. Chalmers winked at Colbie and tossed a hearty grin at me.

He let me go and cuddled Colbie in a hug. "And you. As

always, you're the talk of the recital." Dr. Chalmers released his student and clapped his hands. "Come to the auditorium. Both of you."

I needed to allow Colbie time to enjoy her day, not that I wanted to leave. "I really should be going."

"Nonsense. Come." Dr. Chalmers didn't leave room for an argument and started toward the reception.

I extended my arm to Colbie the same way I had the night of her brother's rehearsal and wedding. She took it and let me escort her. As soon as she entered the room, people turned toward us and started clapping and whistling. The blush that overtook her cheeks complimented her milky complexion. I'd never seen the subtle smile she wore for the people who now surrounded her. Colbie was pure class and the epitome of elegance.

I stood back and admired the way she moved through the crowd and worked the room. She was born for this, but I wondered if she'd ever get to embrace a life that welcomed her the way these people did. Leaned against a wall with a glass of sparkling punch, I couldn't tear my eyes away.

"I'm glad she's found you."

I nearly jumped out of my skin when Dr. Chalmers spoke. "Pardon?" If I'd had anything in my mouth I would have choked on it. I hadn't thought coming here would alert the media to my feelings.

He raised his hand that held his drink and pointed toward Colbie. "I've been worried about her."

"How so?" I had to be careful how I approached this. I didn't know what he referred to, nor how close he might be with her parents, although I doubted they had much of a relationship since they never attended these things.

Dr. Chalmers hadn't turned toward me, instead he watched Colbie as though he needed to be certain of where she was in the room so he couldn't be overheard. "You love her?"

"I'm sorry, I don't know—"

He shook his head with a smile. "Son, that's nothing to be ashamed of. A fool could see it a mile away. Colbie needs that. That unconditional devotion, love."

There was no point in denying anything. The old man would believe what he wanted. What he didn't need to believe or even be aware of was that I was also her teacher.

"Colbie has been a pupil of mine for over a decade." He chuckled. "I remember how tiny she was when she first started. About Maggie Chan's size. Delicate, almost fragile, until her fingers touched those keys and her soul caught fire. In all my years, I'd never seen anything like her, and to date, I still haven't."

"I sense a *but* coming."

"For years, that flame burned without kindling. Colbie was intense, even as a small girl. She confided in me as she got older, but sometime last year, something snuffed out her fire and she quit talking. I have my thoughts about what it might have been, but nothing concrete."

God, I wanted to pry. Compare notes. Get him to tell me anything he could. Except, in order to do that, I had to offer the same. And I couldn't break her confidence or risk anyone finding out.

"Your silence tells me you know what I'm talking about, Eli."

I hadn't taken my eyes off her. She was as happy here as she was when we ran together. This moment was a reprieve for her. A sanctuary of sorts. I wanted this for her every day. "I do."

It got harder to hear him when he lowered his voice. There was a healthy crowd that mingled in the room around us, and classical music played overhead, but I strained to listen to every word. "Her parents mean well. They're just a little..." He clicked his tongue and rolled his hand, trying to come up with the right word.

"Distracted?" That was a polite way to say oblivious and neglectful.

"Precisely. I think it goes beyond them, though. I can't put my finger on it, and I don't want to speculate or hint at something I can't confirm. But Colbie's health is suffering." He'd seen it, too.

A lady interrupted to say goodbye to Dr. Chalmers and tell him what a wonderful recital it had been. I stood to the side to allow him time with others. He was quite the charmer. The old ladies flirted like crazy, and I wondered if he'd ever dated any of them.

He kissed the woman's hand and then turned back to me. "She's a perfectionist. Always has been." It was as if he hadn't stopped talking to me for five minutes. He picked right back up where he'd left off. "School. Music. Being *good* has never been *good enough* for Colbie."

"She has to be flawless," we said in unison.

"Eli, years ago, she cracked when she felt she couldn't win her parents' love. Now...now she's crumbling. She's lost weight, those circles under her eyes, her cheeks are hollow." He shook his head and closed his eyes; I couldn't help but think it was to stave off overwhelming emotion he felt for his pupil. "Colbie is a beautiful girl, but I don't think she's eating. And Lord, did you know that girl has to have new tennis shoes every other month?" He waited for me to answer.

I hadn't noticed new tennis shoes. I also hadn't bothered to look at her feet when she had on shorts and a sports bra. "For what?"

"Apparently the treads on tennis shoes are only good for about five hundred miles?"

It didn't surprise me. Five hundred miles was a long way on a single tread. I did the math, and it was roughly seventy-five days or less, depending on Colbie's whims down country roads. And I imagined there had been more of that recently than I knew. "Have you mentioned any of this to her parents?"

Maybe Dr. Chalmers could be the outside force that brought

this to their attention. "I don't see them. They pay for Colbie's lessons online, and as you can see, they don't attend her recitals, much less her lessons."

I hadn't meant to let out a sigh so loud that a group of people turned to stare at me. I waited until they went back to their own conversations. "She's having trouble in school, too."

Colbie would kill me if she found out I'd breathed a word of anything going on. This man was her confidant, and I was turning him into a conspirator.

"Her grades?" There wasn't a single word to describe the horror staring at me through Dr. Chalmers's expression. "Eli, if she loses that spot at graduation, she'll never recover."

I hadn't been referring to her grades, because I'd let her get by with subpar work and still given her *A*s. "No, not her grades. Her best friend and her little brother started dating. It cut her pretty deeply when she found out they'd lied to her for months."

"Jess and Caden?"

"You know them?" That surprised me.

He waved at someone across the room who tried to get his attention. "I've met Jess several times, but I haven't seen Caden since he was small. She's talked about both often."

The same man waved again, and Dr. Chalmers's couldn't avoid him any longer. He reached into his pocket and pulled out a business card. "In case you need me." He handed me his number. "Colbie is like a granddaughter to me. Don't hesitate to call...for anything."

I took the card. "Of course."

Again, Dr. Chalmers clapped my shoulder, and this time, he gave it a squeeze. "Colbie will be okay with you in her corner, Eli. That I'm quite certain of." He winked and mingled his way across the room.

I wanted nothing more than to be what she needed, although I doubted Dr. Chalmers would feel the same if he were aware of who I was in Colbie's life. As an educator, he too knew the dos and don'ts of student relationships. I had so far overstepped the moral line that I couldn't even see it in the sand behind me. Yet somehow, I twisted his blessing into encouragement.

As the crowd thinned and finally dwindled, Colbie seemed to float across the room. Her dress hid her feet and the layers of fabric concealed the movement of her legs. There was no hesitation in her approach. I could get lost in her radiant smile and the glitter that lit up her eyes.

She laid her hands on my forearms and used them for balance when she leaned close to whisper in my ear. "Thank you for coming, Eli. You'll never know what it meant to me." And when she pressed her lips to my jaw, I lost it.

My guard.

My demeanor.

My resolve.

It all went straight out the window and cast my soul into a fiery pit of hell, and I didn't give a single damn.

There, in front of the few people that remained, I captured her jaw in both my hands, threading my fingers through the back of her hair. My lips met hers with undeniable passion that left us both breathless when Colbie finally broke away.

"Eli." Her eyes darted around the now empty room, and then she held the back of her hand to her lips. Stunned.

I didn't speak. I took her hand and led her to the parking lot. Again, she searched for witnesses, and I started to wonder if she thought I'd hurt her when she got into my truck.

"You don't have to come with me, Colbie."

The confusion she felt rested at my feet. "I just don't understand."

I wanted her to trust me, but I'd given her nothing to go on. "Come home with me. Let's talk where prying eyes can't see. I'll bring you back to get your car."

She stared up through the distance between us. The innocence I loved so much hung in her eyes like stars in the sky. And as the horizon grew dusky-dark, Colbie whispered, "Okay." She lifted onto her toes and touched my lips with hers in a soft peck.

I helped her into passenger seat, evening dress and all. Before I closed the door, I watched as she settled her gown the way she had at the piano. Pure fucking class.

11

COLBIE

All it took was a glance into Eli's eyes, and I'd follow him to the ends of the earth. He was the only person I'd ever known who could communicate more with one look than a thousand words. If eyes were the window to the soul, I'd just entered the gates of heaven with a golden key.

I didn't have a clue what I planned to do with him alone in his house, nor did I know what he wanted to talk to me about. But after a kiss like that—that *he* had initiated—there was zero possibility of me turning him down.

He pulled himself into the truck by the steering wheel, and the muscles in his forearm flexed, popping the vein I loved. Heat pooled between my legs, and I clenched my thighs together to stave off the desire. Eli was far too cautious to allow this to get out of hand, and I needed to push those thoughts aside. Not to mention the promise I'd made to myself...that I seemed to break every time I was in the same room with this man.

The ride to Eli's house was relatively quiet except for the country station that played over the radio. He hummed along to most of the songs and tapped a beat on the steering wheel. I couldn't help but giggle.

"What are you laughing about?" A grin tickled his lips, and when he took a quick peek at me from the driver's seat, his eyes were alight with amusement.

I pointed to his hand steadily marking time. "You have your own little private concert going on over there."

He feigned hurt and slapped his hand across his chest to hold his aching heart. "What? You don't like my singing? I'm wounded, Colbie. Wounded."

"Hush. You are not." I swatted at his arm. "If you're going to sing, make it worth listening to." I turned up the radio, and with it came Eli's voice.

As he got stronger, I added in the harmony. "I had no idea you could sing like that."

"That makes two of us." But I didn't want to stop singing to talk.

He had this smooth tenor that felt like warm honey. I bathed in the sound of his voice and found comfort in the way our tones blended into one perfectly. It was impossible to pick the two apart. And as we sang a ballad, he slid his hand across the bench seat and on top of mine. Eli never took his eyes off the road, and he gave me a gentle squeeze when we pulled into what I had to assume was his driveway.

I searched the area around us for onlookers, but it was fairly dark, and the streets were empty.

He hopped out of the truck and came to my door to help me down. I imagined the two of us together on our wedding day—me in an elegant dress and Eli all dapper in a black tuxedo. I wished we were able to capture the way we looked today. The matte black dress and his white shirt and grey slacks—any woman standing next to Eli Paxton would be gorgeous. And that was exactly how he made me feel.

Eli placed his hands on my hips and, with little effort, lifted me out of the truck to set me on the driveway. I felt weightless in his embrace.

"You're just a little whiff of a thing," he joked as he closed the door behind us. He wrapped his arm around my waist, and I couldn't stop myself from nestling into his side.

I'd been so caught up in Eli and what went on around us that I all but missed his house. I couldn't remember what color it was once we were inside. He released me to toss his keys onto the counter and turn on a couple of lights. In the meantime, I surrounded myself in a hug to ward off the chill he'd left in his absence. With my shoulders hunched forward, I hadn't realized the gap I created in that position between my braless chest and the fabric of my dress. The second I saw my nipples by glancing down, I pulled my shoulders back and dropped my arms to my sides. My mother would be appalled if she'd thought I'd been indecent.

"What's wrong?" Eli returned to my side, clutching my bare biceps.

"Nothing, why?"

"You just groaned. Are you cold? You have chill bumps." He ran his hands up and down my arms to warm me. This man couldn't be any more perfect if I'd created him myself. Eli pulled back and assessed me from head to toe. "I didn't think this through, Colbie. I'm sorry."

Disappointment encompassed my entire body, and I felt myself shrink at his dismissal. "You can take me to get my car. I understand."

"Huh?" Three lines appeared on his forehead and one between his brows. It would be cute if he hadn't just told me he'd made a mistake. "No. I meant the dress. I can't imagine it's comfortable to hang out in, and I doubt I have anything that will come close to fitting you. You're tiny." He waved his arms from his chest to his legs. "And I'm not."

I felt foolish. These were the times my inexperience shined like a beacon. Etiquette classes and cotillion didn't prepare a girl for a night alone with a man in his house.

Eli stepped forward again, draping his hands loosely around the small of my back. "Don't get shy on me. I promise, I won't bite." He wiggled me to elicit a smile. "At least, not tonight." That wink did me in every time.

I'd become a mute. I didn't have a clue what to say or how to open up dialogue, much less relax. Eli was right, the dress wasn't something to lounge around in, and now that he'd brought that to my attention, I was extremely uncomfortable. But when his grip tightened, pressing my hips to his, I almost choked. My cheeks flushed with heat, and I was fairly certain my panties were wet. And Eli was just as aroused.

"I love when you blush," he whispered as he bent down to kiss my neck.

It was that spot just below the ear, close to my jaw. His touch was so feather-light that goose bumps erupted on my flesh. The tingle that followed might as well have been a drug. I tilted my head to give him better access as his lips moved slowly toward the dip between my clavicles. Eli's touch was better than any food or purge or control or high from running. He was my weakness, and I craved that vulnerability.

My head had fallen to the side when his lips disappeared from my skin. Before I popped my eyes open, he cradled my face and kissed me deeper than he had at the church. My fingers found his hair while my tongue danced with his. The need to be closer to him overwhelmed me, but there was no space between us now. Confusion teased desperation, and my mind clouded over with lust that lacked rationale.

He slowed the kiss until I had to stop for air, and then Eli tilted his forehead to mine. His pupils surged and his nostrils flared just a hint. "I don't want to stop. God, I don't want to...ever.

But if I don't, you won't have to worry about that dress not being comfortable because you won't be in it."

That didn't sound so bad to me, but I could tell it had been hard for him to resist taking me there. To that place of no return.

"Don't misunderstand." His breath was warm against my face, and I couldn't turn away if I'd tried. "At some point, every inch of you will be mine, and I'll be damned if another man ever touches you." Eli's lips were soft and full against my own. He didn't open; instead, it was sweet and reluctant, as if he were as disappointed he had to stop this—whatever *this* was—as I was.

I nodded. "I'm going to hold you to that." That was rather brazen for a girl who'd never even been kissed—me kissing him didn't count—prior to tonight.

"I'd expect nothing less." His thumb stroked my cheek, and his eyes searched what he could see of my face while being this close. "But Cole, you need to understand, once you give me that gift... there's no turning back. Ever."

I'd seen a lot in Eli's eyes, but this intensity was new. Part of it frightened me, but mostly, it turned me on.

He released me, and I instantly hated his departure. "Now, would you like a shirt? Maybe some boxers? You could probably fold them down."

There was no way in hell I'd refuse an opportunity to swaddle myself in Eli Paxton's shirt and boxers. I'd stand in a blizzard with nothing else on just to share that casual intimacy with him. "Please."

I followed him down an unlit hall, and when we stepped into what I assumed was his bedroom, he didn't turn on the overhead light. The lamp cast a more subtle glow that I hoped would flatter my body the way a candle would.

Eli rummaged through the drawers in his dresser and then handed me a shirt and boxers. When he held up the boxers, he shook his head. "Those are going to swallow you whole."

"Hardly," I scoffed and snatched them from him. With his stuff cradled against my chest, I gave him my back. "Would you mind undoing the zipper?" It started midback at that spot I couldn't quite reach—I'd had to use a wire coat hanger to pull it up when I put it on—and ran the length of my spine to right below the dimples above my butt.

He kissed my shoulder, and the zing of the zipper stung my ears. If he didn't stop breathing on my neck, he wouldn't have to worry about me giving him the gift he craved. I'd be on him in a skinny minute, daring him to turn me down. Eli ran a finger down my bare spine in an achingly slow fashion. And when he reached the bottom, he slid his hand into the dress and around my side. Then the other. As slowly as they had descended, they rose up my ribs until he cupped my breast and teased my nipples.

My arms dropped to my sides, and I barely held onto the clothes he'd given. The dress hadn't stood a chance. It pooled on the floor at my feet. And there, in Eli's bedroom, I stood in nothing other than black-lace panties and heels.

"Jesus. I've never seen anything so beautiful." It was almost as if he talked directly to the Almighty. Just before he paid reverence to the offering.

He was gentle in his appraisal, and instead of turning me, he circled the spot in which I stood. It didn't occur to me to cover my chest with the clothes in my hand or with my arms. I let him look, explore, memorize, and the more he stared, the more confident I became. Eli might have put the brakes on things in the kitchen, but that didn't mean we couldn't start the engine again.

I held his gaze when I reached for the top button on his shirt, searching for any sign that he wanted me to stop. My fingers fumbled with the tiny pearlized plastic until, one by one, they all came undone, and then I tugged the tails from inside his waistband. Eli didn't stop me from unbuckling his belt or his pants. And when I lowered his zipper, I didn't miss the warning in his heated stare. The moment I dropped his slacks to the ground, I would be in unchartered territory, and Eli didn't know if he could turn back once I'd crossed the line.

He caught my wrist in his hand. "You don't have to do this."

"I want to." And I did. I couldn't speak to how far I would take it. I was beyond thinking. I merely acted on instinct, and everything in my body told me I was safe with Eli.

I waited for him to release me, so I knew he wanted me to continue. It wasn't reluctance in his stare; it was fear. I was the one who should be scared.

"What are you afraid of, Eli?" My sultry tone was foreign to my ears, as was the sound of his slacks falling to the floor.

His chest expanded, and his Adam's apple dipped. "That you'll never look at me again the way you are right now." His thumb brushed my cheek, and he searched my eyes. "That I'll never hear you tell me you love me." His lips swept softly over mine, more like a breeze than a kiss. "But most of all, that you'll regret anything that happens tonight." He tucked a strand of hair behind my ear.

"I love you, Eli." I hadn't planned to say it, yet he clearly needed to hear it. "The only thing I'll ever regret is not showing you just how much." Every word I'd uttered was pure and simple truth.

He still hadn't moved, and it occurred to me that he wouldn't. I didn't doubt that he would participate once I got it started, but Eli would not be the initiator. My fingers trembled when I lifted my hand to his chest and took a step closer. The beat of my nervous heart thumped in my ear. Had there not been evidence of his arousal, I likely would have chickened out.

One of the worst parts of being a perfectionist was trying something new, something I wouldn't likely be good at on the first go—and the pressure to get this right should have been overwhelming. I'd never asked, but I didn't believe Eli was a virgin.

Even if he'd only had sex once—which wasn't possible—he'd at least know what he was doing. I'd never even watched porn. But being with him quieted my spirit.

I dragged my fingers down the well-defined dip between his abs. I didn't have a clue what to do, I just wanted to explore. It might prove to be torturous for Eli. His nipples pebbled and bumps prickled his skin in the wake of my touch. Each reaction I witnessed grew my confidence that much more. It didn't seem right to just go for gold, and the truth was that I wanted to know every inch of his body the way my heart was familiar with his. When I reached the patch of hair beneath his navel, I added my other hand to the exploration and trailed it up the insides of the prominent *V*. That might have just become my favorite part of him, more so than the veins on his forearms. The muscles on his stomach tensed as my nails started up his sides.

When I dared to find his eyes, I expected to see him holding back laughter; instead, his lips were set in a firm line and his jaw ticced. "Am I doing something wrong?"

His hand caught my wrist in a cat-like reflex when I tried to pull back. Eli moved his head from side to side and then licked his lips. "Uh-uh." It was more of a grunt fueled by longing than an actual word.

He freed my wrist to allow me to continue; only, this time, he draped his hands over the dips in my sides and slid them behind me to cup my butt. I stumbled forward, closing the few inches that had remained between us. Instinct took over when my naked body fell flush with his. Eli dipped his head, and I took the opportunity to steal a kiss. Once I'd closed my eyes, my hands roamed free, no longer bound by fear, and the warmth that spread throughout my body felt feverish.

My mind went blank, leaving me without stress or worry, and my heart soared at the love flowing through my veins. Each swipe of my tongue against his shot electrical impulses straight to my pussy, and I had to fight the urge to find relief by grinding against his leg. I dug my nails into his skin, and he kneaded my ass with one hand while lifting his other to palm my breast. The pinch of his fingers around my nipple had me gasping for breath. My head fell back and exposed my neck, which Eli took as an invitation to feast. The nip of his teeth on my skin teetered on pain until the swath of his tongue and lips soothed away the sting. It was delicious and divine, and I'd lost control.

Control I freely gave to the man before me.

I lost my hold on his back when he dropped to his knees, but before I could question where he'd gone, his lips latched on to my breast, and I threaded my fingers through his thick hair, holding on for dear life and praying Eli didn't stop.

I couldn't keep track of his hands or his mouth. They were everywhere at the same time, and sensations I'd never experienced swam over my flesh, one drowning the other. Lips kissed and pecked down the center of my stomach, and every once in a while, he'd tease me with his tongue. The need for more drove me crazy, but my mind couldn't sort out what *more* was.

I got desperate when he breathed a warm breath on my pubic bone, and I couldn't find words to confess what he did to me. "Eli..." His name was nothing more than a breathy moan, a begging plea.

He responded, just not in the way I'd expected. His fingers slipped between my thighs, and I spread my legs to offer him what I hoped he sought. I probably should have been embarrassed by my shameless greed; however, I wasn't. His mouth on my hip bones kept me swirling in nirvana, and almost oblivious to him parting my lips. When I tensed ever so slightly, he stilled. I glanced down to find him staring up. *That* was when my cheeks flushed with heat, and an impish grin rose on my swollen lips.

His eyes shined with something I'd never seen. Before I could question it, Eli dipped inside me. One finger, and then two. He held my stare, yet as much as I wanted to keep my eyes open, my lids grew heavy and my breathing hard. In and out, the friction blossomed like a flower in the sun. My knees trembled, so I braced myself against his shoulder, which did nothing for me when his tongue joined his hand, sliding between my folds. Lips suckled my clit, and I couldn't quiet the moan that escaped, followed by another plea. "Eli..."

Chest heaving, breaths short, my skin glistened with perspiration, although I'd done nothing to exert myself. I could barely get out his name again. "E-Eli." I huffed, panting, yet not knowing what I was begging for.

His ministrations continued, his tongue, his lips, his fingers. Tingles, tinges, warmth, electricity. I couldn't decipher one from the other as I climbed toward an apex of ecstasy. I had no idea how high he could take me or what it would feel like after the fall, but like a drug addict, the peak was the only thing I cared about reaching.

Eli got to his feet, taking with him the fullness of his fingers and the wetness of his mouth and the heat of his tongue.

"No, no, no," I murmured. This had to be the sensation guys felt when girls cut them off. Personally, I was on the verge of tears if something didn't relieve the pressure Eli had created.

He ignored my protest and trailed my essence up my side. I tasted myself on his lips when he captured them in a kiss, which built a different kind of fire. My entire body danced on the edge of torture and pleasure—a nudge could send me in either direction.

I broke away and tucked my head into his neck where I huffed out a fake cry. My nipples rubbed against the hair on his chest, and the head of his dick poked me in the stomach. He stroked my back, and my hair began to fall when he pulled out the clip. I all but whined, standing in front of him, nerve endings raw.

The hair that tickled my spine lifted when he fisted it, and so did my head when he pulled back my hair. There was no more denying what I'd seen in his eyes, and mine went wide. Eli growled. It was a low rumble in the back of his throat that had started in his chest. Animalistic, and I dared say, the hottest things I'd ever heard or seen.

"Tell me what you want, Colbie." He still struggled with the right thing to do, but in my mind, that choice had been made when the two of us stood naked in his bedroom. And it sure as hell went out the window when he'd put his mouth between my legs.

With all the emotion I could muster without sounding like a desperate whore, I said the only thing that summarized my answer. "You."

The most seductive smirk I'd ever witnessed formed on his lips just before he bent at the knees and wrapped an arm under each of my thighs. And when he stood, I circled my legs around his waist and clung to his neck.

Eli's breath was warm against my ear. "I won't let you fall."

For a split second, those five words seemed like a premonition, but the instant the head of his dick touched me from that position, that thought was lost, and I jumped a bit in his embrace. The room lost shape as he moved. I had no idea how he carried me across the floor, much less laid the two of us onto the mattress without so much as a flop. Eli positioned the two of us gracefully like a dancer.

My ankles unlocked, and my knees fell to his sides with him nestled between my thighs. There, he supported most of his weight on one forearm. I could have stared into his eyes all night. His regard was tender yet searing, loving although smoldering, soulful. With each emotion I caught sight of, another one floated in and layered itself on top of the last so I couldn't pick them apart.

Eli tucked my hair behind my ear. His lips parted, and I waited for what he had to say. And when nothing came, I softly stroked his cheek with reassurance and lifted my head to kiss his succulent lips. In that moment, he was the epitome of poetry. A silent stanza.

"Don't think, Eli." The last thing I wanted was for him to get stuck in his head, worried about the right and wrong, the should or should not. "It's just us." And I became the seductress. The one to ply him to my will and want.

He huffed, shook his head slightly, and the corners of his mouth tipped up in a bit of a grin. "It's not that." He cooed as much as he whispered, like his words might break me if he spoke too loudly. "This is going to hurt."

I scrunched my brow, trying to figure out what could hurt. Sex was supposed to feel good. Men all over the world had been doing it for centuries. I didn't know much, but he had to be doing something wrong if this was painful.

Eli licked his lips and shifted between my legs. He slipped between my folds and nudged my clit. "The thought of hurting you"—oh, *me*, not him—"guts me."

I lost track of what he said when he rocked his hips again, and my back arched as my eyes closed the next time. God, I didn't want him to stop. I encouraged his motion with my palms on his muscular butt, and I lifted my lids to find him peaceful and happy...and well aware of what he did to me.

Every muscle, from head to toe, had relaxed. Eli warmed me from the outside in. The only thing I wanted right then was to connect with him...fully. My hips found his rhythm and worked to build the pleasure he'd started, and when he covered me, shifting his weight from my side to my center, I never wanted to leave his cocoon.

He found my eyes and waited. I bit my bottom lip and held his stare. Nothing could have prepared me for what it felt like to have Eli fill me. With each inch, he allowed me time to adjust and silently beg him for more. When he stilled completely, I knew what he waited for.

I wasn't sure how he even detected the subtle movement of my head that gave him permission, but I braced my hands on his taut biceps and cried out in searing pain as he tore through my hymen. The burn came from deep inside and ripped across my abdomen. And when I blinked, tears seeped from my eyes and down my cheeks.

As the pain subsided, I realized he was balls deep, seated to the hilt, and I was terrified for him to move. I tensed with apprehension and fear spilled onto my cheeks. I tried to hide behind my hands, but Eli refused to let me shield my emotion.

"Baby." His thumbs brushed away the moisture, and he graced my lips with a kiss. "Look at me, please." He'd never called me anything other than my name, but those two syllables stole my resolve.

My eyes cleared, and Eli rested his forehead against mine.

"Talk to me."

I shook my head like a petulant child. If I spoke, I'd choke on emotion, but if I didn't, I was afraid he'd move, causing me agony.

"Just give it a second. I promise the pain stops."

It had started to subside, but I wasn't ready to admit that. And Eli didn't make me. He took control, starting with my mouth. His tongue parted my lips, and the second mine joined, that familiar warmth that pooled between my legs returned. I didn't know when he'd started to move or when I'd joined him. Eli found our rhythm, and holy hell did he play me a song. It was a quiet ballad of love I never imagined him capable of. Football players weren't tender and gentle; they were fierce and aggressive.

Eli had one hand under my shoulder and one wrapped around my thigh, using both for leverage when he dipped his head into my neck. "Fuck, Cole." He breathed the words onto me. "You're so tight."

I assumed that was a good thing, because the reciprocal side of that was how full he made me. It was a sensation I could easily become addicted to and had no idea how to maintain. But as his pace increased, the thought of making it last flew out the window. The build inside me grew exponentially with each of his thrusts. My nails scraped his back and clawed at his skin, and when he growled, I felt the vibrations in my chest. The two of us had climbed the mountain together, and the sounds he made indicated he was near the top.

"Eli..." I panted his name in his ear because no other words would come to me.

His teeth nicked my neck and then bit at my ear. "I want to hear you."

The warmth of his breath and the scent of sex on the man I loved all but forced me to give him what he craved. My shrill voice reverberated off the walls when I cried out his name in ecstasy. I held on for dear life, wrapping my legs around his waist and locking my ankles. He grunted with each push until he finally roared.

Any other time that sound would have sent me reeling, yet knowing it was for me, because of me, I tried to capture it in my memory to save for a rainy day. Eli now had a piece of me that I could never give to anyone else.

I expected him to pull out, and I tensed, waiting for it to happen, for him to fall to my side in a heap of tired mess, even though I had yet to release him. Instead, he pushed onto his knees, and lifted me up so I straddled his waist. Eli twisted us so his back was against the headboard and his legs were out in front of him. With me settled into his lap, he held me in place with his hands on my ass. And he still hadn't broken our connection.

I stared down into his brown eyes. His smile had changed, and I wondered if mine had, too. A moment of panic struck when I thought that if I could see that change that everyone else would as well.

"I love you, Colbie."

But those three words erased the care from my mind. Nothing mattered other than Eli. The rest of the world could go to hell. I kissed his perfect mouth and then whispered into his ear, "I love you, too, Eli."

Nothing had ever felt so right or more perfect. I never wanted it to end, although I had no idea how we'd get through the next six and a half months.

There was no turning back for either of us.

12

ELI

I WASN'T LOOKING FORWARD TO THE CALL I WAS ABOUT TO make. I'd just hung up the phone with Caleb, and now I had to let Colbie know. Thankfully, I didn't have to do that through text anymore. Once she had given me the green light and assured me that no one cared who she talked to, much less listened in, I preferred to hear her voice as often as possible. Until now.

She answered on the first ring. "Hey."

"You busy?" I knew she wasn't, but it seemed like a good opener.

Colbie giggled. "No." The effervescence in her voice since the recital didn't go unnoticed, nor did her affinity for me. "And if I were, you know I'd stop whatever I was doing." She would, even though I was supposed to see her in thirty minutes.

I hated to burst her bubble, but I also didn't want her to find out from anyone else. "I just got off the phone with Caleb."

"And?"

My relationship with her brother hadn't come into play since Colbie and I had met. His life had been filled with a new wife and football, while mine had been occupied by a new school and his little sister—both of which I loved. "It seems I'll be having Thanksgiving dinner with him tomorrow."

"Okay..."

"At your parents' house."

A door closed in the background and then another before her anxious whisper came through the phone. "Are you *crazy*? Why would you agree to that?"

It wasn't funny, and while her panic was cute, she'd ream me for laughing. "Baby, he's my best friend. And I'm in a town where he doesn't think I have any friends. Caleb knows I can't go home to see my parents and didn't want me to be alone. How could I say no?"

"Easy, you purse your lips, open your mouth, and out comes sound." She huffed and tried to keep her voice down. "Eli, they'll know. This is going to be a disaster."

"No one will know anything. No one at school has." That was the truth.

Colbie did an amazing job of feigning indifference—so much so that at times it bothered me—where I was concerned. It helped that she had never been close to many people, so the only ones who might have noticed would have been Jess, Caden, and Caleb. Any of those three finding out would be catastrophic. I'd followed her lead. I'd also avoided her in the halls at all costs.

We still ran together, but we did so under a cloak of darkness early in the morning. And nine times out of ten, that jog ended in my bed. A smile rose on my cheeks, thinking about Colbie naked and riding my cock. I couldn't get enough of her over me, under me, next to me—at my side. Colbie was more than a lover; she had quickly become my best friend.

"Eli—"

I'd drifted off into thoughts of her instead of focusing on the conversation. "Colbie."

"Don't patronize me."

I loved her spunk, even if she were frustrated with me, she didn't hesitate to call me out on it. "I'm not. I'm sorry. I got lost in thoughts of this morning." And it had been a *great* morning. "I promise, it's going to be okay."

If I hadn't heard her breathing on the other end, I would have assumed she'd hung up.

"Cole, don't work yourself into a frenzy. There will be a ton of people there. No one will even notice me, much less us. Your parents think I'm coming as Caleb's friend, not your boyfriend."

She sniffled and the hitch in her breath came through the line.

"Baby, why are you crying?" There was nothing more I hated than for tears to fall from her eyes—except not being there to wipe them away.

"It doesn't matter."

"Don't start that shit with me, Colbie. Talk to me." I also loathed having to get firm with her, but no one had listened to her in so long that she didn't believe anyone valued her opinion, and therefore, she avoided sharing it.

She sputtered and started and stopped a handful of times before forming coherent words. "I don't want you to see me that way."

I softened my tone to keep her engaged. "I don't understand."

"It's one thing for me to tell you that my family doesn't care. It's another completely for you to witness it and be a part of it."

Even without seeing her face, I felt her pain. "Why would I be a part of it?" Jesus, I needed to hold her, comfort her, show her how wrong she was in her assumption.

"How can you not? If you try to be what you are to me, it will draw attention. If you act like you care at all, Jess or Caden or Caleb will notice. Which only leaves you being there with your best friend and me out in the cold. I can handle being alone with them. I can't fathom it with you."

I didn't know how to ease her fears, nor did I know how I'd

deal with people being anything but adoring toward her. Colbie was my world, and I'd protect her in any way I could. "You should know I won't let that happen. It's not like we don't know each other. Your parents and your brother know you're in my class."

She'd dried her tears and metaphorically stiffened her upper lip the way she always did. Colbie had put on her armor and prepared for battle. A battle she believed she'd fight alone. "And you should know that it won't just be Caleb there. Carson and Casey are both coming home. They'll expect you to talk UGA; you guys will get engrossed in football, and my parents will fawn over you like you're the long-lost son they never had because you're as football as every one of the Chapmans. Every one but me."

I couldn't argue with her. She wouldn't have listened anyhow. All I could do was show her. And I wasn't able to do that until tomorrow night. "You're going to have to trust me."

"Not even you can work miracles."

I let out a hearty laugh that probably would have gotten me smacked had Colbie been with me. "That wasn't what you cried out this morning. I think you even made Jesus believe I could walk on water."

"I hate you."

"You love me."

"Bye, Eli."

"I'll see you on the sidewalk." And then again in my bed after we ran for the second time today since this morning had been cut short. "Love you, Cole."

She couldn't do it. She couldn't hang up without telling me she loved me, and I lived to hear it. Finally, Colbie relented with a huff. "I love you, too, Eli." And there was no question in my mind of just how much.

But Colbie needed someone to prove that devotion and commitment were reciprocated. Tomorrow might be my chance to do it. I'd bitten off more than I could chew, and I'd known that when I had accepted the invitation. Unfortunately, I had no legitimate way to get out of it. I spent every minute of free time I could squander with Colbie, and I'd avoided Caleb for the better part of first semester because of it. Now I prayed I could keep Colbie happy while not rousing any suspicion with the rest of the Chapmans.

Colbie had managed to escape her house this morning, although when she'd shown up at my back door in her running gear, she didn't actually want to exercise. She'd pushed past me, grabbing my hand as she went. I didn't make a habit of questioning her, so I followed along without remark. She hadn't wasted time pulling me into my bedroom and tugging off my clothes followed by her own, nor did I hesitate when she pushed me onto the mattress.

Colbie didn't typically take charge. She was always pliable and definitely involved, but never the initiator. And while I had no idea what had gotten into her, I went with it anyhow. It wasn't until she'd seated herself on my dick with her hands on my chest that I'd finally seen what she'd tried to hide deep inside.

I'd flipped her over, but instead of giving her the punishing fuck she'd believed she needed, I made love to her. Reassured her. Wiped away her tears. And promised, no matter what happened today, I'd still love her tonight and tomorrow. And all the days after that.

Colbie didn't get it. But I'd spend a lifetime proving it to her.

She was it for me.

And now, here I stood with a bottle of wine in my hand for her mom and my finger on their doorbell. I could hear the clamor going on inside from the front porch. And when the door swung open, Chasity greeted me with a smile followed by a hug. Over her shoulder, I noticed Colbie with her mom. I hated touching another woman in any way, but especially now when I couldn't go grab her and show the world who my heart belonged to. So I mouthed "sorry" and broke free from Caleb's wife.

"Eli." Mrs. Chapman dropped what she was doing, leaving Colbie to finish the task, and raced to greet me. "We're so glad you could join us. I can't believe we haven't seen you since you moved into town." She wrapped an arm around my waist and escorted me into the kitchen. "We still do Sunday dinner every week. You should join us. You're like family."

I doubted she'd feel that way if she knew I was in love with her daughter or what we'd been up to only hours before. "Thanks for the offer."

It only took minutes for everyone to go back to what they were doing, and even less time for me to see what Colbie hadn't wanted me to. This wasn't going to be as easy as I'd believed. I hadn't seen Carson or Casey in ages, and as Colbie had predicted, the conversation flowed to football. It was the common denominator for everyone in attendance—including Jess—except Colbie. I looked around and realized Colbie hadn't joined us.

"Eli, you want a beer, man?" Caleb lifted his.

I didn't, but I assumed they kept them in the kitchen, which happened to be the last place I'd seen his sister. "Yeah." I stood. "Fridge?"

He nodded and pointed the way. I glanced back to ensure no one had followed or noticed me leave. Her hair was down and her back to me. Colbie hadn't heard me come into the room. I took a chance I shouldn't have and leaned my nose into her neck, circled my hands around her waist, and inhaled the comfort of her scent. I'd imagined coming home to her—our home—countless times to do just this. "Hey, baby," I whispered into her ear and kissed her slender neck.

Without hesitation, Colbie turned and found my lips. "Hey." Her greeting was soft, but I felt it just the same.

"I'm gonna grab a beer." I pulled away and went toward the fridge. "You should join us," I said as I leaned down to find a bottle.

"Critter's cooking. Don't distract her if you actually want to eat tonight."

I slammed my head into the fridge when I jumped at the sound of Caleb's voice. Tempering the rage I felt at his dismissal of his sister was infinitely more difficult than I'd imagined it would be, likely because I didn't believe they'd exclude her with company around.

"Damn, Paxton. I didn't mean to scare you. What's got you all jumpy? Toss me one."

I flipped my best friend off with one hand and tossed him a bottle with the other. "Colbie, you need any help in here?" I couldn't leave without acknowledging her.

"She doesn't need your help, dumbass. She does this shit every year. Critter likes it, don't you?"

Chasity called from the living room, and Caleb went running. Not literally, but figuratively enough that he couldn't deny the leash she had wound around his neck that one day she'd use to hang him.

"Colbie?" I needed to see her eyes, even though she wouldn't give them to me. I'd find every bit of heartache in her pale blue irises, and she didn't want me to.

She pulled her shoulders back and cleared her throat. "I'm good, Dr. Paxton. Thank you for offering."

I didn't give a fuck if that was for show, it gutted me. She didn't even address me that way at school anymore. She avoided addressing me at all. Because in our world, I was Eli and she was Cole.

The noise from the living room grew as I realized how quiet

the kitchen was. My heart stood sad and alone just feet away, and I couldn't leave her. It might raise suspicion, and I'd probably regret it later, but right now, Colbie was my only priority.

I set my beer on the counter and stepped to the sink to wash my hands. "Hey, Colbie. What can I do to help?"

She watched me dry off with a dish towel, almost mortified. "What are you doing?" she hissed, and her eyes darted toward her family.

"Earning my keep." I tossed the towel on the counter and winked at her. "So, you can either show me what you *want* me to do, *or* I can take matters into my own hands. Although, I have to warn you, no one will be happy with me adding the finishing touches." I lifted my brows and grinned. My back was to the living room that she faced. I could do whatever I wanted without risk of being seen; Colbie, however, could not.

The plastic grin she secured to her lips didn't hide the irritation in her eyes. And when she talked through the fake smile, I almost lost my composure. "You're going to get us both in trouble."

I nipped playfully at her stomach, so no one could see. "Not if you just give me something to do. Then we both get what we want."

Her eyes narrowed yet her lips remained high. "Fine." Colbie ground her teeth together. "You can peel and cut the potatoes. I'm sure Mama will be back in here soon enough."

"Perfect. The more the merrier." I refused to allow her to be alone or panicked about my presence. I couldn't hold her here. We both knew that. I couldn't protect her physically with my embrace. I could, however, keep her from being isolated, and if I knew anything about her family—which I did—one by one, they would end up in the kitchen as well.

Colbie handed me a vegetable peeler and pointed to the food. "Have at it."

I snatched the kitchen towel, spun it in a tight circle, and pegged her in the butt with a tight whip that made her jump and screech. The glitter I normally saw in her eyes returned, and so did her mom.

"Colbie, is everything all right?" Elise had her hand over her heart. "I heard you yelp."

I snickered, hovered over the sink. I could feel Colbie glaring at me.

"Yes, ma'am." Colbie paused. "I slipped. I'm fine." And she lied.

"Eli, *what* are you doing? You're our guest."

I turned toward Mrs. Chapman with a smile that had far less to do with her and more to do with Colbie and shook the peeler at the matron of the house. "Ah, ah, ah, you said I was family. Family helps with dinner."

"Oh, fiddle-faddle. That's just nonsense." She tried to wave me off. "Go back in there and have fun with the boys."

I didn't budge, and I wasn't going to. She could shoo me away from the food and forbid me to help, but I wouldn't leave the kitchen without Colbie. "I'm a firm believer in pulling my weight. I really don't mind helping. Actually, I kind of like it." I didn't have to turn to sense every bit of Colbie's apprehension; I could feel it as if it were my own. "Do you have an extra apron?" I maintained the most innocent expression I could manage.

Mrs. Chapman giggled and handed me one that clearly belonged to her husband. The three of us set to work with idle chitchat, most of which Colbie's mom directed toward me, and I tried to wind around to include Colbie, who took every chance I gave her to stay involved. And as I had predicted, Caleb came to find me, then Chasity to locate him, and one by one, the entire family—both parents, seven kids, one wife, and two significant others—had crowded into what was typically an enormous space.

Several times, I caught a peek from Colbie, and I took every opportunity afforded me to brush up against her or sneak between her and someone else. I needed to feel her, and that was the best I could get. And by the grace of God, Elise sat me next to the love of my life at the table. When it came time to say the blessing, everyone took hands, and again, I thanked heaven to get the chance to stroke her fingers while everyone's eyes were closed, and give her a squeeze when we said, "Amen."

With twelve people seated around one table, even normal conversation was deafening. Everyone carried on with someone else, regardless of where they sat in relation to them at the table—everyone except Colbie. She ate quietly and responded the couple of times someone spoke directly to her, but otherwise, she didn't join in. And it didn't escape my attention that the only time her family spoke to her was to have her pass something.

Except Chasity.

Whom I had started to hate.

She nipped at Colbie with backhanded compliments more than once and did so in a way that no one else heard what she said, except me.

"Do you *ever* get full?" Chasity held her fork in her hand and sipped her tea with the other. Her eyes accused Colbie of something, although I couldn't discern what or why. "I'd be as big as the side of the house if I ate like you."

My eyes darted between Chasity across the table and Colbie at my side while chatter clamored on around us. I hadn't noticed that Colbie ate much, ever. In fact, I worried she never ate and worked out too much, with as much weight as she'd lost since the beginning of the year. I couldn't put a number to it, but I held the girl in my arms daily. I'd memorized every curve and angle of her naked body. Even in the few weeks since we started having sex, I'd seen evidence of weight loss.

"Do you eat like that at every meal? Or just dinner?" Chasity hadn't let up, and I wondered what she thought she knew.

I sucked at this kind of thing. I didn't understand the cruelty of women toward each other, and I'd never get catty behavior, of which Chasity was reigning queen.

"It's all the miles she runs." Jess perked up and into the conversation. "You could eat whatever you wanted if you put in five or six miles a day." She thought she had helped her best friend. "Sometimes she runs more than once a day." Jess grinned at Colbie, and it was heartfelt...genuine. "I wish I had that kind of dedication."

Like a shrinking violet, Colbie turned in to herself, and she quit responding. But Chasity hadn't stopped.

"How many calories do you think you eat a day?" Chasity glanced at Colbie's plate and back up. "I bet it's thousands."

Jess shook her head. "Oh no, she eats like a rabbit at school."

No one other than me seemed the least bit distracted much less concerned about this discussion or why it was even taking place. And I had to sit there and watch it happen. I couldn't add anything or question Colbie. She had eaten a fair amount tonight, but it was Thanksgiving. We had all overeaten. But Chasity had an ulterior motive that I couldn't figure out. As much as I wanted to pin her to a wall and drive a stake through her heart, I was helpless.

Minutes dragged by when Chasity finally got involved in a conversation that didn't involve her sister-in-law. But by that point, the damage had been done.

I leaned over while everyone else focused on one of Mr. Chapman's football stories. "What the hell was that?"

Colbie shrugged, and a tear slipped down her cheek. She wiped it away as quickly as it had fallen.

I slid my hand around the back of her chair and turned slightly to be certain no one heard—or read my lips—what I said. "I love you."

Colbie turned into my shoulder and returned the sentiment.

"What are you two whispering about?" Chasity alerted everyone at the table, causing all eyes to face us.

Colbie scooted her chair back. "I had asked Eli to let me out so I could go to the restroom. I didn't want to disrupt everyone."

The two girls stared each other down, and I waited for Colbie to lash out and claw at her brother's wife. My jaw hung slightly ajar when no one—not even Caleb—told Chasity to back off. But Chasity's smug grin was evidence that she knew they wouldn't.

When Colbie stood, I put my hand on her knee where no one could see it beneath the table, and she glanced down at me, never missing a beat.

"You okay?"

She nodded, and the weight of Chasity's stare almost smothered me. "Yes, sir."

Any other time—particularly if she were naked—that might have turned me on. This time, it was ice water to my libido and morale. Another reminder of who I was to Colbie in her family's eyes...her teacher.

Colbie discreetly disappeared up the steps, and I despised not being able to follow. Maybe she really did just need to use the restroom, although there was one right down the hall, but I gathered it was more than that. She had needed to escape.

Casey and Caden got up to put dishes in the sink, and Chasity helped Mrs. Chapman put leftovers away to prepare for dessert. I sat, bewildered, in the same place I'd been since Colbie had left.

Jess plopped down in the seat next to me, the one Colbie had vacated. She propped her foot on the edge of the chair and put her chin on the knee she hugged. To anyone else in the room, it appeared casual. "She's okay, Dr. Paxton."

I searched for prying eyes or ears, yet found none.

Jess dipped her head toward the stairs. "She's just really... regular." Jess's brows lifted like she was imparting secret information, information I didn't understand.

"What?"

Her eyes danced around. "You know...*regular*." She huffed with irritation at my inability to decipher whatever code she spoke in. "Like her stomach processes things at the same time every day." She hid her mouth with a cupped hand to keep her words from drifting farther away. "Sheesh, she's dropping the kids off at the pool."

And the lightbulb finally went off. "Oh..."

Jess laughed. "For being so smart, you're not so bri—" She stopped herself before throwing that insult my direction. "Is anything I say here going to get me in trouble at school?"

I patted her shoulder and chuckled. "No, Jess. You're fine. Thanks."

"Eli, how about a little round ball in the driveway?" Caleb spun a basketball on his finger, and I couldn't turn him down.

His wife was busy, Colbie hadn't come back, and everyone else was occupied with something else. I wasn't exactly dressed for basketball, but neither was he.

"Sure." I followed him through the kitchen and out the back door.

Everything Caleb and I did became a competition, even when it was hoops in his parents' driveway. In minutes, the two of us were drenched in sweat. Not much had been said, but when you'd lived with someone for as long as Caleb and I had been roommates, you just got a sense they had something on their mind. And while I was afraid to ask, it was either that or be stuck out here, smelling like I hadn't bathed in days.

I went in for a layup, and on my way down, I finally dug in. "What's on your mind, Caleb?"

He took the rebound and dribbled out. "What makes you think I've got something on my mind?" Caleb bent at the knees and lunged up. The ball left the arch he created with his hand, and I watched as it went into the basket, nothing but net.

I grabbed the ball and stopped. "The fact that you didn't say 'nothing' is a good place to start."

He rested his hands on his hips and took a couple deep breaths. "Have you noticed anything going on with my sister recently?"

My heartrate shot up to dangerous levels, and I fought to keep my eyes from revealing my panic. "Like what?" God, I wished I hadn't stopped playing so I could turn away from him. I needed a distraction, a thunderstorm, a car plowing through the house... anything to get me out of this conversation.

"Kendra Cross came to see me right before break."

Listening seemed like a better option than talking at this juncture.

"She had some concerns about Colbie's schoolwork."

My heart stopped beating completely, and a lump formed in my throat that I wasn't certain I'd be able to speak around, so I stared at Caleb, waiting for him to get to his point. Sweet Jesus, there were eleven other people inside; *surely* one of them wanted to join us. "Oh?" It was more of a grunt than a word.

"She thought maybe you'd noticed the same thing. Kendra said you'd asked some questions in the teacher's lounge a few weeks ago, but you hadn't been specific about any particular student."

I couldn't stand here idle any longer. I bounced the ball a couple times and took a shot from under the basket. "Has she talked to Colbie?" I passed off the rebound to Caleb. I'd kill for the scratch of sneakers on the pavement, anything to break the weight of silence.

"She tried but didn't get much response, so she came to me. And I'm coming to you."

"And what exactly are you looking for?" I tried to be nonchalant. This was the same guy who'd warned me not to get close to students; I certainly couldn't tell him how I'd noticed the details that I had.

He shrugged. "Your opinion on whether I need to get my parents involved. You see Colbie every day. You have her in class. You grade her work." Caleb chuckled and added another two points to his score. "You spend more time with her than I do, so I thought you could offer some perspective."

This was where things got tricky, dicey even. I had a split second to make a decision. I couldn't hem and haw over what Caleb wanted to know without giving myself away. But by telling him what he wanted to know, I might be able to get Cole what she needed—not that I was even certain what that was.

"Caleb, your sister is smarter than everyone in that school, including the teachers. Have I seen a dip in her quality of work? Yes. Has it warranted a reflection in her grades? No." I hoped that lie didn't send me straight to hell. "Your sister puts an enormous amount of pressure on herself to be the best." That was common knowledge and not something I could only have garnered from spending time alone with her. "Maybe she's letting that guard down a bit since she's already gotten into college—"

"No way. Not Critter. She'd never willingly give up valedictorian." He shook his head and ran a hand through his hair. "Kendra said it was more than just her work, though I doubt you'd have noticed whether she'd lost weight or had bags under her eyes."

I didn't confirm or deny that statement. "Maybe you should talk to your parents. Surely your mom would notice those types of details about her only daughter." Even though I knew she didn't.

Chasity stuck her head out the back door. "Dessert's on the table. You two come in and get washed up." She squinted to see us better in the dark. "How did you get so sweaty? Caleb, that's gross. Your mama is not going to want pigs at her dining room table."

Caleb faced his wife. "Give me a minute. We'll be right there."

I rolled my eyes with his back turned. Marriage hadn't made Chasity any less of a nag, and I couldn't help but feel sorry for my best friend having to deal with that for the remainder of his life. I didn't even want to consider what she'd be like if they had kids. But I kept my mouth shut.

Caleb slapped me on the chest. "I'll talk to my parents tonight. I'm sure Chasity could be a help."

And then I couldn't keep it shut anymore. "I think you might want to leave Chas out of it, Caleb." The thin ice I currently treaded on was about to crack and drag me under, but I couldn't throw Colbie to that wolf.

He'd taken two steps toward the door when he stopped. "Why?"

There weren't many things that a man gave a shit about, but his football team and his woman always made the list. "She's not exactly nice to Colbie." He pulled back like I'd slapped him. "I really think you should just talk to your parents alone."

"What are you talking about? You're never even around them together." His defenses were drawn, and I couldn't blame him; mine were too, but for a different reason—Colbie was on my list. Caleb just didn't know it.

I turned my lips down and shrugged with as much indifference as I could muster. "You're right. But I saw your sister at the rehearsal dinner—and you yourself told me they didn't get along. Then the following day at the church, I heard rumors about things Chasity said to Colbie in the dressing room. And tonight at the table, she really ribbed your sister for no apparent reason."

Caleb hadn't heard a word I'd said other than something negative about his wife. "It's not like that. You just don't know them. Critter's just as much to blame as Chas."

"Maybe, maybe not. But from the outside looking in, Chasity is the adult. She should be setting the example, not picking fights."

He eyed me for several long seconds. For a moment, I thought he might throw a punch. I would have taken it if it got my point across.

"And as your little sister, you should be insistent that your wife be good to her."

He laughed, but it wasn't one born from humor, more like irritation. "Coming from the single man who's an only child. Dude, you have no idea what it's like growing up the oldest of seven children. I can't babysit them all."

"Then how about just your wife?"

Caleb's face turned Georgia red, and his chest heaved with unspent aggression. "Pax, I love you like a brother, but that's my wife you're talking about."

"And you asked me about your sister. Your wife isn't my concern."

"Is Colbie?"

We were seconds away from this taking a turn neither of us could come back from, but at that moment, I no longer cared where it went. Colbie was an adult, and if it cost me my career then so be it. "Meaning what, Caleb?" I couldn't decipher whether he'd insinuated my guilt or if I had read into something that wasn't there.

"Meaning that if you cared about your students half as much as you say you did then you would have come to me when my sister seemed off course."

The two of us were practically screaming. "Seriously?"

"Yeah!"

"You're the one who told me not to get too close. So which is it, Chapman? Do you want me to keep my distance? Or do you want me to run to you with everything that goes on in my classroom? Jesus, you act like I didn't tell you that Colbie was failing my class. Newsflash, she has an *A*. She shows up every day. She participates"—if I called on her, but that wasn't my point—"I don't know what knowledge you expected me to impart to you. But I'm telling you this, leave your wife out of it if you expect your sister to talk."

"Boys?" Elise now stuck her head out the door. "Is everything all right? It sounded like yelling out here."

"We're fine, Mama."

"Good, then come in and have some cheesecake. Everyone's waiting on you two." Mrs. Chapman didn't wait for us to respond because she expected to be obeyed.

"Look, Caleb. I'm not trying to push your buttons." I took a deep breath. This had to be put to bed before we stepped foot inside. "I just don't think you can approach your parents with your sister the way you would your brothers." I held up my hands in surrender and peace. "That's all I was trying to say. And if you want me to look out for her, just say the word, and I'll do my best."

He wrapped his arm around my neck and pulled my head into his chest. His knuckles rubbed into my scalp as I fought him off. I didn't know if he'd heard me, but I prayed he had. A little attention from her parents wouldn't hurt Cole.

"Thanks, Pax. Honestly, I think Kendra's making a big deal out of nothing. Like you said, Critter puts a lot of pressure on herself. And if her work is still better than everyone else's, I'm sure there's nothing to be worried about."

13

ELI

I arrived at my back door to find a very pissed off Colbie Chapman staring at me through the windows. She'd quit knocking but not glaring. Part of me feared opening the door to a woman on a warpath; I'd learned long ago to steer clear of them.

"Open up, Eli." Her voice didn't sound nearly as angry as the gleam in her eyes appeared.

I unlocked the deadbolt—not that I'd intended to keep her out —and let her in. I'd barely closed the door behind her before she laid into me.

"What the hell did you say to my parents last night?" Colbie marched past me. She didn't turn down the hall to my bedroom. She stayed straight toward the living room.

It was too early for this. I'd been over at her house and came home to nurse a bottle of Jack, worried about what Caleb would or wouldn't say to his parents. That led to a hangover today. The sun hadn't risen, and my girl now dared those rays to shine. I ran a hand through my hair and followed her.

I plopped onto the couch while she stood in front of it, staring me down.

"Well?" Her thin arms were folded under her breasts, and I

wanted nothing more than to feel her front pressed to mine...and for her to lower her voice just a tad.

I held out my hand, and she uncrossed her arms to come to me. Colbie's shoulders dropped, and so did her guard. With my fingers locked with hers, I tugged her onto the couch and nestled her into my arms between my side and the back cushions. "You smell good," I cooed into her hair.

"Eli." She might have softened, but she hadn't given up.

"Baby, I don't know what you're talking about. I didn't talk to your parents last night. About anything." My lids drifted closed, and the heat from Colbie's warm skin seeped into mine. "You were there for everything said." All I wanted to do was breathe her in and keep her close. Talking could wait.

She managed to wiggle her way up and onto her elbow, and I peered through one eye to see just how much trouble I was in. I estimated it to be a seven out of possible ten, which meant I needed to give her my attention.

Relenting, I focused on her. "Okay. Tell me what happened." I propped up my head with a pillow to ensure I didn't fall asleep.

"My mom and dad came to my room last night."

I didn't see a problem there, but I bit my tongue.

"They wanted to talk about school and piano."

Maybe Caleb had actually gone to the Chapmans after I'd left. I remained silent to let her get out whatever she wanted to share.

"Caleb told my parents that my teachers are concerned about my schoolwork. How would that have happened on Thanksgiving, Eli? You were the only one of my *teachers* present at my house. And those same *teachers* expressed concern not only about my grades but over my health and the pressure I put on myself." She sat up completely and scooted to the other end of the couch and out of my reach.

I reacted the way she had and bolted upright. Hangover be

damned, I moved quickly to grab her. "Uh huh. Don't do that. Don't assume I did something and punish me. If you want to talk, we can talk, but you're not going to isolate yourself so you crawl into the box you want to hide in." I wouldn't force her into my arms, but I wouldn't let her cower, either.

"Why do you care if I touch you?" she asked timidly as she inched back in my direction and put her hand in mine.

I wouldn't lie and tell her I didn't care, because I absolutely fucking did. "Because before I told you I loved you, I showed you every time I hugged you or caressed your cheek. And even without words, those same things illustrate that sentiment. It's something I never want you to lose sight of, regardless of how mad you might be. If my hand is still in yours, we're tethered. Partners. I won't let go, and I hope you never do." I meant it figuratively and literally, which Cole was smart enough to understand.

She sighed and leaned her head against the back of the sofa. "Just tell me what happened, Eli." One by one, her fingers laced mine, securing the connection.

"Last night after you went upstairs, Caleb and I went outside to play basketball. Had I known when he asked that it was a way to get me to talk, I wouldn't have gone. But that's neither here nor there." I tucked her hair behind her ear and noticed she was in yoga pants and flip flops versus the running gear she typically had on. "Mrs. Cross talked to your brother before school let out. She's concerned, Colbie."

"About what?" Tears flooded her eyes, and the moment she blinked, several fell. "I still have straight *A*s."

I wiped them away. "Your health. Your schoolwork. Whether there might be something wrong that she didn't know about."

She sniffled and swiped at the trail on her cheeks. "So why would Caleb mention that to you?"

I didn't miss that Colbie didn't deny that things had changed; I just chose to hold that close to my chest for right now. "Because you're in my class. Like it or not, I *am* one of your teachers, and your brother thought I might have some insight."

"And you confirmed what Mrs. Cross said?" Surprise lilted her tone, and her wet lashes went wide. "Why would you do that? Why wouldn't you talk to *me*?"

"Baby, I didn't tell him anything of any significance because I *hadn't* talked to you. I confirmed that the assignments you handed in were still miles above everyone else, although they weren't the level you had submitted at the beginning of the year. And when he asked why I hadn't brought it to his attention, I told him that you still had an *A*, showed up, and participated, even if that last one was stretching the truth a bit."

"What else haven't you talked to me about?"

I pulled her knees toward me and tossed her flip flops onto the floor. "I'm worried about you." With each of her feet on the outside of my thighs, I hooked my forearms behind her knees and brought her to me. "The circles under your beautiful blue eyes." I leaned in and kissed the spot I referenced. "And the weight you've lost." I trailed two fingers down her thin side and then pressed my lips to her collar bone. "That you kill yourself trying to be the best at everything you do."

She let me bring her into my lap, straddling my waist. I cradled her jaw in my hands and tilted her head to give me access to her mouth. Colbie opened for me the way she always did, welcoming me. I tasted her. Drank her in. Showed her how much I loved her with every swipe of my tongue. And as my cock hardened, she mewled and ground against me.

I debated whether to take this further or continue the conversation at hand, but when she pulled her tank top over her head followed by her sports bra, my ability to make the right decision fell short.

Colbie stood and wiggled out of her tight black pants. Then she tugged at the waistband of my boxers until I lifted my ass so she could remove them as well. I straightened myself on the couch with by back to the cushions and feet flat on the floor. Colbie took that as an invitation to climb into my lap. There were few places I'd rather have her than right where she was. I had access to her pussy, her ass, her tits, and her mouth. And when Cole rode me, I took advantage of all four. There was nothing better than watching her come undone in my hands and on my dick and then being able to hold her when she collapsed into my arms. All of which she did.

Completely bare, totally vulnerable, and fully exposed, Colbie leaned back and shattered what we'd just shared. "My mom took away piano last night."

My brow furrowed. Colbie had hid that devastation, although I had no idea why.

"Why didn't you tell me? Jesus, Colbie." That was a tad bit more important than getting my rocks off, regardless of just how good her pussy felt.

She hopped up and quickly got dressed.

I shouldn't have raised my voice, much less yelled. I never wanted to scare her. "Baby, I'm sorry. I didn't mean to holler. I don't understand. What do you mean she took piano away?" I stood—still naked—bringing her to my chest. I held her close with one hand on the back of her head and one on the small of her back.

It only took seconds for her to close her arms around my waist. "Caleb and Chasity think I do too much, and it's taking a toll on me. They suggested to my parents that I give up piano to finish the school year strong." Her words were broken between ragged breaths, but I'd still understood what she'd said.

I also hated Caleb and his stupid fucking wife. I had been rendered speechless. There wasn't a single word that came to mind.

But she wasn't done. "And I'm not allowed to run more than

three miles a day. Daddy tried to insist that I limit that to five days a week." She held on tight, and I waited for more. "But I got my way on that." Her body shook with sobs that I couldn't soothe. "Eli, they locked the piano last night."

Caleb had done the exact opposite of what I'd suggested. Not only had he involved Chasity the shrew, he'd taken the only thing she cared about and the one thing none of them did—music. If they thought this would solve any issue Colbie had, they were sorely mistaken. The four of them had just compounded the problem exponentially. If he'd accomplished this at home, there was no doubt in my mind that he'd cut her off at the school as well. She wouldn't have access to the practice rooms, and I was quite certain, they'd stop payments to Dr. Chalmers.

I didn't have a clue where to begin to fix any of this. "I'm so sorry, Cole. So fucking sorry." And I was. I could have lied to Caleb and said I hadn't noticed anything. If I'd had any idea this would've been the end result, I would have. I would've lied through my teeth and then done everything I could to protect Colbie until the end of the year when I could get her out of here.

Instead, I had to figure out how to care for the broken piece of this fallen woman.

"Baby, please don't cry. We'll figure something out. I promise."

She remained quiet until the sobs no longer racked her body and her eyes had dried. Colbie was tough, but I didn't want her to have to be strong, not about this. I shouldn't be grateful that she'd been able to salvage her workouts because they only aided in her weight loss; however, they were the excuse she used to see me outside of school. Yet if I had to pick which I wanted for her, I would have waited until graduation—as much as that would have killed me—so she could have continued with piano. Knowing Caleb and Chasity, they had likely rallied in her corner for exercise and the mental and physical benefits it offered. I was just surprised her parents had so easily scrapped piano. They were both bright, educated people who should have known the benefits of music were just as valuable as physical activity, which led me to wonder how much they'd actually considered Colbie's wellbeing versus just doing what Caleb and Chasity suggested.

As much as I didn't want to admit it, her parents' response was just further proof of how far removed they were from Colbie's life and needs.

"Is that it?"

She pulled back, although I didn't let her go far. "Is that *it*? Did you hear what I said?"

"I didn't mean it like that. I just need to know if those are the only restrictions they placed on you, or if we have other things to work around."

Her forehead wrinkled as her dark brows drew in. "Like what?"

"I don't know. Did they take your car?"

She laughed, but it wasn't formed from humor. "Are you kidding? That would mean they'd have to drive me to school and pick me up. No, there was no mention of my car."

"How are they tracking how far you run?"

"My watch. Why?" Colbie hadn't thought about what that might mean because she wasn't a manipulative teen, nor did she do things she'd get in trouble for—at least not before me.

I already knew she used the workout app and that GPS tracked her whereabouts. "You might want to stop tracking your runs."

She dropped her hands from my waist to her side, leaving cold spots where her body heat had been. "Why?"

"Because they might figure out that they start and stop at my house."

Colbie covered her mouth when she gasped. Clearly, she hadn't considered their ability to actually follow her. Her innocence shone through in the glimmer of her eyes.

I captured her jaw, and she dropped her hand. Once I was certain I had her attention, I made her a promise. "We will figure this out." Or I would. Either way, I wouldn't let them steal anything from her. "But, Cole?"

She stared up at me with wonder. "Yeah?"

"That means you're going to have to start talking to me about what's going on up here." I tapped her head. "And you've got to stop losing weight."

That hit a nerve. Her expression went from hopeful naïveté to resentment in one breath. "What's that supposed to mean?" She folded her arms and cocked her hip to the side. The woman who'd arrived on my back porch this morning had returned.

I hated doing this. I didn't want to. But Colbie wanted me to talk to her and not her family, so this was me doing just that. "You've lost a lot of weight since we first met. Weight you didn't have to lose."

Colbie's crimson-tinged lips pursed, and her eyes narrowed to a fierce angle.

"I've contributed to that by running as many miles as you wanted because I was selfish and that was the only way I could spend time with you." I had to push forward when she stepped back and out of my reach. "But baby, your clothes hang on your thin frame, and I can't help but wonder if the dark circles under your eyes are from lack of sleep or malnourishment—"

"So Chasity blasts me for how *much* I eat, and you're telling me I don't eat *enough*? Seriously, people wonder why girls have eating disorders. Do you hear yourself? Why does *anyone* care what I do or don't put into my mouth?"

I didn't attempt to close the distance between us; Colbie had her guard up. I had to bring it down. "I don't know about Chasity, but I care because I love you. And I need the healthiest version of you for *us*." We hadn't talked about the future beyond graduation, but just because we hadn't discussed it didn't mean I hadn't thought about it. I hoped it wasn't too much for her to handle with everything else that had been thrown at her in the last twelve hours. "At some point, I want you to take my last name. And after you finish school and get your practice set up, I hope that you'd want to carry our children. I want to see the world with you, I want to see you on stage again, I want to see you do everything your heart desires. But you can't do any of those things if you're sick."

"You're being melodramatic, Eli." Her words said one thing while her body language said another. Even the roll of her eyes didn't deter me, nor did her dismissal of my heartfelt confession regarding our future.

I took the chance and stepped forward. Thankfully, Colbie didn't push me away, even if she hadn't reciprocated my touch. I was okay with that as long as she knew I wasn't going anywhere. "Baby, I'm not asking you to make any drastic changes. I just want you to keep letting me in. Talking to me about what you want, what you need, what makes you happy or sad."

"I already do that," she whined. And she did to some extent.

"I'm greedy. I want it all. The good, the bad, the ugly and everything in between. You're mine to love and care for, to protect." I tucked her hair behind her ear, and she leaned into my palm and placed a kiss there. "I have to know where the demons are to battle them. I can't bring light to darkness if I can't find the switches. I'll go to the ends of the earth for you, but I have to have a map to get there, Cole."

A tear slipped past the corner of her eye, and she nodded just enough for me to know she heard my sentiment and not just the words I had said. Colbie never had anyone fighting for her, but I'd come out of the corner with guns blazing if she'd just give me the ammunition.

"I'm scared." That was a start.

I took her hand and led her back to the sofa. My erection had long since gone soft, but I still stood in front of her with nothing on. I slid my boxers to my waist and sat next to her. "About what?"

Colbie couldn't look me in the eye, and I didn't try to encourage it. If she needed to get something out and was more comfortable doing it while staring at her fingers, then I'd take what I could get. "That my dragons will be too big for you to slay. And my darkness too deep for you to penetrate."

"Then we'll learn how to ride the dragons and carry a flashlight. I don't care what it means. I just need you to know I see *you*. I want *you*. Every perfection and every flaw. I love all of you equally."

She still refused to take her focus from her lap. "You wouldn't if you knew what they were."

"Try me."

That got her attention, and she lifted her chin. "What?"

I leaned back and relaxed as if this were an everyday conversation. "Tell me one of your flaws. One you think will turn me away."

Colbie stood abruptly and put her ass in my face. She grabbed the sides of her butt where saddlebags would be if she had any. "This." Her hands jiggled up and down, shaking her money maker. "I'm afraid of being so fat that you won't want me anymore."

While I wished she were joking, it had become painfully obvious in the last day between Jess's comments and Chasity's that Colbie's weight was more than a fad diet gone terribly right. I grabbed her ass and pulled her onto my lap. "I happen to love that ass. And I'd like it even more with more meat on it."

She unclasped my hands that I'd just secured on her abdomen. "Yeah? You like for your girl to have a pooch before she's even had kids? I bet that's a huge turn on."

There was no pooch. I grabbed the spot she referred to. "Baby, that is nothing more than skin from sitting down." I shifted her in my lap. "Look, I have it, too. Does it turn you off?"

"It's not the same. Guys aren't held to the same standard women are." Her fingertips played with the smattering of hair under my navel.

I bounced her on my knees to get her attention. "Does that mean you'd love me less if I gained a few pounds."

"Of course not." The echo in the room was more prominent with the rest of the house silent, and she jumped a bit at the force behind her voice. "I don't care what you look like."

"Yet you think I'm so shallow that I want you to waste away to nothing?"

"That's not what I meant."

I hated not being able to hold her and see her at the same time. While I wanted to reassure her with my touch, I needed her to see the sincerity in my eyes. "Colbie, I am not going to lie to you and tell you that I don't think you're gorgeous. You're the most beautiful woman I've ever laid eyes on, hands down."

"But?"

I snickered when she rolled her eyes and waited for what was to come. "But... I didn't fall in love with the way you fill your jeans or how many ribs I can count on your back when you don't have a shirt on. I don't give a shit about the size of your bra *or* your panties. I fell in love with your mind, your wit, your determination and drive." I shook my head and grinned like a jackass. "The day we met and you put me in my place, I'd never been more turned on in my life. But for the life of me, I can't tell you a single thing you had on or how you looked. I can, however, tell you exactly what you said that put the first chink in my armor."

Colbie raised one brow. She didn't have to tell me she thought I was full of shit. It was written all over her expression.

"Don't believe me?" I asked, excited to burst her fucking bubble.

"Nope."

I cleared my throat and licked my lips. My impression of Colbie might not be spot on but the words were. "'With all due respect, sir, your relationship with Caleb isn't my concern and holds little interest in my life. I don't make a habit of arriving late, but even more so, I don't *slide* in anything academic. Where my brothers want to be star quarterbacks, I'm aiming for valedictorian, and I didn't get there by resting on my laurels or my brother's friendships. Vanderbilt doesn't give a shit who Caleb Chapman is.'"

Her jaw dropped, and I had to force back a laugh. I sucked at throwing my voice, but I got my point across.

"I can't tell you how many times I've jacked off to your voice in my head, saying those very words. And that had nothing to do with your weight or appearance. It had everything to do with the way you challenged me. *That* was the sexiest fucking thing I've ever seen, not a Playboy model or some Barbie in porn. *You.*"

Her fingers slid up my stomach and then moved to my hair. "I want to be perfect for you." Her tone was soft and moved through the air like a spring breeze.

"You already are simply because you're you."

Colbie leaned her side under my shoulder and rested her head in the crook of my neck. This all went much deeper than her desire to please me. It started with her desire to please her parents. And that might be a goal she would never accomplish. What Colbie had to realize was that was on them, not her. She couldn't force them to see her or love her differently. Colbie had to learn to love herself as she was.

And it had just become my mission to help her fall for herself the way she had for me.

I'd been right. The Monday after Thanksgiving break, Colbie came racing into my classroom at lunch. She had been on the verge of tears, but I knew she wouldn't let a single one fall at school.

I closed the door behind her, although I kept my hand on the knob in case anyone tried to enter. It also kept me in sight through the glass in the door if anyone wanted to peer inside. No one would catch me with my hand on her in school—ever. "Take a deep breath, and tell me what's wrong."

She followed my directions, and when her chest rose with her inhalation, my thoughts returned to the memory of her naked in my lap the Saturday before. Her frustration today kept me from grinning. "Caleb!"

I needed more than that to go on. "What did he do?"

"I can't play in the practice rooms." The vein on her neck bulged, and I worried her blood pressure had skyrocketed to an unsafe level as red as her face and chest were. "He got to Mr. Bledsoe and explained the restrictions my parents had put on me." She stomped her foot and clenched her fists. "This has gone too far. Why can't he just leave me alone?"

Colbie plopped down on the edge of my desk in defeat. Jesus, I wanted to go to her, comfort her, kiss her. But there were cameras in every room. And while I doubted the school monitored them all around the clock, neither of us ever needed that indiscretion uncovered. So I held firm at my post.

She looked up expectantly. "He's never given a crap, Eli. *Never*. Why now?" Her color was no longer the crimson color it had been when she'd stormed in, and while I could still see the pulse in her neck, the vein had calmed substantially. "Caleb has nothing to gain from this."

"I don't know, Colbie. If Kendra"—I corrected myself—"Mrs. Cross told him the things she did me, he may be scared."

"You didn't tell me she said anything to you." Her spine straightened, and her brow dipped.

I'd managed to jumble this up because thinking straight took far more effort with her in my classroom alone. "Not about you. She had another student a few years ago, Michael somebody."

"Martin."

I pointed at her. "Yes! Michael Martin. Anyway, she saw a decline in his performance and other warning signs that she regretted not addressing." I shouldn't be discussing any of this with another student. I prayed to God no one listened on the other end of that camera. "Mrs. Cross believes she might have been able to help him had she reached out to his parents or made anyone aware of what she saw."

"Michael Martin killed himself, Eli. I'm not going to put a gun to my head." This was where her short life worked against her. Colbie didn't have the wisdom to go along with the intelligence that simply living brought.

"She didn't think Michael would, either."

"Fine, then why not call my parents instead of my brother?"

That I didn't have a positive answer for. "I can only assume that since Kendra and Caleb grew up together and are now colleagues that she believed he would know how to best handle her concern."

She hopped off the desk and adjusted her backpack that had slid off her shoulder. "Great. My fate rests in the hands of Rudy and Gidget. Lucky me."

I shouldn't have been surprised by Colbie's references, although she probably meant the movies and not the novel. Either way, it was funny. Caleb saw himself as inspirational as Rudy Ruettiger, and Chasity embodied the personality of the boy-crazy surfer girl. "This won't last forever." My level of reassurance sucked. In a high schooler's world, six months was forever. And that was how long her parents and her brother could make her life painful.

"Good talk, Coach."

If we were home, I'd spank that sarcasm right out of her tone. "Colbie, I will find a way to get you in front of a piano."

Her defenses fell and hope brightened the blue in her eyes. "Okay."

"Now, get to class before we both get in trouble." I flicked my stare up to the camera, and her focus followed. "I'll see you tonight."

She nodded and pulled her lips between her teeth. I couldn't swear she did it on purpose, but I had a hard time believing she wasn't aware of the effect she had on me. And that little gesture had me adjusting my slacks when I opened the door.

I glanced at the clock, noting I had about twelve minutes before the next bell. I'd spent my planning period trying to find a used piano online, and while I wanted more than anything to surprise her with one that she could play at my house anytime her heart desired, they were so far out of my price range that they might as well have been mythical creatures—in my world, they didn't exist.

There was only one other thing I might be able to work out, and even that was a long shot. I grabbed my cell from my bag and the card I'd kept in my wallet since I'd received it.

"Hello?"

"May I speak with Dr. Chalmers?" I had no clue what I'd say if he answered. I just knew I didn't have anywhere else to turn.

"This is he."

I glanced out my classroom door and into the hall at the occasional student passing by. "Hey, this is Eli Paxton. I don't know if you remember me—"

"Colbie's boyfriend. Of course. What can I do for you, son?"

Maybe her parents hadn't cut this part off; he certainly didn't sound like he'd lost his star pupil.

I didn't really know where to start. "I, uh— Have you heard from the Chapmans?" I had to remember this man believed I was a high school student, college at best. He had no idea I was Colbie's teacher. "I mean, I know it's none of my business, but—"

"Stop right there. I'm glad you called. I heard from them this morning."

There was no delicate way to approach any of this, so I dove in head first. "Did they end her lessons?"

"Umm, well, I guess that depends on how I interpret what her father said." There was mischief in his tone, and I wondered what the old man had up his sleeve. "Mr. Chapman said they wouldn't be *paying* for lessons for Colbie anymore."

I let out a sigh of relief. This I could swing. I could work it into my budget. "Can you send me the invoices, Dr. Chalmers? I'll take care of them." I didn't have a clue what he charged, but I doubted it came anywhere near the cost of a Steinway.

"Eli, I told you when we met that I love Colbie like a granddaughter. I also told you to call me if you needed anything. I won't bill you for spending time with her."

There was no doubt he believed I was a poor student who would scrounge around to put together the funds to cover his services. "Really, I want to pay you."

"Son, I know how much teachers make. Even those with doctorates. I also know what kind of legal bills you might rack up if anyone finds out that you've taken a special interest in a student. Keep your money. Tell Colbie I'll be waiting for her at four o'clock just like I always am."

My heart hammered in my chest. I wouldn't have to worry about Colbie stroking out if I had a heart attack first. "Sir, I uh—" Stammering only made me appear guilty. "I—it's not... Colbie is just—"

The good-natured chuckle on the other end of the phone stifled my attempt at an explanation. "Life doesn't necessarily present opportunity at the times it's easiest to seize them. They come when they're needed, regardless of the price. Just be careful."

Thank you seemed inappropriate, not that any other words were more acceptable. Stunned, all I could do was agree to his terms. "I will."

He disconnected the call, and I stood next to my desk wondering what the hell had just happened and whether or not I could trust a man I'd only met once. Dr. Chalmers loved Colbie, and that was what I had to keep reminding myself. Sometimes we do things for people we love, even if the world says we shouldn't. Jesus, I hoped to God I never had a daughter. I'd likely have to add murder and body disposal to my list of felonies.

I still had a few minutes before the bell. I had no idea where to begin looking for Colbie if she couldn't be in the practice rooms. The lunch room was empty except for a handful of kids I didn't know. Then by chance, on my way back to my room, I passed her with Jess. Either she read my mind or saw something in my eyes.

"Dr. Paxton, wait."

I turned to see her talking to Jess, who glanced at me and then back to Colbie. Jess waved, and Colbie came in my direction and made sure to announce why she'd stopped me.

"Hey, if I give you my outline, can you give me your feedback before I start the project?" There was no outline nor project, but the teachers in the hall heard her request which was nothing unusual for the star student.

I jerked my head toward my class. "Sure. I've got a few minutes before next period."

We stepped out of the hall and into what would be a cocoon for roughly ninety more seconds.

"What's wrong?" Her panic-stricken eyes darted back and

forth between the door and me. She'd conjured up a lie to tell her friend to make sure I was all right.

"Nothing. I tried all morning to find a used piano that I could put at my house."

"Aww. That was sweet, but they're really expensive, even used."

That I already knew. "You aren't kidding. Anyway, I wanted to tell you before school let out. Dr. Chalmers will be waiting for you at four."

"Why? My parents said they were going to call him to cancel. My dad was supposed to do that this morning."

I nodded. "He did. And I undid it."

"I don't understand."

"Dr. Chalmers gave me his card at the recital and said if you ever needed anything that I should call him."

She gasped. "Please tell me you did *not* call my piano teacher!" If she weren't careful, her shock would ring out into the hall for other people to hear.

"Okay, I didn't call him. But he's still expecting you this afternoon. So don't miss it." I winked, and as much as she wanted to be upset, her eyes twinkled, and she might have danced on her tiptoes in a circle.

The bell rang, and Colbie stopped her pirouette. "You can tell me the details later." She leaned around me to see if anyone could hear her. "And I'll find a million ways to thank you." Colbie waggled her brows in a less than seductive fashion that made me laugh, and then she raced off to her next class.

I'd do anything to see her smile.

14

COLBIE

"Something's different about you." Jess eyed me up and down, standing next to my locker.

I closed the metal door and spun the lock. "Nope. Same old same old."

She leaned her shoulder against the wall, adjusting the strap of her backpack. "Don't lie to me, Colbie. I know you better than anyone. What is it?"

I kept my face free of emotion and stared at her blankly. There was too much water under the bridge to divulge this secret. I loved her. I hoped we could get back to the place we'd been last year. But I didn't trust her. She'd lied to me for months—not just avoided the truth, flat out lied. There was too much at stake.

Jess gasped and pushed off the wall. "Oh my God, it's not *what*, it's *who*!" She smacked my arm and practically knocked me over with the force behind it. "Sorry, that was a bit much. You *have* to tell me."

I turned toward English, dreading walking into his class. Not because I didn't want to see him, but because I didn't want *her* to see *us*. Jess had already told me once that she noticed the way he looked at me. Now she noticed something in me. If she connected the dots that could be disastrous. "There's nothing to tell, Jess."

She grabbed my bicep. "Cut the crap, Colbie. Caden told me about your parents. You should be huddled in a corner rocking back and forth, not glowing like you had the best orgas—"

I clamped my hand tightly over her mouth. "What is wrong with you?" I searched for eavesdroppers and thankfully found none. And when I didn't think she'd holler again, I grabbed her wrist and forced her to move. The faster I got into class, the fewer questions or accusations I'd have to face.

Jess dug in her heels just outside of English and crossed her arms. "I'm not moving from this spot until you tell me what's going on. You've practically been a ghost the last few weeks, your parents annihilated you, and instead of sulking, you're shining. Spill it."

I had to give her something, and I didn't want it to be a lie. It also couldn't be the truth. It was a precarious position I found myself in, and the irony wasn't lost on me. The difference between what Jess and Caden had done and what I was about to do was the detail. "If I tell you, you can't tell Caden."

Jess crossed her heart and salivated for what she thought would be a salacious secret. And in a way, it was, just not the way she expected. "Scouts honor."

I rolled my eyes at her ridiculous pledge—she'd never been a scout—and lowered my voice to keep from being overheard. There were eyes and ears all over this school, and anything could get back to Caleb and, therefore, my parents. "I'm still seeing Dr. Chalmers every day after school."

Her jaw dropped as did her arms. "You're kidding me, right?"

I shook my head with a smile.

"*That* is your big secret? You have clandestine meetings with your hundred-year-old piano teacher?" She cocked her head to the side, bored by my life. "You really need to get out more, Colbie.

That's just pitiful. And totally not worth getting in trouble over if your parents find out."

The indifference in my shrug must have been convincing because she started toward the door.

As we walked in together, she kept talking. "I don't even want to know how that happened. The less information I have the better."

Eli glanced at me with worry lining his brow. With an almost imperceptible shake of my head, I reassured him it wasn't what it sounded like without saying a word. The bell rang.

"Ladies, gossip after class. The next fifty-one minutes belong to me." Eli held his hand out to show me which seat I belonged in.

It was the first time things had felt normal in months. Jess acted like my best friend instead of my brother's girlfriend. Eli had showed me just how much he loved me after our three-mile run this morning. And while I hadn't exposed all of my demons, I felt like I was doing better keeping them at bay. My parents had never asked what I did in the afternoons after they cancelled my piano lessons, so I hadn't been forced to make anything up there, either.

My stress level was manageable, even with midterms fast approaching and Christmas on the horizon. I'd made it three days without sticking my fingers down my throat or eating my emotions. And while that might not have seemed like much to anyone other than me, it was a hard battle fought. One I promised myself I'd keep fighting. It didn't matter that I only fought it to keep from admitting it to Eli. The end result was the same. I cringed each time I stepped on the scale, and I diverted my eyes from the mirror when I got out of the shower. I hadn't gained any weight, but I hadn't lost any more. Nevertheless, I had to have one day before I could manage one year.

"Ms. Chapman?" Eli stared at me, expecting a response to a question I clearly hadn't heard.

I stared at him, willing him to repeat what he'd said...or for anyone to blurt out the answer and save me. No one did. "I'm sorry. I didn't hear the question."

He pointed toward the chalkboard while staring me down. "Have you heard *any* of the discussion?"

I sucked on my teeth and wished he'd call on someone else. Thankfully, Jess and Joey came to my rescue. I didn't have a clue what they were talking about, but it distracted Eli enough to let me off the hook. I'd hear about my lack of focus later, but I'd be able to show him just how well I could focus outside of his classroom.

When the bell rang and he dismissed us, I darted out the door with Jess on my heels. She caught up with me not far down the hall. It was about the same time my phone chirped with a text message.

Not thinking, I pulled my phone from my pocket right as she sidled up next to me.

Eli: What the hell was that, Cole?

"Cole?" The sassy smirk and raised brows said everything she hadn't.

I slid my phone back into my pocket and ignored Eli. "Jess, please." For once, just once, I hoped she respected my privacy. After the stunt at dinner about the track team, I couldn't chance her slipping anything to Caden or in front of my parents.

She relented, threw her arm around my shoulder, and turned us both down the hall. "At least I can take satisfaction knowing I was right. Is he everything we thought he'd be?"

"Jessica McLean, you're gross. I am *not* doing this."

"You know you want to compare notes. And you're dying to tell someone what you've been up to. That someone should definitely be me."

Even the noise of a couple hundred kids padding down the corridor didn't drown out her plea for information. I reached up and pulled my hair into a messy ponytail, anything to distract myself and her.

"Not here." If I got her to concede to another time, I might get lucky and she'd forget, or at the very least, it bought me time to determine what I would willingly share.

She spun in a circle. "My house after piano then. My parents have a charity benefit. Actually, I think your parents are going, too. I'll order pizza, and we can kick back while you dish out the goods."

Jess skipped into her next class. And I stood there watching her go, unsure of what I'd just agreed to.

"Colbie?" Mrs. Cross held her door open. "Care to join us?"

I just wanted the day to end. That wasn't true. I needed school to end and whatever time I had to spend with Jess to pass quickly, so I could get to the part of my night that I enjoyed. Eli.

The anxiety had built all day, and while I'd managed to avoid eating lunch, my willpower waned when I reached Jess's. She'd ordered from our favorite pizza place. I smelled it the moment I walked into her house. The hollow feeling created by nerves turned into hunger. I kept thinking the apprehension would cease once I got there and we started talking. It did not.

"Are you ever going to admit it?" Pizza dangled from her fingers, and the cheese threatened to slide off if she didn't take a bite.

I picked at mine, trying not to overindulge. One piece wouldn't hurt, and I wouldn't have to run it off. Although, obsessing about that didn't help. "Admit what?" I pulled a piece of pepperoni from the top and tilted my head back to drop it in my mouth. I counted the number of times I chewed to make sure I got the full flavor. And if this turned into more than I wanted it to, having chewed well would make the ending much less painful.

"Don't play dumb. You're sleeping with Dr. Paxton."

This was unfamiliar territory for me. And Jess for that matter. The two of us had never gossiped about boys or dating or sex. "Can you keep your voice down?" I searched the house, swiveling the bar stool I sat on.

"There's no one here, Colbie. I'm not going to tell anyone."

I huffed and grinned.

She pulled her foot onto the seat where she sat. Her thin leg looked like the stem of a flower, and her jeans fit her perfectly. "Hey! That's not fair. I've never spilled any of your secrets to anyone."

My pizza hit the paper plate with a splat. "You tried to." And I wiped my fingers on a paper towel.

"When?" Jess was on the verge of laughing at my accusation.

"Dinner with my parents. Track. Cross Country. Ring a bell?"

She smirked and took a bite of her pizza. When she began to speak with a mouth full of food, I would have given her anything she wanted to get her to stop. "Are you still talking about that? That was ages ago. Admit it." Her leg fell to the side, creating a triangle. Jess's stomach was flat and her breasts perfect for her size. It was hard not to envy her. She was as close to a walking goddess as I'd ever seen.

"It was like a month ago!"

"You're stalling."

"You're prying."

She leaned forward and put her forehead on mine, our noses almost touching. Jess hadn't done that since we were little. I'd always hated how distorted she looked that close up, which was precisely why she did it now. To get me to give in.

"Fine. *Yes*. I'm sleeping with him." *Shit*.

Jess sat back, stunned, and a bit of slimy crust fell from her mouth. "Seriously?" She tried to catch the food as it fell, but when she missed, I watched that crumb bounce off her leg.

I slapped my hands on my thighs. "You already knew. Why are you acting so shocked?"

She snorted. "I just thought you had a serious crush on your older brother's best friend. I didn't *really* think you'd had sex."

This was why I didn't do this type of thing. I sucked at it. "Well, now you know." I snatched my slice off the plate and tore at it with my teeth. "I bet you're super glad you asked." It was difficult to understand as I talked around cheese and crust.

"What was it like?" She swallowed and then hit my knee. "Wait. You said *sleeping*, as in present tense, meaning more than once and still happening." Her eyes grew and the whites outweighed the blue.

Jess wanted details, to compare notes. The problem was, I wasn't interested in hearing about my little brother and them sneaking around, having sex in random places. And I didn't want to tell *anyone* about Eli, not because I was ashamed, but because it was private. I couldn't imagine he'd be thrilled to know Jess had asked about the size of his penis and what he looked like naked, much less the nuances of how he took my virginity and the first time he told me he loved me. Even though I knew those were things best friends shared, my tongue got thick and my mouth went dry. In order to keep from sharing more than I had to and listen more than I wanted to, I shoveled slice after slice of crusty goodness into my mouth. Each calorie laden slice went down with ease until I'd lost track of how many I'd consumed.

The weight in my stomach settled my nerves, and the peace in my head calmed the anxiety in my heart. Until the weight turned to lead and my thoughts raced. It had happened before I could stop it, and now, in order to relieve it, I had to find solace, control, and a bathroom.

"So you guys have sex like every day?" She kept talking, even though she wasn't really getting answers. "I can't imagine how hard it would be to pretend like he's just your teacher every day." Jess had no clue she rambled to herself. "Is it hard to watch other girls at school flirt with him?" She cocked her head. Apparently, she thought that question deserved a response.

I pushed my stomach with the heel of my hand. "No. Is it hard to watch girls flirt with Caden? It's no different." The gurgling started, and I guzzled water. It didn't matter how well I'd chewed, bread always came up in painful clumps. And by the time I'd started on piece number two, I'd stopped counting the number of times my teeth came together before I swallowed.

That wasn't a thought she'd considered. "Who flirts with him?"

"Every underclassman he comes in contact with. Even a couple guys. Are you blind?"

"No more so than you are. What are you going to do after graduation? You're still going to Tennessee, right?"

This was the problem with not dating throughout high school and waiting until our senior year. Questions other girls didn't have ran rampant in our minds. "Of course I'm going to college. Are you planning to ditch Georgia Tech for Caden?"

She popped the top on a can of Diet Coke and sipped. "No, but it's not that far away. He can come see me or I can come home every night if that's what we want to do. That's not the case with Nashville. Are you guys going to stay together?"

I didn't know. We hadn't talked about any of this. He'd indicated he wanted to, but we hadn't had an actual discussion about the logistics or commitment that would follow when I left. "I don't know, Jess. It's still six months away. A lot can happen."

"You better hope your parents don't find out." She set down her can to pick absentmindedly at her nails.

There had to have been a reason I came here other than to be tortured; however, I couldn't think of it. "I need to use the bathroom." Panic had risen in my chest. My train of thought only went one direction, and that track led to a commode.

I hopped up—as casually as possible—and went to the bathroom I'd always used at her house after meals. No one else ever used the guest bath, so they wouldn't have to endure any lingering smell. She believed it, and I had kept using it until it was habit. And even though it had been a while, I followed the same routine.

My eyes burned by the time I locked the door and flipped on the fan, and a knot had formed in my chest. If this ache weren't familiar, I'd swear it was a heart attack, or at the very least, the worst case of indigestion I'd ever experienced. My stomach stretched and bent to my will, accommodating, albeit briefly, the amount of food I'd needed to ease the emotional pain. The three days I'd fought so hard for were about to go down the drain, literally.

I wanted to stop it. I didn't want to do it. But I had to let it out—the torment, the pressure, the stress, and most importantly, my own disappointment.

Tears filled my eyes before my fingers ever touched the back of my throat. By doing this, I failed. My emotions had ruled, and I'd bowed to their reign. No one would ever understand the power the mind had over reason. It was a war I'd lost before I ever stepped onto the battlefield. Eli deserved better, but I couldn't give him the best of myself if I felt the way I currently did. That would only come when I'd expelled all the bad that I'd consumed.

I had to be in control.

The guilt would pass.

Without another moment of hesitation, I stuck my fingers in my mouth. And I kept doing it until the first burst came. My esophagus expanded and stung as I wretched. The water hadn't helped as much as I'd hoped, and the clumps kept getting stuck in my throat. I'd gag and choke with my air passage clogged with dough, and forcefully have to swallow just to breathe, only to repeat the same process until I was empty.

Except this time, it wasn't just my stomach that was void. I'd never felt more reckless than I did in that moment. The tranquility that normally followed a binge and purge never came. The racing thump of my heart took residence in my ears, and I gasped for air when I slid down the wall and onto the floor. Every rib, up and down both sides, were as bruised as my pride.

There was no relief.

No calm.

Nothing but shame.

"Colbie, you okay in there?"

I wiped my tear-stained face, realizing my hand was covered in thick saliva and bile. "Yeah, my stomach was just a bit upset. I'll be out in a minute."

Her voice was muffled through the wood of the door. "Are you crying?"

I swallowed hard and prayed I was able to mask the edge in my voice. "Not at all. Why?" I stood, holding my hand out as I pushed off the floor. And my face crumpled at the reflection staring back at me from the mirror.

Her frantic knock echoed in my head. "Open the door, Colbie. I'm not kidding." The knob rattled and the wood shook. "Colbie!"

I couldn't let her see this. Not the mess in the bathroom. If she found me crying, I could lie my way out. There would be no getting out of the vomit all over my hand and her toilet.

"Let me in!" Jess had gone from knocking and speaking, to banging her hand flat on the surface and screaming.

Ignoring her cries, I flushed the toilet and then turned on the faucet to wash my hands. When the sound of rushing water no longer filled the room, I realized Jess's voice didn't, either. But I couldn't open the door until I had composed myself. Maybe she'd recognized that I just needed a minute. I took the reprieve she offered and curled up in the corner. Once I caught my breath and cleared my head, I'd go out and tell her I had a panic attack. Or that I got a bit overwhelmed. She'd be shocked, but she wouldn't believe I was lying.

But each time I started to inhale, tears rushed and flowed over my lashes. I couldn't stop them no matter how hard I fought. My lungs refused to fill, and fire ate at my insides. The demon was winning because I hadn't been strong enough to keep him in the cage.

The knob rattled again, and I peered up through puffy eyes and pools of tears just as the door swung open.

Eli didn't say a word when he moved toward me or when he bent down to slide an arm under my legs and one behind my back. And he remained silent when he lifted me and curled me into his chest where I buried my head and hid.

"I'll figure out what to do about her car." Step after step, Eli held me. "Thanks for calling, Jess."

Jess had reached out to Eli. Which meant Eli knew I'd spilled our secret. I'd freaked out my best friend and betrayed my boyfriend.

My entire body jolted in sobs. "I'm sorry, Eli." It was incoherent at best.

"Shh, there's nothing to be sorry for." He helped me into his truck, fastened the seatbelt around me, and closed the door.

When he got in the other side, I unbuckled my seatbelt and slid across the bench into his side. He welcomed me with a protective arm, and held me tightly without so much as a word the few blocks to his house.

Eli gingerly untucked me from his body when he put the

truck in park and turned off the ignition. The door swung wide, and he stepped down. "Cole?" His voice was gravelly and thick as though my name had caught in his throat.

I peered up to his trembling lip and then took his outstretched hand. My fingers weaved through his, and I squeezed until he did the same. Walking took energy I didn't have; nevertheless, I followed him through his back door, down the hall, and into his bedroom. Eli didn't turn on a light, and the moon only provided enough light to see his silhouette when he removed his shirt.

My eyes adjusted to the darkness about the time he kicked off his shoes and then dropped his pants. I had no idea what he was doing, but I was surprised sex was on his mind when he'd just picked me up off a bathroom floor. I'd never seen him move the way he did right now, it was more than just slow—he was heavy. Every motion laborious.

I reached out with trembling hands. The tips of my fingers were cold against his heated skin. His sudden movement startled me, and I yelped when he grabbed my wrist. The sound hadn't even left my mouth completely before Eli had yanked me to him and cradled the back of my head in his palm. My cheek was flush with his pec, and I wound my arms around his waist.

"You scared the fuck out of me, Colbie. I had no idea what the hell was going on when Jess called from your phone." He struggled to speak, overcome with emotion. "She didn't know what was going on or what you were doing. She couldn't get to you..." When he swallowed, his arms constricted, and the muscles in his chest moved. "I would have torn that door down if I'd had to."

The darkness clung to the silence, and the moon gave us privacy. His hands slid down my back and beneath the hem of my shirt. Like a child, I raised my arms. The fabric swooshed to the ground and puddled at our feet. Eli leaned back just a hair to unbutton my jeans so I could shimmy out of them. He made no attempt to remove my panties, and he'd left on his boxers.

Before I realized what he had done, Eli had me in his arms, moving to the bed. Cradled in his embrace, I worried what would come next. He laid me down and pulled a blanket over me before crawling under it himself. I lifted my head to allow him to slide his arm under my neck and went willingly when he splayed a hand across my stomach and got as close to me as he could.

"What happened tonight?" He'd gotten me undressed, surrounded me with his fortress, and ensured I felt protected so I'd open up.

Skin to skin.

Halfheartedly, I raised one shoulder and let it drop. It was futile. Eli wouldn't let this go.

"Colbie."

The tears started again and before I lost control, I gave up something he wanted. "A dragon got loose."

"Do you want to tell me about it?"

I didn't, not even a little. I also didn't want him to leave me. "I got overwhelmed."

He released a breath I hadn't realized he held, and it was mighty. Eli allowed his hand to roam over my hip and down the outside of my thigh. His touch soothed the ache that burned inside. Maybe he'd expected more, or possibly, he didn't realize what "overwhelmed" encompassed.

"Jess asked me to come over."

"Baby, she's your best friend. That should be a good thing, especially with all that's happened with Caden."

Blood tinged my taste buds when I bit my lip and fought against yelling. This wasn't Eli's fault, and I couldn't attack him. "She wanted to *talk*." I let that sink in for a moment. "She kept badgering me about why I was glowing and demanding that I tell her what was going on." God, I didn't want to tell him the rest. "And I slipped. I yelled at her that I was sleeping with you." And then it became word vomit. "I thought it would stop once I told her the truth, but it didn't. She wanted details. Details I didn't feel right sharing, and not because I'm ashamed but because they're ours. I didn't want to tell anyone about how you took my virginity or the size of your dick." My chest heaved as I let it fly. "I don't know how to do that type of girl talk. And I don't want to learn. By the time I escaped to the bathroom, I had nearly hyperventilated, and I'd exposed us to someone I wasn't sure I could trust. It spiraled." *This* purge felt better than any I'd experienced recently, and quite possibly ever.

He took note of every word I said. Each sentiment he accounted for. Eli felt my pain, my embarrassment, my anxiety. And I knew he did, because he loved me and never quibbled over showing me just how much.

I was out of breath and waiting for a reply when he pushed me to my back and rolled on top of me. It didn't take him long to settle between my legs, flesh to flesh, eye to eye. He tucked away my hair and kissed my nose. "I'm not upset with you." He kept his weight on his forearm, although I'd give anything for him to halt the discussion in favor of a kiss. "I'm honored that you want to keep the details of our love life away from prying eyes. I'm a little jealous you were able to confide in someone. I want to shout from the highest mountain how much I adore you, tell the world of your unexpected arrival in my life. But baby, any time you reach a point that you're uncomfortable—in any situation—call me."

"Eli, I can't just call you anytime I freak out."

The pad of his thumb brushed over my lips like he tried to wipe away what I'd just said. "You can. I expect you to." He searched my face, even in the darkness. "I will always come for you."

I averted my eyes, staring at something I could see in the dark. "Do you think I'm a basket case?" No part of me cared to hear him say yes, but I needed to know.

He nudged my chin and found my gaze. "Not at all. And I

won't the next time you call me or the time after that or a hundred breakdowns from now. My job is to protect you. I can't do that if I don't know you need help."

"You're going to get tired of the damsel in distress routine."

He rolled over and pulled me with him. "It's anything but routine. And I'll take every opportunity afforded me to show you how much I love you. Plain and simple. I'm sorry that you're in a position where you get so worked up you get physically ill. If we can get through the next six months, that won't be an issue again."

I pushed myself up and straddled his lap. "Physically ill?"

"Jess said she heard you throwing up and crying." His hands drifted from my butt around my hips and down my thighs.

I'd given him a sliver, and thankfully, he hadn't asked for the whole pie. Eli accepted that my anxiety worked me up to the point of panic, and he let it go at that. I took his hand and leaned back to pull him to a seated position. Once he sat back against the headboard, I leaned in, needing to taste his mouth. Just before our lips collided, I realized I hadn't brushed my teeth and stopped myself.

"What's wrong?"

I covered my mouth so as not to expose him to what had to be horrible halitosis. "I haven't brushed my teeth."

He chuckled and popped my butt. "Hop up. There's an unopened toothbrush under the sink. I need to call Jess back anyhow."

"What are you going to say?"

Eli pressed his lips to my forehead. "I'm going to have her tell her parents that you didn't feel well and fell asleep. And I'm going to ask her to text her parents to let your parents know that you'll come home before school tomorrow to get ready."

There were some benefits to being in love with an older man. He'd done things six years earlier and could coach me through them. Like this.

"Then, I'm going to come back in here and take the rest of my clothes off. And I hope to find you the same way except under the blankets."

A grin spread my lips and lifted my cheeks. The anticipation of his return emptied my head of negative thoughts, and that tingle just below my pubic bone caught my attention. Eli wasn't ashamed of me or my meltdown. He'd clear things up with Jess, and I could apologize to her in the morning. No one had to know that I'd stuck my fingers down my throat. I could start over tomorrow and have three days under my belt again in no time.

SURPRISINGLY, OPENING UP, EVEN JUST THE LITTLE THAT I had with Eli, had lifted a weight. We'd spent more time just hanging out and talking. I loved sitting on his back porch, staring at the woods while we shared stories of our childhood or friends. The two of us sat there watching lightning bugs flicker as the sun set, and I told him how my brothers and I tried to catch them and keep them in jars when we were all little.

His phone vibrated on the table, and he leaned over to see who it was. "It's my mom. Do you care if I take this?"

"No." I giggled. "Go ahead." I didn't know what his mom knew or didn't know about us. I hadn't had the courage to ask.

He watched me intently when he slid his thumb across the glass, and his stare became heated as he lifted the phone to his ear. "Hello?"

I put my bare foot on his knee and pretended like I wasn't trying to overhear both sides of the conversation. The damn birds chirped like they were co-conspirators at keeping me in the dark. If they didn't shut up, I'd miss the whole thing.

"Colbie and I are on the back porch."

My toes drifted under the space between his shorts and

thighs, but he didn't stop me as I approached his crotch. Instead, he spread his legs wider to give me better access and allowed me to play until my heart was content. It seemed a bit devious with his mom practically on the porch with us, but if he wouldn't push me away, then I wouldn't pull back.

"No, Mom. I can't bring her home with me. I'm fairly certain her family expects her to be at their house for Christmas. Maybe next year."

Eli ran his hand up my shin as far as he could reach and teased my calf on his way back down without ever missing a beat in his conversation. I wondered how far I could take this game without so much as a hitch in his breath, but I wasn't brazen enough to try. Not yet.

"I realize I went to their house for Thanksgiving, but I live here, Ma."

His mouth remained closed, and every once in a while, I'd hear a bit of a murmur from her end, but between the frogs, the crickets, and the birds, I was none the wiser to anything she said to her son.

"Yeah, I know. I promise. I'll see you in a couple weeks."

My head jerked up from where it played eye spy with his shorts and the temptation that hid inside them. By the time he had disconnected, it was obvious he'd flipped a switch of concern.

"You're going to Michigan?"

"Just for a few days over break."

I withdrew my foot from the game I'd been playing, folded my arms over my chest, and pouted. It wasn't fair to punish him for going to see his family; nevertheless, it didn't change my frustration. A hole started to open in my chest, an ache, a longing—he hadn't even left, and I was already going mental.

The rumble of Eli's laughter drowned out nature's white noise. He leaned forward and pulled my chair close to him. His lips met my cheek, then my jaw, down my neck, and finally my collar bone. I couldn't help the visible reaction that pebbled my skin every time he touched me. "Don't pout, baby. I won't be gone long. And after this, there won't be a holiday we have to spend apart."

"I'm still not happy."

His fingers slid behind my ear, likely moving hair from my face. Every time he did it, my heart melted at his gentle approach. This man was muscle and brawn and everything testosterone on the outside. The complete opposite of what I got from him. Sincerity, kindness, love. Eli was as tender as he was strong. If hearts could bench press, he'd be a world champion lifter.

I relented when I gave in to the softness of his warm brown eyes, the crinkle of his crow's feet, and the tip of his lip when he smirked. "I'm just going to miss you. It's silly, I know."

"It's not silly. I don't want to go without you, and had my mom told me before she bought a plane ticket, I would have found a way to get out of it."

Being mature wasn't what it was cracked up to be. "That's not fair to you or them. I'm sure they miss you."

"They can't wait to meet you. My mom was still trying to buy you a ticket to come with me."

I had a hard time believing his parents knew the details of our relationship. "How much have you told them?"

He sat back and propped his feet on the table, clearly quite pleased with himself. "Everything."

"I'm sorry, what?" That could mean a lot of things. Technically, it couldn't. Everything only had one definition, but maybe he meant everything about my personality. Or everything about what we did together. Not *everything*, everything. "Surely not."

"Why are you so surprised?"

"They know *every*thing?" My mouth hung in waiting while he nodded. "Like my age?" *Yes*. "My family ties?" *Yes*. "That I'm in high school." *Yes*. "That you're my teacher?" *Yes*. Every question received the same smirk followed by the same nod of confirmation, and truth danced in his eyes, twinkling. "That you took my virginity?" I raised my brows, expecting him to finally concede that they didn't know quite as much as he wanted me to believe.

"That was a little more difficult ground to cover, but yes."

I swatted at his arm. "Eli! Why would you tell your mom that? She's going to think I'm awful."

He flinched, even though I'd barely touched him. "I tell my mom and dad everything. We've always been really close. And she loves you because she knows I do."

I covered my face, embarrassed. Heat seeped from my neck up my cheeks, and I imagined I was as ripe as a tomato on the vine. "Oh my God," I muttered through my fingers.

"Baby, I promise you, it's not a big deal. As a matter of fact, she threatened me—so did my dad—after I told her."

"I don't even want to know why." I couldn't bring myself to quit hiding.

"Because my dad is the only man she's ever been with. And my dad told me I had damn well better have known before I accepted that gift that you were *it*, or he'd beat my ass himself."

There wasn't a world I could picture where children were that frank with their parents and their parents were that receptive to the children. "They don't care that I'm your student? Or that I'm six years younger than you?"

Eli hesitated to answer and chewed on the inside of his cheek. "There were some lengthy—and rather heated—discussions, but in the end, my mom asked me if you were worth taking the chance of losing my career and my best friend."

My hands fell to my lap, and I held my breath until he spoke again. My heart didn't beat, the world didn't spin. Reality ceased to exist for just a split second.

"I told her I'd walk away from it all. And that's when she

knew. It also became the point that she started driving me insane to meet you."

My pulse sputtered and ticked back into gear, nature started to sing, and the earth resumed its rotation. Eli Paxton was the epitome of perfection, or possibly just perfect for me.

15

COLBIE

I HAD DONE A FANTASTIC JOB OF NOT FOCUSING ON ELI leaving, so much so, that I pretended it wasn't happening. But the night before his flight, the sight of his suitcase on his bed prevented me from lying to myself any longer.

His neatly folded clothes in his luggage twisted that success into a fear of failure, and my imagination took flight with what ifs. The walls hummed and breathed, swelling with each inhalation, closing in. The fan spun overhead with gale force winds. And I struggled to clear the panic away and grasp reality. Weakness shook my knees, and my legs trembled without their support.

If I hadn't seen his face, I would have thought the wind had blown me away or the walls had swallowed me. It was neither. Eli had scooped me up and carried me out of the room.

"Colbie, stay with me."

I clung to his voice like a life raft. And each time I started to slip away, he roped me back in.

"Baby, talk to me." There was no fear or worry in his tone, just love and patience. "Breathe in." He did as he instructed so I could follow along. "And out." Slowing down his intake and exhale with each set. "In...and out."

The quicksand I'd found myself standing in dissipated. The electric roar of the walls died off. And my heart decided to beat in time with Eli's. The fog cleared, and all that remained was a man with endless patience and faithful love.

He stroked my hair and held me in his arms on his couch. "Panic attack?"

How the hell he recognized that I'd never know. "Yeah. It came on really fast. I normally have warning and can control them." There was no reason to admit all that other than to try not to feel like I was broken. I didn't have them often, or maybe I'd just learned how to stave them off before they turned into full-blown incidents.

"You know I don't want to leave you tomorrow, right?"

Another thing I loved about him—to add to the already extensive list—he understood without explanation. "Yeah."

"I'll be back in a week."

Seven days had never seemed that long until I thought about living them without Eli. I hated that I'd gone from not needing anyone to panicking at the notion of being away from someone. It was weak. That was the last thing I ever aspired to be. "I'll be fine." Rationally, I was well aware that I wouldn't die without Eli around. Emotionally, I was a train that had already left the track.

I just needed to be close to him. As close as possible. That connection would tide me over until he got back, or so I hoped when I lifted my torso so my lips could bond with his. Eli always gave me what I needed, and this was no different.

"Eli..." I breathed his name between kisses. "I need you."

"I'm right here, baby." His whisper drove me as mad as his touch; I felt them both the same way.

I shifted in his lap, trying to get situated under him. When he pushed up onto one arm so I could move, I tugged his shirt over his head and left it hanging on the arm that held his weight. He tossed it to the floor as he stood. Eli pulled me up from the couch. My shoulders slumped, and a groan of disappointment might have passed my lips.

My complaining did nothing to deter Eli. He removed my shirt, my bra, and then my shorts and panties. As quickly as mine had disappeared, his did the same, freeing his firm erection with a bit of a spring. I immediately reached for it. I wanted my fingers wrapped around it and then my lips, to taste him, to hear him moan my name. But he stepped out of reach, crouched at the waist, and lunged forward—not with any force—tossing me onto his shoulder. My ass stung from the smack of his hand, and the reverberated slap in the room made me grin.

Then, with each foot he put forward, my smile fell. But Eli turned off the hall before he reached his room and flipped me off his shoulder and onto the guest bed. Relief washed over me. Eli didn't have to be reminded that his room had triggered the panic attack.

Once he covered me with his body, I forgot about the anxiety I'd felt and the fact that he was leaving. Being with Eli, having all of him devoted to me, was all-encompassing. It numbed me to the outside world, it shifted my thinking, it strengthened my resolve. He made me better.

He also made me scream.

"Eli," I panted his name on the brink of euphoria. It was a high I never wanted to relinquish.

And when he followed me over the edge and into the orgasm, he nestled his lips near my ear. His breath as devoted as his words. "I love you, Cole."

As I LISTENED TO THE MOST UNLIKELY THING I'D EVER heard—Chasity and Jess making plans to attend a bowl game together with my brothers—I feasted, although not mindlessly. It was calculated. Every bite I took was used to drown them out and feed my relentless need for satisfaction.

For most teens, Christmas break was the best time of the school year. For me, it was torture. Since the lessons I took from Dr. Chalmers were at a college, the campus was closed, and thereby took with it my daily dose of piano. Eli would have been a fabulous distraction, but he'd been gone since the day Christmas break started and wasn't going to return for another three days. Jess had tried to be a friend, but I wasn't terribly good company. After the incident at her house, she'd kept closer tabs on me than ever before. Even though I'd relentlessly attempted to assure her it had been the anxiety of admitting the truth, she hadn't bought into it. Either that or she and Eli had some sort of pact I wasn't aware of it. Both were highly probable.

My nerves were raw and frayed, and I tried at every turn not to rouse suspicion. This was the time seniors kicked back. I'd gotten into college. I had a full ride. I'd be leaving at the end of the school year. Except for the valedictorian spot, the spring semester should've been a breeze. I wished I could adopt the laidback attitude Jess had this year, but I refused to let myself slide—regardless of what my parents thought, thanks to Kendra Cross. And while they had some control over things I did, they didn't have anything absolute. I'd managed a work-around for piano—thanks to Eli—and I took my watch off midway through my runs to avoid their three-mile rule. I'd upped my game at school, too, making sure to talk to each of my teachers daily. They all bought into the routine, and I was fairly certain that Mrs. Cross would give my brother a glowing report on her next update.

But no matter how well I'd patched things over to meet my internal needs, nothing I did fixed the hole caused by Eli's absence. Text messages and phone calls were nice, but they weren't the same as his touch or the way his breath floated across my skin. His voice was distorted by technology. And what made matters worse was that he seemed to be having a great time. Eli was home with his parents and people he hadn't seen in ages, friends from high school. It was hard not to be jealous or envious—both words had a negative undertone in this context.

The two weeks purge-free that I'd had before he left were long gone by the end of day one of his absence. Each time we talked resulted in a binge after we'd hung up. It felt good at first—just like it always did—but that gratification, the perfect fullness, quickly turned to disgust and disgrace. Every gag, every retch cleansed a part of me that soap couldn't reach and wouldn't have washed away even if it had. The flush of the toilet was my finale in a solo performance no one witnessed.

It left me high.

Then I crashed.

Alone.

And I'd reached that point once again in the day. My skin stretched tight against my abdomen, and my ribs ached from the bloat of my stomach. Each time I shifted in my chair, I grew a little more uncomfortable. I wouldn't be able to sit through dessert, and cheesecake was my favorite.

"May I be excused?" I pushed back from the table before I'd finished my question not expecting anyone to stop their conversation, much less care.

Mama glanced at Daddy, and I wondered when she'd last had Botox. The line between her brows sunk in when she frowned. I hadn't seen that in years. "Colbie, dear"—another cursory glance around the table—"I made cheesecake just for you. Aren't you going to have any?" She acted as though my neglecting dessert was a personal attack on her.

Everyone at the table had their sights set on me thanks to my mother's pity party.

"My stomach is a little upset. I just need to use the restroom."

And if I didn't return before the cheesecake were put away, then so be it.

The mark on Mama's brow evaporated when her smile appeared. "All right then."

However, Jess's face went sour when I scooted my seat in and turned away from the table. I doubt I would have noticed it, except that everyone else resumed the conversation they'd been in the middle of while she stared at me. Her attention tugged at my sleeves and pushed on my shoulders, and I wondered if she sensed my guilt.

By the time I'd reached the bottom of the stairs, she'd engaged in fits of laughter alongside my brothers, forgetting me. This was the one time I relished being ignored. No one was the wiser. And as much as I didn't want to do this twice in one night, I could be in and out, and then back at the table before Mama had the dinner dishes cleared.

I hurried without running and then stopped outside my bedroom to listen. The sounds of my happy family floated up the steps and settled in the back of my throat like a rock. Heavy and sharp, it made breathing difficult and swallowing nearly impossible. Saliva pooled in my mouth, and my gut gurgled in anticipation. I hated that their happiness ended with this. I wanted to be part of it. To be normal. To fit in.

I slammed the bathroom door behind me, raced to raise the lid, and barely had my fingers in my mouth when the first wave rose like a geyser. Old Faithful had nothing on the power behind my diaphragm. The tears that came weren't just my eyes watering. My mind pummeled me with remorse and acknowledgment that I'd played a huge part in my own misery, and suddenly, I hated myself as much as I'd hated their perceived neglect.

The second expulsion tried to rip my esophagus to shreds, but I wasn't done. I'd yet to reach the salad I'd started dinner with, and I wouldn't give up until I had...regardless of how much it hurt.

I opened as wide as possible, stretching my lips until the corners of my mouth split, to get my fingers further in. The door creaked as I tried to jerk my hand away, but I couldn't stop what Jess had already seen.

Thick spit clung to my hand, and bits of vomit remained in my palm. It wasn't over, either. I choked on fragments I hadn't chewed well enough, gagging until I retched again. And while I couldn't outline the details of her expression, I saw enough to realize I couldn't pass this off as an accident. It had obviously been intentional, but all those lies I had rehearsed in my head had never taken into account an eye witness. They'd been written for someone standing on the other side of my stage's curtain—out in the crowd.

Jess hadn't moved. When I stood upright and faced the door, fear flashed across her expression and then panic set in.

"Colbie..."

I waved her off and realized I'd done so with the paste of vomit and vile still clinging to my nails and sides of my finger. Drool had run down to my wrist, and Jess now had a first-row seat. "I'm fine, Jess. Really."

I turned the faucet on and made the mistake of glancing up. The mascara I'd put on to look nice at Christmas dinner painted my cheeks in streaks of charcoal. My eyes were not only bloodshot, but a vessel had broken in the white of the one on the right. And my lips cracked in more places than just the corners.

Her head turned from side to side, almost in slow motion. "Is this what you do after every meal?"

I stuck my hands under the water and then reached for the soap. I had to clean them before I could even begin on my face. "No." I huffed in exaggerated irritation. I hoped it deterred Jess enough to get her out of my bathroom without further incident. "I just ate too much."

"Nope." The shake of Jess's head had become more

pronounced, and I did my best to ignore it in favor of making myself presentable. "I've seen you eat like that a thousand times. And after every single meal, you go to the bathroom. It doesn't matter where you are. You find a restroom. Every. Time."

My tongue swept across my rough lips. I desperately needed to brush my teeth, but I couldn't argue with my mouth full, and keeping Jess quiet was of utmost importance right now. "You're making something out of nothing. I promise."

"You need help, Colbie."

I grabbed her wrist when she tried to leave. "I'm fine." I enunciated those two words, certain she'd understand how seriously I meant them.

Jess was going to make herself sick if she didn't stop twisting her neck. And the tears. "It's all there. The pieces fit together. I can't believe I've been so stupid that I didn't notice."

"Jess, I'm not kidding. Lower your voice." I'd clamp her mouth shut or shove a washcloth into it if I had to. I was not above gagging my best friend.

The door to the hall stood open from where she'd entered, and her tone rose with each word. She had me trapped, unable to bypass her, much less keep everyone else from listening.

"No. If you didn't have anything to hide, you wouldn't be worried about anyone hearing me." Snot ran from her nose, and she hiccuped when she talked. "How long have you been doing"—she waved her hands in circles around the bathroom—"this?"

I took a deep breath, unable to come up with a response to settle her. The truth would only make matters worse.

"Is this what happened that night Eli came to get you at my house?"

I shook my head and stared at her shoes.

"Every Sunday dinner, is this what you do after?"

Still I didn't respond.

Jess stomped her foot on the ceramic tiles, but her shoe didn't make nearly the noise her voice did when she shouted, "Answer me, dammit! Tell me why you're killing yourself." Her fists shook at her sides, but I couldn't determine if it was anger or disappointment that made her tremble.

The stampede had begun at the bottom of the stairs, closing in rapidly. I tried to push her out of the way, but she latched onto the doorframe and held on for dear life. "You're being ridiculous."

"This is why you've lost so much weight, isn't it? And why your parents are freaked out. They just don't know it's the catalyst for all the other stuff." As if she needed each person in the house to hear every word she said, her clarity didn't come quietly.

My defensive walls went up, thick and strong. If she wouldn't shut up then I'd shut down. Which was precisely what happened when Caden stumbled through the door, followed by my brothers and parents.

Caden spun Jess toward him. The change in his expression gave way the second he had realized she was crying. Chasity appeared confused. And none of my brothers said a word. My parents brought up the tail end, but before either could express concern or question, Jess sobbed into my little brother's chest.

"She's going to die, Caden. I've told you a hundred times there was something wrong, and you wouldn't listen." Jess's fist beat on Caden's shoulder as her knees decided to quit holding her weight.

It was a melodramatic performance to say the least. I rolled my eyes as Caden caught his girlfriend's weight and scooped her up. He sat on the bed with her in his arms, and all I could think of was the way I felt when Eli cradled me.

God, I missed him.

"Colbie, what's going on?" My mother's prim yet surprised voice barely made it through the commotion of the multitude of people now hovering in the entrance to my bedroom. She glanced at Jess and Caden and back to me for an explanation.

I crossed my arms. "Nothing."

"It's not true." Jess was a blubbering mess, and Caden needed to get his girlfriend under control. "Look at her face."

I swiped painful strokes under my lashes to remove mascara residue, knowing it was futile. I hadn't gotten to wash my face before Jess went into hysterics. The water still ran next to me. In fact, she'd thrown my entire sequence out of order. If anyone took the time to look behind me, I hadn't cleaned up the toilet, and the seat was still raised.

"Look at her eye, Dr. Chapman." She sniveled, and I wanted to wring her damn neck. "Just look."

My father pushed through the group, but before I could slam the door—that Caden had removed Jess from—and hide behind it, he slapped his palm against the wood and forced it open. I couldn't remember the last time Daddy had put his hands on me, but he grabbed my chin so he could see my face.

Jess continued to wallow from the bed. Meanwhile, my family waited with bated breath to see what Jess referred to. My dad was a doctor. If Jess had seen it, he would instantly. He tilted my chin to the side and used two fingers to pry my lids apart.

He went from looking *at* my eye to looking *in* them. "Colbie, what's going on?" The gruff tumble of my father's gravelly voice had taken on a softer, concerned tone. It was the voice of my childhood, the one that had tucked me in bed at night. I hadn't heard that man in years, and I realized I missed him as much as I did Eli.

I shrugged him off, but trying to get by him was pointless. And even if I had, there was layer after layer of people between me and freedom. "Nothing, I'm fine." If I'd taken a gentler approach than snarling, I might have convinced my father that was true.

"It's not true, Dr. Chapman. Ask her what she was doing in the bathroom. Ask her what she does every time she leaves the table after dinner."

My brother tried to calm his girlfriend. "Jess—"

"Ask her!" Jess was on the verge of hyperventilating, and my dad's medical expertise would be better suited toward getting her under control before she passed out.

"Shut up, Jess. Nobody cares." The walls breathed in, stealing my air. "Shut up." The room rotated, side swiping my equilibrium. "Shut up." Gravity squeezed every inch of my body, ripping apart my flesh. "Shut up." I no longer knew if I'd continued yelling the same words on repeat or if that was an echo smothering the bathroom. I didn't care.

Pandemonium had ensued, and I lost my grip on reality. Brother after brother leaned into my face and disappeared to allow the next to demonstrate their disapproval in my mind's funhouse mirror. None of it was real, or maybe all of it was. The voices around me faded into each other until they were all unrecognizable.

"Cole?" But it wasn't Caden's voice that called my name. "Cole, baby, open your eyes."

He wasn't here.

"Cole, look at me." The warmth of Eli's voice, or even the hope that it could really be him, pried my lids apart.

There were his sweet brown eyes, staring at me with love. "Eli." My voice cracked, and tears replaced the panic. I took the phone from Jess and ignored everyone and everything else in the room.

"Don't cry. Wipe your eyes and tell me what happened."

I glanced up to horrified expressions, and Jess mouthing "I'm sorry." I didn't know what had happened or how long I'd been in the state I was. It had to have been bad for Jess to call Eli...with my parents and my brothers—including Caleb—in the room.

Eli didn't speak and neither did I. Instead, I waited for each relative to see themselves out until my dad and Jess were the last two in the room.

Daddy reached out and squeezed Jess's hand. "You stay. When they're done, come get me."

She nodded and sat on the bed, leaving me in the bathroom with my phone. I leaned my back against the cabinets and hugged my knees. Jess had a full view of me, but she couldn't see Eli. Not that we had any privacy regardless.

"How did you end up on the phone?" I already knew. There was only one person who could have made that life-altering decision on mine and Eli's behalf. I gave her the evil eye from my vantage point.

Jess had no idea what she'd just done. I wouldn't have died from a panic attack. Eli could go to jail because she'd freaked out and called him.

"Jess called me."

I realized I had her phone in my hand, not my own. "My whole family heard you."

He nodded and gave me a reassuring smile. "I know." Eli didn't appear the least bit concerned. "I'll deal with that. Right now, I need you to tell me what's going on."

Foolish didn't begin to describe the level of embarrassment that painted my cheeks. I had no idea why this man cared for me; all he saw these days was a blubbering mess of mental instability. "I had a panic attack." It was true. My world had sucked itself into a tiny vortex. I just hadn't admitted why.

"Any idea what caused it?"

I shook my head.

From the peanut gallery, my best friend corrected me. "Liar." She'd stopped crying, but the evidence of her emotion remained all over her cheeks. Jess had gone from sobbing to angry, and if she had any boobs to speak of, they'd be smashed by her arms crossed over them.

"You can tell me anything, Colbie. You know that. Nothing is going to change how I feel."

My mouth refused to open, and my throat closed tight. I couldn't admit what Jess had all but accused me of. Not to Eli.

"Breathe, baby. Don't get stuck in your head. It's just you and me talking."

I squeezed my eyes shut with my entire face, hoping that when I opened them this would all be a nightmare that had ended. I'd wake from the horrible dream, sweating and breathing heavily, but it would be over.

That didn't happen.

"Jess overreacted to something she saw, and she managed to get my entire family involved." I cut my eyes her direction again. I wished she'd leave. "And you."

"Colbie, we've been over this. It's my job to take care of you, even when I'm not there. I'd told Jess if you needed anything to call me. And when she did, *I* made the decision for her to put me on FaceTime to see you. *I* made the choice not to hide when I might be able to help. Don't be upset with Jess." Eli wasn't the slightest bit riled up. His only concern at that moment was me.

I'd been reduced to a whisper. "But your job..."

Eli had just thrown himself to the wolves and likely the school board and police. "The only thing I care about right now is you." His voice, his presence—albeit virtual—calmed me.

We spoke for a few more minutes, and he made me promise to call him later when I could talk. He'd given me a pass tonight, and that might continue until he got home, but at some point, in the not so distant future, I'd have to confess. I wasn't looking forward to it. Convincing him there was nothing to be worried about would be far harder than Jess. I'd promised him I'd open up, expose my demons, release my dragons, and for the most part, I had.

This was the only secret I'd kept closely guarded—from everyone.

How I'd managed to escape my parents' thumbs for even a few minutes, much less long enough to drive to Jess's house, was beyond me. They were awfully trusting to believe I'd come back after the bomb they'd just dropped on me, especially now that they were aware—even if they didn't know the extent—of my relationship with Eli. There had been hushed conversations behind closed doors late into the night, and when Caleb had finally left, he had refused to look me in the eye.

I'd worried that inability to face me had to do with Eli, and then my parents had me come to the formal living room to "talk." I'd never been in trouble, but the twins had. That spot on that couch didn't bode well for me. And it had only gotten worse the longer I sat there.

By the time I had stood, I wasn't certain my legs would hold me, much less carry my shaky body. And driving probably hadn't been the best idea, either. But this wasn't a conversation to be had by phone—not that I had one to call her on since Mama had taken my cell—and there was no way in hell I was leaving town without saying what I had to say.

Luckily—for Jess, not me—her parents weren't home. I pulled all the way down the drive and turned around so leaving wouldn't be difficult. I hadn't called before storming over here, and I doubted my arrival would be well received by my "best" friend. That term held little meaning at the moment since it was synonymous with enemy.

I rang the bell at the back of the house and then started banging my fist on the glass until she appeared in the window. "Open the door, Jessica."

She appeared apprehensive, but she unlocked the deadbolt and swung open the door to silently invite me in. That had been a smart move. Neither her parents nor mine would want the gossips in this small town to get ahold of what currently dangled on the end of my tongue.

"What has you in an uproar?" She closed the door but didn't come any farther into the house.

I was almost surprised she didn't know, but I guess it spoke to the truth of my parents' threat. "Thanks to that little stunt you pulled on Christmas night, I get to spend the spring semester..." I tapped my finger on my lips to formulate the perfect wording. "Abroad."

She pushed past me and into the kitchen. "Like internationally?" Jess reached into the fridge and grabbed a bottle of water. She offered me one as well, but water would just get in the way. It was hard to be theatrical with unwanted props.

"You're joking, right?" I deadpanned.

Jess recapped the bottle after taking a sip and then set it down. She fidgeted with her hair, putting it into a ponytail while she played twenty questions. "You said abroad. So no. Where are you going? And why are you so mad about it? Is it because of Eli?" Either she was a damn fine actress or clueless.

Eli was another issue that I'd get to. "My parents are sending me to an inpatient treatment center, Jess. Out of state so my 'reputation isn't tarnished in the community.' You have them convinced I'm on a fast track to death with that hysterical performance of yours on Christmas."

She took a seat on one of the bar stools with a huff. "I'm sorry, Colbie. I don't want you to be mad at me, but you have an issue that you need to get help with. And it's better to do it now than face it on your own when you're in college." There wasn't a hint of remorse in her tone or carefree expression. She felt justified in what she did, not guilty.

"There's nothing to *deal* with, Jess. That's the part you seem to be missing."

"Cut the crap, Colbie. I saw you with your fingers down your throat, inducing vomiting. You hadn't swallowed poison; you hadn't consumed too much alcohol. You had eaten your emotions. And you've done it before."

I slapped my hand on the counter. "How would you know? You're never around to have a clue what I do or don't do. That could've been the first or the hundredth time." My body temperature started to rise with my anger, and my underarms began to sweat.

Her eyes softened, as did her tone. "I wish I believed it was the first. I wish I could go back and do things differently so I would have recognized it when it started. I wish someone had been paying close enough attention to hear you when you cried for help. But I wasn't there for you when you needed me. I can't possibly make up for any of that if you're not around, so I don't regret your parents finding out."

"Newsflash, Jess, I won't be around to ease your guilt."

She snorted and shook her head. "I don't mean in Brogdon, Colbie. If you're dead, there's no salvaging anything. And that's the path you're heading down if puking is your choice for problem resolution."

"It's not!" Screaming didn't do any good; she didn't get it.

"Then you'll be in and out of this place in no time. If you get there and we've all blown this out of proportion, they'll send you home."

I dropped my hands to my sides with exaggeration. "And come home to what, Jess? You're shoved up Caden's ass, and Eli will be lucky if he's not in jail."

She shot out of her seat. "That's not fair. He made that decision, not me."

"What choice did he have? You never should have called him!"

Jess had maintained her composure for the most part, until now. Her cheeks heated with color, and her dark-blue eyes lightened the way they did when she cried. "If you'd seen what I did, you would have done the same thing."

"I've seen people puke, Jess, and I didn't rat them out."

"No, not that. The way you zoned out. You didn't hear anything around you. You weren't reachable, Colbie. It was worse than the day at my house. Your dad was ready to call 9-1-1, and he's a doctor! I can't explain it to you, and you may never forgive me, but I didn't see any other choice."

I wasn't buying it, even though I couldn't remember a section of time from Daddy coming in to Eli's voice. "So you did *what*? Just grabbed your phone and in the midst of the commotion, reached out to my teacher—who I happen to be sleeping with—to update him on my mental condition which was rather crazy at that moment? At any point, did it occur to you that you shouldn't have made that call with *any* of my family within earshot?"

"I didn't." She barely whispered, and I had to strain to hear the rest. "I left while everyone tended to you. I went down the hall to Caden's room. No one heard me. I needed him to tell me what to do, Colbie. I was scared."

"And you thought he had some secret weapon?"

"He does. I don't know what it is about him. Honestly, I don't care. All I know was life came back to your eyes when he said your name. That vacant stare all but disappeared when he called you 'baby.' And like it or not, Eli made that choice. I could have put the phone to your ear to hear his voice. He wanted you to see his face. He *chose* to refer to you in a way that would reveal your relationship to anyone who heard him. And he did both because he loves you."

"But he wouldn't have had to if you'd just kept your mouth shut. Talked to me instead of screaming so everyone within a five-mile radius caught wind of what was going on." Some of my anger had faded into acceptance, but I still blamed her. "All you've done is make things exponentially worse for me, Jess. Eli would have been home in a couple days. Now, I won't get to see him before my parents ship me off. I can't even tell him I'm leaving because my parents took my phone. I won't be able to spend my last semester of high school at home. And as if I hadn't quite felt lonely enough, I will have the pleasure of living in a facility where I know absolutely no one, and no one will give a shit about me. At least here I had Eli and Dr. Chalmers. There..." I shrugged, defeated. "It's game over."

"Colbie..." She didn't have words to fix any of this. Jess had outdone herself this time. "You still have me. Even if I haven't been the best—"

"Save it, Jess. You've helped enough."

I didn't stand around to chitchat or listen to her crap excuses for why she hadn't been a better friend. I'd said what I had to, and now, I needed to go. The damage was done.

16

ELI

Jess's second call of the trip sent me flying to my old bedroom to pack. I'd expected to hear from the Chapmans, or possibly Caleb—not Jess. And when her voice cracked, I feared what would come next, with good reason.

"Ma," I called as I climbed the steps. It wasn't a huge house; she had to hear me. "Ma!" I didn't wait for her to respond.

My closet door jammed when I tried to open it, and Ma appeared in the midst of my struggle to free my stuff. "Elijah Paxton. Stop that." She swatted at my hands. "What's gotten into you?" One of her weathered hands rested on my chest, and the other took hold of the knob. It opened with ease. The weight of her touch calmed my racing mind.

"Colbie." I took a deep breath. I didn't want to violate Colbie's privacy, but there was no way I'd get through all of this without my parents' support. "I've got to get home, Ma."

She knelt to grab the handle of my suitcase. "Slow down." My mom didn't try to stop me as she lifted the empty bag onto my bed and unzipped it. "How can I help?" This was what parents were supposed to do, and it killed me that Colbie didn't have it. I wondered if she ever had.

I sat with a slight bounce on the edge of my mattress next to the empty luggage. Pulling my hair out by the roots wouldn't change anything, but it might make me feel better. And while it did provide a bit of relief when I tugged, it didn't fix jack shit. "I don't have all the details." My chest heaved, and I fought off the emotion that threatened to overtake me, but my voice still cracked. "Jess called. Colbie's parents are sending her to a treatment facility." I struggled to form words that could wiggle through the tightness in my throat.

"For what? When?" My mother hadn't even met Colbie, yet she was outraged.

This was the hard part. As soon as I gave a voice to the issue, there wasn't a doubt in my mind what her reaction would be. "Bulimia."

Her spine straightened, and a wrinkle formed under her neck when she pulled back, as if she hadn't heard me correctly. "Were there not signs, son? How could you not know your girlfriend was sick?" It wasn't judgment so much as shock. "You've always been such an astute boy." *Boy*. If she had to scold or teach, I reverted to adolescence from manhood.

I dropped my elbows to my knees and my head into my hands where my poor hair continued to take a beating. "She's an overachiever." It wasn't an excuse, even if it was true. "Everything Colbie does, she has to be the best."

"That didn't answer my question."

"Yes, she's lost weight. More than I wanted to recognize, I think." I raised my head and stared my mom in the eyes so she could see the pain I currently felt at the part I'd played in not helping the woman I loved. "And yes, I was a contributing factor, but I didn't have any idea this was going on." And I didn't. "I thought it was just stress." And that was the truth.

Other than the one time at Jess's house, I had no clue she binged or purged. Although, Chasity's comments now made sense...the bathroom trips, the overabundance of running. Separately, none of it amounted to much; together, the puzzle had been in front of me all along.

Beating myself up for the countless miles the two of us had run together wouldn't change where things were now. Had I known the truth, I would have done something different, although I'd be damned if I could figure out what it would've been.

"When does she leave?"

"I don't know. Jess didn't know anything more than it's before I'm supposed to leave Michigan. Jess doesn't even know where Colbie's going, Ma."

She patted my knee in a motherly fashion. "You'll get there in time, Eli. I'm sure of it. But are you prepared for what you're going to go back to?"

I hadn't thought that far ahead. "No. I'm not."

"There have been a lot of secrets kept since the two of you met. Once you get Colbie taken care of, you need to address the situation with the Chapmans *and* with Caleb. They have been a second family to you over the years, and I'm sure their trust is broken. The school is a whole other can of worms."

My head bobbed on its own while I took in what she had to say. I'd only allowed myself to briefly consider anyone other than Colbie in this scenario, and I'd justified my actions out of love for her. But in a way, I'd betrayed my best friend and his parents. I should care about the school, maybe more than any of the other. I'd spent years fast tracking through college and graduate school to get my PhD, and it was quite possible I'd thrown all of that away with one phone call.

"It's never too late to make amends. Just be sure you're honest with yourself and them, and that Colbie remains your top priority." She stood and then started out of the room. Before she left, she turned to face me. "Son, if you're not prepared to see this through, you need to be a man and let her go."

She had no idea. None of them did. Not my parents, not the Chapmans, and not Caleb. But that was something I'd have to prove. Words simply wouldn't do it justice, and time wasn't on my side.

I pulled my phone from my pocket to check flights and quickly found one that left in two hours. With the ticket purchased by credit card, I threw my clothes into the bag, zipped it, and raced down the stairs.

My dad stood at the door with keys in his hand. "You ready?"

I nodded. "Ma, you coming?"

The three of us were in the car minutes later. The two of them talked continuously, telling me what I needed to do. I listened without comment and tried to make note of all they pointed out, but my only concern was getting to Colbie. And when we arrived at the terminal, my goodbyes were short and sweet. My parents knew I loved them and that I'd call with an update.

I'd never been so thankful for an empty airport as I was today. I blazed through security and made it to my gate with little time to spare. Rolling in the plastic seat to lift my hip, I pulled my phone from my back pocket.

She had no idea I was on my way home, and when I tried to reach her, I got her voicemail. I had to assume her parents had taken her phone, which was why she hadn't called me herself, but I left her a message anyway.

"Hey, Cole. I'm about to board a plane. I'll be home in a few hours. I'll call you back when I land." I paused, not wanting to leave it at that but not caring to expand on the reason for my early arrival. "I love you, baby. We'll figure this out when I get home tonight."

I hung up and hoped she called right back. Unfortunately, that didn't happen. And once I boarded and the stewardess forced the passengers into airplane mode, I'd have to wait hours to hear her voice and reassure her.

I HAD TRIED REPEATEDLY—AFTER I GOT OFF THE PLANE, through baggage claim, and on my way home—but Colbie's phone was turned off. The side of my hand hurt from beating my fist on the steering wheel every time I called with no luck. It had cost me a fortune to get here. I'd be damned if she would leave without seeing me first.

My driveway was empty when I got home. The lights were off inside my house. I didn't know what I'd expected, but Colbie hadn't been there waiting on me, which would have been the most ideal situation. I threw my bag onto my bed once I had gotten inside and plopped down next to it. I didn't know what to do from here. If I couldn't reach her, then I couldn't see her. And if I couldn't see her, then I couldn't help her. None of which worked for me. For all I knew, Colbie could be leaving first thing tomorrow morning, and waiting to make a move could prove catastrophic. I didn't have a choice.

Before I lost my nerve, I grabbed my keys off the counter and went to get into my truck. Her house wasn't far from mine, so it left me little time to contemplate what I'd say when her parents answered the door, or how I'd explain my actions with their daughter, much less my reason for standing on their stoop. If I had to beg for a chaperoned visit in their living room, I'd do whatever was necessary.

I breathed a sigh of relief when I passed her driveway and pulled the truck next to the curb in front of her house. Other than Colbie's SUV, there weren't any other cars there. There also wasn't any movement inside the house, and I prayed they hadn't already left. When I got out and rounded the hood, I stared at her piano just briefly. It sat with the top closed, and I assumed still locked. My chest tightened at the thought of the pain they'd inflicted with that move, yet now, I wondered if it had been the right one.

If Colbie were really sick, they needed to get her help. I just couldn't help but think they'd gone about it the wrong way, robbing her of everything she loved. Dwelling on it wouldn't change their mind or that it had happened. My legs felt like anchors dragging the bottom of the ocean as my ship was tossed by the waves. My feet tried to preserve my wellbeing while my heart pushed forward.

There wasn't enough air in the sky to take in a calming breath. Nevertheless, I tried repeatedly to suck in enough to keep me from passing out. I was a grown man. This was ridiculous. With more determination and courage than I truly had, I rang the doorbell. When it went unanswered, I clanked the knocker three times.

I took several steps back to peer into Colbie's bedroom window, but the blinds were closed. Just as I admitted defeat, the lock clicked, and the door opened. Yet instead of Dr. or Mrs. Chapman or even Colbie, Caleb appeared on the porch.

With his arms crossed and jaw set, he took an offensive posture on his parents' steps. Caleb could be down and ready to charge before I could fully turn to face him, and he had the power behind his stature to take me out. "What are you doing here, Eli?" *Not Paxton or Pax, Eli.* "I thought you were in Michigan for another couple days?" There was no air of curiosity in his tone, only accusation.

This scenario hadn't even crossed my mind—her parents yes, Caleb, no. I walked toward him, prepared for whatever he dished out. It was time to take my stand the way he'd taken his. If it became a showdown, so be it. "I flew home early."

"Clearly." The muscles in his jaw flexed, and I hated that I was close enough to see the pulse in his neck because it meant he could reach out to wring mine. "Why?"

I let down my guard and ran my hand through my hair. "I had hoped to see your sister before she left."

The chuckle that parted his lips didn't include a smile or the slightest bit of humor. "You've got balls, Paxton. I'll give you that." At least Caleb was back to using a nickname despite the circumstances. "Colbie's not here."

I didn't know if that meant she wasn't here right now or she'd already left. My priority had been getting to Colbie first, then Caleb and his parents, but if I had to rearrange the order of things, I'd work with what God offered me. I gave him a half-hearted shrug. "I'm sorry, Caleb. I didn't mean to fall in love with her. I tried like hell to keep it from happening."

"Not hard enough."

"Maybe not. But I can't change it. And I won't walk away."

"You might have to be carried." His biceps tightened beneath his T-shirt that already stretched to accommodate his arms.

I couldn't help the sarcastic chuckle that blew through the air like the wind. "Why do you care? You haven't noticed a thing she's done as long as I've known you, so why now? Because we're friends? Because you believe I've crossed a moral boundary? Or is it that you can't see what I see and you're blinded by confusion?"

"Critter and I have always been like this. You—"

I threw my hands in the air. "Stop calling her that. She's not a rodent. Jesus, Chapman. Your sister is a beautiful, insanely intelligent, witty, talented, and loving *woman*! Regardless of her being my student, she's an adult. She's eighteen, in case you missed it."

"She's still in high school."

"So was Chasity when you started college. The only difference is my role in her life being the way I met her. But Caleb, it wouldn't have mattered if I had met her at Brogdon High or tailgating at one of your brother's games. That's what I'm trying to tell you. She's *it*."

He closed the space that remained between us when he came

down the three steps to the sidewalk. "Colbie's a kid. You're a grown man who preyed on her." He poked me in the chest to enunciate his point. "That's sick."

"I wish you could see her the way I do, man." I couldn't stop shaking my head. "I wish I could convince you that the way I love her is as pure as the way you do Chas. If she were a freshman in college, we wouldn't be having this conversation."

"You're right. We'd be having the conversation about bro code and not sleeping with your best friend's little sister, much less taking her virginity."

I didn't want to know how he had that information—maybe he'd just assumed it—so I didn't ask. I also didn't deny it. I did, however, look around for witnesses to our discussion that became more heated with each word that flew from Caleb's mouth. His parents would have heart attacks if they were aware this conversation had taken place on their front lawn.

"I'm not going to apologize for loving her, Caleb. I won't even bother pointing the finger at the reasons why she sought security in my arms instead of the people she shares a last name with."

"What's that supposed to mean?" He blanched.

The heat of the moment had a way of taking over, and words came from my mouth that never should have held residence on my tongue. "Your family is oblivious to Cole's needs."

Caleb's hands fell to his sides where he cracked his knuckles when he balled his fingers into fists. "What the hell are you talking about?" If he wanted to fight, we could throw down right here. I wasn't above defending Colbie.

"Have you ever met Dr. Chalmers?"

He pulled back, confused. "Her piano teacher? No. Why would I?"

"I have. Do you know how much your sister loves music?"

"I know she hates football." He hit that nail on the head.

"And why do you think that is?"

"Who cares, Paxton? She's just not into sports. Big deal." Caleb had gone back to being the oaf Colbie knew.

"She hates it because your entire family revolves around it, and it was something she could never do. As a girl, she couldn't put on pads and race onto the field. Piano is her sport, and not one of you cared enough to show up for the biggest performance she's had to date. It was like the NCAA Championship game for her."

He grimaced. "You mean her little recital? It was the weekend of the UGA-Auburn game—" Clarity reached his eyes, and he now knew why I hadn't attended as an alumnus with his family.

"Her *little* recital drew hundreds of people. Strangers come annually to watch the only performance she gives each year. A couple next to me *cried* because it was the last time they'd hear her play." I groaned in frustration. "Your sister is a musical *genius*, Caleb. Not only have you missed that, but your *entire family* has. Can you imagine what it would've been like if your parents and brothers had never shown up for your games? If you'd won the Heisman and they hadn't been there? That's the equivalent here."

Caleb shoved his hands into his pockets. "It's not the same. My parents can't be everywhere at once, Eli. They went where the majority of their kids were."

"It was one day, Caleb. *One*. She spent months conquering a piece of music, and I was the only person there to see it."

"She should have said something."

I'd never thought my friend was daft before today. Blind, oblivious, distracted, but never stupid. "It's not just piano. It's school. It's running—"

"Critter's been that way since she was little." If he called her Critter one more time, my fist would leave my side and land squarely on his jaw. "You didn't know her then. She's always wanted to be the best."

I closed my eyes, counted to ten—and took as many breaths—

before opening them to try one more time. "Has it occurred to any of you to ask *why* she chased perfection?"

"Since when did you become a psychologist?" Deflection. Great.

I couldn't keep my voice down any longer. "Don't you get it?" The door opened behind him, but I didn't bother to see who it was. "Her perfect was never enough for any of your family's attention!"

Chasity came out on the porch. "You two realize people in the town over can hear you bickering?" She sidled up next to her husband and rested her palm on his shoulder, staring at me, daring me to challenge her. "Phillip and Elise are not going to be happy when they find out about this." She clicked her tongue and shook her head.

I scrubbed my hands down my weary face and took a deep breath. "When's she going to be back, Chapman?" I dropped my arms, and my shoulders slumped.

"My parents aren't going to let you see her, Eli. And trust me, she won't be alone until they leave for Tennessee tomorrow morning. They aren't going to take the chance that any of this might get out."

I huffed, unable to process the words I'd heard. "What are they planning to tell people?" They were out of their ever-loving minds. "No one is going to believe Colbie just decided not to finish her last semester of high school, Caleb. Get real."

"No, but they will believe that she's studying abroad," Caleb responded. "My parents don't want anyone to know differently. My brothers don't even know."

I stared at him and raised my brows, utterly shocked by their bullshit and his willingness to go along with it.

"It makes sense for the class valedictorian to spend time overseas. It's best for everyone. This way, rumors won't get started." Caleb's continued explanation of this valiant effort their parents were making didn't change how stupid it was. "She can return for graduation at the end of the semester, and no one will know the difference."

I didn't have a clue how they thought "no one" would find out that this small-town girl had gone into treatment, but that was neither here nor there. I wouldn't be discussing it with anyone.

I couldn't fathom five months without her touch, her voice, her laughter—her.

17

COLBIE

Five hours was a long time to sit in the back seat of a car, brooding in silence, but that's exactly what I did on the ride to Nashville. I'd never felt the type of fury that seeped into me and surged through my veins, filling every ounce of headspace and each fiber of my being. My parents had been indifferent for years, yet now, when I didn't need their help and no longer wanted it, was the time they decided to step up and take note.

The three of us had barely reached Atlanta when Mama'd had enough of my huffing, and in her own, polite way told me to shut up.

I had never argued with either of them, but I didn't have anything else to lose. "You're wasting your money and my time. This is asinine. I do not have an eating disorder."

"Sugar, the decision has been made." Daddy's term of endearment didn't take the finality or the bite out of his words.

I threw myself against the seat back. "How can you take Jess's word over mine?" It was a futile fight. "Prior to her sleeping with Caden, the two of you never even noticed her." It was a low blow, but if a sucker punch got me out of this then I'd throw them all day.

Mama turned around. "Colbie Chapman! That's enough. You are *not* going to say such vile things about your brother."

My face contorted into some awful expression that left a sour taste in my mother's mouth. "You think just because you pretend Caden's a virgin that it makes it true?" I huffed a sarcastic laugh. "Dream on, Mama. He's no more a virgin than anyone in this car. And Jess wasn't his first."

This wasn't my brother's fault, and I really should leave him out of it. Unfortunately, it was Jess's fault and, well...guilt by association.

"Colbie, I'm not having this discussion with you. It's inappropriate and unbecoming of a lady." She cleared all emotion from her expression the way I'd seen her do my entire life and then faced forward as though that ended my tirade. It did not.

"Don't you get tired of that? Pretending nothing affects you? Turning a blind eye to reality? Always putting up a front?" I didn't get a response. *Typical.* "It has to be exhausting to lie to yourself and everyone around you constantly."

Daddy hadn't said much, but that was his breaking point. "Enough."

Fine. I'd take a different approach. "You realize that I'm eighteen, right? I don't *have* to go. You can't *make* me check myself in." I sat back with my arms crossed and a smug disposition.

Daddy didn't seem the least bit put off by my proclamation. "I hope you have an alternative plan then because you won't be coming back to our house until you've successfully completed the program."

"I have other options." Eli had a house. Jess's parents wouldn't turn me away.

They both stared out the windshield. Daddy didn't so much as glance in the rearview mirror. "If you think the McLeans are going to help, I've ensured that's a dead end. And if you value

Eli's freedom and reputation, you won't consider that an option, either."

I didn't know if my father's bite was as vicious as his bark, and I didn't aim to find out. The last thing I needed was him going after Eli. I hadn't dared to ask what their plans were in regard to my relationship with him, but I wouldn't risk him facing any more trouble than he already did.

So, for the next four hours, I kept my mouth shut. When they stopped for food, I didn't order, nor did I eat. Eli would be disappointed by my behavior, but that didn't stop me from being an ass. And when we arrived in Nashville, I didn't allow myself to take in the buildings or the streets or the people because *this* was not my introduction to this city. This was not how I would come to my new home. The awestruck wonder and excitement of going to college would not be tainted by this venture with my parents.

It wasn't until we turned at the sign for the facility that I bothered with the details. The facility or housing or whatever it was called here, sat a long way back from the road. Lush gardens and gorgeous landscape reached as far as the eye could see. It looked more like a luxury spa than any rehabilitation center I'd imagined. The pictures online didn't do it justice. Nevertheless, I wasn't fooled by the appearance which came at a price—a price my parents were all too happy to pay to save face in Brogdon.

I tried one last time to reason with them. "Don't you think this is a tad extreme? Couldn't we turn around and try counseling or round-the-clock babysitting?" *Anything* other than being dumped here. "For the love of God, Daddy, you're a doctor. Why can't *you* treat me?"

I didn't even get the courtesy of a response or a reprimand for taking the Lord's name in vain.

My father pulled in front of the building and got out as a man in a black suit rounded the front of our car. *Valet.* I couldn't roll my eyes far enough back to illustrate how vulgar and pretentious I found this. The same man retrieved my bags from the trunk, and I relented to my fate. Although, I did not go gentle into that good night. Dylan Thomas brought Eli to mind, and I fought to stave off the tears that burned my eyes.

Mama rubbed my arm. "See, this won't be so bad." *Utterly clueless.*

And then as quickly as we'd arrived inside, my parents played the devoted role of loving caretakers...right before they announced their departure. They didn't stay for the tour, they didn't see me to my room, or meet the staff. Phillip and Elise Chapman had done their duty—dropped me off and paid for the trip; none of which should've surprised me. Yet there I stood, dumbfounded, as they pulled out of the circular drive.

"Why don't I show you to your room?" Emily—I thought that was her name, but I only vaguely remembered the introduction—wrapped an arm around my shoulders. It was meant to be comforting; it gave me hives, and I shrugged her off.

There was no intake process, and I'd yet to see another living soul besides the valet. "Don't you need to get my name and information or something?" I searched for an office or triage and came up empty-handed.

"Your parents provided that by phone." So, all Bright Horizons had were statistics my parents lifted off my driver's license along with their credit card number to pay the tab. Good to know.

I followed Emily down the corridor to a suite that looked more like a fancy hotel room than a mental health facility. There, on the plush bedding, sat my suitcases, unzipped and open. My jaw dropped about the same time Emily—who I shall refer to as Satan going forward—snapped the edge of her latex gloves one by one.

I didn't have time to close my mouth, much less stop her grubby paws from digging through my things. "What are you doing?"

Satan didn't even look up. "Checking for contraband."

"Contraband? What is this? A prison? I don't have a shank or anything."

The devil herself pulled out my razor and set it on the mattress.

"You know I'm not suicidal, right? Why are you taking my razor?" I stared in disbelief when she added to the pile. "Seriously? It's Tylenol." I picked up the travel container and looked inside. "I can hardly overdose on..." I counted them in the bottle. "...eight pills."

Lucifer snatched the plastic cylinder from my fingers and put it with the razor. Seconds later, she added nail clippers and mouthwash to her pile. Seemingly satisfied, her horns retracted—or so I'd thought—and she turned to me with her hand held out.

"What?" I had no idea what she wanted.

"No jewelry." She raised her brows and pointed to my diamond studs, and then she pulled a plastic bag out of her pocket. "Put them in here, sign the front, and seal it. You'll get them back at discharge."

They weren't all that expensive and certainly didn't hold sentimental value, but it still seemed absurd. I did as she had instructed, but before I sealed the bag, she stopped me.

"Necklace too."

I adamantly shook my head and reached up to touch the pendant. "No." I refused. "I just got it. It was a Christmas present."

Eli had slid the chain around my neck right before he had left for Michigan. It was dainty and elegant, resembling a snowflake. A reminder of just how unique I was—his words, not mine. The little diamond chips sparkled. They made me feel special. I wasn't about to give up the only piece of him I had with me—the only piece I might ever have after this charade was over.

"You can earn it back when you move out of the dorms."

My mind spun. "Like check out?" That would be months

from now.

She dropped her hands to her sides. "Has no one told you anything about this process?" Her eyes no longer flickered with the flames of hell. Instead, they appeared forlorn, sympathetic maybe—an emotion I was quite certain the devil could not embody.

I shook my head, still clutching Eli's gift that hung around my neck. "No. It was all sprung on me two days ago."

Emily set the plastic bag on the dresser, removed her gloves, and motioned toward the small sitting area near the window. There, she proceeded to tell me the basics of Bright Horizons. Ideally, I would be in the "dorms" for thirty days or less, depending on my progress—which was up to me to determine. I would have individual therapy, group therapy, nutrition classes, a meeting with a nutritionist one on one to develop my daily meal plan and goals, and a personal trainer. Meals were served in the cafeteria—it sounded more like a restaurant—and they weren't optional. Exercise was limited until I proved I could use it responsibly. And therapy was the driving force behind wellness.

My days were outlined, every minute accounted for—structure, structure, structure. "What about school?"

"What about it?"

I had to remind myself that Emily didn't know me, and she only had the limited knowledge my parents had imparted, if that. "I graduate in May. I'm in the running for valedictorian. When do I do my schoolwork?" This could become a huge sticking point, even bigger than the necklace. I didn't know what other options I had, but I would not give up valedictorian for anyone. I'd worked too hard to maintain that spot, and I'd be damned if I'd hand it over to Jess without a fight.

"You'll meet with Raine this afternoon. She coordinates those additions into each patient's routine."

Raine. What kind of name was that?

"Do you have any other questions?"

I had so many that I couldn't formulate one. "I guess not."

She hopped up and went to get my contraband and the earrings in the baggie. "Necklace."

"Not going to happen."

Emily glanced at her watch. "I'll let you take that up with Raine. Your appointment is in ten minutes, so I'll walk you to her office."

An hour later, I'd lost the jewelry, shed a deluge of tears, and already hated everything and everyone in this damn place, starting with Raine. I'd never wished pain or death upon anyone, but I was tempted to ask God for this one favor. Although I was fairly certain He'd deny that request since He hadn't answered any of my others in recent years.

The only thing I'd left that horrible woman's office with was the knowledge that I could earn rewards, although here they called them "privileges." If playing by their stupid rules got me a phone call to Eli or out of the "dorms" where I wouldn't have the level of restrictions I did as of now, then I could play the game. *I had to.*

Dinner was the first test. Internally, I shook my head and snickered at their stupidity. I could eat a well-balanced meal and not feel the weight of guilt. They prevented my ability to overeat, thereby eliminating the desire to purge *and* the need to be here.

I didn't socialize with anyone at my table or participate in the after-dinner activities. I went back to my room to complete my homework for Raine—journaling. My schoolwork would resume when classes started back in a couple of days, but it would be monitored. There would be no contact with anyone at the school or in Brogdon, and they would make certain of that.

The next morning, I met with Raine, my nutritionist, and personal trainer, together. The three of them derived a plan while I listened. When they were done, I expressed my thoughts.

"I'm a runner. I'm not giving up running. I don't care if it's on a treadmill, but I'm not scratching it off just because it burns too many calories. So, if I have to eat more to get to run, so be it." I wasn't sure how I'd manage that since the idea of eating to run defeated the point of running, but I'd cross that bridge when I reached it.

The trainer cocked his brow in interest. "How many miles do you typically run per day?"

I decided to be honest. I doubted I'd get my way anyhow. "It used to be about seven." I didn't mention my parents setting a limit at Thanksgiving because I hadn't adhered to it. "But there've been times it's been over ten and others where it was less."

Chewy—he resembled Chewbacca, and I hadn't bothered to learn his name—leaned back and folded his arms in a relaxed position on his chest. "Part of this process is learning to curb excessive tendencies, Colbie."

"So, by that rationale, I won't be forced into hours of daily sessions that I might become dependent upon? Or encouraged to write in excess to explore my emotions? And the facility—"

"*Unhealthy* excessive tendencies," he corrected.

"When did running become unhealthy?"

Raine and the other guy kept their mouths shut while Chewy argued Bright Horizon's case. "Why do you run?"

There were a host of reasons, none of which would help my situation. "Is everything I say going to be psychoanalyzed?"

"You're evading."

"Questioning for clarity." I could banter with this guy all day long.

Chewy grinned. "Helping you to understand your pattern of behavior will help you to manage negative tendencies."

I crossed my legs, held my knee with my hands, and rocked back. "Or, at least those you deem excessively negative."

"It's a simple question, Colbie. Why do you run?"

It wasn't a simple answer. I ran because it was good exercise that used plyometrics and cardio to strengthen muscles along with aiding in heart and lung health. The high—I knew better than to use that term—accelerated me past exhaustion like a needle in the vein. It eliminated stress, gave me time to think, and countless other reasons like burning calories. "I enjoy the solitude."

"Then walking alone on a treadmill for an equal amount of time would provide you that same emotional fulfillment, correct?" One of Chewy's eyes narrowed just a smidge, and I'd swear I noticed a hint of a grin. *Bastard.*

An hour walking on a treadmill *might* get me five miles. Whereas an hour of running could yield seven to eight, depending on my hustle. I didn't have much time to debate. Chewy saw me calculating numbers in my head and weighing my options.

"Yes." It was a blatant lie; we both knew it. But they'd never agree to my running habits, and it was better to log more miles even if it were at a slower pace. If I were limited by distance, my workouts would be over before I started.

God I missed Eli. With no way to communicate, I hadn't had so much as a text message to cling to. For all I knew he'd given up, or he *would* when he found out what a basket case I was. I hated thinking he'd be so fickle, but I couldn't bear the thought of him facing the firing squad to defend us, either.

"Colbie?" Chewy said my name like a cheese, and I hated it.

I glanced up to find him waiting on something. "Yeah?"

"You have group down the hall."

Raine opened the door and put her hand on my arm. "It all becomes routine pretty quickly. Just don't fight the process."

That was easier said than done when my entire life had been thrown into a paper bag, shaken up like chicken in flour, and then thrown into a fryer.

"You need to lower your voice, Colbie." Raine would do better to close her office door than tell me to be quiet.

"Why don't I get a phone call?"

"If you'd like to sit and have a discussion, we can. I won't tolerate yelling."

I hated who I was in this minute. I'd never been confrontational because I'd never had a need. But I'd absolutely fight over getting to call Eli. "I've been here two weeks. I've done everything you guys tell me to when you tell me to do it. I've played by the rules, participated in all these stupid classes and therapy sessions. I've even met with a nutritionist named Ralph without making any jokes about the irony in putting someone you believe is bulimic with a guy whose very name conjures the thought of purging! Why does everyone else get a phone call and I don't?" I sat in the chair I often occupied across from her desk.

"You broke the rules. Privileges are earned...and lost."

I didn't understand. "I haven't broken *any* of the rules. I don't know where you got your information, but I've done exactly what you told me I had to do."

Raine scooted her chair closer to her desk, put her elbows on top, and then fiddled with a pen in her hands while she smiled. "What time is lights out?"

I hated the smug expression on her thin lips and the patchouli she wore like deodorant. "Ten."

"What time did you turn yours off last night?"

"Five after." This had to be a joke. "I was finishing my homework, Raine. It had to be turned in before the weekend. Remember, I'm not in class because I'm here." I spread out my arms just in case she didn't realize which *here* I referred to. "Meaning, not only do I have to do the work, but I have to teach myself the material."

She set down the pen and laced her fingers together. "The

rules are in place for a reason, Colbie. And you have to learn that you can't bend them to suit your need."

"So I should ignore school to adhere to an arbitrary rule some psychologist put into place for the masses without consideration for the individual?"

Raine slid her glasses off her nose and set them next to the pen I wanted to stab her with. "Colbie, I realize this is a struggle for you. It's always the intelligent patients who struggle the most because your mind doesn't want to relinquish control. But that same control issue is what landed you here to begin with. Your life would not have been altered by handing in your homework five minutes earlier."

"I wouldn't have gotten an *A*."

She shrugged. "*And*? That's one assignment. Not your entire academic career."

My lips were drying out from breathing through the hole between them. "It *is* my entire academic career. I'm vying for valedictorian, Raine." My blood boiled, and my heart raced. I couldn't recall ever being as angry as I was right now. "All it takes is one slip-up to lose that spot. A spot I've spent nearly four years trying to procure."

"Then you made a choice."

I threw my hands in the air. "A choice for what?"

"That your class rank was more important than the phone call you profess to so desperately want."

"Why does it have to be either or?"

"Because you can't relinquish control. Nothing in your life is done in moderation. When you can learn to balance life's requirements, you won't need the restrictions. You're not there." The blank expression on her face infuriated me more than her words.

There was nothing left to discuss. I'd tried to look at this as a vacation, a reprieve from my parents. I convinced myself that there were things I could learn here to help me relax and not take life so seriously, and I'd done so to prove to Eli that I didn't need to be here but also that I loved him enough to try. That I could follow the rules, get the rewards, and be home to him at the end of the semester. Then he'd have nothing to worry about after graduation—assuming there *was* an after graduation for the two of us. As it stood, I hadn't talked to him in two weeks. No letters, no carrier pigeons, no calls, texts, telegraph, or even smoke signals. Nada. Zilch. I had no idea where he was in this, what had happened in Brogdon after I'd left, whether my parents notified the school, or if our relationship still existed. I had nothing.

And now, that silence would continue because I'd failed at something that should have been elementary, something I'd done my entire life without falter—follow the rules. Never had I been penalized for making school a priority; it was what every parent dreamed of for their kids, but it killed my drive to have another perfect week. One tiny mistake. Five minutes had cost me the only thing I'd cared about having. Time with Eli.

I sulked back to my room where I skipped group and nutrition. I hadn't even bothered to go to the gym during my scheduled workout—it was a joke anyhow. This was ludicrous. I hated being here, and I wanted to go home. Yet there was nothing there, either. My parents wouldn't welcome my return, and whether Eli wanted to or not, I couldn't live with him and finish school. I had nowhere to go until this was over.

Despite Raine's insistence, I refused to get out of bed the next day except to pee. I abdicated my responsibilities, school included, in favor of wallowing in depression. And the things that I could have counted on to bring me pleasure weren't within reach. I couldn't stimulate that satisfaction through food or running or sex—they were all off the table. Perfection wasn't attainable. I couldn't play the piano or read a book. Every joy in my life had been stripped away, and all I was left with was myself.

And that was a painful mirror to look into.

18

COLBIE

I COULDN'T FIND RELIEF.

I couldn't run. I couldn't work out. I couldn't even do yoga. There was nothing to pour myself into to regain the control I'd lost since coming here. There were no phones available. I could write until my hand fell off, but without correspondence, I didn't see the point. I'd been cut off from the outside world, severed, and until I resumed therapy, that isolation included school. I needed something, anything.

Walking down the hall, peeking my head into cracked doors, I realized I'd reached the lowest of lows, and I didn't care. There were people on this floor who suffered from the opposite of what Bright Horizons believed my affliction to be. There were yins to my yang. I just had to find them. Befriend them. Or at the very least, buy one off.

Bella sat on her bed, reading a book about nutrition. I rolled my eyes before I knocked. The girl was cloyingly thin—and I had apparently become incredibly judgmental—but we had something in common. She didn't want to eat, and I needed to binge. If there was one thing I'd learned while being here, it was that people went to elaborate measures to handle their body the way they wanted. No treatment facility in the world could change someone who didn't want help. Bella didn't want help, and I didn't need it.

I'd seen her conceal things when she left the cafeteria, and I knew she was hiding food in her room to keep from having to eat it. Sadly, I didn't care what it was. I'd take anything. My heart longed for that full sensation, the happiness that came from a satisfying meal. My brain needed the flood of endorphins that was almost as good as sex, although not quite. I hadn't had a runner's high, an orgasm, or food euphoria since I'd arrived, and my mind whirled in a frenzy of uncertainty and confusion. I couldn't grasp anything because it all moved too quickly.

"Knock, knock." I tapped on Bella's door. "Hey." I smiled when she peered up from the pages of her book.

She had beautiful teeth and full lips. Her nose was straight, and she had the most unique green eyes I'd ever seen. Bella's blond hair had probably been spectacular before her nutritional habits stole the life and body from it. "Hi, you. I haven't seen you in a couple of days. Everything okay?" Bella placed a bookmark in her spot and closed the cover.

The two of us weren't friends. I wasn't friends with anyone here. They were all sick and needed help. I had school to worry about—well, until recently—and trying to get by until I could get out. Going through the motions here was taxing, not to mention time-consuming, and I hadn't managed to create relationships in addition to the things that were required of me. The last couple of days, I'd forgone those things as well.

I glanced in both directions down the hall outside her room and then stepped inside, closing the door behind me. She watched me approach with her large, round eyes, but she waited for me to tell her what I wanted.

"I was wondering if maybe we could help each other out?" I chose my words carefully.

Her eyes sparkled when she nodded. "Sure, what's up?"

Bella—like everyone else here—was not hurting for money. She was a B-list actress who'd made some serious cash on a daytime soap opera. Bargaining with her wouldn't include using my ATM card.

She must have seen my hesitation because she laid her hand on my knee. "I'm happy to help you if I can, Colbie. What's wrong?"

I took a deep breath and went for the gusto. "Do you have any snacks you don't want?"

Her shoulders slumped, and her expression sank. "Did Raine send you in here to ask me about lunch?"

"Raine? What? No. Of course not." I twisted my fingers in my lap and chewed my bottom lip. "It's just..." I wondered if this was how drug addicts begged for their next high when they were out of money and dope. "I'm..." I couldn't maintain eye contact. "I'd be willing to barter. I mean if there's something you need. I just thought maybe we could help each other out."

"Oh." The surprise in her voice wasn't that of disappointment, but rather clarity. She squeezed my knee and then patted it. "I don't know if I have anything you want, but you're welcome to it." Bella stood and then moved around the room.

She shifted the vent from the air intake and pulled out a pillowcase before replacing the cover. One by one, she removed small items from her drawers, then she went to the closet and pulled stuff from the pockets of her pants and jacket. By the time she returned to my side, she had collected enough food to kill a small horse and deposited her loot onto the mattress.

"Wow." There were apples, granola bars, a couple of snack cakes—I didn't have a clue where she'd gotten those. They certainly weren't on the menus I'd seen. Bagels were wrapped in napkins, and I wasn't sure I wanted to know what had caused the grease stains on the paper towel.

Bella shrugged. "Some of it you probably shouldn't eat. It

might make you sick. I try to get rid of things before they go bad, but it can be hard. And the packaged stuff won't go down the toilet."

I didn't want to know how she'd managed to get all this food out of the cafeteria. I just needed to know what she wanted for it. "How much?"

She plopped onto the bed next to me, but as light as she was, the mattress barely shifted. Her frail fingers pushed the food around as though she were sorting through it to see how valuable it was. Then she met my eyes. "Can you get any laxatives?"

I'd known this would all come at a price. I had hoped it wouldn't include theft, but in my mind, I justified that by telling myself that the patients paid a steep tab to be here. That money was what Bright Horizons used to buy the medication they had on hand. So technically, I wasn't stealing. I was taking something my parents had paid for when they enrolled me in this place.

I nodded to answer Bella's question. "I'll be back." I didn't reach for the food. This was an exchange, not a handout. I wouldn't get the goods until I'd given her the payment. That was the way deals worked.

The door remained ajar when I left. I didn't bother to look back. I could feel Bella's hopeful eyes staring holes into my back. She had her own needs that craved attention, and I was desperate to find a mutually beneficial solution.

In the time I'd been here, I'd kept my head down. I might have been naïve, but I wasn't stupid. The adage everyone has a price proved itself over and over again within these walls. There were ways to get things you wanted, needed. Contraband was only unobtainable if you didn't keep your eyes and ears open. I stayed alert. I knew where to go to get what Bella had asked for and whom I'd have to pay off to be able to swipe it. What I didn't know was how long that would take to facilitate.

It wasn't as easy as just walking down the hall to the nurses' station and swiping it off a shelf. Braxton was the rumored conspirator, and he had just come in for his shift. I sat in my room and watched the hands tick by on the clock, trying to give him time to get in and get the previous shift out. The fewer people around, the better my chances would be. After twenty-two minutes, I'd waited as long as I could. My leg bounced in nervous anticipation, and I'd nearly chewed a hole in my lip.

I stuck my head out my door and strained to peer around the corner. Braxton sat alone at the computer. He was a cute guy, in a nerdy sort of way. And clearly, he was intelligent, or he wouldn't have a nursing degree. What he wasn't was ethical, and that worked in my favor. So did the fact that he'd made no secret over finding me attractive.

God, I missed Eli. One phone call—just to hear his voice—would end this nonsense. I wouldn't need the fix I currently sought. I wouldn't feel justified in breaking a rule much less a law. This idea that eliminating outside distractions somehow benefited a patient was nothing short of ludicrous.

Before I talked to Braxton, I checked myself in the mirror. I couldn't imagine what he saw in me, but if he fancied patients in rehab centers and that got me what I needed, then I'd play the game. I took a deep breath and pulled down the front of my shirt a smidge to expose my cleavage.

I hated myself for this.

The hall was clear coming and going. I waltzed down it like I had all the confidence in the world when in actuality, my hands shook, and adrenaline pumped through me causing my heart to hammer in my chest. The pounding nearly drowned out Braxton's overly friendly welcome.

He stood as I approached. "Hey, Colbie." His gaze dropped to my neckline before quickly rising back to meet my eyes. It was a tad creepy, but the smile he tossed out made this a little easier.

I glanced around like a crackhead checking for cops. "Hey, Braxton." I kept my voice low to prevent drawing attention or being overheard.

His head of dark curls leaned in close, and I could smell the peppermint on his breath. "Why are we whispering?"

I straightened my back when it dawned on me that whispering might draw more attention than casually talking. "Sorry." I cleared my throat, touching it lightly with my fingers when I felt heat rise up my neck. "I heard you provide a service for people here."

He clamped a meaty hand over my mouth as quickly as the words had left it. "Keep your voice down."

I rolled my eyes and pushed his arm away. "Can you help me or not?"

Suddenly, Braxton appeared sketchy, on edge. "Yeah, yeah. Sure." His eyes darted up and down the hall, and he checked over his shoulder before saying anything else. "What do you need?"

I wasn't sure if I needed to make as big a show of checking for onlookers and eavesdroppers as Braxton had, so I raised my brows and waited until he gave me a visual go ahead. "Laxatives."

"Child's play. That it?" His dismissal irritated me. Braxton had no idea how hard it was to be trapped here, cooped up like an animal. Prisoners had more freedom than those of us still in the dorms.

I shrugged. "Unless you can get me a conjugal visit, yes, that's it."

"Two-fifty for the service and a hundred for ten pills." He swiped his thumb under his nose and continued to glance around.

I nearly choked. Three hundred and fifty dollars for ten laxatives. That wasn't just highway robbery, it should be punishable by death. "Seriously?"

He crossed his arms and shrugged one shoulder. "Take it or

leave it. I'm not the one who needs it." Braxton cocked his head to the side, eyeing me like a sirloin on an all-you-can-eat buffet. "Unless you want to work out another form of payment."

I sighed and realized why Braxton carried a flame for women in treatment. Not only did he lack game, but he was also a slime-ball. "Does cash work for you?"

He smirked. "Good as gold."

Five minutes later, I returned with money from my commissary fund. I didn't see the point in having a commissary when I was forbidden from buying half of what they offered and wasn't interested in the other fifty percent. Thankfully, it provided me with an influx of cash—the only sign that my parents remembered me being here. When I handed over the bills, Braxton sidled up next to the counter in order to discreetly tuck a small blister pack of laxatives into my jeans' pocket.

He leaned in, and the heat of his breath on my skin crept down my spine like spiders. "I'm more than happy to work out another form of payment anytime you're ready." The sound of his voice was worse than nails on a chalkboard, and it made my toes curl. A person could go from decent to despicable in the blink of an eye.

I stepped back and thought he ought to be grateful Eli wasn't here to show him just how little he thought of Braxton's violation of my personal space. "Cash works. Thanks."

I didn't stop to analyze the way my skin crawled or the gleam in his eyes. This had a purpose, and I'd accomplished my mission with relative ease. As fast as my feet would carry me, I beelined toward Bella's room, and there I exchanged her want for my need. It all felt like a covert operation that could go wrong at any point, but I didn't care. No recourse could have stopped me from what I was about to do.

Consequences be damned.

I'd made sure to wait as long as I could into our dinner hour before I started eating so that once I got back to my room, I could add to it what I'd gotten from Bella. I was giddy with excitement and felt a bit like a rebel when I rose from the table to go to my room.

"Hey, Colbie?"

I turned at the sound of my name called to find Bella still in the dining room. "Yeah?" My hand tapped the side of my leg in anticipation. I was wasting precious time.

"You want to watch a movie with us tonight?" She thumbed over her shoulder to two other girls. They all stood with smiles, awaiting my reply.

I didn't want to think about a movie right now. "Sure. I'll come find you in a bit." It was hard to keep my voice level when all I wanted to do was scream at her to leave me alone.

Bella had to know my plans. I hadn't bothered her when she'd downed her laxatives or raced off to the bathroom. Surely, she could give me some time to enjoy satisfying the beast that clawed inside me. I didn't need long. Bella bit her pouty lip and nodded. Yep, she knew.

I waved, but my clenched fingers and balled fists probably didn't do much to ease my awkward reply.

Trying desperately to remain discreet, I shuffled down the hall and kept my head down. The corridor was relatively quiet since most people went to the recreational rooms—there was no *recreation*, only movies and board games—after dinner. It was the only place we were encouraged to socialize. Apparently, getting a bunch of people with eating disorders together was a recipe for disaster. I'd heard through the grapevine that patients exchanged secrets for how to. It didn't matter if it was anorexia or bulimia, meetings of the minds became strategizing sessions when they were unsupervised. Hence the reason we were discouraged from having visitation outside of the common areas.

Personally, I didn't care what anyone else did. I was just here to do my time and get out. That was more difficult than I'd assumed it would be, which was what currently had me at the brink.

There were no locks to our suites, so I moved a chair against the door and under the knob to prevent anyone from casually wandering in. I retrieved the pillowcase of food I'd hidden in the suitcase in my closet. I also grabbed my headphones and the MP3 player I'd bought from the commissary. I'd picked the device loaded with classical music—they offered country, pop, rap, and some alternative grunge—because my fingers could dance on an imaginary set of keys as I listened. It was as close to a piano as I could get, and without Eli, I had to make do.

I crawled onto the bed and covered my legs with a blanket. A strange nostalgia washed over me as I sat Indian-style with the pillowcase in front of me. As a child, this had been how I'd gone through my Halloween candy. Caden and I would sit on my bed and dump out our loot. He'd toss me his Snickers, and I'd give him all my Kit Kats. But Caden wasn't across from me, and there wasn't any candy in my bag. I was alone. My family had dumped me here. They'd stripped me of everything I loved.

I ripped open a granola bar and took a bite—that was for music.

The dark notes of Mozart pounded into my ears and washed out everything around me.

I didn't even taste the little bits of chocolate as I tore through the first snack.

The bag of pretzels didn't stand a chance as I demolished them—that was for running.

Puccini killed Mimi in *La Bohème* as I ate through an apple.

One bagel, then two—they were for Eli—gone through like the

men in *Platoon* when Samuel Barber's "Adagio for Strings" rang through my headphones.

And Bach brought it home when he stole every ounce of happiness, and I begged him to take me like "Come, Sweet Death."

It was mindless.

My memories played on fast-forward as I ate my way through thousands of "healthy" calories. My stomach swelled, and for the first time since I'd seen Eli before Christmas, a glimmer of euphoria danced around my thoughts' edge. It was so close; I could almost touch it. I reached with each bite, desperate to hold its hand for just a fraction of a second. I stretched every time I chewed, grasping for a shred of happiness.

But when Henryk Górecki's Symphony No. 3, "Sorrowful Songs," echoed in my ears, I lost the battle. The tears won out as the chilling music, inspired by the words of an eighteen-year-old girl—a World War II prisoner—engrained themselves into my soul. The war was over. My heart ached. My body was weary. I was crushed in the agony of defeat. The days I'd gone without bingeing or purging had been shattered in this moment of weakness.

The food rose in my esophagus, threatening to make its way free before I lifted the lid to the toilet in the bathroom. I ripped the headphones off and tossed them onto the bed with the MP3 player and trash and remnants of food and all of my sanity.

Eli.

Dr. Chalmers.

Jess.

Caden.

I'd failed them all. They'd been right, where I'd been wrong. Each of them had known, and I'd been blind. I'd let them down. Fools rushed in. I was lost. More lost than I'd ever been. Drowning in the weight of my choices and the unhappiness it always brought in the end.

The control was an illusion, and I was sick.

Not just sick right this second.

Sick as in *sick*.

Worthlessness.

Hopelessness.

Betrayal.

Demise.

Hatred.

I purged those words into the water before me. Tears streamed down my face and neck. My fingers couldn't go deep enough to rid myself of the self-loathing that ate at me like maggots on rotting flesh. There was nothing good in what was left of me.

Saliva clung to my fingers like a web, and bile ran down my palm. I fell to the bathroom floor and begged God to have mercy on me, to show me a light that would point me in the direction of happiness. I pleaded with the Almighty for compassion right before I tried to bargain with the Devil. I'd take either or; I just needed something.

But God didn't rescue me.

Satan wasn't interested in my pleas.

I was alone. In a bathroom. In a rehab facility. With vomit on my hands and nothing left of my heart. Maybe I'd never made enough effort and just blamed everyone else. It was possible the entire fault fell to me.

Epiphanies didn't always come with brilliant light; sometimes they happened in the dark. This was one of those times.

There were always counselors on the clock at Bright Horizons. Twenty-four-seven. Any patient had access to a psychologist. It might not be the one we typically worked with, but one would be available. And it took a lot of effort to pick myself up off that floor to go find that person.

I'd managed to blow another blood vessel in my eye with that purge, and it was clear I'd spent a substantial amount of time crying. But I'd washed my hands and done my best to clean up my face before I moved the chair away from the door.

I stopped myself, recognizing how metaphorical that velvet chaise lounge actually was. The comfort of that piece of furniture, the luxurious feel of the fabric on my skin, the barricade it provided to the inner workings of my mind as it kept the door sealed shut. Moving it wasn't about the physical effort; the strain came from knowing that once I pushed that hurdle aside, ripped off the cushy upholstery, and got rid of the plush pillows that the real work had to begin.

The pain of that acknowledgment was greater than believing my brother and Jess had betrayed me or that my parents had ignored me. It was more substantial than the loss of Eli's touch or missing the way he loved me. There was no one on the other side of that door who could do this *for* me. No one could help shoulder the burden.

It was entirely up to me.

I took a deep breath and lifted my hand to the knob. Each step required a monumental effort. I twisted the handle, cracked the door, and then took the first step into recovery.

And she was a scary bitch.

She taunted me as I walked down the hall. With each breath I took, recovery reminded me of how hard this would be. I wanted to turn around, go back to the safety of my room. If I could hide from the world until May, then I could leave and never deal with any of this.

"Hey, Cole—" She hadn't meant to call my nickname—the

one Eli and Caden used—but Raine had stopped herself mid-name when she'd seen my tear-stained cheeks.

And *that* was the sign I'd asked God for. *That* was the mercy He'd sent to show me the way. *That* was the one thing I'd needed to plead for help.

My eyes met hers, and the tears started before I could stop them. I cupped my face in my hands and sobbed. Right there in the hall. I let out every fear, every worry, every imperfection that haunted me. Raine wrapped me into a firm embrace, and there she held me until I was able to move. She didn't try to talk to me or ask what was going on. In some innate way, I believed she knew. Or maybe she'd just dealt with enough basket cases not to need words.

My legs were wobbly, and my emotions just as unstable.

"Why don't we go down to my office," she whispered into my ear, and her tone reminded me of the way my mom had talked to me when I was little—before she'd forgotten I needed her just like my brothers.

Raine helped me into a chair and took the one next to me instead of the one behind her desk like she usually did. Then she reached behind her and snagged a blanket from a basket to offer me. There was something comforting about that layer of protection that reassured me I was safe.

AFTER MY BREAKTHROUGH AND SUBSEQUENT BREAKDOWN, Emily slipped into my room and closed the door behind her. "I could get fired for this."

I sat on my bed cross-legged and stared at the girl I'd not so long ago believed harbored Satan's spirit. "For coming into a patient's room?"

She took it upon herself to get comfortable on my mattress and tossed an envelope into my lap. "No." She huffed and rolled her eyes. "For that."

I picked up the mail and turned it over. The handwriting was as familiar as his kiss.

"You looked like you could use a pick-me-up." She might not have had any of the details behind what had gone on in therapy over the last couple weeks, but I was certain she caught wind of patients who finally "got it." "But if you get caught with it, you didn't get it from me." Emily jumped up as quickly as she'd sat down and escorted herself out, closing the door behind her.

I stared at the mail—at his handwriting—and my heart swelled. Tears came to my eyes. The letter was thick, but it wasn't a card. I stuck my finger under the flap, not wanting to destroy any piece of Eli that I could physically cling to. Inside, there were several letters.

As I read, I heard his voice as though he whispered the written words into my ear. One by one, they comforted me, fueled me, and then drove me.

Even through my silence, Eli hadn't given up. In fact, he'd made sure that I knew beyond a shadow of a doubt that he'd thought of me in everything he did. He told me the parts I would have liked and hated and how he wished I could have shared them with him.

When everything here is familiar and I still struggle to breathe, I can only imagine how hard it is for you to be away.

The sky was the color of your eyes today. And I was convinced it was your way of staying with me.

Even as much as I miss you, I'm immensely proud of the step you've taken to be the best you *that you can be.*

I only thought I loved you before you left...now I know I'll never let you go again. Not without me by your side.

If you get lonely, know that we're under the same sky with the same stars and moon and that not even the Montagues and the

Capulets kept Romeo and Juliet apart. I giggled when I finished the next part. *Okay, that might not be the best reference, because you're not fifteen, neither of us is going to poison ourselves, and our families aren't at war. But you get the gist of how deep my love for you runs. One day, it will be our story the greats write about.*

Each letter professed a more profound love, an unwavering devotion, a commitment that renewed my desire to see this through. I'd already messed up this week, so there was no hope of a phone call, but I might get to write him a letter if I played my cards right. And maybe at the end of next week, I could hear his voice. After nearly a month, I wondered if I'd be able to contain my excitement.

By the time I'd actually been granted any freedom, I'd been at Bright Horizons for forty-six days, and it felt like Christmas. While I hadn't been moved out of the dorms—yet—I'd had a large envelope full of mail delivered to me, and in just a few minutes, I'd get to use the phone.

Unfortunately, the letters were given to me during my counseling session, and Raine felt it necessary to discuss the emotions that seemed to explode from me upon seeing who'd taken the time to write. She didn't understand why I was shocked to have received anything from Caden and the twins. Nor did she get why my parents would lie regarding my whereabouts. And while I'd anticipated getting in trouble for not doling out all of this information in one of our earlier sessions, she praised me for my openness now. Raine hadn't given me a hard time or attempted to convince me that I had merely misunderstood my parents' intent. She listened. She heard me.

And then she did something no one other than Eli had. She validated me.

At the end of our session, I realized we'd gone over our appointment slot. Raine hadn't shut me down or told me we'd resume the conversation the next day. I read a couple of the letters, sitting in front of her. It was obvious my brothers really believed I was out of the country. My parents acted like *they* believed I was on holiday. It was all superficial, but I didn't expect different from the boys.

I had refused to read Eli's mail in Raine's office, and I had only skimmed a couple of Jess's letters. There was a lot of hurt there—on my part anyway. Forgiving her wouldn't be as simple as her saying she was sorry. And a lot of how I moved forward would depend on how Eli had faired in all of this. Which I still didn't know because I hadn't talked to him.

At this point, he could be back in Michigan because he'd been fired. I wouldn't know the difference unless he gave me insight on the phone. School hadn't been in session during the first week I was here, and those were the only letters Emily had smuggled to me. I wanted to believe that the school board would have called him in before classes started back if, in fact, my parents had reported him, but I couldn't be certain of anything.

Seven long weeks had passed since then. Forty-six days was a long time to be out of the loop and away from daily life. In the letters I'd read this afternoon, Eli had mentioned work—so at the very least, he wasn't unemployed—but only in the vaguest sense. He focused on articles he'd read or books he thought I'd enjoy. Every word was perfectly chosen to bring a smile to my lips and keep worry from my heart.

He'd written every day, and I now had a pile of his thoughts to go through any time I needed to feel close to him.

There was a light tap on my door just before Emily stuck her head in. "Phone's all yours. You've got an hour. Use it however you want." She started to leave but poked back inside. "I'm really proud of you, Colbie. I know it was hard to get here." Emily referred to having the privilege of phone calls.

It had been hard, but not because I'd wanted to binge and purge—that had only happened a couple times. The self-exploration here was impossible to avoid. And that journey was more difficult than any nutrition or exercise plan they could have put me on. Because my unhealthy eating habits were a result of my internal disdain and shame. But knowing that didn't mean I'd fixed any of it—just that I acknowledged it.

I squealed and nearly fell off the bed, trying to get up. My hair bounced around my shoulders and got in my face as I scrambled to my feet. If Eli had been standing here, this was the time he'd reach out to tuck the tendrils behind my ear. *God, I missed him.* I raced down the hall in my socks, sliding on the tile floors when I tried to stop.

"Slow down, Colbie." Emily giggled and shook her head when I nearly fell, rounding the corner.

There were several little rooms along a corridor, none of which were bigger than a small closet. However, they contained the most coveted things in the building—resident phones. With one phone on the wall per room and a lounge chair with down cushions, they were comfortable and made for privacy. I took the blanket from the back when I sat, and then I covered myself.

Suddenly, my heart fluttered with nervous anticipation. Eli had no idea I'd be calling, and there was no guarantee that I'd reach him. Not getting to hear his voice was enough to make my stomach churn.

I took the cordless phone and dialed the number I'd waited weeks to use. Tears welled in my eyes after the third ring, and my bottom lip quivered on the start of the fourth.

"Hello?" He was out of breath, and I couldn't be certain that had been the actual word he'd said.

"Eli?"

He huffed into the phone, trying to catch his breath. "Cole? Is that you?" Either the connection was horrible, or Eli was skydiving. "Hang on, baby. Let me get inside."

The seconds ticked by, and so did time on the phone's receiver. It had to have been wind ripping around that caused the static on the call, although I had no idea what he'd be doing.

And then the line was crystal clear. "Hey. I'm sorry. We have a horrible storm coming, and I was trying to get my patio furniture into the garage. The umbrella's still out there, but it might have just become a sacrifice to the god of bad weather." He chuckled, and his laughter filled my chest and wormed its way into my soul.

"Do you need to go take care of stuff? I can let you go." Brogdon didn't typically get hit by hurricanes or tornados, just the wind and rain they brought with them. Those tropical storms could do a lot of damage though. But in February, neither should have been a threat.

"Not a chance in hell. I don't care if everything out there blows away."

I hadn't expected this to be awkward, yet now that I had him on the phone, I wasn't sure what to say. And the seconds of silence unnerved me. "How have you been?" Great, we'd managed to talk about the weather, and I'd asked how he was.... I was a riveting conversationalist.

"All things considered, I've been okay. Hearing your voice just upped okay to fantastic. Jesus, I miss the hell out of you, Cole. Things just aren't the same without your sassy mouth."

"Have you gotten my homework? How'd I do on my test? Oh, and the essay on Poe?" I had turned in my assignments—albeit some were late, and others hadn't been my best quality—but I didn't get word back about grades. I wasn't in danger of failing, that much I knew, but that was where it stopped. The rest was a work in progress.

"Baby, I don't want to talk about school or grades or class. I want to know what you've been doing for forty-six days—and yes, I'm counting. Tell me about the people you've met. Your counselors. Life here is status quo."

"Oh, well, I um...I just wanted to make sure—"

"Colbie, please don't worry about your grades."

"I wasn't. I just didn't..." I trailed off, unsure of how to ask what I needed to know without slicing open a wound that might never heal.

"What? Don't go shy on me."

I licked my lips and debated whether or not to question him. It was something I needed to mark off my list, and the only way I could do that was to ask. "Did you get in trouble at school?" The words raced from my mouth and tumbled into the phone.

He sighed, which didn't sound promising. "Shit, I'm sorry. You've probably been worried about that since you left, and I haven't said anything or written about any of it. I didn't want to bring any of it up."

"Oh God..."

"No. That's just it. I worried for days—*weeks*—after classes resumed that Caleb would say something or your parents would call the principal. But nothing."

I didn't want to spend a lot of time contemplating the ins and outs of what that actually meant. "I wonder if that's their own special brand of torture."

Eli's deep belly laugh rang through the line. "I don't think so. That was just a special gift that came with purchase. Honestly, Cole. I haven't heard so much as a peep from your parents, and Caleb steers clear of me at the school."

"Are you afraid they're going to?"

"At some point, I'm going to have to deal with the situation with both your folks and your brother, but no, I don't believe they plan to take it to the school district. Although, I can't say I'd do the same if it were our daughter."

I nearly choked on my saliva. "We have kids now?" The broken chortle did nothing to hide my shock.

"No, clearly not. I'm just saying that I don't understand. I don't even have children, but I'm so overly protective of the *idea* of the ones we *will* have someday, that I'm blown away by your parents' indifference. I'd string me up by the balls and threaten any grown man that touched my baby."

"Eli..."

"And God help me. If we have a son, and he doesn't take it upon himself to handle his best friends to protect his sister, I'll beat some sibling devotion into him."

"Eli."

"Don't *Eli* me." His tone had taken on a playful lilt, but there was no doubt in my mind just how serious he was. "Caleb should have beat my ass, Colbie. Plain and simple. And I would have taken it like a man."

The thought of my brother and Eli throwing punches at each other was humorous, even if it shouldn't have been. "Oh yeah? So you'd just let Caleb take some cheap shots and then walk away with your tail between your legs?"

"Fuck no. I said I'd take it like a man. I didn't say I was a pussy."

I loved hearing him laugh as he talked. The way his voice changed warmed my heart, and I knew every word out of his mouth was true. He would fight for me. And I deserved that kind of love. Coming to that realization had been hard-fought.

"If it comes down to it, or ever comes up before you get home, I promise, I'll let you know. Otherwise, don't waste another minute thinking about it. Okay?"

It was on the list of things I had to work on. Letting go came right after loving myself. Or maybe it was relinquishing control and then letting go. Or, possibly realizing my power of persuasion. I didn't know. The therapy sessions were endless, and each time I thought I'd made progress, something else came up. "I'll try."

"Is that something they've taught you there?"

I hated that I had to admit these things, but even I knew Eli would have to be part of my healing process, or he'd be part of what hindered me. The only way to allow him to choose which role was to give him information.

I took a deep breath that I was quite certain he heard. "I'm not sure that I'm quite as great a student here as I am in a real classroom, but yes. I'm learning to prioritize."

"Meaning?"

"That I don't have to be the best at everything." I hated even thinking those words, much less *saying* them. "And that sometimes my best might only be my ability to try something and fail." And those words were cringe-worthy.

Eli and I spent the entire hour talking about my therapy and the things the staff here tried to teach me. He joked about how hard-headed I was and said if they'd attach grades to the work, I'd be an honor's patient. "Oh, shit, Colbie. I'm didn't mean that."

I didn't interject or tell him it was okay. He'd made the mistake, and I allowed him to be responsible for it.

"That was insensitive. I shouldn't have even joked like that. Please forgive me."

And instead of getting offended or feeling sorry for myself that someone stopped to correct something they shouldn't have said, I released him from that burden. "I do." And it felt freeing.

Neither of us allowed it to stunt the conversation, and we talked until the very last minute when a voice came on the line to warn me I was out of time.

"I'll keep my phone on me at all times. If you can call, I don't care when it is. Okay, babe?" The disappointment in his tone made my chest constrict.

"Of course." I tried to keep the pain from coming through. I didn't want him to know just how hard this process was to go through alone.

The automated voice came on again with a thirty-second warning.

"I love you, Eli, and I miss you like crazy."

"Same. I love you, Cole."

19

ELI

IT WOULDN'T BE LONG BEFORE THE SCHOOL STARTED handing out contracts for the following year, and I hoped like hell I'd have another offer before I had to turn theirs down. Several of the other teachers had confirmed what I already knew, the AP English teacher wasn't coming back, and the school would extend that position to me for next year.

Regardless, I wouldn't accept. Even if Colbie didn't want me at the end of this, I couldn't stay in Brogdon. There was nothing for me here. What I'd believed to be waiting for me when I'd accepted this position hadn't proven to be here at all. Yes, the job itself was open, and just as Caleb indicated when he threw the idea at me, the teacher on medical leave wouldn't return. However, I had foolishly—or maybe I was just naïve—believed that living in the same town as my best friend would be like college. Not the parties and all-nighters, but the camaraderie. Getting married shouldn't have changed much. It shouldn't have made Caleb completely unavailable. He and Chasity had been together since I'd known him, and he'd never had a hard time juggling friends and his relationship. The reality was, that had been life at UGA, not in Brogdon, Georgia. Here, he had the guys he had grown up with, his family, and the life he made with his wife. And I'd never been part of those things. I was the outsider, his best friend from college, not childhood.

Most of the teachers at school were women, which was fine, but they weren't people who would throw a football or that I could go have a pint with at the local bar while watching college sports.

And then there was Colbie. She'd changed everything.

I no longer cared about fitting in here or making friends or creating a life. I didn't give a shit about being contracted for next year at Brogdon High or hanging out with the Chapmans at UGA games. I just wanted Colbie to graduate so we could leave. I'd never ask her to change her plans, and since mine weren't fixed, it made sense to follow hers.

She could live in the dorms at Vanderbilt if she wanted. We could date while she attended undergrad. I wasn't set on the logistics, just that I was nearby. I missed her. Never in my life had days crept along at such a slow pace. I'd done more writing since she'd left than I had when I worked on my dissertation. I wrote to her, for her, about her. Anything I could to keep my mind occupied. Most of what I'd written, I had sent to her to ensure she knew I thought about her constantly, that she was missed, but most importantly, loved.

I had not, however, told her that I had set up interviews in Nashville. One was with the Metropolitan Nashville Public School District, and I also had two with private schools closer to Vanderbilt. I hated not being able to talk to her about it, get her thoughts. I wanted nothing more than to drive to Tennessee with Colbie in my passenger seat as spring took over the mountains. The two of us could look at the schools, check out neighborhoods, have lunch. Stay for the weekend. But as it stood, I would make these trips alone. To make matters worse, I'd be within a few miles of Colbie yet not be able to see her.

I didn't want to make these decisions on my own, and it wasn't because I wasn't capable of doing so. I wanted her in on everything we did. In my mind, that was how relationships that turned into marriages worked. My parents talked about the small stuff and worked together through the important decisions. They never made a move without the other. I used to believe my mom was dependent upon my dad, and that she somehow wasn't capable of being assertive or decisive. Now I understood. It was never that she *couldn't* be those things. She didn't *want* to.

But when I only got an hour on the phone with her after forty-five days of silence, talking about my job, interviews, and next year wasn't how I cared to spend our time. My only goal had been to hear her laugh. If I could have made her moan, that would have been at the top of the list as well. It hadn't been until the end of the call that she'd mentioned she had privacy, but even still, I wouldn't risk their being cameras. No one would ever see Colbie Chapman come undone but me.

The bell rang, snapping me out of my thoughts. Groans sounded around the classroom as students murmured complaints about not having had enough time to finish their tests. The only one who hadn't complained—and who promptly stood to hand in her paper—was Jess.

I had to give it to the girl. She'd managed to find a way to ask me about Colbie nearly every day since she'd left—text messages, locating me in the hall or the teacher's lounge. She was worried and feared she'd destroyed the friendship. Daily, I reassured Jess that if Colbie's silence was an indication of her anger, then she was pissed at me as well. I needed to tell Jess that I'd talked to Colbie, but it would likely have to wait until after school.

I winced, thinking about texting Jess. If anyone ever got ahold of any of our phone records, I'd never be able to show my face again, much less teach. My texts with Jess were filled with concern for her best friend, but it was still a teacher interacting with a student. There was nothing that would make that okay. Even if it weren't illegal, it was unethical and immoral.

As the last kid filed out of my room, I stacked their tests into a pile and put a binder clip on top of them. Grading them would go on tonight's list of fun-filled activities to keep my mind off Colbie. I slid the work into my bag and grabbed all the stuff I needed to enter into the grade portal.

I'd found myself assigning more graded work and homework to the AP English class than I had forecasted in my lesson plans. At first, I hadn't realized what I was doing. Then it dawned on me, that every assignment they had to do, Colbie did as well. I hadn't been able to talk to her, but I still got to read her words. She might not have hidden messages in the paragraphs, but I pretended she had. It also gave me the chance to look at her grades in her other classes, as well as her class standing.

Colbie hadn't mentioned it, and I wouldn't bring it up. But I had the inside vantage point. I knew where she was in class rank and whether or not she still held the number one spot. Jess no longer had a clue which one of them outperformed the other. And every time I logged in, my heart would skip a beat, and my chest would tighten until I saw the number next to her name. While her work in my class remained *A* quality, there had been a couple bobbles in others. I didn't have a lot of information other than Colbie said part of what she had to learn to manage was her time, and that had come at a price.

Even if her work had slipped below that of the rest of the class, I couldn't have given her less. It was wrong and unfair to the other students. I just didn't care. She didn't deserve to have been ripped out of town, much less to lose what she'd worked for because of it. However, I couldn't control what other teachers did, nor would I mention it to them.

"I have a favor to ask." Colbie's uncertainty bothered me, mostly because I couldn't soothe her worry while she was away.

"You know I'll do anything for you." And I would. If it were in my power, I'd make it happen.

Whatever she needed, she clearly didn't want to say. Colbie started and stopped several times.

"Baby, just tell me."

She groaned. "Fine." And she huffed. "My counselor thinks it would be a good idea for you to join us for a session or two. Bright Horizons believes it's imperative for those who will be involved in my life post-treatment to be involved during treatment as well. I know you won't want to, and I hate having to ask. And since we haven't really talked about what happens after this, you probably think I have the cart before the horse, but it's just—"

"I'd be happy to—" It also gave me a segue into another topic that had to be addressed.

"I'm sorry, Eli. I know it's a long drive—"

"Colbie. Stop." I waited to make sure she'd quit rambling. "I'm happy to. I am going to Nashville in a couple weeks, anyhow."

"You are?" Her pitch escalated in surprise.

"Yeah. Over spring break, I'll be there for several days."

She shuffled around, and the phone picked up the static of whatever it had rubbed against. "For what?"

God, I wished I could see the curiosity in her eyes and the way her lips remained parted when she asked a question. "I have three job interviews lined up."

"In Nashville?" By now, I knew she'd sat straight up, and if she had a blanket covering her, it would be puddled at her feet. That sexy space would still remain between her lips as she inhaled a deep breath. "I don't understand."

I had thought I was reasonably clear, but I could certainly

draw her a map to my conclusions. "Colbie, you're not going to be in Brogdon next year, and neither am I."

"...You're going to be in Nashville?" Her naïveté was cute.

"Is that where you're going to be?"

She huffed as if she didn't understand. "Well, yeah. Vanderbilt is there."

"And you thought what? That I would just let you leave for four years and hope that you would return between undergrad and med school? Maybe get hitched before you raced off to become a doctor?"

There was dead silence on the other end of the line. I couldn't even hear her breathe.

"Colbie?"

"Yeah. I'm here. I'm just...in shock."

I'd been wandering around my house while we talked, but at that point, I dropped onto the sofa and got comfortable. "About what?"

"That you'd re-plan your life around mine."

I shook my head, even though she couldn't see it. "You still don't get it, do you?"

"I guess not." She was young. She'd also never really had anyone devoted to her, much less a guy. Colbie had never had a boyfriend, and Dr. Chapman hadn't been what she deserved—not to say he wasn't a good man, he just hadn't been attentive to his only daughter as I believed he should have been.

"I want to be where you are. Plain and simple. I don't want to do the long-distance thing any longer than we have to. And right now, we have to. Come June, it's a choice. And a choice I'm not willing to make."

"But what about Brogdon?"

I chuckled at her concern. "The high school or the town? Because really, neither hold any further interest." I hated not being able to see her or hold her or reassure her with the stoke of my thumb on her hand.

"Oh."

"I know we have a lot to work through. And I hope that maybe your counselors can help us figure out how to navigate it. There are things you will need when you leave there, and I'll do my best to ensure you have them. But if I can get a job in Tennessee, it makes that a whole lot easier."

A few seconds of silence passed before she hesitantly confirmed, "You're getting a job in Nashville?"

"Yes."

"So we can be together?"

"Yes."

"In Nashville."

"Yes."

"As a couple?"

I burst into laughter and talked through the gales. "Yes, baby. I want to be with my girlfriend in Nashville while she goes to Vanderbilt and I teach. I want to buy a house that you help me pick out. I'd love for you to live with me, but if you want to live in the dorms, I'll be happy with that as well."

Colbie remained quiet, and I wondered if it was too much, not just for her age but based on everything else she had going on. The two of us didn't get to talk a lot about Bright Horizons, but what she did share was overwhelming for me; it had to be like a tidal wave for her.

The sniffles she tried to hide came through, scaring me, yet still, she didn't say anything.

"Cole?"

"What if I don't want to live in the dorms?" *There* she was, the strong-willed woman I loved who had an opinion on everything and preferences she couldn't be deterred from.

Nothing would make me happier than coming home to Colbie

Chapman every night, going to bed with her, waking up next to her. The two of us would be able to share the details of our day without worry, have dinner, go on dates. It was ideal for me, and I'd never tell her no. "I want you with me, always. So, do you think you can schedule time with your counselors around my visit and my interviews? I'm off that whole week, so I can come earlier and stay later. Whatever you need."

Her tone changed into one I'd never heard before. The only way I could describe it was carefree. We spent the rest of the call discussing her nutritionist and trainer. I didn't get the impression that she cared for either, although she clearly understood the power they each held. And little by little, she gave me bread crumbs to her recovery and the painful pieces of what had brought her to what sounded like acceptance.

She still danced around what had gotten her to this place—the reasons behind her excessive need for perfection—but it was the first time she hadn't denied her need to be in Tennessee. It wasn't my place to bring to light the nuances, the intricacies. Colbie had gone from hating the idea to hating the process—and that was progress. Hopefully, her counselors would get her there. And maybe while I was in Nashville, I could help.

She was an incredibly bright young woman. Her mind had shut off this part of her brain to protect her. There was no doubt these were the pieces of the puzzle that she hadn't put into place—the pieces that kept her in the dorms for nearly sixty days when most moved out in the first thirty. But I was fairly certain she'd made improvements that I wasn't aware of. I was okay with that. I didn't need the painful details if Colbie didn't want to share them. I'd help her carry the burden of the load blindfolded.

The voice I dreaded hearing made an appearance on the line to let Colbie know her time was up. "Find out the dates and times for me so I can plan my trip around them. Will I get to talk to you again this week?"

"Unless I screw up." She wasn't indifferent to the possibility, but she wasn't as averse to the idea as she had been when she'd left two months ago. "I don't plan on it though. So, I should get to call you Tuesday night."

My calendar revolved around those two calls, and they came like clockwork. I probably should have encouraged her to call her parents or spend some of her phone time on Jess. However, I was a greedy son of a bitch who didn't play well with others. Sharing had never been my forte. If her parents had been more attentive, none of this would have happened. Jess, on the other hand, I felt sorry for. At least I had the knowledge that she and Colbie had been exchanging letters. I didn't know the content from either of them. I did know that communication would result in reconciliation. The girls had been too close for too many years for a boy and a confession to come between them...or so I hoped. Colbie needed Jess as much as she needed me.

"Then I guess you need to make sure to do what you're supposed to. I look forward to hearing from you."

"I'll do my best."

I hated that for anyone else, doing their best was what most people asked for. With Colbie, doing her best had jeopardized her health and created a monster she couldn't contain and certainly couldn't control.

"You always do, and I love you for it. But working on you is more important. We've got the rest of our lives to talk." Not hearing from her would hurt like hell, and it would drive me insane until I knew what had happened, but none of that was anything she'd ever know. I'd just keep writing to her and covet every second I got until I had her home.

The electronic woman gave her final warning.

"I better let you go." The sadness at the end of our calls cut me like a knife, shredding my insides with grief. "I love you, Cole."

"I love you, too, Eli. And I miss you."

We disconnected, and I sat on my couch still holding the phone for ages. The moment I set it down, I'd be separated from her. As long as I held it, I clung to the connection. It probably wasn't any healthier for me to be as dependent upon her as she was on perfection, but I'd never stop myself from loving her with everything I had.

20

COLBIE

"Colbie, why are you so anxious?" Raine sat across from me at her desk.

I was fairly certain she already knew the answer to this question, but part of working through my emotions was learning to express them, to talk about them, to share them instead of bottling them up. This was where I struggled most, not because I couldn't accept the emotion, but I hated exposing my vulnerability. "I'm afraid for him to see me like this."

Raine leaned back in her chair and folded her hands in her lap. She was much easier to deal with when she sat next to me rather than in her power chair. "Who?"

I tried to communicate through my stare just how unimpressed I was with her question, but as usual, Raine didn't take the hint. "Eli."

"Why?"

Saliva pooled in my mouth, and my heart beat a little faster. My anxiety ratcheted when I got uncomfortable, so I took several deep breaths and swallowed hard. "Because he hasn't seen me like —" I didn't know how to phrase my thoughts without using degrading words—which weren't allowed—so I glanced down my body and then met Raine's stare. "*This*."

"And what exactly does *this* refer to?"

I huffed, but Raine didn't react; she never did. "My weight, my body. Here." I waved my arms just in case she wasn't sure what I referred to.

"What are you afraid he'll see?"

"Imperfection."

Raine smiled. That one word didn't imply much, but in my case, it said everything. "Flaws are reality, Colbie. We all have them. You have a choice on how you deal with them."

We'd been through this more times than I could count, and I was trying to come to terms with that, but the truth was that I struggled to accept it. I didn't have to have flaws. I just needed to get better at managing my life so I didn't resort to unhealthy coping mechanisms.

"You're doing it again."

My eyes had drifted to the floor in my thoughts and popped back up to Raine. "Huh?"

"You're dismissing whatever you're feeling to figure out a way to hide it, fix it, or avoid it. It's time to face it, so it doesn't hinder you when Eli gets here."

But I didn't want to face it. I put my hand on my stomach and pressed. It was no longer firm and taut. There was a layer of softness that hadn't been there in ages. When I looked in the mirror, there was an innertube around my midsection. But when I got on the scale, I'd only gained five pounds in two months. The number was small, yet in my world and on my body, it was monumental and uncomfortable. "He's never seen me at this weight. What if he doesn't love me anymore?"

She tilted her head, and a gentle smile parted her lips. "I don't know him other than what you've told me, but I believe you're selling him short. Do you really believe his love is tied up in your waistline?"

"No. Rationally, I know it isn't. But this isn't a rational process. If I were rational, I wouldn't be here."

"And you have to find ways to combat that mindset, Colbie. Your impression is not necessarily his."

"But what if it is? What if he doesn't love me because I'm not the person I was at Christmas? What if he doesn't like my flaws? What if he doesn't want me?"

"All those are real possibilities, but Colbie, those are possibilities in *any* relationship. It's why people date—to find a person they're compatible with. It doesn't mean that your flaws are unlovable. It could just mean that Eli's not the one to love them."

I shook my head. I couldn't handle that level of rejection. Eli was all I had. I hadn't spoken to anyone in my family. Jess and I had only exchanged letters. And Eli had done all of the communicating with Dr. Chalmers since I'd left. "No."

She didn't wait for me to explain. "There are going to be things you can't control, Colbie. Other people are one of them. We've talked about this with your parents and your brothers, but the same is true of friends and boyfriends."

I wanted to believe I could let everyone else's opinion go, that it wouldn't matter to me if I didn't have their acceptance, as long as I had Eli. But that was an unfair burden to place on another human being—Raine's words, not mine. It was also just another form of dependency. *Ugh.* I'd never get this right.

There was a knock on the door. Emily stuck her head inside, and her smile radiated when she found me in the office. "You have a visitor."

I scrambled to unwind myself from the ball I'd curled into so that my feet hit the ground before my face. My inhibitions disappeared with the notion that I'd get to see Eli. He was here...somewhere. I glanced at Raine who'd stood. She shooed me away with the flick of her wrist. I hoped her eyes still glittered with excitement for me when I returned.

My feet had a mind of their own, and nervous energy came bounding out in little dance steps down the corridor. "Is he in reception?" I grabbed Emily's hand for support.

"He is." She squeezed my fingers. "I love seeing you this happy, Colbie." Emily lowered her voice. "And oh my God, can I just say your beau is smokin'."

Eli was absolutely hot as hell. I'd noticed that the moment I'd laid eyes on him in third period, right after I'd thought he was a pompous ass.

I stopped in my tracks and jerked Emily's hand toward me. "How do I look?" I straightened my spine so she could assess me.

Emily tugged me in for a quick hug before pushing me back by my biceps. "Radiant. Happy. Healthy. Beautiful. He's a lucky man." She patted my cheek. "Don't forget that."

We started walking toward the reception area, and when we rounded the corner, I could see him standing at the end of the long corridor. He turned at the sound of our approach, and even from a distance, it was impossible to miss the smile that spread on his face. I dropped Emily's hand and took off running. It might have been overkill to anyone else, but I was desperate to be in his arms, to smell his scent, to feel the heat of his breath on my skin. The sound of his voice was different on the phone than in person. It all was. And three months had been too long.

Eli opened his arms just as I launched myself into them. He closed around me and spun in a circle as he held me tight against his chest. A sense of peace washed over me that I hadn't felt in ages. It was the relief of being home. And it was at that moment that I realized, home wasn't a dot on a map, it was a state of mind.

I clung to his neck and sucked air through my nostrils, drawing in his woodsy scent. I wanted to see him, but I didn't want to let him go to pull away.

Eli's hand held the back of my head, and he dipped his mouth next to my ear. "Hey, beautiful." The coo of his affection warmed my heart, and I relaxed enough to slide down his front.

But when I pulled away, Eli had other plans. He apparently didn't care if I got to see his face. He took my lips with his and kissed me unapologetically and unafraid of what onlookers might think. Breathless. When he finally broke free, my cheeks were heated, and I couldn't take my eyes off his.

Eli stroked my hair. "God I've missed you." He pecked my lips again.

Emily cleared her throat behind me, and I turned, embarrassed. "Raine's waiting on you both."

I held Eli's hand when I introduced them, and when I said his name, I couldn't help but look up with love through the distance our heights created.

Emily stuck out her hand to shake Eli's. "It's nice to finally meet you. Colbie's told me a lot about you."

He beamed when he glanced down at me. "So, you want to take me to meet this Raine person?"

"Not particularly, but she's going to make me if I ever want to get out of the dorms." I'd been in this part of the facility longer than anyone else since I'd arrived. I wanted out, but until recently, I hadn't thought I was ready—well, after I admitted that I needed to be here. What I wanted were the phones so I could contact Eli regularly, but what scared me was the rest of the freedom that came with living in the villas.

Emily pushed open Raine's door once we'd reached it and motioned us in. She quietly disappeared. And once the introductions had taken place, Eli and I took the seats on the opposite side of Raine's desk.

"I'm glad you could join us, Eli. I know Colbie's excited you're here." That was an understatement.

Raine took the lead on the conversation, telling Eli how important it was to have family and friends included in the recovery process, and I snickered or maybe scoffed. "Colbie, what's funny about that?"

I glanced at Eli who appeared uncertain, and then I shrugged. "I don't know. None of my friends or family have been interested in any of this. Does that mean I won't be successful because I don't have their help?" My voice wavered with the emotion I tried to contain.

Eli reached out and put his hand on my forearm before sliding it down to tangle with my fingers. "Baby, we're going to get you through this. I promise."

Raine set down her pen and leaned forward on her elbows. "No, but having a support system is critical to your recovery."

I clenched my fists and bit my cheek, desperate to keep the tears from falling. My effort was in vain.

Eli stared at me, lost. He didn't have a clue how to help or what to say. "Talk to me," he whispered, as if Raine weren't sitting three feet from us.

But just like I always did where Eli was concerned, I dropped my guard and opened up. I put on blinders and hoped like hell Raine let me pretend she wasn't there. I hiccuped and tried ineffectively to wipe the water from my cheeks. "It's just another example of how they're not around. They're never going to be around. I'm on my own. And now, I can't even get healthy because I don't have a net like most kids do."

He turned to face me, keeping a firm hold on my hand. "Then we create a new network of healthy people who will be in your corner, Cole. I hope like hell your parents and your brothers see what they face losing, but at the end of the day, we'll make our own way."

I already knew the answer to this. I had heard it a hundred times from Raine if I'd heard it once. "I can't control what anyone else does, but I don't understand why my parents don't care more.

I can't wrap my mind around how the hierarchy in our family works." I sniveled and took the tissue that Raine offered across the desk. "Why aren't I as important as the boys, Eli?"

He reached out and brushed my hair behind my ear. His soft brown eyes filled with a mixture of sorrow born out of love. Eli's tone was calm and soothing and everything my heart needed. "I don't know, babe. I hate that you waste your time and energy worrying about it."

"Nothing I ever do is going to be good enough." I made the statement under my breath and mostly to myself, but I wasn't surprised when Eli tilted my chin to keep me from looking away.

"Colbie, *you* are enough. And I love you. The rest will come. It just might take time."

"Eli's right, Colbie. Your focus needs to be you." She paused for a moment before asking, "Have the two of you talked about what your plans are when Colbie leaves Bright Horizons?" Raine looked to Eli for an answer.

He straightened in his chair and put his arm around my shoulders, keeping a protective, although casual, embrace surrounding me. "That's why I'm in town." He proceeded to explain to Raine that he didn't think either of us had a life waiting in Brogdon, Georgia.

I sat back and listened intently as the two talked, occasionally asking my opinion or including me in the conversation, but most of it I'd already heard from him or her or both. They just hadn't talked to each other.

"Colbie is still working on her self-image and coping mechanisms. Her fight against control will be hard won. But I have to agree with you; a change of pace and scenery would probably do you both good. If Colbie is nearby, we have an outpatient facility that she can make use of as well. She's going to have setbacks, and if she doesn't have a network of people to fall back on, being close to Bright Horizons would be second best."

I already knew what one setback, in particular, she referred to, but I hadn't talked to Eli about it, and I didn't want to with her as a witness. So I made a mental note to discuss it with him later—if there was a later.

Our hour with Raine came and went, and when she opened her office door to escort us out, I didn't know what the protocol was for Eli's visit. I didn't want to ask, but I didn't want to get in trouble, either. I was too close to successfully completing phase one, and I wanted to move out of the dorms and into the villas.

"Hey, Raine?" I stopped in the door while Eli waited in the hall. "Can he stay for a while?" I felt like a child asking my parents for permission to have my boyfriend over.

She nodded, and I thought I caught a glimpse of pride in her eyes. "Of course. Common areas and courtyards only—no private visits." Raine raised her brows to indicate what she meant, and I burst out in laughter.

"Okay, mom." I couldn't help it; she had become a matronly figure in my life. And as much as I hated to admit it, I admired her.

However, I knew better than to grow attached. Raine was in my life because my parents paid her to be; nevertheless, there was still a special place for her in my heart. She'd shown me tough love, been compassionate, and most importantly, a cheerleader. Raine had wanted my success more than I had at times. And for that, I'd forever be grateful. I wanted her to be proud of me the way I was learning to be proud of myself.

Eli held out his hand for me to take. "Want to show me around?"

"Of course." I didn't care what we did as long as I got to have him with me. I escorted him out the side door and down the pathway that made a circuitous route around the property. "How was the drive?" I sighed. "That was lame. I'm sorry."

"For what?"

I stopped and faced him. "This. All of it. Putting you in a position to even be here. Asking about the trip. A million things, Eli." It was hard for me to acknowledge being in this position. "It won't always be like this." And I believed it wouldn't.

"Colbie, we all stumble. I want you to be healthy. The only thing about *this* that bothers me is being away from you. I miss you, and I'm ready to leave Brogdon. But good things come to those who wait...even if it's forced patience." He winked, and I loved him a hair more than I had sixty seconds ago, although I didn't know how that was possible.

He pulled me down the path, refusing to allow me to dwell on something I couldn't change. I pointed out the different buildings, some of which I had visited and others I hadn't. When we got to the villas on the backside of the property, it looked more like Fiji than Nashville. The little huts were occupied by two residents per dwelling and coveted by those of us in the dorms. Me more than others.

"Is this where you'll go next?" Eli peered into one of the windows.

I swatted at him playfully. "Stop. You're going to get me in trouble."

"There has to be one that's not occupied." He smacked my ass, and I jumped, afraid he'd see it jiggle. Eli didn't wait long enough to notice anything before he snagged my waist with his arm and tugged me to his chest. "Do you have any idea what I'd do to you with an hour and privacy?" He nipped at my neck and kissed me under my jaw.

"Hmm, I'd let you do whatever you wanted. But there's no such thing as privacy here." I pulled back, giggling and then pointed up.

On top of the light pole sat a small camera. They were on all the light poles along the paths and at the entrances to all the villas. No one was ever *really* alone at Bright Horizons.

He cocked his head and then looked at me. "If I'd had to wait much longer to see you, I might not have been able to resist." Eli bent down, taking my lips with his. His touch had slowed. Gone was the vigor to take me, and in its place was the longing that lingered just beneath the surface for us both, always.

"I wish I could go home with you." I pressed my forehead to his, hoping I could transmit my thoughts through osmosis.

"It won't be long, and I'll be here." He pulled back and started to walk, swinging my hand like we were kids. "Have you decided what you want to do about graduation?"

This had been the same topic that Raine had hinted at without mentioning it, and one that I'd successfully avoided with Eli until now. "I go back and forth on whether I want to be there." It was a shift from when I'd left, but there was also uncertainty now that hadn't existed before. "If I'm the valedictorian, then I don't want to miss it, but if I fall from that spot, I'm not sure I want to face that failure in front of hundreds of people."

"You know that whether its valedictorian or salutatorian, there's no shame in either, right? You've worked hard, and you deserve the recognition for whichever spot you land in."

I tried to analyze each word Eli had said to see if there was any indication to which spot I currently held. His demeanor gave nothing away, and I couldn't tell if he even knew. Without asking, I wouldn't have an answer. Fear kept the words trapped in my mouth, but it was an opportunity for me to ask for something I wanted. Granted it was just information, not someone's time or attention, but I had to start somewhere. "Do you know what my rank is?" My entire body tensed waiting for his answer, except my heart. That damn organ beat like a tympani drum, reverberating into my chest.

Eli stopped and ran his fingers through his hair. Frustration, or possibly worry, marred his brow. "I'm not sure I'm allowed to tell you that." His face scrunched, and he shook his head. "I mean because of Bright Horizons, not the school."

"What does this place have to do with it?"

"I'm fairly certain that your grades are on some sort of hush list."

I laughed so hard I snorted. "What? Like my class rank is part of a covert operation or something?"

Eli inhaled and then exhaled sharply. "No, more like a deterrent from your recovery. Good or bad. Like if it's number one, then you're going to obsess about keeping it there. If it's number two, then you're going to worry about getting the top spot back. When in actuality, the only thing that matters is your health."

It wasn't what I wanted to hear, nor did it answer my question. "You're not going to tell me?"

He shrugged. "Honestly, Colbie, I don't think it benefits you in any way. You're not going to lose your acceptance to Vanderbilt. Nothing changes whether you're number one or two. So why worry about it now?"

Every part of me wanted to scream in his face so loudly that his cheeks pushed back from the force of my wind. However, that wouldn't solve anything, and it wouldn't get me what I wanted. I clenched my teeth and yanked my hands from his to ball them at my sides. The energy I tried to contain was rolling itself into anger as I forcefully slowed my breathing and became aware of each one I took until I calmed down. The itch to wallow in sorrow or a cake nagged at the back of my mind. It would scratch that part of me that needed satisfying. It was also the first time Eli had ever triggered it.

"Colbie?" Eli reached up and tucked my hair behind my ear. "Baby?" His voice pulled me back from the ledge and acted as the calamine lotion my emotional hives needed.

I closed my eyes. "Just give me a minute." My tone was harsh and more of a bark than intended. "Please." I lost count of how many breaths I took, but when I opened my eyes, Eli remained.

"I'm not trying to upset you."

I licked my lips and swallowed. My cheeks heated with embarrassment when I realized he'd witnessed my freak out. Yet, nothing in his expression said he was bothered or irritated by what had happened. "I know you're not, Eli. It's just hard to be kept in the dark about things I've worked so hard for."

He sighed and looked around. "I want to do what's best for you. If Raine says it's okay, then I'll tell you what I know. Fair enough?"

I nodded, knowing what the topic of conversation would be for our session with Eli tomorrow. And I promptly changed the subject. "Are you excited about your interviews?"

Eli proceeded to tell me what he knew about each school and the residential areas surrounding them. "Honestly, I'm pretty nervous." There weren't many chinks in Eli's armor, and if there were, I didn't tend to see them.

We'd moved through the villas and the gardens and taken up residence on a bench near the edge of the property. I didn't spend much time out here. It was too easy to get lost in thought, and most days, I tried to stay busy to keep my mind from going idle. Now, with Eli, there was nothing I wanted more than to lose myself as the sun kissed the horizon and day welcomed night.

"What's there to be nervous about? You're great at your job." Regardless of my personal opinion of Eli, Dr. Paxton was a phenomenal teacher, and any school would be lucky to have him. "Is it the girls?" I narrowed my gaze and tilted my head to the side. "I bet it's hard to go into a new flock each year and pick out the eligible ones, huh?"

"You think that's funny?"

I did. Which was why I laughed, continuously. "A little."

He prodded me in the side which fueled my giggles, but when

he finally responded, his answered silenced me instantly. "Because if I don't get one of these jobs, I won't be in Nashville."

I reached up and captured his jaw in my hand. "Eli. Don't put that kind of pressure on yourself. There are tons of schools around here and tons of time to find the right one." My thumb stroked his jaw and the five o'clock shadow that resided on it. "You keep telling me not to worry, and when this is over, we will figure things out. Right?"

He swallowed, and his Adam's apple bobbed in his throat. "Yeah, but it's my job to take care of you, Colbie. Your job is not to take care of me."

"Is that some primitive notion you have going on in that ruggedly handsome head of yours?"

Eli smirked, and mischief danced in his eyes. "You think I'm handsome?"

I dropped my head back with a laugh before facing him again. "Depends. Me Jane? You Tarzan? If so, then no. If by *take care of you*, you mean the two of us lean on each other and provide for each other in all ways—not just financial—then yes, I find you incredibly hot."

He kissed my lips and then talked against them. "Then you leave me no choice but to accept this liberal attitude. I will bury the caveman in favor of partnership."

I pulled away, smiling. "I think you're mocking me."

"Meh. If we were home, I'd be trying to get you naked. Here, I just want you to know how much I love you."

The bell chimed in the distance, and I felt my face fall.

"What was that?"

"The chapel bells. It's our call for dinner...."

"And my time to leave?"

I nodded as tears filled my eyes. I didn't want him to go. I never wanted him to go.

Eli's tongue passed over his lips, and his eyes met mine when he cupped my jaw. "Baby, I'll be back. Every chance I have, I will be here. Don't cry."

"I just hate to see you go." My words were as broken as my heart.

Eli healed a part of me that no one else could touch. He wasn't my cure, and he wasn't a fix. He was simply a piece of my heart that I didn't like living without.

He wiped my tears and pulled me to my feet. The warmth of his hands on my hips and his lips on my mouth would have to be enough to tide me over. His fingers dug in as his tongue swept past mine. The tingle grew between my legs, and I wanted nothing more than to connect with him. His fingers dipped under the hem of my shirt, and his palms splayed against my back. Searching, soothing, tracing. His touch was everywhere. Thankfully, he was stronger than I was and broke the kiss. "Mmm. What I wouldn't give to taste you right now."

I glanced around. We were isolated and alone. No one knew we were out here. I could have my clothes off in seconds, and his would follow. The bench would work. The two of us could reconnect. The vision ran through my head like trashy porn, and that turned me on more than the idea of sinking onto his length. The possibility of getting caught made my heart race, and a reckless abandon tried to take over my spirit. "We better go before I take you up on that." I panted, standing next to him.

My chest heaved, my pussy was wet, and I was beyond ready to get out of Bright Horizons. Sadly, that wasn't going to happen today or even next week. And if I didn't play my cards right, the little freedom I'd managed to garner over Eli's visit this week would be lost. And that was a consequence I couldn't risk facing.

"Come on, Eli. We better get back."

21

ELI

It was mid-April before I began to receive offers from the schools I'd interviewed with in Nashville. I'd started to sweat, worried that I wouldn't hear from any of them. As much as I wanted to take one of the positions at the private schools, the public school had better pay and state benefits. It wasn't just me I had to worry about.

Right now, I didn't have to decide about health insurance to include Colbie, but I didn't want to have to change jobs when that was a concern whether that was two or five or fifteen years from now. What I did have to consider, however, was my income covering all of our household expenses and anything she needed.

We'd talked extensively about her moving into on-campus housing instead of living with me, and at the end of the week I'd spent visiting Bright Horizons, all of us—Raine included—had agreed that it was too much freedom for Colbie starting out. I had no problems with that; in fact, I loved that I would get to be the one to care for her and provide for her. Her parents were the wildcard.

Her tuition and acceptance to Vanderbilt weren't conditional upon her parents' approval. She'd gotten a full academic ride.

That, however, did not cover activity fees, campus identification, parking stickers, much less clothes, cell phone, insurance, or anything else that came up. And if she didn't take the housing, she didn't get the meal plan. Every penny counted for the next four years if her parents cut her off. And at this point, neither one of us knew which way they'd lean.

While I'd been to multiple counseling sessions on several different occasions since Colbie had first invited me, her parents hadn't attended a single one. Her brothers—other than Caleb—still had no idea she wasn't backpacking across Europe. I rolled my eyes every time I heard that. Colbie was not into the great outdoors. Anyone who'd ever spent more than five minutes with her could have deduced that. I just kept my mouth shut whenever it came up at school. No one was the wiser that I knew any differently, and the staff all seemed envious of her freedom. *If only they knew.*

Jess had even made an appearance at Bright Horizons on visiting day last week. The two were on their way to mending fences, but it would take effort and time. Colbie still didn't know where she stood in class rank—Raine had agreed with me that imparting that knowledge wasn't beneficial to her recovery—so there was a part of her that held a smidgen of resentment toward Jess, who also knew and wouldn't tell her. It had taken little effort to convince Jess that Raine was right. Until Colbie accepted the fact that she might not be at the top of the class, there was no benefit in her knowing where she ranked. It actually had started to help her work through those emotions with Raine, who had promised to give Colbie the information she wanted once she believed that Colbie could handle either outcome. Colbie wasn't there.

There were parts of me that worried about her coming home to spend any time in Brogdon. Even though Colbie was now aware of her triggers, the things that sent her into the panicked state that craved perfection for acceptance, she hadn't been able to face some of them. Her parents and brothers were top on that list of red flags.

Between now and the end of May, dealing with those issues was at the top of Colbie's treatment priorities, along with her self-image. She was a work in progress, but I'd learned through this that most people are. Every time I went in for a session with her, I ended up with as much to work on as Colbie did. I'd never realized how many emotional withdrawals people made without replenishing themselves with deposits, especially women. They thought their reservoir was limitless, that the bounty would always be refilled. Colbie had siphoned every resource she'd had into a tank she'd hoped would feed everyone else. Not only had she not gotten what she wanted out of that, she hadn't even come close to getting what she needed.

So with three offers in hand and three schools to choose from, I made the decision to wait until I could talk to Colbie tonight. Part of creating an overflow in her well was ensuring she not only thought but knew beyond a shadow of a doubt that I valued her insight.

I closed my laptop as my AP class started handing in their work and filing out of my classroom. Jess took her time packing up, and I sat back, waiting for her to come out with whatever was on her mind. She zipped her bag and lifted it from the floor to her shoulder.

"Dr. Paxton?" She had my attention, so I wasn't sure why she addressed me. Jess adjusted the strap to her bag and fiddled with the buckle.

"What's up, Jess?"

Anytime she talked to Colbie, I usually heard about it from Jess the next day. She tiptoed around Colbie's treatment and recovery, not knowing what to share about life here and what to spare her from. And with that uncertainty came insecurity. No one other than Raine and I knew that Jess had talked to Colbie. And Jess did everything she could to keep Colbie's secret, including lying to—or evading—her boyfriend. Caden was still just as clueless as he'd been the day Colbie left.

She sighed and continued to fidget. "Are you really leaving?" Her eyes met mine after she'd asked the question.

It shouldn't have surprised me. I should have thought that Colbie would tell her best friend her plans for next year. Nevertheless, I hadn't considered that, and it caught me off guard. I wasn't going to sugarcoat things or mislead Jess. There was no reason to; she wouldn't be here anyhow. "I am."

Jess glanced at the door and squared her shoulders. "For Colbie?"

That was a trick question because it didn't have a simple answer. "Yes and no." I swallowed and thought she deserved more. "More yes than no." I leaned forward and put my forearms on the desk. "I can't hold her back, Jess. And the things that brought me here don't really exist." I shrugged one shoulder.

"You don't think it would be best for her to come home for a while? Maybe delay Vanderbilt for a year?" She worried her bottom lip with her teeth, and I prayed she didn't cry.

There was a lot of information I was privy to because of Colbie's counseling sessions that I wasn't certain needed to be or should be shared with anyone. "Have you asked Colbie about that?"

She shook her head and continued to gnaw on her lip. If she weren't careful, she'd chew a hole into it. "I don't want her to think I'm questioning her. But I'm worried. I think it's too much, too soon."

In the split second that I had to make a decision and the few minutes I had to discuss this, I opted to support Colbie while encouraging Jess to talk to her friend. "Her counselors are in agreement that a change of scenery is best." I wouldn't elaborate any more. "You should talk to her. Let Colbie explain why she doesn't want to come back to Brogdon."

Jess gasped. "Ever?"

"To live. Probably not." That was as honest as I could be. I tilted my chin toward the clock. "You don't want to be late."

Jess nodded, and for a moment, I saw the similarities in Jess's and Colbie's appearances. The girls could be sisters, although their personalities were night and day. She stopped at the door and turned back. "I hope you know what you're doing. If not, you'll end up destroying her."

I didn't have a clue what I was doing other than trying to plan a life with the woman I loved. It all sounded cliché and stupid when I said that out loud. Colbie was young, a baby by most standards. We had an uphill battle in front of us. If she were following me, I would absolutely question my motives for taking her away from family. The opposite, however, made the reasoning far more pure. "Do any of us ever truly know what repercussions our actions will have?"

"Probably not, but most of us don't hold someone else's lives in our hand, either. I'm just worried about her, Dr. Paxton. That's what friends do. And since I'm limited in what I can say, do, or ask on *every* front, I have to challenge what I'm able to. I can't help but feel at fault for a lot of this. Right or wrong. Beneficial or not. I cost her a lot, and the only thing that will make that suffering worthwhile is if she gets a happily ever after or a pot of gold at the end of the rainbow." Jess was a good girl and a better friend. She'd made mistakes, but I wasn't foolish enough to believe Colbie hadn't made some where her friend was concerned as well.

"The only thing I can assure you of is that she is my number one priority. If she wanted to be here, I would stay. I'm not her reason for going."

Jess nodded and took a step into the hall.

I called after her. "Talk to her, Jess. It will help you both."

"I will, Dr. Paxton."

My phone buzzed on my desk as Jess went to her next class. Colbie's face lit up the screen when I reached for my cell. "Hey, beautiful."

Since she'd moved out of the dorms a couple weeks ago, I heard from her a lot more often. When she had free time, she was allowed to use it differently than she had been in the dorms. Colbie hadn't really made any friends at Bright Horizons other than Emily and Raine, so her free time typically fell to schoolwork, Jess, and me.

"Did I catch you at a bad time?"

I closed my classroom door to have a little privacy. "Not at all. I'm glad you called." I took my chair and opened my laptop to go over the offers I'd gotten.

"Oh yeah?"

"Well, I'm always happy to hear your voice, but I didn't want to have to wait until tonight to talk to you."

She groaned on the other end. "That doesn't sound good."

I chuckled. "Don't assume the worst. It's actually good news."

"You won the lottery?"

"I don't play the lottery."

"You should. It benefits Georgia's education system."

"Noted. If I should ever teach in Georgia again or have a child in a Georgia school system, I'll make sure to buy a ticket. As it stands, I will be relocating to Tennessee and want your help deciding which offer to accept."

Colbie squealed into the receiver, piercing my eardrum. "You got an offer?"

"Three."

"Eli, that's fantastic. You got an offer from each school?"

"I did."

She clapped in the background, and I couldn't stop the smile that spread across my lips and made my cheeks hurt. Six months ago, Colbie wouldn't have been the type to squeal or clap. She had been reserved and modest, never wanting to stand out in the crowd. Now, her eagerness and happiness curbed any sense of embarrassment she might have over someone witnessing her exuberance. "Which one did you pick?"

"None of them." The line went silent, and I pulled the phone away from my face to see if the timer had stopped. "Colbie?"

"Why not? Did you decide against moving?" And as quickly as joy had sparked, it was squashed.

"Of course not. I didn't want to make the decision without you." That wasn't a line to make her happy. It might have benefited her recovery, but it was the truth regardless of what it did for her self-esteem or her ego. "I got the last one this morning."

"Which one do you want to take?" The innocent happiness in her voice made me realize that I didn't really care which one as long as it kept me near her.

I told her about the three schools. We'd discussed each one after my interviews while I'd been in Nashville over spring break, but she listened dutifully again. Then we compared salaries, and the public school's was more robust, as was their entire compensation package.

"The insurance and retirement plans are better with the state." I didn't expect Colbie to see the value in these things because she'd yet to have to pay for insurance, and no one in high school thought about retirement.

"The fact that you pointed that out tells me that's not the job you want, Eli. So which one do you think is the best fit?"

I proceed to list the pros and cons of each offer, and Colbie kept bringing me back to what I wanted, not what I thought had the best long-term possibilities. "I have to think bigger than what I *want*, Cole. It's not just me I'm considering."

"Huh-uh. You're not pinning a decision to be unhappy on me or our relationship."

"I'm not—"

"Nelson Hall."

"What?"

"That's the offer I think you should take."

Obviously, I hadn't made myself clear. Maybe I needed to send her the offers so she could read them herself. "Colbie, that's the offer with the least stability." Financially, contract, promise—they couldn't guarantee anything beyond one school year. It paid the least of the three. They had the smallest campus and student body.

"It's also the one you want." She was right, even though I'd tried my best to conceal a preference.

While they were a relatively new school, they had a lot of money backing their endeavor. They had a huge endowment for arts, and those were the kids they catered to—those with money and talent. Their library rivaled that of any college, and I'd be heading up their creative writing department, which not only included fiction but poetry. These kids were the cream of the crop, and they had their parents' support. Nelson Hall also ran a summer program and needed a teacher who could take over at the beginning of June.

"Nelson Hall wants the summer school teacher, Colbie."

"Doesn't that make it a perfect fit?"

Or the worst one. "That means I won't be home to help you when we move. I don't want to dump that responsibility on you."

She laughed, although I had no clue why. "Eli, you've taken on the responsibility of procuring a new job, moving to another state, and soon, you'll have to find a place to live. I think I can handle a few hours alone unpacking over the summer." Her resilience and strength were two of the things I loved most about her.

It wasn't that I didn't think Colbie could handle doing it on her own. I didn't want her to have to. "Maybe I want to do it with you." I sounded like a pansy and was grateful no one other than Colbie had heard me hide my mancard.

"Okay. Then I'll find stuff to entertain myself while you're at work. Seriously, Eli. This is the job you want. It makes the most sense. It's closest to Vanderbilt and Bright Horizons. The pay is good. The vacation and perks are decent. But the job itself was the one you raved about after the interview. I want you to be happy. We'll figure out the rest. Isn't that what you're always telling me?"

"Nothing like having your words thrown back at you."

"Nelson Hall, Eli. That's the job."

When we hung up, I emailed Nelson Hall and accepted the position to start in June. And then I walked down the hall to the Principal's office to officially hand in my letter of resignation. I'd already declined the offer to teach at Brogdon High the following year; I just hadn't made my last day this year official. The letter had been in my bag for a week. Now I just had to hand it in. It was bittersweet. I'd come here with so much hope and the idea that this would be my home. And while I hadn't gotten any of *that*, I was taking away so much more.

Traveling back and forth to Tennessee on weekends was tough. The only thing that made it bearable was being able to see Colbie. I'd had to go twice to take care of hiring and contracts with Nelson Hall, and once I'd gotten that squared away, I had to deal with the housing situation.

I didn't have the luxury of a best friend living there who told me where to rent or what neighborhood to buy in like I had in Brogdon. Thank God I hadn't taken Caleb's advice about buying in Georgia. Selling a home on top of finding a new one would be a nightmare with work and Colbie being out of state. I also wouldn't have the funds to make a down payment on a property in Tennessee. Colbie was okay with renting, but I wanted a place that was ours. A place where she could paint the walls or plant flowers.

Nelson Hall had also included a small relocation package that included a realtor, Samantha. She was a parent of one of the students, so I was hesitant about what knowledge she gained about Colbie. But once she'd heard my girlfriend would be attending Vanderbilt in the fall, nothing else I said mattered. She was an alumnus, and her oldest daughter was a legacy.

Colbie wrangled a day pass out of Bright Horizons, and the rest felt like history. Samantha took to Colbie immediately—never once asking how we met, how long we'd been together, how old Colbie was, or what Colbie was doing in town—and I faded into the background. The three of us visited the four houses I'd picked, but I left the final decision to Colbie.

She pulled my hand into the master bedroom of the last place we'd gone to see and closed the door behind us.

I quirked my brow. "Miss Chapman, are you thinking what I'm thinking?"

Colbie rolled her eyes. "Down boy. As much as I'd love for you to take me on a stranger's bed in a home that belongs to people we don't know, I think we need to talk about the houses without Samantha's input."

When Colbie and I had met, I'd loved her sassy mouth. Her willingness to put me in my place had been a huge turn-on. The girl had spunk and maturity in spades, not to mention, she was flat-out gorgeous...although that might have taken me a while to fully appreciate. However, the four months she'd spent at Bright Horizons had brought out a side of her that I adored even more. Every minute I got with her was better than the last. All of those things I'd originally fallen for still existed, yet now, they came with a more fun-loving spirit, a person who wasn't inhibited by fear of failure or rejection. She wasn't immune to those things, but they no longer ruled her life.

"Not even a quickie?" It had been months since Colbie and I had done anything other than kiss. I wanted to adhere to Bright Horizons's policies, but at the end of the day, I was still a man. And a man who had Colbie Chapman on his arm was a man who remained in a constant state of arousal. Mentally, physically, emotionally, or sexually—one of them was always at its peak.

Colbie settled her hands on my waist and licked her succulent lips when she stared up at me. Her crystal blue eyes pierced my heart, and when her pupils contracted, I didn't care who stood on the other side of the door. My mouth took hers, and I didn't bother to hold back on the kiss. Her knees went weak, and she broke away, breathless. Colbie's cheeks were flushed, and it wasn't embarrassment. I loved to see her affected by me. Her chest rose and fell quickly, and the vein in her neck pulsed rapidly. She wanted me as badly as I wanted her.

"Can we focus?" She took a step back and made sure she wasn't within arm's reach.

I laughed, but when I reached for her hand, she ducked out of my way with a smirk. "Fine. What do you want to focus on?"

Colbie stomped her foot and grunted. "Eli..." Even her whine couldn't wipe the grin from my lips. "Come on."

"Baby, I told you. I like them all. I've looked at seventeen houses to narrow it down to four. Which one do you like the best?"

She rubbed her hands together in front of her, twisting them with worry. She might not have wanted me to frisk her in this master bedroom, but I wouldn't let her anxiety take over, either.

I stepped forward and took her hands to stop the fidgeting. Our fingers wound together, and I stroked the backs of her hands with my thumbs. "What's wrong?"

Colbie did some little dance while standing still that

reminded me of a child about to throw a tantrum. "They're really expensive, Eli. It's a lot of pressure. Could you not find something at a lower price point?"

For Nashville, they were lower-middle class homes. Albeit, the rest of the nation would consider them all upper-middle class. Yet when you had singers, songwriters, and celebrities all over the county, normal people didn't amount to much in terms of dollars in real estate. "These are modest, Colbie. Plus, I don't want to have to move in a few years."

Colbie and I hadn't really talked a lot about children. The one time it had come up in a therapy session, Colbie had shut it down rather quickly. Raine pointed out that Colbie wasn't at a point in her therapy where she was ready to consider what children would do to her body. And I was quick to ensure Colbie that I wasn't interested in starting a family until she'd finished school and started her practice. That meant at least eight years and probably longer. I wasn't in a rush, although I didn't want to take the option off the table. And whenever that time came, even if it were adoption, I didn't want to have to move to accommodate a change. It might be overly optimistic to believe that we would move into our forever home before we ever got married, but I was a guy. We had simple minds and even simpler expectations.

She rolled her ankle and refused to look anywhere other than the floor. The hardwoods were nice, although I doubted they held her attention.

"Colbie?"

"Yeah?"

"There's not a single house in the group that I can't afford. I don't have any debt, no student loans, no credit cards. I've saved more than I've spent. I promise, I only gave you options that are comfortable for us."

She lifted her chin hesitantly. "We don't have to offer what they're asking, right?"

Interesting. My little brainiac was also a negotiator. "Nope. We can go in at whatever you want. But you have to tell me which one you want to make the offer on."

"I love the porch on the third one we looked at. And the rounded front windows..." Colbie didn't have to say what she was thinking. The room was perfect for a piano.

It also had a pool, which had made it my first choice as well. I had visions of Colbie in a swimsuit—or without—on a warm summer day and me next to her...or inside her. I wasn't picky about how we spent our time in the backyard as long as it was together. And I'd envisioned her sitting at a piano in our living room more times than I could count. Maybe I had romanticized life with Colbie, but I'd do everything in my power to make that fantasy my reality.

"Let's go tell Samantha." I nudged Colbie in the side with my hip as I wrapped my arm around her. I planted a kiss on her temple for good measure. "I love you, Cole."

She tilted her mouth to mine as we walked and pecked my lips. "Love you, too. Thank you for this."

Before we left, Colbie and I had filled out a contract and made an offer on the house we both loved. And by the time Samantha had driven us back to her office, the owner's agent had responded and accepted the deal with only minor changes. We were set to close the day after graduation, and then I'd start the following week at Nelson Hall.

I'D PUT THIS OFF AS LONG AS HUMANLY POSSIBLE. WITH Colbie coming home tomorrow, graduation in two days, and us moving in three, I was out of time. I'd sent Caleb a text and asked him to come to his parents' tonight, but I never received a response. In all fairness, I had no idea if they'd even speak to me. I hadn't tried to contact them for fear they might say no. And I hoped like hell they were home, because if not, I was pretty much screwed. I wanted to do this the right way, or as right as possible given the circumstances.

My own parents would likely have permanent hearing loss from listening to me role play with them about what I would say to the Chapmans. I was surprised they even answered the phone when I called anymore since that was all I ever talked about—that and Colbie. They loved learning about Colbie and the house and the move. I don't think they were as eager to take in my bemoaning over having to be a man and ask for forgiveness. I just had such a hard time with the whole thing.

None of the Chapmans had visited Colbie since she'd left. And when I apologized, it wasn't going to be for what I'd done or what we were about to do. It would be for the way I'd gone about falling for their daughter. I would apologize for not being more respectful of the relationships I'd had with each of them. But in no way, shape, or form would I apologize for loving Colbie.

To my knowledge, neither her parents nor Caleb had any idea the two of us were still together. Jess had remained tightlipped with Caden, but not to protect our relationship. She'd done it to protect her own with her boyfriend and her best friend's family. Caden and Jess were still pretty hot and heavy from what I'd seen around campus, and that girl was smart to stay in the neutral lane.

The last time I'd stood on this stoop, I'd lost my best friend. I didn't think I had anything left to lose here and hoped there was something to gain. I wanted nothing more than to facilitate an open door to Colbie and our home, but that would be by my rules. In my house, Colbie reigned, and anyone who did anything to take away from that, make her feel less than worthy or inhibit her health and happiness, would get a one-way escort out my front door.

I took a deep breath and rang the bell. I could hear the movement inside and Mrs. Chapman calling out that she was on her way, so I stepped back. I wasn't interested in being within striking distance once the door opened, which it did seconds later.

Her smile was as wide and pretentious as the day was long until she saw who it was. Mrs. Chapman's expression fell, and she braced herself to put forth the front of a lady. "Eli. I wasn't expecting you." She called over her shoulder to her husband and turned back to me.

"Yes, ma'am, I know. I was afraid if I called that you and Dr. Chapman might not be willing to speak with me. Please forgive me for intruding, but I hope I can have a few minutes of your time." I looked behind her to see Dr. Chapman join us. "Both of you."

Mrs. Chapman pursed her lips and shook her head of perfectly coiffed hair. "I don't think that's a good idea—"

"With all due respect, there are some things you need to know. Five minutes. That's all I'm asking." I needed a hell of a lot more than five minutes if this turned into an actual discussion, but if they just listened to what I had to say, then I'd be back outside in less time.

"Elise, let the boy in. The neighbors don't need any reason to gossip." Dr. Chapman spoke, and his wife listened, opening the door to allow me inside.

"Eli, can I get you some tea?" Elise was ever the hostess. She escorted us to the kitchen table and pulled out a chair.

I wasn't here for beverages or idle chitchat. Pleasantries need not be extended. "No. Thank you." I took a seat across from Dr. Chapman and her.

Neither of Colbie's parents said a word, and it dawned on me they wouldn't. I'd come to their home, and I'd have to initiate the conversation.

I looked Elise and then Phillip in the eyes, and every practice run I'd had at this performance went out the window. "I'm sorry I haven't come by sooner. At first, I thought it would be best to let things die down, then I was angry, and it wasn't until recently that I believed there was any point."

Her dad folded his arms over his chest, and her mom tucked her hands into her lap. And they waited. It was funny how they'd mirrored each other's reactions in their own way.

"I can only imagine your frustration with my relationship with Colbie and that we hid it from you—"

"Son, I'm not really sure what kind of *relationship* you can have with a child. *That* is where my problem starts."

"Colbie isn't a child, sir. Just because she's your kid doesn't mean she's not an adult." I didn't want to be disrespectful. "I admit, I was in the wrong to allow anything to happen and feelings to get involved before she graduated. But it happened. I tried like hell to keep it from turning into anything more than friendship..."

Dr. Chapman bared his teeth and then drew his bottom lip in, still showing his pearly whites. "You might want to stop there, Eli. Whatever happened between you and our daughter is over. She graduates the day after tomorrow, and then she's going to Vanderbilt in the fall."

There was the confirmation—not that I'd needed it—that Colbie's parents had no idea what had gone on in their daughter's life for the last five months. "Yes, sir. She is graduating in two days. And the following day, I will pick her up and take her to Nashville. To the house we bought. Together. She will continue treatment at Bright Horizons on an outpatient basis over the summer while I start a new job, and in the fall, you're correct. She will start classes at Vanderbilt."

Dr. Chapman stood so quickly that his chair tumbled to the floor behind him. Mrs. Chapman rose seconds later, grabbing her husband's hand to calm his temper. "Who do you think you are, boy?"

There was no point in staying in my seat. I'd be escorted to the door shortly. "I'm the man who loves your daughter, and I hope and pray that at some point, you recognize that. Colbie desperately wants a relationship with you both, but she's strong enough now to make you earn it." I pushed the chair under the table and stepped toward the door. "Our home will always be open to you both once you're ready to love Colbie the way she deserves. Until then, I hope you'll let her go with little fanfare."

"She's not going anywhere with you."

I reached for the knob to let myself out. "You're going to be disappointed when she walks out that door, Dr. Chapman. I assure you, the day after tomorrow, you will lose your daughter if you don't reconsider your position. Because I'm not going anywhere."

I didn't wait for a response. There was nothing to say. Colbie would have a fight on her hands when she got home, but she was expecting it. Raine and Colbie had been working on it for weeks. Oddly, I wasn't the least bit concerned. Colbie had no reservations about what she wanted and how she'd go about getting it. She had begged her parents for years to see her shine, and they'd continuously turned on the lights to dull her glow. I'd pay her power bill for the rest of my life just to be in the warmth of her shadow.

The Chapmans would be without.

I would not.

22

COLBIE

The ride home from Bright Horizons might have been worse than the ride there. Eli had called me last night after he left my parents' house, so I anticipated...*something*, just not total silence. When they'd come into the facility, they'd acted like they were happy to see me. They talked to the counselors, found out what the aftercare plan was when I came back—next week—and they'd all wished each other well like they were long-lost friends. Ever the dutiful Southerners. My parents would never allow that painted-on perfection to slip in public.

Raine and I had spent a lot of time talking about reuniting with my parents, and we discussed it at length again last night after Eli had called. She was a parent and sympathetic to their concerns. However, she'd also gotten to know Eli. He—and Jess—had been the one to make the trips to see me, and he had been the one to invest time in my therapy, time in me. My parents hadn't done any of that, not once. So while Raine wanted me to keep an open mind and recognize that wounds don't heal overnight, she also warned me against allowing them to trigger a relapse.

Every mile I rode without so much as a whispered word, the urge to binge grew stronger. I talked myself down in my head. I did breathing exercises. I was limited by my surroundings and my company. Without a cell phone, I couldn't even text Eli or Jess. So I finally gathered the courage to talk to my parents.

"How's life in Brogdon?" I wanted to smack myself for not being able to come up with an opening line any better than that, but my parents and I had never really carried on casual conversations.

My mom turned her head to look at me over her shoulder, briefly. "Same as always. Nothing new to report." She forced the smile she gave everyone during polite conversation, and then she faced forward.

"How are the boys?" I was desperate for any kind of connection. "I got a couple letters from Caden and a card from the twins. But that was months ago."

"They're good. They're all gearing up for summer ball. Caleb's got them on a grueling schedule starting next week."

"What about Carson and Casey? Are they coming for graduation?" I didn't know if either of my older brothers planned to come home for the summer, but I hoped I would get to see them before I left.

It was my dad's turn to reply, which he did after my mother gave him that glance that said, "Why don't you take this one." And I was certain it wasn't something I cared to hear.

"Sugar, your brothers aren't going to be able to make it home. They didn't know for certain that you'd come back for graduation, so they didn't plan for it."

My mother clapped her hands together and turned in the seat again. A genuine smile lifted her aging cheeks; it was the first time I'd noticed her age and the greying hair. "Carson's going to propose to Heather."

It sounded like I should know who Heather was. "Who's Heather?"

"Oh, Colbie, sweetie. You really should pay more attention to what's going on in your brothers' lives. He'd be crushed to hear you ask that."

He'd be crushed. He'd be crushed. And I lost the grip I had on reality. "*He'd* be crushed? Are you kidding me?"

Mama chuckled and situated herself better in the seat, so she faced me instead of the windshield. "What's gotten into you?"

I closed my eyes and counted to ten, taking as many deep breaths. When I reopened them, she hadn't moved and waited on me to answer. "Mama, I haven't seen Carson or Casey since Christmas, and that visit was short-lived. I never talk to them, and I've been gone for months...you know, traveling abroad? How on earth would I know who Heather is?"

She raised her brows to chastise me with a look. "Maybe this summer you can make catching up with your siblings a priority. That would be a lovely thing to do before you leave for school in the fall." Mama turned to my father. "Wouldn't that be nice, Phillip?"

"Your mother's right, Colbie. I'm sure Carson would love to have you come see him for a weekend. We could plan it so Casey would be around, too. Maybe Caleb could take you."

I rubbed my temples. I had three more hours to endure, and I was about to make things more than uncomfortable. "You two don't listen, do you?"

"Colbie! When did you become so disrespectful?" My mother scoffed and righted herself in the seat next to my father.

I shook my head, even though she couldn't see me. "I don't mean to be disrespectful, Mama." I breathed in through my nose and slowly released it through my mouth. "I just wish the two of you would listen to me."

Daddy laughed. "Sugar, you haven't said anything for us to hear."

Fair enough. "I know Eli came to talk to you last night. And based on that conversation, you are aware that I won't be in

Georgia this summer. So inferring that I should spend time with brothers who have never bothered to spend time with me is not only asinine, it's an impossibility; at least it is in the manner you suggested."

My father gripped the steering wheel so tightly that his knuckles went white, and my mother laid her hand on his forearm. This was about to get ugly. If Phillip or Elise Chapman ever lost their cool, there was no coming back from it. I'd only seen it a handful of times in my life. Once with each of the twins, once with a football coach my three oldest brothers played under, and once with Casey when he'd been caught *with* a girl in my parents' house. This would make number five, and as far as I was concerned, it would be the last.

"You're not leaving with that boy, Colbie. There won't be a discussion. We raised you to be a lady, and only tramps live with men before they're married—"

"If that's the technicality you need to be remedied for you to be comfortable with our relationship, I'm quite sure Eli would be happy to oblige." I quirked a brow and folded my arms in the back seat, knowing Daddy could see my defiance in the mirror.

My mother swung around like a revolving door. "You will not marry some random man the day after you graduate. Why would you want to throw your future away?"

"You don't get it both ways, Mama. You don't get to tell me that I can't leave with him because I'm not married and tell me that I can't marry him because I'm throwing my future away. Eli is not some hoodlum off the streets. He has a doctorate for the love of God—"

"Don't you take the Lord's name in vain." My mother shook a bony finger in my face.

"Oh for Christ's sake, Mama. Listen to me." I'd raised my voice, my mother blanched, and my father was pulling over the SUV. "You lost your ability to have a say in my life—both of you—

when you abdicated your responsibility to a treatment center in Tennessee and lied to everyone we know."

"Colbie—"

I held up my hand, halting my father. "No, Daddy. I've listened to the two of you for eighteen years; now it's time you hear me." I had prepared myself for this in therapy; I'd just never believed it would come down to it. The deep breath I took did nothing to make it any easier. "I didn't want to go to Bright Horizons, but I'm grateful you sent me. I learned more about myself than I think would have ever been possible on my own."

My mother gave me a satisfied smirk, the one that said, "See, mother knows best." Daddy had stopped the SUV on the side of the highway, and both now turned in their seats, giving me their undivided—albeit unhappy—attention.

"But what I hadn't expected was to get confirmation of what I'd believed all along about the two of you. I was insignificant. Every visiting day that passed that neither of you showed up, I pushed you a little further from my life. Every family counseling session you didn't attend sealed that fate a little tighter."

"Colbie," my mother huffed. "You can't expect us to just stop what we're doing to drive to Tennessee for an hour or two during the week."

I smiled and shook my head. "You do it for Georgia football." And I let that comment sink in. "And I get that we all prioritize things in life. We make time for what matters. Who matters. And while neither of you made time for me, Eli did. Over and over. Jess even came to a couple sessions." I stared at them, knowing what they were thinking. "But don't worry, she never told Caden where I was or that she'd seen me. Your lie is a well-guarded secret."

My mother's lips parted as if she might say something, but then she licked them, and three wrinkles marred her forehead. It might have been confusion or worry. I didn't know which, but it wasn't my problem to deal with anymore. I could only control me.

"Today, when I get home, I will pack my stuff. Tomorrow, I'll find out if I'm valedictorian or salutatorian, and I hope you'll be there to congratulate me on either. I've written a beautiful speech about overcoming adversity and finding yourself that I hope I get to deliver, but if not, I'm still going to be proud of what I've done." I prayed like hell that was true. God, I wanted to be okay with wherever the chips fell on this, but that was tomorrow's struggle, not today's. "And the following morning, Eli will pick me up, and we will leave for Tennessee."

My mom shook her head with so much vigor that strands of hair fell from her perfect up-do. "No, ma'am." She closed her eyes and kept shaking. "Nope. That is not how things are going to go."

I reached out and touched her hand and then placed my other hand on my father. "Your option is to have a couple of days before I leave, or I'll leave when we pull into the driveway. This isn't up for debate. The only questionable part is your role in it." I managed to keep my expression stilled, or at least I thought I had. My vibrato was strong, as was my voice, yet inside, I trembled like a leaf. That little girl still craved her parents' approval and love.

There wasn't another word said. My mom removed her hand from mine and gave my dad a look that communicated something between them. Daddy put the SUV in gear, and we spent the following three hours in complete silence. Not even the radio played as we traveled the highway back to Brogdon.

My homecoming was bittersweet. I knew it would be, but I'd prayed it would be a happier occasion. My parents didn't give me the opportunity to see anyone last night. I felt like a hostage in a large, plantation-style cage. The piano was still locked —I didn't bother asking for the key. My brothers were home, and Mama made dinner.

I'd called Eli as soon as I got my hands on my cell phone, and he gave me the option to see it through at their house, or he'd come to get me. We both hoped a little time would help my parents ease into acceptance, and I decided to stay. I'd almost regretted it the moment Mama called me to dinner.

Mounds of food sat before me, steaming hot in the bowls from my childhood. I'd always loved my mom's cooking. I hadn't seen or smelled it in months. Between that and the tension that surrounded us, I struggled not to eat everything in sight.

There on that table sat emotional fulfillment. *And relapse.* That was the thing about an eating disorder. Unlike an alcoholic or a drug addict, I couldn't remove food from my life. Moderation was not a word that I enjoyed. I hated saying it. The sound of that word made me cringe because reminding myself I needed to use it meant I was out of control. I'd allowed someone or something else to dictate my happiness.

"Cole, you okay? You look like you've seen a ghost." Caden's concern warmed my heart. Regardless of what had happened between us, my little brother loved me.

That was enough to bring a tender smile to my lips and calm the beast within me that wanted to feed. It also made me realize that everything about this environment was unhealthy. Everything here was a trigger that could send me soaring down the rabbit hole of destructive behavior.

"I'm sorry. Please excuse me." I touched the napkin I'd had folded in my lap to my lips, and then I set it on the table next to my plateful of food.

"Colbie, you haven't eaten. Sit down." But my father's command no longer held jurisdiction in my life.

I slid the chair under the table. "Mama, thank you for making dinner. I'm sure everyone will enjoy it." And I walked away with my father hollering after me, and my mother's confusion working the table in whispered worry.

I climbed the stairs, knowing no one—except maybe Caden—would follow. But I'd heard my father stop that from happening as well, and Caden wouldn't go against him unless he thought I was in duress. Oddly enough, I wasn't. I'd left my parents' dinner table with a smile.

Once I was tucked inside my room, I found a free spot on the bed among the boxes and bags of my stuff I'd packed, and I called Eli.

"Hey, beautiful."

My heart filled with joy at the sound of his voice. It was never anything other than love. "Hey."

"Everything okay?" Eli was the only person besides Caden who instantly knew when something was off with me.

I sighed, but it wasn't one of frustration. It was a realization. "I don't think I should stay here anymore."

"Did something happen?" Endearment morphed into panic.

I ran my hand through my hair and twirled the ends. "Yep. I decided I'm worth more, and the Chapman house isn't where I need to be."

"Okay." There was zero hesitation in his voice or his question. "How much time do you need?"

I dropped my hair and ran my hand down my thigh to stall my bouncing knee. "I'm ready whenever you are."

"Baby, I've been waiting months to be able to act on that. I'll be there in a few minutes."

True to his word, Eli was on my parents' front porch by the time I'd rounded up the rest of my things from the bathroom and tossed my car keys into my bag. I was coming down the stairs when Caden opened the door.

Like most teenage guys, Caden stuck his hand out to Eli in some manshake sort of greeting that Eli reciprocated. "What are you doing here, man? Caleb's at home."

Eli's eyes shifted to me on the stairs. "I'm here for your sister."

Adoration dripped from that sentence, and I knew I'd made the right choice.

Everything that had happened in the last months had all led to this moment. The time where I got to pick him, and he got to pick me. Openly.

"Hey, babe. You ready?"

Caden turned toward me, then back to Eli. "Wait. What?"

I continued down the stairs, and Caden opened the door to allow Eli inside. The commotion from the dining room indicated my parents were on their way, which meant the twins would follow.

I met Eli in the foyer and took his side. I resisted the urge to lean up and take the kiss I so desperately wanted. My parents might not have any respect for me, but this was still their house. He slipped his arm around my waist, providing a certain level of emotional protection.

"I'm totally lost. When did the two of you become an item?"

My father made sure to answer that question before either Eli or I could. "They're not. Eli, you need to go home. Colbie, upstairs."

"Afraid not, Dr. Chapman." Eli leaned down to whisper in my ear. "Go get your bag, beautiful. We'll come back to get all your things." He kissed my cheek, and I did as I was told. "Sir, Colbie is leaving with me. We will see you at graduation tomorrow. And Wednesday, we'll come back to get her things while everyone's out of the house."

I didn't listen to the rest. I needed to hurry before this turned into a brawl in the entranceway. With my cell phone and bag in hand, I raced back down the stairs to find my dad less than two inches from Eli's face, Caden trying to work himself between them, and my mother glaring holes through me like I'd caused the scene in her home.

"Daddy." I cleared my throat and tried again when neither man stopped talking. "Daddy!"

They both faced me with emotion thick in their expressions.

"Stop. Now." My chest heaved as I tried my best to diffuse the situation. "Your problem is with me, not Eli. I've given you ample opportunities to discuss it, and neither you nor Mama have taken them. So now I'm making the best decision I can for me and my health."

I kissed my dad on the cheek and then my mom. "I hope I'll see you all at graduation tomorrow. I love you." Then I took Eli's hand, and Caden opened the door—shell shocked—to let us out.

There was something final in the click of the latch behind us when we walked down the steps.

"Eli." I stood with my hand on the knob. "Please don't make me walk into the auditorium to find out who got the spot." I'd tried the best I could not to ask about this. I wanted to be okay with waiting until I got there. "If I'm going to break down, I don't want to do it in front of the entire town." My eyes glistened with unshed tears, tears I fought hard to keep at bay. It wasn't my rank that overwhelmed me, but the thought of my public reaction I couldn't contain. I wanted to handle either outcome with grace because I deserved that, and so did Jess.

Eli's eyes softened, and he lifted his brows just a hair. And that was my answer. He took my hand in his, and I blinked, causing the emotion to slide down my cheek. "Second is an honorable position, Colbie." His arms secured my body in a fortress of protection, a shield from the world. "I know how hard you worked."

I didn't have to see Eli's face. I could hear the emotion in each choked-up word. There wasn't much to say, nothing actually, so I nodded against his chest and held on tight. I'd prepared myself for this. In my heart, I'd known. There were too many months that I wasn't in a classroom and too many bobbles. When you want to be the best, a minus sign next to an *A* was the difference between success and failure. Six months ago, I would have been defeated by this. It would have consumed me. Today, I was proud of the choice I'd made. I'd chosen myself over valedictorian.

Eli stroked the back of my head, and when I finally pulled back, I did so with a smile on my lips despite the tears hanging from my chin. I lifted onto my toes and pressed my mouth to his. His hands left the small of my back and cupped my jaw so he could deepen the kiss. And while Eli didn't get crazy, he made sure to love me well.

"I'm proud of myself." I stroked his cheek with my thumb and stared into the chocolate-brown eyes that did more to soothe my soul than any binge ever had. "And I'm happy for Jess." I hoped he saw the truth. I'd fought hard to get to a place where second best didn't sting. I'd be lying if I said I hadn't wanted to be first, but in the end, I had something far better than a title no one would remember a year from now. I pulled the speech I'd written from my pocket and placed it on the counter at my side, knowing I wouldn't need it.

The warmth of his lips pressed to my forehead was a stamp of approval that I no longer needed but loved having just the same. He wasn't my crutch; he was my partner. In everything. Eli stood at my side where he could hold my hand or help hold me up. There was no doubt in my mind he'd step forward if I needed him to lead or behind if I needed him to catch me when I fell. And I'd do the same for him. Forever.

"You ready, beautiful?"

I swiped the tears from under my eyes and grabbed a paper towel from the counter to dab my face. "Did I ruin my makeup?"

Eli shook his head. "Nah, you're still stunning." He looked me up and down. "Even in that horrible black gown." And then he winked. He'd loved everything about this gown an hour ago when he'd lifted it to my waist along with the skirt of my dress beneath it, removed my panties, and shown me just how stunning he thought I was.

Together we left his house, but he dropped me off at my parents' to get my car. They may not have wanted me to take it, but there was nothing they could do. It was in my name, and it was paid for. Luckily for me, they'd done that for each of their kids to help establish credit. I didn't need their permission, and I didn't ask for it. Eli waited at the curb while I went to the garage.

No one was here, and my car was the only one in the garage. I pulled the keys from my pocket, lifted the door, and backed out. Eli followed me to the high school for the ceremony, but I'd insisted we take separate cars. As far as I knew, no one—other than Jess, and now Caden—knew about our relationship, and I wanted Eli to be able to watch his seniors walk across the stage. I wanted him to be able to watch *me*—without whispers and accusations. The two of us showing up together would have been nothing short of scandalous in Brogdon, Georgia.

He winked at me when I went a separate direction to join the rest of the seniors, and he hung out in the auditorium. I couldn't stop the joy that overflowed knowing he was mine and I was his. And in a few short hours, the two of us would start our lives together, or at least the next chapter.

I searched for Jess in the back, and when I couldn't find her, I finally asked Mrs. Cross—who was delighted to see me—if she'd seen her. My teacher pointed down the corridor to Eli and Jess. He handed her something, but from this distance, I couldn't make out what it was. Then he patted her shoulder, she nodded, and they separated.

"Line up, everyone." Mrs. Cross's command boomed in the small space and bounced off the lockers that surrounded us on two sides. "Where's my valedictorian?" She stood on her toes, trying to find Jess in the crowd of kids. "Jess, up front. And my salutatorian?" Mrs. Cross slid me in behind Jess in line. "Everyone else in alphabetical order."

While Mrs. Cross checked the roster against the line behind us, Jess turned to me. She threw her arms around my neck, and I was sheathed in horrible, black polyester. I was also covered in a friendship and love that would stand the test of time, even if she was in love with my brother. I'd always wanted a sister, and Jess was the closest thing I'd ever had. Maybe in time, it would be legal, as well.

"Can you believe it?" She pulled back with bliss brimming her expression. If her smile could have dripped off the sides of her cheeks, it would have, it was so infectious and big. "In an hour, we will be out of high school." Jess squeezed me again. "Eep. I'm so glad you're here, Colbie."

I held on for a second longer than Jess, and when we stepped back, I admitted, "I'm proud of you, Jess. Congratulations. You deserve this."

She rolled her ankle and bobbed nervously. "I'll just be glad when it's over."

Before I could question her anxiety, Mrs. Cross clapped, and we started to file into the auditorium. It was surreal to see so many people here. Brogdon didn't have that many residents, so I had to assume family members had come from all over to see their loved one graduate. I wondered if any of my family was in that crowd, or if it was only Eli here to support me. I had to assume my parents were as well. Not because of me, but rather the perception their friends would have had they not shown up. And in the Chapman household, appearances were everything.

I didn't bother looking for them, and Eli was with the rest of the faculty up front, so finding him hadn't been hard. I couldn't focus on anything being said by the principal or the guest speaker

—I'd never heard of her, either—nor the prayer that commenced before Jess took the stage. It wasn't until my best friend started to speak that my ears perked up, and my heart went sideways.

"As many of you know, I've been in a hard-fought battle with my best friend for the crowning glory of valedictorian since the start of high school. And while I stand here with that honor on my record, I can't help but thank the person who made it possible. Colbie Chapman turned her final semester of high school into a journey of self-discovery." Jess made eye contact with me from the stage, and I had no idea where she was going with this or why. "That choice opened the door for me to an honor I never would have won on my own. And while life opens doors and provides opportunities, they all come at a price. Colbie's price was standing up here this afternoon."

I'd promised myself I wouldn't cry, but Jess had thrown me a curve ball I couldn't have prepared for. There wasn't a peep from the audience, not even a murmur or a screaming baby—nothing. There might not be another soul in this room who waited with bated breath, but I'd pass out soon if I didn't give my lungs the oxygen they needed.

"I wanted to find a way to honor Colbie, since, without her, I wouldn't be here." Jess stuck her hand into the pocket of her gown and pulled out her speech. "I doubt I'll do this the justice she would have, but as our graduating class leaves here today, I want her words to be those that remain in your heart and on your mind. Our journeys to self-discovery are far more valuable than the time we spend in a classroom." She flattened the paper onto the podium and found my eyes again.

My best friend proceeded to deliver my valedictorian speech to our class, the one I'd slaved over and poured my heart into. The one that had been as honest and as real as it could be. It opened every window and door to allow people in that room to see just how real my travels had been. But they weren't travels around the world, they'd been travels around the heart—the soul.

And when she finished, there wasn't a dry eye in the building. She'd had a hard time getting through parts, but she'd brought me to her light and kept me out of the shadows. Jess had sacrificed her glory for our friendship. Nothing could ever mean more. When the audience stood and continued to clap, and every student hollered and cheered, Jessica McLean took her cap from her head, held it against her heart, and blew me a kiss. It wasn't cheesy or cliché. It was Jess to a tee. It was who she'd always been, even when I'd doubted that person still existed.

I could barely see her through my tears, and my hands stung from clapping so hard. Nevertheless, I watched her descend the stairs and round the rows of faculty to join me at my side. I'd never know which of us initiated that embrace; I'd only know that it sealed our bond forever.

Jess and I held hands throughout the remainder of the ceremony, only letting go when each of us took our diplomas. At the end, she hugged my neck again. "I know you said you're proud of me, but girl, I'm so proud of you. Be good to Eli." She took a step back but held my hand. "And let him be good to you."

I kissed her cheek. "You act like this is goodbye forever, silly." I shook our still-clasped hands to ease the seriousness of the conversation. It was a good day. A happy day. A day she deserved to enjoy.

Her parents interrupted, and I stepped to the side. I wasn't sure what to do with myself. Most of the kids had met up with family, but the one person I wanted to go to, I couldn't. I finally spotted Caden, who stepped away from our parents when I got close and another couple joined them.

Before Caden could utter a word, I heard my mom speak to the woman in front of her.

"Yes, well. It was a choice that we believed would benefit

Colbie in the long run. She got to see the world, traveling the last few months, and it was a sacrifice that will serve her well in the future. Phillip and I both agreed that it was worth it when Colbie asked us about it over Christmas." She turned to my dad with a smile. "Isn't that right, Phillip?"

My brother stood next to me, watching me watch them. "Congratulations, Colbie."

I hugged him, but I was too lost in the reality of what I'd just witnessed.

They were never going to change. They were never going to own up to mistakes or admit that their life wasn't the picture of perfection. My parents would always worry more about what people thought went on in their home rather than about the toll their inability to live in reality had on their children. Maybe that was only true for me. Perhaps my brothers experienced something different. I'd never know because they'd never see the world through my eyes.

And in that moment, I let go of that hurt and that regret. I couldn't shoulder their burden anymore. I could wish on every star in the sky, and it wouldn't change our relationship until they were ready to work on it.

I smiled at my little brother. "Thanks, Caden. I hope you'll come spend time with me in Tennessee this summer." I punched him playfully in the arm. "Maybe bring Jess."

"Okay." Caden appeared a little confused, and I knew I had explaining to do.

"I'll give you all the details then. Promise."

I hugged my little brother, who wasn't so little anymore, and left to find Eli. I couldn't hug him or kiss him—not here, anyway—but I could tell him I was ready to go.

My parents weren't home the next day when Eli and I

went to get my things. I'd let them know when I'd be coming by, and they'd chosen not to stay. There wasn't a note or anything to say goodbye, and I was okay with that. It took us about an hour to load my things into his truck and my SUV, and when I closed the door to my bedroom, I acknowledged that I'd never be back.

I hated driving separate vehicles all the way to Nashville, but it couldn't be helped. The moving truck had all of Eli's furniture and things, and we had to have both cars once we got there. As I traveled the highway behind the man I loved, I thought about the trip I'd taken up here to start at Bright Horizons. The anger, the hurt—it all seemed like a lifetime ago, or maybe it was just someone completely different who'd experienced that trip. A girl who'd wanted to conquer the world but needed to know she couldn't do it alone.

My tribe was small but true—and one day, I'd make a difference.

EPILOGUE—ELI

SIX MONTHS LATER

It was far too early on a Saturday morning for the doorbell to ring, although Colbie and I had been up for a couple of hours. I'd groaned when she pushed me out of the bed at seven to go running, the same way I did now at the thought of a solicitor on my front porch at nine. I only had a couple weeks off for Christmas break and zero desire to spend two hours trying to convince a Rainbow salesman that I didn't need a new vacuum.

The bell rang again, and I had to give up hope that Colbie would answer the door or that the person would go away. I got up from the kitchen table but went back to grab my coffee. If I were going to be stuck listening to someone's spiel, it would be with caffeine.

On the third ring, I hollered at the door. "I'm coming."

People were so impatient. Maybe if they'd waited until a respectable hour to wake the dead, they wouldn't have such a slow response time from their victims. I ran my free hand through my unruly hair that I hadn't bothered to brush after showering with Colbie. The thought of her naked brought a devious smirk to my face when I opened the door.

That smile dropped the moment I saw who stood on my front

stoop. This was not how I planned to spend the Saturday before Christmas, or hell, any Saturday in the near or distant future.

"Good morning, Eli."

I held onto my coffee with one hand and the edge of the door with the other, while my sanity threatened to fly out the door. "Hi." I was at a loss for words when I stuck my head outside and looked both directions. "What are you doing here?"

She clasped her hands in front of her and pulled her lips into a prim greeting that would make Emily Post proud. "Might I come in?" Her expression was hopeful, and I prayed her visit would be positive.

I didn't have a clue what to say to the woman in front of me, although I was fairly certain my silence conveyed the message of shock. I stepped back, taking the door with me and allowed her inside. My heart raced with uncertainty, and I glanced up the stairs when I heard footsteps bounding down them.

As soon as Colbie rounded the corner—her foot hadn't even touched the next step when she jerked to a stop—she halted in her tracks, and the happiness that had been painted on her face for months fell. "Mama?"

Elise stared at her daughter and then glanced at me. "Oh, my." She let a tiny huff of uncertainty escape. "I told Phillip we should have called before we came. Please forgive me for intruding, dear."

The three of us stood there staring at each other. One of us had to make a move, and Colbie determined that person was me. "Eli." My name was a plea, a question, and a command all wrapped into one.

I didn't know which one my name was meant to represent in this context, but I assumed it was a cry for help first and foremost. And the only thing I knew to do when unexpected company showed up was to be hospitable. "Would you like some coffee?" I didn't wait for anyone to answer when I headed back to the kitchen.

They both followed, and Colbie sidled up next to me, suddenly afraid of her own shadow. Once I'd started the pot, I turned to face Mrs. Chapman with my arm around her daughter's waist. Colbie had come to my side for security, and I'd give her anything I could to reassure her. It was our house, and I didn't like that she wasn't comfortable.

"What are you doing here?" Colbie's voice quivered with uncertainty, but as long as I held her next to me, she stood her ground.

Elise motioned toward the kitchen table that was bathed in morning sun. "May I?"

Colbie and I were being rude, but I wasn't really sure what the protocol was for one of your girlfriend's parents showing up unannounced when neither of you had spoken to them in over six months.

"Of course." I encouraged Colbie toward the same seats her mother had taken. "Are you in Nashville alone?" I sat first, and Colbie chose my thigh instead of a chair. This wasn't quite how I envisioned any of this ever happening, and I was quite certain that Colbie perched on my leg with my arm around her waist didn't make her mother terribly comfortable.

"Oh, heaven's no. Phillip will be here shortly."

Great. Not one unexpected arrival, but two. But it wasn't their presence that concerned me so much as their motivation for being here. Everything with them always came at a price, and Colbie was typically the one paying the tab.

"Mama, why are you here?" Colbie tried again to get an answer all while keeping watch over the coffee maker, likely to be able to have something to occupy herself with once it was done.

Elise waved Colbie off as if this were an every-Saturday occurrence. She'd driven hours to get here not knowing if we'd even let her in or be home; it was far from the casual affair her hand gesture indicated. "Can't a mother come see her only daughter without having a reason?"

This was just odd. Any other mother, yes; Elise Chapman, no. Colbie had talked to Caden a couple of times since we'd moved, and Jess and Caden had come to visit once over the fall break, but that was where the communication ended with Brogdon, Georgia.

It had taken Colbie a couple months to reach a point that she was okay with that limited communication. She'd finally accepted that her parents weren't going to change; she could either accept them for who they were and what they offered in an emotional connection or sever ties. For the time being, she'd decided to stay disconnected until she could come to terms with who they were. I knew for a fact she still worked on her lack of a relationship with her family during counseling sessions because we'd talked about it recently.

While Colbie had made the decision to leave and to go to Vanderbilt, she hadn't made the decision about her family lightly. For weeks, she had raced to the mailbox every day, hoping for some sort of correspondence. She had asked regularly if I'd heard from Caleb. She was always met with disappointment on both fronts—there were never any letters or phone calls. I had no idea what this visit would undo in her recovery, but right now, I wasn't thrilled that it was happening.

The knock on the front door indicated her father had arrived as well. I didn't have the foggiest clue what to do. Tempering my anger currently took all of my energy. They didn't deserve the benefit of the doubt, but I knew how much Colbie wanted them in her life in a healthy capacity.

I patted Colbie's thigh. "Babe, why don't you go answer that and then get coffee for everyone?"

She needed something to do besides fidget. I snagged her by the fingers and squeezed before she got out of reach. Colbie turned her baby blues toward me, and even if the rest of her was a nervous wreck, her eyes filled with warmth and love at that one simple gesture.

As soon as I was certain Colbie was out of earshot, I hardened a glare in Elise's direction. "What are you doing here, Elise?" I'd never called her by her first name—not to her face—but here, we were equals. I was a grown-ass man, and this was my house.

Colbie's mom sighed, and the plastic expression she always wore cracked. "Trying to mend a fence, Eli. I'll admit it's something I'm not very good at, but I'm doing my best."

I didn't buy it. I wished I wasn't skeptical. I wanted to accept her explanation as the gospel's truth, but it was too simple. Too easy. "Why now?"

"My daughter isn't coming home for Christmas."

I couldn't help but think her motivation was how that looked to the people of Brogdon rather than Colbie's decision not to leave Nashville for the holiday. "Last time I checked, she hadn't been invited to your house."

Colbie and Phillip joined us in the kitchen before Elise could respond. My girlfriend appeared terrified, and her father looked perturbed. I stood, although it was more out of habit than respect. Colbie veered off toward the coffee, and Phillip extended his arm.

"Morning, Eli. Beautiful house you've got here." He shook my hand and took in what he could see from where he stood.

"Maybe Colbie will give you two a tour. She's done all the work." It was true. I just lived here and lifted the heavy objects when she asked me to. "We're quite happy here." I added that in unnecessarily, but I couldn't resist the dig or the opportunity to ensure they knew there was no regret on either of our parts.

Phillip took a seat next to his wife, and I couldn't shake the uncomfortable silence that captivated the room. Colbie brought the pot of coffee and a little tray with cream and sugar, and seconds later, she returned with mugs. The four of us remained silent while she busied herself in the kitchen, and I wondered what went through her mother's mind, watching her daughter perform the hostess role Elise did daily.

It wasn't until Colbie joined us that her parents finally made eye contact with their daughter. I vowed to myself to stay out of this as much as possible, but I wouldn't leave her side, nor would I allow them to venture into territory that made Colbie uncomfortable. She might be their daughter, but she was my heart.

Her dad was the first to speak, and he didn't mince words. "Sugar, this nonsense has to stop." He poured himself and Elise a cup of coffee, and then met his daughter's stare.

Colbie cocked her head to the side. We glanced at each other, and she grimaced. "What nonsense, Daddy?"

"This not speaking." His Southern accent was thick, and I thought maybe he had a show of his own the way Elise did. "It's gone on long enough."

If the room were black and white, I would have sworn we'd been transported to Mayberry through some strange space, time, and television continuum.

"Is that why you drove all the way here from Brogdon?" Colbie's voice cracked, and she furrowed her brow. "To tell me that I'm not doing something the way you want me to?"

"No, honey." Elise reached across the table to take Colbie's hands, but Colbie pulled back before she could touch her. Her mother was visibly put off by her daughter's reaction, but she forged ahead. "Sometimes your daddy isn't good with words." She patted her husband's hand as if to excuse his poor behavior. "I think maybe we just all need to talk. The four of us."

I leaned back in my seat, folded my arms over my chest, and let out a heavy sigh. Elise's gaze darted between Colbie and me, but it dawned on me that she was as nervous as Colbie.

"I don't know how you and Eli formed your..." She paused before giving our status a title, "...relationship. Or how you kept it going when you were gone. Daddy and I were confused by everything that happened." Her shoulders slumped when she exhaled. "Colbie, can't we all agree that none of us handled any of this very well?" That was a huge admission of wrongdoing coming from the woman who did no wrong.

My jaw might have dropped, but I concealed it well; however, I didn't try to hide my eyes going wide at her willingness to shoulder some of the blame.

Colbie wrapped her hands around her warm mug of coffee and stared into it for a second before she lifted her head. "I can agree to that. There are things I wasn't honest and upfront about. But one thing I was clear on was what would take place if you continued to shut me out. I told you what my plan was for this past summer and what the school year would look like. You both buried your heads in the sand. And whether you like my relationship with Eli or not, it isn't going to change."

If they were smart, one of them would interject before Colbie got on a roll. Once she found her voice, there'd be no stopping the months of disappointment that had resulted in countless hours of counseling.

"There's no use crying over spilled milk, sugar. The only thing we can do is move forward."

Colbie leaned back and laughed. "Daddy, with all due respect, this isn't just *spilled milk*. It's my life. And you've invaded mine here. One I've worked hard to normalize without anyone in the family—other than Caden—supporting me."

Caden had come to visit with Jess, and he and I had talked, man to man. He hadn't had nearly the issue with my relationship with his sister as his family had. Caden's greatest concern was Colbie's happiness and health.

"And Caden is a large part of the reason your father and I are here. He and Jess."

"Why?" Colbie narrowed her eyes, wondering how her brother had played a part in the odd encounter, probably imagining ways to hurt him the next time she saw him for putting her parents up to this.

"Jess has shed some light on your relationship with Eli since you left. We saw her a good bit over the summer, and she argued in favor of your being here with him. And when Caden came home after they visited, he told us how well you were doing. How happy you seemed."

Her dad's face lit up when he smiled. "I heard you got all *A*s this semester. I'm proud of you, Colbie. Vanderbilt's a tough school."

"Thank you." Her response was hesitant. Colbie had no idea what to do with their praise. She'd wanted it, coveted it for years, and now that she was receiving it, her confused expression looked like she was listening to a foreign language and trying to comprehend it.

Phillip put his forearms on the table. His brows dipped, and his eyes darkened. When he leaned forward toward Colbie, I dropped my arms from their folded position and prepared myself to pounce if necessary. "I also heard you're considering dropping your minor next semester." His statement wasn't accusatory. Instead, it was possibly disappointment that lingered in his tone, or maybe even regret.

If Jess had been here, I would have laid into her right after I strangled her. This was a really touchy subject in our house. With a music minor, Colbie needed to practice. The rooms on campus were frequently booked and difficult to get into to say the least, especially as a freshman. Without a piano at home, music had been a struggle since the start of the year. I'd looked at new instruments; I'd looked at used instruments; I'd look at renting. But Colbie wasn't a novice. She not only needed but deserved a decent one, and it was as expensive as buying a high-end car. So, the rounded windows that faced the street currently sat empty until I could figure out a way to put a piano in that spot.

"Yes, sir." Colbie chewed on her lip not wanting to admit the reason.

Elise sighed. "Colbie, I don't expect to fix things in a conversation around your breakfast table." She reached across the space, and Colbie finally let her mother connect with her. "But we brought you something, and I hope that you'll see it as us trying to lay the foundation to start to build a bridge that we should have constructed years ago."

There was only one way to buy Colbie's attention, and they'd known it.

"I don't understand, Mama."

I did.

Part of me hated them for being able to do it when I couldn't, and part of me wanted to hug them for giving her something she needed when they'd done nothing for so long.

"Are they in the driveway, Phillip?" Elise appeared excited to give her daughter something she knew she'd love, and in that minute, I set aside my petty jealousy. The Chapmans had the means, and it was important to Cole.

Colbie stood. "Who?" She didn't wait for a response, and I followed on her heels.

Her parents talked behind us, but Colbie raced toward the door without shoes on or a jacket. When I finally caught up with her in the driveway, she stood with her hands clasped over her mouth and tears streaming down her cheeks. She didn't speak when the driver and the passenger hopped out of the large, white box truck. The driver rolled up the back door, and Colbie's shoulders shook.

Her eyes went to her parents. "For me?" She was choked up, and while I'd never condone buying off kids, in this case, the Chapmans had done the right thing.

Her mom tried to play it off. "It was just collecting dust in our house, and Jess told me all about your front windows and how beautiful your piano would look there." Elise stuck her hand in her pocket and held out the key to Colbie, but before she released it, a tear of her own slid down her cheek. "I'm sorry we locked it, Colbie. I promise, if you'll give us a chance to fix things, we'll never shut you out again."

Mrs. Chapman wasn't just referring to the piano lid. That key had as much metaphorical meaning as literal. I didn't get the impression that the gift came with any stipulations though...just the most sincere apology two people who didn't apologize could find.

"Sugar, I hope you'll consider sticking with music. Your mama and I'd love to come hear you play this spring." And there was her dad's first brick in the mortar of the foundation to a relationship with his daughter.

She nodded, unable to speak. There were times I couldn't get the girl to stop talking, and others when her silence said more than all the words in the English language. This was one of her moments of incomparable silence. Colbie was vulnerable, bare, and completely exposed, and the best thing I could do was step up. I wrapped my arms around her and pressed her head to my chest while she let out the emotions that overwhelmed her.

This wasn't the solution to Colbie's problems, and it wouldn't guarantee a reconciliation with her parents. It was, however, a start. Colbie had a heart of gold and a forgiving spirit. And all she'd ever needed was for them to see her for who she was and love her as she came. But if they'd done that as flawlessly as Colbie had done everything else, then I wouldn't be standing here. Their imperfections had given me a gift I never would have had a chance at receiving otherwise.

We stepped back as Elise and Phillip directed the piano delivery, but I never let Colbie go. "You okay, beautiful?"

She nodded and looked into my eyes. "A bit overwhelmed. Raine is going to have a field day with this one." Colbie giggled, but it was her way of recognizing that what she'd wanted had come full circle, and now, she had to put in the work to keep it going.

I'd be there every step of the way, whether it was to hold her hand or carry her when she couldn't walk. "One day at a time, baby."

She smiled, and the purest form of joy I'd ever witnessed radiated from her soul, a contentment I hoped to see for the rest of my life. Colbie lifted onto her toes and gave me a quick peck.

"I love you, Cole."

"I love you, too, Eli." It was the way those five words came together, the curve of my name on her lips, the heat of her breath on my skin, the pulse of her pupils when her nostrils flared.

From the moment I'd met her, I had never stood a chance against loving her. It was in me, who I was designed to be. Loving Colbie was as natural as breathing, and without her, I'd cease to exist.

My lids closed, and our lips met. I didn't kiss her with passion; I kissed her with promise.

Promise to be patient.

Promise to be faithful.

Promise to protect.

But most of all, promise to love.

Everything about her was perfect—for me.

THE END

ABOUT THE AUTHOR

Stephie is a forty-year-old mother to one of the feistiest preteens to ever walk. They live on the outskirts of Greenville, South Carolina, where they house two cats and two dogs in their veritable zoo.

She has a serious addiction to anything Coach and would live on Starbucks if she could get away with it. She's slightly enamored with Charlie Hunnam and Sons of Anarchy and is a self-proclaimed foodie.

ALSO BY STEPHIE WALLS

Bound (Bound Duet #1)

Freed (Bound Duet #2)

Redemption (Bound Duet Spinoff)

Metamorphosis

Compass

Strangers

Beauty Mark

Fallen Woman

Girl Crush

Unexpected Arrivals

Small Town Girl

Family Ties

Beaten Paths (The Journey Collection #1)

Gravel Road (The Journey Collection #2)

Dear Diamond

Her Perfect

Made in the USA
Las Vegas, NV
26 December 2020

14755920R00216